VOLUME 1

Obsessions
of
an Otome Gamer
Elementary School Years

NATSU

ILLUSTRATION BY SHOYU

Obsessions of an Otome Gamer, Volume 1
Natsu

Translation by Charis Messier

Illustration by Shoyu
Editing by Ingrid Chang and A.M. Perrone
Proofreading by Robert Fox
Book Design A.M. Perrone

Obsessions of an Otome Gamer
© 2014 by Natsu
English translation rights reserved by
Cross Infinite World.

English translation ©2018 Cross Infinite World

Cross Infinite World
contact@crossinfworld.com
www.crossinfworld.com

Published in the United States of America

Visit us at www.crossinfworld.com
Facebook.com/crossinfworld
Twitter.com/crossinfworld
crossinfiniteworld.tumblr.com

First Digital Edition: March 2018
First Print Edition: March 2020

ISBN-13: 978-1-945341-33-5

TABLE OF CONTENTS

Prologue (Rika)

IN the spring marking the beginning of my second year of high school, I encountered the game that changed my life. People may say I'm over-exaggerating, but it's true. *That* game started it all.

It was a love simulation game marketed toward women, making it part of the genre popularly referred to as "otome games." In the vast catalogue of otome games, there was a game particularly infamous for being called, "The most difficult, crappiest game for sale. Anyone who manages to get a single ending is a gaming god."

And that's the game I became totally obsessed with.

My sister, who's older by a year, didn't think highly of my newly acquired addiction. In any other situation, I would've obediently taken her advice with how close we were. But not this time. Maybe I was being juvenile, but I couldn't help myself. She was concerned about me gaming all the time and took every opportunity to tell me to quit.

On that fateful day, I was browsing a bookstore with the fashion magazine and new romance novel my sister had asked me to pick up tucked under my arm. Yet it felt too pitiful to leave the store without buying something for myself. For that simple reason, I stopped to browse the magazine rack. An oddly shiny, illustrated book printed to resemble a magazine leapt out at me.

"Let me hear your sound."

Sound? Curiosity piqued by the line printed on the book's wrapper, I approached the rack. On the cover was an enlarged illustration of a handsome young man with light-blue hair, standing shoulder to shoulder with another handsome young man sporting flaming-red hair, their hands extended toward the viewer. I furtively reached out and snatched the glossy book. My heart raced.

A perfectly shaped nose sat between almond-shaped indigo eyes, leading to sexy lips; his build was slender and toned. Perhaps it would be easier to understand how I felt if I said this character was the pure embodiment of my ideal man. This dashing red-haired young man on the cover checked every mark on my must-have list and then some.

I fell in love for the second time in my life with a two-dimensional man made from paper and ink. I should note that my first love ended in heartbreak last year. A troublesome love marked by bitterness and pain. The sooner I forget the experience, the better.

I scanned through the book and learned his name—Kou Narita. Even his name was wonderful. From the looks of it, he was the main character of a dating simulation game.

...Wait a minute. A dating game?! I can date this hot guy?!

Tightly clasping the book to my chest, I hurried to the store's game section.

It's not here! I can't find it! The game where Kou Narita moves and speaks isn't here!

Heart set ablaze, I purchased my books at the register and promptly searched the four game stores in the area. I pedaled my bicycle like a madwoman, wearing an expression too ghastly for a maiden in love.

Finally, at the fourth store, I found the game.

Let Me Hear Your Sound ~Melody to My Heart~

I ogled Kou's portrait on the game package and lined up at the register in high spirits. A nice lady who looked like a college student rang me up. She frowned when she saw the game I put on the counter.

"...Um, I don't know how to put this, but I own this game too." Concerned about what others might think if they overheard, the part-timer lowered her voice and leaned toward me. "This game is super hardcore. Are you sure you want it?"

The game caused her enough strife to go out of her way to warn a customer not to buy it. That must be some difficulty level.

But I'm still going to buy it. I've come this far. I'll do whatever it takes to see

Kou move and speak with my own eyes! I have experience playing games. I foolishly dismissed her warnings. *I've only played puzzle games, but aren't all games the same when it comes down to it? My cousins just bought a new system and gave me their old portable game console. I'm sure I'll be able to handle it.*

"I'm sure. I can handle it," I declared, and got my hands on *Hear My Heart*—the shorter name fans call the game.

Who was I kidding? I wasn't able to handle it at all. No wonder the shop clerk felt the need to warn me. From what I looked up online, almost every major otome game company has released several different types of popular game series in the music genre. In order to break into the intensely competitive otome game market, the new company behind *Hear My Heart* filled the game with a lot of experimental elements.

One such experiment was decreasing the typical number of romanceable characters to develop a longer, unique scenario for each character, rather than having repetitive scenes across multiple characters. The industry bare minimum of five romanceable characters had been reduced to only two—Kou Narita, who had captured my heart, and the blue-haired Sou Shiroyama.

Kou is a sexy *oresama* type who exudes pheromones at all times, while Sou is a *tsundere oresama*. What's an oresama and tsundere? They're popular character archetypes often found in otome games and Japanese media. Oresama characters are generally pompous, overconfident, and narcissistic. Meanwhile, a tsundere acts coldly toward the heroine until she melts his frozen heart to reveal his soft side.

Otome game fans threw a huge fit when it was announced that the game only had two romanceable characters, both of which were oresamas. Of course they'd be upset. No matter how much you like the oresama archetype, it's off-putting for every dateable character to be pompous.

To add insult to injury, there are as many as twelve endings. What's so bad about that? Only one ending is actually *happy*. Of the remaining eleven endings, six are considered Friend Ends and five are Bad Ends. The Friend Ends are broken into: Best Friends End; Good Friends End; Friends who Occasionally Text Message End; Friends who Chat when They Bump into Each Other End; Friends who Know Each Other's Name End; and Friends who Recognize Each Other's Face End. I strongly believe more than half of those can't even be called friends anymore.

The game takes place at a music school, but all the bad ends revolve around failing tests. Yup, you guessed it, *Hear My Heart* wasn't your typical visual novel otome game where you simply read the story and make choices, but a full-on simulation game.

You have to pass a total of four tests. If the various requirements aren't met, the heroine will be kicked out of school. What standards are those four tests conducted on? This is exactly why players have cursed *Hear My Heart* as *Break My Heart*. Put briefly, the parameters displayed on the in-game menu are just decorations and have absolutely no effect on the tests whatsoever! To pass the test, the player has to run the heroine all around the campus collecting music notes, scales, and musical notations and compose a song with them.

The player faces the screen and earnestly composes a song on the in-game keyboard. If you want to see any of the sweet, romantic, or enjoyable scenes, you must compose and compose and compose away. What the heck kind of game is this? The first test is within the realms of playable. After all, the song's melody only needs to be sixteen bars. On the other hand, the nightmarish final test requires the player to compose a string quartet's whole first movement. How is that even possible?

As the player is graded on the musical intervals, scale, rhythm, harmony, and even the counterpoint, randomly lining up music notes and failing will make the principal appear on screen and coldly declare, "I can no longer allow you to remain at this school."

Game over. People on the Internet went crazy, raging that the game system had gone far beyond the bounds of a simulation game. Rumors say only university music students could clear the game and for some reason, near the end of the game's life, large music stores started selling it alongside instruments.

How do you capture the two romanceable characters then? By chance. If one of the characters happen to enter the area where the heroine is composing music, his affection for her increases. Whether they show up or not is random. This system is ridiculously, pathetically painful. The sheer pitifulness of the heroine, wholeheartedly composing music while nobody appears, brings the player to tears. Even if someone set out to make a game as crappy as this one on purpose, they wouldn't be able to do it.

This is a game that even I never reached an ending to. Even so, my love for Kou continued to grow. People would refer to my obsession as escaping reality. True by all accounts, but I couldn't give up. I desperately needed it at the time.

Kou occasionally wandered onto the screen and murmured some sweet, confusing lines like, "Hi there. Looks like you're working hard. I'd give you a reward, but you'd have to beg for it first."

You wouldn't believe how hard I fell for him each time he showed up, said those lines, and strutted off the screen. Looks, voice, and way of speaking—everything about him was what I wanted and had me squirming in my chair.

Now that I think about it, I've played the game over a hundred times and never once encountered Sou. What kind of mechanics does this game run on? I looked it up online and found out that Kou appears when you're composing songs in the major key, while Sou appears for songs in the minor key. Whenever I lined up the musical notes, it always became a merry and carefree melody. No wonder I never saw Sou.

The shiny magazine book I bought at the beginning of my obsession wasn't a guidebook, but a fanbook with illustrations and data on the romanceable characters. In other words, it was worthless when it came to gameplay.

Foreseeing that very few fans would ever reach the endings, every CG and image in the game filled the pages of the fanbook. Players who despised spoilers avoided it like the plague. But I was extremely grateful for it. I only ever managed to unlock three CGs during my gameplay. I ogled Kou's CGs enough to wear holes in the images as I indulged in my fantasies.

To someday reach Kou's Love End was my greatest aspiration.

♪♪♪

JANUARY—THE month of sporadic snowfall. I finished my university entrance exams and was on the road home. I did the best I could, but my best didn't even scratch the surface of what was needed to score decently. I've never had a knack for studying. Depressed, I glanced upward and sharply inhaled—Kou was right in front of my eyes.

"The great *Hear My Heart* is coming for you to experience up-close and personal after its massive remake!"

A pompously smirking Kou gazed at me from a pose that awkwardly kinked his neck. Apparently, they weren't releasing a sequel, but a remake of the game. Fixated on the promotion poster in the game store window, I walked toward it—until I was suddenly floating. Right where I had stepped was an open manhole. Swallowed whole by the gaping hole of darkness, the hair on my arms and the back of my neck stood up as I fell.

Ah, I'm going to die. Those were my last thoughts. Without a second to think of anything else, my consciousness cut off.

CG 1: Footbridge (Sou)

I remembered my past life when I was in the second grade. My memories returned when I spotted a blue-haired boy on the footbridge on my way home from school. He rubbed at his wet cheeks with tiny fists while shouldering a fancy, leather backpack that instantly gave away the fact he attended private school.

I've seen him somewhere before. Struck by an intense wave of déjà vu, I stood rooted to the ground. *I can't stop looking at him standing in the middle of the footbridge. He looks like someone. But who? It's on the tip of my tongue, but I can't place it. I feel sick.*

He noticed my rude stare and glared at me. "What's your problem? I'm not here for your entertainment."

"What? Ah...I'm sorry."

He cried in the middle of the road rather than waiting until he got home. Something pretty terrible must've happened to him. I quickly shook my head and went back to walking. I tried not to look, but I was irritated that I couldn't remember, and kept sneaking glances at him.

"...Is it that strange to see a man cry?"

"I'm really sorry. You just look like somebody I know and I keep wondering who... Anyway, it doesn't matter if you're a man or woman, you should cry when you want to. I believe emotions rot and eat away at you inside if you force yourself not to express them when you feel sad," I bluntly voiced my thoughts. His eyes darted around in confusion. The traces of tears on his cheeks tugged at my heart.

"...I don't know you."

"I see. Hmm. I was sure I'd seen you somewhere before… Um, sorry for staring."

As an apology, I dug through my pockets and handed him the origami grand piano I had secretly folded during class. It was the painstakingly complicated masterpiece I carefully folded using a single sheet of black and a single sheet of white paper.

I was born with unusually nimble and dexterous hands. Amused by my ability, Mom taught me origami at a young age and bought me a ton of books on the craft. Only she knows why she chose origami to focus on, but it's thanks to that decision that I was able to fold origami at the master level by the wee age of seven. It's one of the few skills I can boast about.

"Wow! What is this?!"

Yup, it's awesome, isn't it? I felt completely confident in this masterpiece that had my classmates and teacher staring at my hands in wonder as I folded it, while they exclaimed, "How are you doing that?!"

"Did you fold that yourself?"

"I did! It took tons of time though. But I've memorized the steps, so I should be able to fold a prettier one next time," I explained proudly.

Nimble fingers and origami are about the only things I've got going for me since I suck at anything athletic and am below average in my studies.

"Amazing! You're seriously amazing!" the boy innocently blurted out after carefully resting the grand piano on the palm of his hand.

Despite the don't-approach-me aura he gave off, his smile completely changed my opinion of him. His adorable, darkly colored eyes were like a puppy's, reflecting the glittering light of the setting sun in an absolutely stunning way. I took a better look at him and noticed that he was actually pretty handsome, with a cute face and fine physique for a boy close to my age.

My heart fluttered at that realization. I blushed and got ahead of myself, "If you want, I can fold something else for you right now."

"Okay! Can you fold this for me then?"

He pulled a paper out of his backpack titled: "Bring Your Mother to School Day."

"Eeeh?! I can't use this. You need to show it to your mom at home."

"I don't need to. That woman won't come anyway," he spat out sounding like a grown-up. Sounds like his family situation is complicated. I could tell even as a second grader, so I was reluctant when I took the paper.

"It'll be difficult to make something complicated with flimsy paper like this." As I folded the corners into a square, I asked, "What do you want me to make?"

"A dog!" he immediately answered. "I want to have one, but my parents said I can't. Can you do it?"

"Piece of cake. Okay, I'll make it so that you can go for a walk with it." I placed the paper on the footbridge railing and creased tiny lines into it, folding a three-dimensional dog. An ash-colored dog formed within a few short minutes.

The boy's eyes sparkled in admiration, and he grabbed my shoulders. "You really are amazing! Thanks!"

"Hehe. I'm not that amazing... Oh no, I should get home soon."

The color of the sky returned me to my senses. What time was it? *If I don't hurry home, I won't make it back in time for my anime!*

"Hang on. What's your name and school?"

"I'm Mashiro Shimao, a second grader at Tada Elementary School!" I turned and shouted as I ran off.

He shouted back, "I'm Sou Shiroyama, a second grader at Seio Academy's Elementary School! Let's see each other again, Mashiro!"

I was surprised that the boy called me by my first name within seconds of hearing it, but I replied as I waved from below the footbridge, "Yeah, see you later, Shiroyama!"

Shouting our names at the same time makes it Mashiroyama—pure white mountain! I was thinking about stupid things as I returned home.

Later that night, quite suddenly—and I mean out of nowhere—I remembered my past life.

"Now that I think about it, Sou Shiroyama is the same name as that Sou... Huh? AAAAAH!"

It happened the moment I got in bed and started to close my eyes. My words had triggered my memories, which flooded into my brain with the force of a raging storm! My reflexive shout sent my parents frantically stampeding up the stairs to the second-story.

"What's wrong, Mashiro?!"

Both of my parents are kind and serious people, but they're also seriously flawed in that they completely lose their heads over their children.

Dear Father: please leave the metal bat downstairs.

My sister, who's older by eight years and a freshman in high school, popped over from her room next to mine. "What's up? Is there a bug somewhere?"

She must've been in the middle of washing her face, because she looked like a ghost when she appeared in the dark doorway with cotton pads stuck all over. To be honest, she was scarier than any bug.

"N-Nothing. Hang on…is it okay for our hair to be this color?!"

I've never paid attention to it before, but this hair is really disturbing. Aren't Japanese people supposed to have black eyes and hair? My sister has pink hair. Not a dyed pink either—her roots are pink. Like she's some sort of anime or video game character…

"It looks like someone was just half-asleep," Mom giggled, her short, orange hair bouncing along.

After the three of them left the room, I lay in bed, face up, and had a sudden realization—Sou Shiroyama's hair was blue too. And I was way too familiar with the name "Seio Academy."

That's right, that was the name of the music school in Hear My Heart. The instant that dawned on me, the final moments of my last life came rushing back.

I most likely fell to my death. Maybe I was reincarnated into Hear My Heart's world through some sorta freak accident. I did fall into a manhole while being captivated by a poster of Kou.

The simple answer my mind came to was practically a supernatural fantasy. *Reincarnation, huh? This is amazing.* I must've been in a significant amount of shock since I instantly accepted this crazy idea.

I wormed out of bed and checked my face in a hand-mirror. Aside from the hair color, my plain old face was staring back at me. Nothing had changed. But *Hear My Heart*'s heroine was a beautiful girl with long, brown hair.

Looks like I was reincarnated as an NPC. I guess I don't get to be reincarnated as the heroine and spend a magical childhood with the romanceable characters. I'm disgusted in myself for hoping even for a second that it'd happen. I should've known such an amazing coincidence wouldn't fall in my lap.

I returned to bed feeling disappointed and relieved.

I never fathomed that this world was actually based on the remake version of *Hear My Heart*.

Heroine's Results
Target Character: Sou Shiroyama
Encounter Event: Comfort Him on the Footbridge
CLEAR

The game menu floating in the air sounds the start of the game. A man smiles with satisfaction and folds his arms over his chest.

♪♪♪

HAVING regained memories of my prior life, I naturally recalled my love for Kou.

Aah, how many times had I spoken to him through the console? Stopped by the LCD screen, I could hear his sweet whispers yet never get close to him. But in this world, there's a chance I can meet the real Kou! The living, breathing, moving, blinking Kou!

At the moment, nothing had happened besides meeting a boy who was the spitting image of the game character Sou Shiroyama. Yet I got so worked up about it; I hope you can sympathize with me. My body wasn't mature enough to completely understand all of the memories I had suddenly regained—it was still that of a seven-year-old girl. I simply latched onto the convenient half of my memories and daydreamed.

Since I've successfully encountered Sou and he's the same age as me, Kou must be the same age as well. I let my imagination take over. *An elementary school Kou! I bet he's super cute. I want to be his friend!* I didn't hope for anything out of my league.

I have no doubt that Kou is fated to meet the beautiful brunette heroine. As long as I can gaze upon him from afar as one of the many background characters, I'll be happy.

"That's right! I have a chance to meet Kou!"

I sat up and hugged the teddy bear sitting next to my pillow and rained kisses on its adorable lips. Holding both of Becchin's—my fluffy teddy bear's nickname—hands, I stood and spun around in my room.

"Voi, che sapete che cosa è amor, donne vedete, s'io l'ho nel cor!"

'I feel an emotion full of desire, that is now pleasure, and now suffering. You who know what love is, ladies, see whether it's in my heart.'

From the Second Act of Mozart's The Marriage of Figaro opera.

I sang Cherubino's famous aria, "You who know what love is", as it was written in Italian at the top of my lungs and raised Becchin over my head as I knelt on the floor.

O Becchin. Let me tell you that this emotion full of desire is love!

Short of breath, I began to consider my life plan. I had the good fortune of regaining the memories of my past life.

I can now redo my life that tragically ended at eighteen! I wish I had worked harder. I should've taken things more seriously back then. Whether it was in my studies or love, I have a lot of regrets. I want to live a regret-free life this time around. I'll devote all my energy to the things I wanted to do before! With a new resolve, I balled my tiny hands into fists.

By the way, memories were the only things I could recall from my prior life. Although I had been a high school student studying for university entrance exams, I couldn't remember anything knowledge-related. The sole knowledge I retained was what I had learned about music in order to complete *Hear My Heart*.

My inexplicable passion for learning music was ferocious enough that it frightened my high school music teacher. "Could you check if my harmony is off here?" I'd demand when I frequently intruded on the teacher's lounge with handwritten sheet music in hand.

You know, I'm pretty sure they were scared of me. I eagerly studied musical composition when I hadn't even been learning how to play an instrument.

I had saved up all my birthday money and allowance to buy every classical music CD I could get my hands on. Eventually, I could read music scores with ease. I don't doubt that there's some sort of meaning behind being able to remember all of that in my reincarnated life.

Kou played the violin.

Then shouldn't I start playing the violin as well? A great idea suddenly occurred to me. *That's it! I should learn the violin and attend Seio Academy. If I do that, I can spend the sparkling days of youth, known as high school, with the object of my desires! Even if he never acknowledges me, I'll be able to breathe the same air as him!*

"Mommy!"

I hastily changed, slipped my backpack over my shoulders, and ran down the stairs. Everyone, from my mom putting breakfast on the table, to my dad reading the newspaper, to my sister Hanaka who was checking her daily fortune on TV, turned from what they were doing to look at me.

"Good morning, Mashiro. You're spunky this morning."

"Make sure to wash your face. Bread's almost toasted."

"Mashiro, what were you singing?"

They all started talking at once, so I couldn't understand what they were saying. Instead of trying to figure it out, I placed my backpack next to my feet, then I knelt so that my knees were flat against the wooden floor.

"Wh-What are you doing...?"

My parents froze with their mouths open. Hanaka stared at me, wide-eyed.

"I have a favor to ask! Please let me learn how to play the violin!" I deeply bowed my head.

Violins come in various sizes. As a child grows, new violins need to be bought to match their size. Not to mention, there are lesson fees and instrument fees. Seio Academy is a private school, so with tuition and obligatory donations, my school expenses would be enormous.

Our family is an extremely normal middle-class household, and Dad is a company man who only recently got promoted to chief clerk, so it's probably a stretch.

But I'll work hard at it! I'll give it my all!

Mom regained her composure and laughed at my unusual determination. "I was wondering what this was all about. We don't have the money to let you pick up such an expensive hobby."

"Sorry, Mashiro. Daddy's job is just doesn't pay enough..."

Seeing Dad's sad expression clued me in to just how little leeway we had in our budget.

Right. I'm a minor character, so things aren't going to be easy for me. I sighed heavily as I was overcome by shock. *I see. It makes sense. Just because I was reincarnated into an otome game doesn't mean I'll get to live a life connected to Kou, especially if I'm just Pedestrian 1.*

"You're right. Sorry. I just asked because I figured I should give it a try." I stumbled to my feet and sat at the dining table. The bread and ham with eggs were tasteless.

"Why the sudden interest in the violin?" Hanaka asked, peering at my face, concerned.

Not like I could say, "Because I want to meet a romanceable character from an otome game." Instead, I changed the subject with a vague laugh.

It was time to go, so I put on my backpack and left the house.

♪♪♪

"MORNING!" Eri, my childhood friend who lived in the neighborhood, chased after me and lightly rammed into me from behind.

"Morning," I greeted, after pulling myself together.

"Hey, did you see it? Yesterday's IdRev?!" Eri's soft cheeks were flushed from excitement.

IdRev is an abbreviation for a show that's all the rage with elementary schoolgirls right now. It's short for *Idol Revolution ☆ Sparkling Stage*, an anime with a typical pipe dream story where a normal girl with pigtails suddenly becomes an idol. It's got your typical Cinderella storyline. Since it's backed by a major toy company, they're milking the preteen girl market and getting huge amounts of money from them and their parents.

As part of the herd, I had become engrossed in the trading card games. Mom looked on disapprovingly every time I had her take me to the shopping center to buy the next deck of cards to add to my ever-growing collection.

Agh. Now that I think about it, that was such a waste! I wonder how many music books I could've bought with that money?

"I forgot to watch it."

I totally wasn't in the mood for it yesterday. *Sou must know Kou for sure!* is the only thing I thought about all through dinner, bath time, and bedtime.

"No way! Mashiron, how could you?!"

"You're right. Tell me what I missed on the way to school!"

My interest in IdRev had completely vanished, but I needed to stay in character. I forced on the most disappointed expression I could manage.

Eri took on an all-important sounding tone as she caught me up, "Rune's quick change into her stage outfit was to die for! I want the card with that new outfit!"

Until yesterday, I would've thrown a fit in horror of missing the episode. I wanted so badly to copy Rune, that I even had my hair cut like hers.

It's only been one night, yet I see everything differently now. It's gonna be tough to wait eleven years to reach my former age.

Eri happily chatted away, oblivious of what I was thinking.

Restlessly, I stared at my homeroom teacher during class.

Aah, I want to hurry home and study. This isn't the time to be doing my multiplication tables. I was impatient because I remembered the game's fanbook from my prior life. I hadn't given up on my obsession even after being reborn in another world, and Kou's type was listed in the fanbook as, of all things, "Intelligent Girls."

I couldn't keep up with school in my past life, but if I start seriously studying now, I should make it in time. There's nothing that says we have a zero percent chance of meeting by accident, so I want Kou to have a high opinion of me when we do.

"What's wrong, Shimao? You don't need to hold it if you need to go potty."

We called the male teacher with a gruff appearance, who always wore a dark-blue jersey, Mr. Kumaja—a pun on his name and the word for bear. He was a kind teacher who was considerate of his students, but I think I just learned the reason why he was still single despite being over forty.

While all my classmates around me laughed, I thinly replied, "I don't have to go."

...Boy, it's painful to be an eighteen-year-old who's being laughed at by seven-year-olds over bathroom jokes.

♪♪♪

I somehow made it through an agonizing half-day amid the earsplitting ruckus kids make and left through the school gates beside Eri. Elementary schoolers are seriously noisy and annoying. They talk constantly to the point that you'd think their flapping lips would help them fly. They're like a swarm of flies buzzing around your ears for hours. Realizing I had been a part of that very swarm until just yesterday made me sigh inside.

Elementary school teachers are incredible. Definitely not a job you can take on unless you love children.

"Hey, can you play today? Takkun and the boys said they're gonna play dodgeball at Kujira Park. You're going too, right, Mashiron?" Eri peered meaningfully at me in my silence.

Takkun was the name of the most popular boy in the second grade. He was fast and great at dodgeball. Meeting those two requirements will easily win you the hearts of seven-year-old kids. If I remember correctly, I had ogled him at one point thinking he was kinda cute before my memories kicked in.

"I'm good. You should go, Eri. Didn't Takkun pull your hair today? Isn't that because he likes you? They say elementary school boys tease a girl the more they like her."

I just can't play dodgeball with a bunch of seven-year-olds. I kept my thoughts to myself and turned her down in the nicest way.

Eri gave me a curious look and burst out laughing. "Oh no, Mashiron! You're starting to sound like my mom!"

…I want to hurry back home.

♪♪♪

"I'M home!"

My voice was the only noise in the empty house. I opened the front door with the key hanging from my neck and put my small sneakers inside the aromatic wood shoe shelf. Mom was at her part-time job as a cashier at the local drugstore, and Hanaka usually didn't come home until around seven at night.

I checked out the kitchen to find homemade pancakes sitting on a plate covered in plastic wrap. After putting away my backpack and washing my hands, I took a seat on the couch in the living room. It felt awfully spacious. My feelings spiraled into depression from being alone in the silence. Just a little while ago I had wanted to get home as soon as possible too.

The various details of my past life that I had been doing my best not to think about were trying to burst past the mental locks I had placed on them. I blinked repeatedly.

Stop it. I don't want to think too deeply about it.

"I'm going to eat!" I declared in a purposefully cheery voice, then chomped down on the pancake dangling off the end of my fork.

Large teardrops tumbled down my cheeks.

They taste the same as the ones my other Mom used to make.

Obviously, they would. As long as you're using a pancake mix, the flavor's going to be the same no matter who makes it.

What am I crying for? Isn't this stupid?

I knew it was, but the tears wouldn't stop.

You made me snacks every night to encourage me while I studied for exams, and yet I died. I'm sorry, Mom.

You were looking so forward to drinking together once I became old enough, and yet I died. I'm sorry, Dad.

I wonder if my big sister yelled, "That's why I kept telling her to stop playing games!" while crying.

I fell into a manhole directly in front of a game store, so I'm pretty sure they figured out the cause of my death. I can't see them again, no matter how much I want to. I died and left them behind.

Through my sobs, I focused only on devouring my pancakes. If I stopped chewing, my heart would break.

This time I'll outlive my family. And find happiness. That's the only thing I can do now to make up for leaving my last family behind.

I cried my heart out as I strengthened my determination.

♪♪♪

THE sunlight spilling in through the curtains had turned orange when my tired mom came home and gawked at me in shock when she found me in the middle of ironing Dad's formal white shirt, having already done the laundry. Don't underestimate a seven-year-old's small hands. I'm confident in my dexterity.

"Oh dear! Why aren't you playing with your friends today? D-Don't tell me…b-bullying…you're being bullied? Oh no! I have to call your dad!" Mom pulled her cell phone out of her purse, trembling, and tried to dial Dad's number.

All I did was help out with chores, right?

I gave Mom a horrible shock since I had been a carefree elementary schooler who only played and did absolutely nothing to help out until yesterday.

"W-Wait a minute! I'm not being bullied! Calm down!"

"Mashiro, are you worried about something? Now that I think about it, you were acting funny this morning too… No matter what happens, I'm always on your side, Mashiro. So please talk to me about anything."

What wild things did she imagine as she tightly hugged me with teary eyes? For starters, I'd better get her to loosen her grip on me.

"Nothing is wrong! Mr. Kumaja said moms work hard for the family every day and it's important to help out. So I got the idea to start trying to help out now!"

The number one way to get parents off your case is to mention your teacher's involvement.

"He did? Mr. Kumazawa is such a nice teacher. I'm so proud of you, Mashiro! It's not easy to take advice from your elders."

I love this about Mom. She doesn't try to force her children to mindlessly listen to adults like parents and teachers. I nodded, grinning, and put away the ironing board.

Mr. Kumazawa? Mom, Mr. Kumaja's actual name is Nobuo Takemitsu. I laughed and kept the correction to myself.

At any rate, I had finished helping out around the house, so I went upstairs to study. I completed my homework in a flash and secretly set out to borrow the middle school textbooks from Hanaka's room. I felt bad for entering her room without permission, but it was necessary to solve my problem. If I asked her directly, I'd be interrogated. I wouldn't have good answers either.

Saying that I had memories of a past life or that we actually live in an otome game world would sound weird and crazy. I'm positive no one would believe me if I told them. And I'd question them if they did.

Since the last time I had visited her room, it'd transformed into a pigsty. I couldn't even see the floor! At least put the clothes you took off on a hanger!

Avoiding the personal items she probably wouldn't want me touching, I tossed out the garbage and lightly cleaned her room. Oh, and I couldn't forget to open the windows to let in fresh air either.

Mission accomplished, I returned to my room and spread out the textbooks. They were in perfect condition, leading me to believe that she barely cracked them open.

Sis, I'm surprised you made it to high school…

I switched gears and carefully read through the textbooks, underlining important passages. Math, Japanese, and English seemed like they'd probably be okay, but social studies and science were going to be a problem. All the subjects that required memorization were in the worst state. I had forgotten practically all of the details.

Next chance I get, I need to go to the bookstore and look for workbooks.

"Mashiro! Dinner's ready!"

I glanced at the clock when I heard Mom's voice—it was already seven. Dad returned home just in time for me to greet him.

"Welcome home!" I exclaimed, jumping into his arms.

"I'm home." He caught me with a lopsided smile and patted me on the head.

Hanaka happily descended the stairs. "Mom, you cleaned my room for me despite yelling at me this morning!" She winked playfully and added, "Thanks a bunch!" with a salute.

My big sister was a slob who found doing things annoying. At the same time, however, her big heart and simple-minded personality always filled our world with cheer and laughter.

Unable to scold her, Mom half-smiled and shook her head. "It wasn't me… Was it you, Mashiro?"

"Yup. I thought it wouldn't be fair if I only helped out Mommy, so I gave Big Sis a hand because she's doing her best at school."

I felt strangely guilty since I had snatched her textbooks and wouldn't be returning them anytime soon. *Am I being too sneaky?* I thought, as I used a sickeningly sweet voice to explain. But hearing my response seemed to delight Hanaka, because she suddenly pulled me into a hug.

"Gosh! Such a good girl! You're seriously adorable! Your big sis will be your devoted follower for life!"

For some reason, after that, Dad joined her in cheering my name, "MA! SHI! RO! MA! SHI! RO!"

Wow. She's got a bad case of the doting older sister disease.

My older sister in my last life had been the same way. She doted on me and spoiled me rotten. I rushed to my seat before my thoughts prompted waterworks and focused only on gobbling down my steak.

Dad often praised me cheerfully, and Mom was kind. My entire family got along insanely well, and the four of us had always laughed together.

"Come on now. Quit causing a ruckus and eat before it gets cold," Mom said, casually scolding them because of my sudden silence.

Filled with mixed feelings of happiness and regret, I continued to intently chew my food.

CG 2: Bookstore (Kou & Sou Common Route)

"SEE ya later, Mashiron!"

"Bye-bye, Eri!"

Although we usually went home together, I parted ways with Eri as soon as we left school. Eri had penmanship lessons today.

Two weeks had passed since I regained memories of my past life. I'd finally grown accustomed to living as an elementary school student, and the days passed by peacefully. What was there for me to get used to when I'd already been living as an elementary schooler until two weeks ago, you say? School. Being at school is when I sorely felt the gap between my mental age and body the most.

Inadvertently, I started to wonder whether it was really okay to go through life like this without taking action. *My information on my dear Kou ends when he graduates from high school. After that, I have no idea what happens to him. If I don't meet him while we're still students, I'll lose the chance to interact with him for life...* I was plagued with worries.

When I announced that I wanted to buy workbooks, Mom gave me the most suspicious look. And I mean *suspicious*.

"Are you the same girl who recently whined about how you don't want to do your homework?" Mom replied doubtfully, handing me 2,000 yen. She went on to specify that showing her the receipt and change were the conditions. I promptly nodded.

So here I was today. After I had bidden farewell to Eri, I crossed the footbridge to visit the massive bookstore facing the road. Then a miracle happened.

Natsu

I stopped in front of the high school exam's reference book corner, carefully scrutinizing the workbooks. I needed to find the most effective learning tools. A middle schooler fishing through the books on the same shelf kept glancing at me. Pretending like I hadn't noticed his questioning eye, I narrowed down my selection to four possibilities. Considering my budget, I could only buy two.

Constantly asking Mom for money wasn't going to be an option. After all, any bystander was bound to see me as second grade runt. Even if they thought I was an eager student studying for her middle school entrance exams, they'd laugh their heads off and say I didn't have a need for workbooks like *500 Questions You Need to Know for Your High School Exams.*

Should I narrow it down to social studies and science? Or go with a workbook that reviews all five subjects? Honestly, I want all four workbooks! I wish I could pick up a part-time job. Why am I still so young?

Just as I was contemplating what to do—

"Oh? Mashiro?" a high-pitched, meek voice rose from behind me.

Hm? This voice is… I turned around with a workbook held tightly to my chest to see a certain boy for the second time.

"Sou! Long time no see." I accidentally called him by his first name because that's what I was used to thinking of.

How could I call someone I met just recently by their first name?! I panicked, surprised by my own actions.

The Sou Shiroyama I knew from the game would've curtly shut me down without a second thought and say something like, "Could you please not speak to me as if we're friends?"

But the real world Sou beamed. "You remembered me. I've been looking for you since then, hoping we could meet again."

He must've also been on his way home from school, since his backpack hung off one shoulder and his school uniform blazer was unbuttoned. His refined pose was undeniably cool.

"Ahaha. You were?"

Sou gazed at me with such earnest eyes that I gradually felt an increasing urge to run away. If possible, I hoped he'd hurry up and walk away. Contrary to my wishes, he came closer and noticed the four other workbooks I had lined up across the shelf. He looked back at me, his eyes wide.

"Wow. Mashiro, you're already doing such complicated problems?"

"No…um, I guess. Just thought I should study properly…"

It's no use—I can't think of a good way to deflect the question. I've always been horrible at handling situations where you have to think on the fly. Good liars are the ones with quick wits.

"You're amazing! I have no idea how to solve these problems!" Sou exclaimed in the same way he had when we first met, as he started flipping through the workbook pages.

Getting the feeling that this conversation was going to be dragged out, I gave up on two of the workbooks, returning them to their former positions on the bookshelf. I wanted to take my time weighing the options, but getting out of here came first. The look Sou had in his eyes since he appeared made me uncomfortable.

Was it admiration? Adoration? Either way, it felt like he was extremely impressed by me. With zero experience with being looked at in such a way, I didn't know how to react.

"Well I'm going to go buy these now," I said, hoping he would catch on to the implied goodbye. Instead, he followed me, as if it were the obvious thing to do.

Seriously?! What am I supposed to do about him now?!

"Sou? Are you done already?"

At that moment—that exact moment—I heard what sounded like the younger version of Kou's sweet voice, which had entranced me on more than one occasion through the earbuds connected to my handheld console. I violently spun around.

His trademark fire-red hair was still short. Donning the same blazer as Sou, the top button of his shirt was undone and his necktie hung loose around his neck. I was overwhelmed by a sexy, pheromone-exuding seven-year-old. Narrowing his deep indigo-blue eyes like a cat, he glanced at our faces.

"What? Is this the girl you were talking about, Sou?"

His voice hadn't yet changed through puberty, but its sweetness still had the same power to resonate through my body.

Oh my gosh. It's the real Kou. I think I'm gonna cry.

I'm a woman at the mature age of eighteen crushing on a barely seven-year-old boy! My other half suddenly regained her composure, immediately raising a red flag.

I know! But if I don't look at him while I can, I might never get the chance to again!

Sou noticed my fascination with Kou and frowned. He grabbed my arm and pulled me behind his back.

"…Don't look at her, Kou. Tone down the fake sweetness."

My unhappiness about having Kou removed from my line of vision went right out the window at Sou's remark.

Huh? What did he just say? Was that some kind of jealousy? Yeah, as if! Impossible. I don't have anything that would attract this pretty boy. Talk about overconfidence.

"Heh… She's got you that attached, huh? Now I'm curious."

You're ten years too early! But I can forgive you! I thought, as Kou swiftly came around Sou's side to get a better look at me.

"I'm Kou Narita. I've been friends with Sou since preschool. Won't you be friends with me too, Mashiro?" Kou said smoothly, with a charming smile. Then he purposefully winked at me, as if to ensure that I would accept.

He winked! I got to see my precious Kou wink in person! This is the same line as the one Kou rewards the heroine with after she clears the first in-game test, and he finally starts to acknowledge her ability a little. Is it all right for you to be using that on a random minor character?!

Flustered, I turned bright red and fervently nodded. Feelings I couldn't put into words gushed inside me. I've no doubt that it was the same bliss felt by someone who meets eyes with or gets waved at by their favorite idol at a concert. If I wasn't careful, I'd turn into a puddle of fangirling goo.

I can't remember how I managed to purchase my books and go home after that. I just dashed upstairs without looking at anyone, tossed aside my newly purchased workbooks and backpack, and dived onto my bed.

"Becchin…! I met Kou! I was able to meet him!" I squeezed my teddy bear Becchin and excitedly rolled around on my bed for a good while before I found myself staring up at the ceiling. Countless unrestrainable sighs slipped past my lips.

He was super kind to me even though it was the first time we met. He's a thousand times lovelier than I'd ever imagined!

I was completely unaware at the time that Kou's wink and smile were a ruse.

I was also unaware of the conversation the two boys had once I left the bookstore.

"Sou, do a better job of picking your friends. No matter how you cut it, she's just after our looks."

"Shut up. Mashiro isn't like that."

"I'm tellin' you not to trust people until you know what they're like."

◇◇◇

Heroine's Results
Target Character: Sou Shiroyama
Second Event: Reunion at the Bookstore

Target Character: Kou Narita
Encounter Event: Who's That Girl?
CLEAR
◇◇◇

A huge turning point arrived the year I turned eight. A used upright piano found its way to our home.

"Mrs. Tanaka on Third Street asked us to take it off her hands because it's been collecting dust in her house for ages! Apparently, her daughter used to take lessons as a child, but got sick of it. It hasn't been used since, and by now she's an adult. Still though, isn't this an expensive instrument? I tried to turn Mrs. Tanaka down, but she told me to accept it without reservation, so here we are."

I immediately realized that Mom had actually spoken to our neighbor for my sake. One day out of the blue, her young daughter suddenly became abnormally passionate about learning music. I wonder exactly how much of a shock my parents had experienced. At first, they took me to a shrine for purification, then had me undergo counseling, but none of it influenced me whatsoever, so they finally gave up on fixing me.

And then there's my sister, who remained completely unaffected, making remarks like, "Mashiro's latent ability has finally awakened! I'm sure of it!" She readily accepted the dramatic change in her younger sister.

"Thanks, Mommy! I'm so happy!" I was so overexcited that I had a hard time sleeping the night I heard the news.

The price for transporting the piano to our house and the fee for tuning it added up to a rather hefty amount before I could even play it.

...I've stretched my parents on this one. The very least I can do is teach myself how to play instead of taking lessons.

At the time, I hadn't realized that Mom had already searched for piano lessons for me.

"Violin lessons may be beyond us, but we should be able to dig up money for monthly piano lessons. I talked with your dad and we decided we'd let you play the piano since you love music so much."

My heart ached painfully at her words.

I'm sorry, Mom. My motives for learning the piano are impure, dyed in a dark pink. But you've gone so far to support me, so I'll be sure to never give up! I definitely won't quit halfway through!

Thus, I became an incredibly busy third grader.

♪♪♪

I hadn't run into Kou again since the bookstore. Instead—not to make it sound like he was a replacement—Sou's path often crossed with mine. However, everything I knew about *Hear My Heart* revolved around my darling Kou. I hadn't seen a single one of Sou's events, so I had no idea what kind of person he was. I couldn't even recall the information on him that would've been printed in the game's fanbook. So I remained unsure of why he'd taken an interest in me.

The one time I asked him if he knew *Hear My Heart*'s heroine—Kon Genda—he promptly replied, "Don't know her."

Hmm, I thought the heroine had a default name, but maybe I was wrong.

On another day, I found Sou standing on the footbridge again. My route home after school seemed to overlap with the area he showed up in as if it corresponded to his territory as a character.

If possible, I wish my path overlapped with Kou's instead.

Sou was leaning on the handrail with a glum face. Whether I liked it or not, it reminded me of him crying on the day we met. His light-blue hair swayed in the wind, getting into his gloomy eyes. I couldn't bear to watch any longer.

"Souchi! What's up? Why the long face?" I called out to him, my voice deliberately perky. I tried to imitate Hanaka, but instead it looked like I'd seriously startled Sou. Sorry, that was accidentally *too* cheerful.

"I was just secretly hoping, 'maybe I'll be able to meet her again today?'" He made a tired smile, the corners of his lips curling up slightly. My heart broke at his overly mature, stressed expression—it didn't suit his age.

Sou looks like he's worried about something. I've got no idea what kind of worries the eight-year-old Sou has, but I'll bet it's not bullying. Wait, actually, that might unexpectedly be plausible. My thoughts drifted to the possibility of other boys at school becoming envious of his popularity and bullying him for it.

Even if the bully doesn't really care one way or the other, scars that'll never fade are carved into the victim through their actions. Consequently, some children choose to die.

Once my thoughts took a turn for the worse, I couldn't stop them. *Kou has a traumatic past; Sou might have one too.*

I wasn't sure how far to pry with someone I'd only recently gotten to know, but I couldn't just walk away without doing something.

"Sou, if...and I mean if...you're being bullied, you need to tell somebody. I get that you might be embarrassed. You might not want anyone to worry about you. But it could escalate if you keep it a secret. You should talk with an adult you can trust sooner rather than later."

Sou watched intently as I cautiously breached the topic of bullying, then suddenly burst out laughing. "So you're worried about me! I'm not being bullied. I don't have that kind of problem."

His carefree laughter meant my worries were misdirected.

Relieved, I laughed along with him. "You're not being bullied? I'm so glad."

"...Yeah. I'm okay. But thanks anyways," he said, with a bashful smile.

If affection meters exist in this reality like they do in otome games, I think his just went up a bar. Sou's honest, affectionate gaze left me unsettled.

"N-No problem. I mean, we're *friends*. Anyone would be concerned if their friend was feeling down," I said, overemphasizing the word "friends".

He chuckled again.

What should I do if his type is, "a girl who makes him laugh"? ...No way. Sou is one of the romanceable characters in Hear My Heart. He wouldn't have an ending with a trivial side character.

"By the way, have you folded anything new lately? What did you say you were attempting now?" Sou changed the topic, a smile still on his face.

At his requests and further pestering, I'd occasionally given him the origami creations I made.

"I've been attempting to fold Angkor Wat for a while now, but it's not going well. Reproducing the small details of three-dimensional buildings is hard!"

"What's Angkor Wat?"

"A temple in Cambodia that's a World Heritage site."

"Heh. You really know a lot of things, Mashiro." Admiration twinkled in his eyes.

Huh. Maybe most elementary schoolers don't know about it? I began to get nervous that maybe I'd let onto the fact that I reincarnated from another world if I kept talking.

"Th-That's not true. Oh yeah, guess what? We'll be getting a piano at my place today!"

Sou played an instrument as well, so I thought music would be a good topic. That was my casual reasoning for announcing my big news. Well, there was also the fact I was unbearably happy and wanted to share it with someone.

Contrary to expectations, Sou knitted his brow. But his frown lasted for only a second before he returned to his usual expression, as if nothing had happened.

"…Heh. I didn't know you played the piano, Mashiro. So, what did you buy? A Bechstein? Or a Steinway?" he asked as if it were normal, rendering me speechless.

There was no way I could buy expensive grand piano brands like those. Some cost more than a car. I knew he wasn't trying to be condescending since his expression had a simple innocence to it, but…

We live in different worlds. He's been blessed with a life where he can get anything he wants, so there's no way he would understand the happiness I feel over something this simple.

"…It's a normal upright piano. Our neighbor didn't have a need for it anymore, so we got it from them," my voice trembled.

It felt like he was looking down on the piano Mom went through so much trouble to get for me.

"Ah...I see," Sou mumbled awkwardly, and his lips parted to continue—

"I have to go now! I need to help out with the chores," I declared, one-sidedly ending the conversation before he could say anything else. I managed to wave at him before dashing down the footbridge.

I know I live in a completely different world from Sou. Kou's setting is the rich young son to a wealthy family, so Sou probably is too. So much so that he'd casually ask me if I got a Bechstein. Those start at twenty grand and some even go for half a million dollars!

Sou didn't call after me. I glanced over my shoulder to see him silently standing still in the middle of the footbridge.

♪♪♪

I meticulously polished the first instrument I had ever owned in my entire life—including my past life—with a soft rubbing cloth. The perfectly tuned piano, which was placed in my room at my request, shimmered and sparkled under the lights.

I needed to give the piano a name before I did anything else with it. In one of the *Hear My Heart* events, after the heroine becomes more intimate with Kou, they discuss their instrument names.

"Treat your instrument as dearly as you would a lover. If you do, it'll whisper its love back to you," Kou had said through the LCD screen.

I planned to follow suit and do the same with my piano.

I went downstairs and asked Mom while she was preparing dinner, "Hey, do we have a name book for babies anywhere in the house?"

It looked like we were going to have breaded pork cutlets for dinner. Mom tilted her head curiously as she dipped the meat in breading. "I think we still have one. What do you want it for?"

"I want to give my piano a name! A super cute name!"

"A name for your piano? I see. Hehe. I'm so happy to see you like it that much. You know where we store the albums in the closet shelves? I'm positive I put it there."

"Okay. Thanks. I'm going to borrow it for a bit."

I found the book I was after covered in dust and wiped it down before returning to my room. The old book, *1000 Names You Want to Name Your Precious Child*, appeared to have been opened and closed many times, so that the binding was worn and the edges of the pages were snipped. The book naturally opened to the pages containing the names "Hanaka" and "Mashiro". They must've considered other names too, since different areas had been methodically underlined.

Unexpected heat stung the corner of my eyes. I could easily imagine my parents from my last life going through the same process in order to name me and my sister. Somewhere in the back of my mind I still felt guilty for making them mourn for me. I blinked repeatedly to keep the tears from escaping and searched through the book for the perfect name.

Thinking about the past now won't change anything. No one can redo the past. I can only do my very best at the present.

Flipping back to the first page, I started my search from the letter "A". Ami, Akari, Ayu…an endless number of names covered the pages. My eyes stopped on the name "Aine". Isn't it a wonderful name that reminds you of Mozart's famous composition "Eine kleine Nachtmusik"? The fact that Kou's favorite composer was Mozart gave me the extra push to decide on this name.

"All right! From today on, you are Aine!" I said to the piano, then played the main melody from "Eine kleine Nachtmusik" that I vaguely remembered with my right hand. A broken melody rose from its keys, filling my room.

Wow! It's the real sound of a piano! The keys are heavy.

I brought my ear to the keyboard and listened attentively to the quality of its sound coming from the keys I pressed. What an incredibly lovely sound. Thirty minutes passed as I struggled to get to the right sound. Eventually, it began to sound like it should. I learned the fingering techniques for playing a piano in my past life, but there's a remarkable difference in difficulty between reading about something in a book and actually doing it.

I have to psych myself up for this one!
Do-re-mi-fa-so-la-ti-do
123 12345

I pressed the key for fa with my middle finger (corresponding to the number 3), then replaced it with my thumb (corresponding to the number 1).

I can't increase the speed smoothly. My left hand's definitely gotten more awkward. As if I were possessed, I practiced the C major scale obsessively. *Separate the four octaves with a staccato. With syncopation. Until it becomes one smooth sound. Go up, up, up, and up and then down, and repeat.*

"I CAN'T TAKE IT ANYMORE!"

My bedroom door flung open. Hanaka stood in the doorway panting with a maddened expression. "Seriously, please don't make me suffer through any more of this racket! You've been repeating the same sound for an entire hour since I came home. I'm freaking out here. Please cut it out!"

The sky peeking through my lace curtains was completely dark.

"Ah, I'm sorry for being so noisy. Next time I'll use the soft pedal to bring down the volume."

"It's not that it's too noisy. It's really not that, but—gah, forget it. Let's go eat." Hanaka slumped her shoulders.

Everyone regarded me differently at the dinner table. Starting with Hanaka, my entire family unanimously emphasized, "We're all here for you if you have anything you want to talk about."

♪♪♪

THE day of my first piano lesson arrived. This lesson was for meeting and getting to know the piano teacher and to purchase the necessary music books—we weren't going to actually touch the piano. Regardless, I was a nervous wreck as I tightly clasped Mom's hand. I was led to a lesson room on the second-story of a large mansion. I was overwhelmed by the excessively spacious, completely soundproof room, when a slender, beautiful woman, who appeared to be in her mid-twenties, entered.

"How do you do? I'm Ayumi Matsushima. Is it all right for me to call you Mashiro?"

Overcome by the image of her polished beauty, my mouth hung open.

"I-It's nice to meet you! I'm Mashiro Shimao. I'm eight. This will be my first time playing the piano, but I'll try my very bestest!" I was too nervous, and my greeting abruptly came out sounding like a typical eight-year-old.

"Haha. You don't have to be so stiff. Relax. Okay? Play the piano a lot with me so you can start thinking music is fun!"

Not only is she a beauty, she's super sweet as well. She's way too cool. My piano teacher was thoroughly captivating.

I secretly stole a glance at Miss Ayumi's fingers while she spoke with Mom about business details like the monthly lesson fee. Her dainty fingers were exceptionally long and looked like they could make the sound of an octave chord resound. As I dreamily gazed at her fingers, Mom awkwardly cleared her throat.

"…I'm sorry. Mashiro, don't stare so much."

"Ah, sorry." I quickly averted my eyes.

"It's all right. Don't worry about it. Mashiro, if you like, why don't you wait in the drawing room next door until we finish talking? I left books and manga in there," Miss Ayumi suggested, out of consideration for my boredom.

Drawing room? Curiosity piqued by the unfamiliar term, I nodded excitedly. Following Miss Ayumi, I crossed the threshold into the room next to the one we were chatting in. Miss Ayumi pushed the solid wood double door open to reveal the embodiment of a drawing room.

A white porcelain vase decorated an antique side cabinet. The chic-colored, striped upholstered sofa seemed like it could comfortably sit about five people. On top of the exquisitely crafted Draw Leaf Table rested a crystal bowl filled with colorful candies. Miss Ayumi pointed to the built-in floor-to-ceiling bookshelf with her perfectly manicured fingers.

"Read any book you like and wait here, okay? You are always welcome to relax here before your lessons start and while waiting for your parents to come pick you up. My other students may be present sometimes, but they are all very good children, so you can rest at ease."

"Okay! Thank you very much!"

She watched me respectfully bow my head to her, and left the drawing room with a gentle smile.

I immediately made my way to the bookshelf. Manga about ballet and music filled the shelves, unexpectedly side by side with shounen (for boys) sports manga. Naturally, there were normal books, music books, musical grammar books, and a lot of essay compilations on music in general.

What should I start with? I was cheerfully rummaging through the bookshelves, when—

"Hello. Oh…?" A girl entered the drawing room.

It wasn't like I was doing something I wasn't supposed to, but I frantically pulled my hand back from the bookshelf.

I wonder if she's one of the students Miss Ayumi mentioned.

I timidly turned around and tried my best to greet her without sounding funny. "Hello."

Long, brown hair; big, beautiful eyes with several layers of color; and perfectly white skin caught my eye. An undeniably beautiful girl like the genuine incarnation of a two-dimensional character was standing there.

Huh. I feel like I've seen her somewhere before. Who is she?

The girl intently stared at me as I racked my memories for who she was, then, for some reason, she struck a triumphant pose in the middle of the room.

"YEESSSSSSS! I found you! I finally got to meet you!"

Her graceful appearance and aggressive speech and manners were seriously at odds. Bowled over by her reaction, I took a big step back.

"Ah, sorry. Don't creep away from me! I mean, don't be creeped out!"

Why did she say it twice? Does she mean both mentally and physically or something?

The girl's eyes shone with joy as she closed in on where I stood frozen and looked straight into my eyes. Then her big eyes wavered, tearing up.

Why does she look like she's going to cry?

"I'm Kon Genda. Am I right to assume you're Mashiro Shimao?"

Kon Genda...

Kon Genda?!

A smile bloomed on her face when she saw my eyes widen with astonishment. Her eyes were still misty, and she looked like she was about to cry any moment now.

"How do you do? I'm the old game's heroine. You're the remake version's heroine, right? Do you understand what I'm talking about? Or are you thinking, 'what the heck's this strange woman blabbing about?!'"

H-Hang on a minute! I'm too shocked to process this information!

"I-I understand...I think. B-But what remake version? Um, Genda, is it possible you also—"

"You can call me by my first name. I don't like this last name very much. And yes, I've also reincarnated into this world."

"I-Is that even..."

Possible?!

I guess it's not impossible. It's not like there's a set rule that only one person can be reincarnated per a world. Now that I'm studying her carefully, it's not just the name and appearance that matches—she also has all the traits of Hear My Heart's *heroine. Just as she announced, this girl must be the heroine.*

The remake version must be the game that was advertised on the poster I saw right before I died. I never got to play it myself, so I've no idea what has her so excited.

"It's a real surprise, isn't it? By the way, how old were you in your last life?" Her initial explosion of excitement seemed to settle down, because she asked me that in a calmer tone.

"Eighteen."

"I see... I was twenty-four, so that makes me like your big sister,

Mashiro." Her smiling face was perfectly refined in every way, like a doll's.

It's seriously disorienting when you see an eight-year-old girl saying she's twenty-four. Although I was in no position to judge her, being in the same position, so instead I etched into my mind to be sure not to make the same mistake.

"Do you have time to talk right now?"

"Probably not. I think my mom will be coming over here soon."

"Okay, then can you tell me when your lesson days are decided? I'll book a time close to yours!"

"O-Okay."

Kon pulled a smartphone out of her lesson bag, which I recognized instantly as an expensive brand. "You don't have a cell phone, right? Gimme a second to write down my phone number."

How did she know that I didn't have a cell phone? I was surrounded by middle-class students at school, but a good percentage of my classmates owned smartphones. Maybe that was one of the elements added to the remake version.

There were so many things I wanted to ask her.

"Here you go, Mashiro! You can call me anytime, so give me a call when it's good for you. I'll add your house phone number to my contacts when you do."

So that's how I met another person who was reincarnated into this world.

CG 3: Piano Lessons (Kou)

I stretched as far as I could in the bathtub. I still wasn't used to this body. My gaze shifted downward to my stick-like calves and I scrutinized my spread-out fingers. No matter how I looked at my hands, they were the smooth, soft, tiny hands of an eight-year-old.

Maybe I didn't actually reincarnate into this world? All along, some part of me had been doubtful. *There's a chance I mistook a lucid dream or something like that for "memories of a past life".* These thoughts hid in the back of my mind.

But the truth I was unable to prove on my own, yet believed in, had been suddenly verified by the appearance of Kon Genda.

Or is it possible both of us have a few screws loose?

"Agh! I just don't know anymore!"

SPLASH! I submerged my face in the hot water.

At any rate! Even if this is a delusion or my imagination running wild, I'll do whatever it takes to get admitted to Seio Academy and find a way to interact with my dearest Kou.

Maybe this alarming obsession with him is what makes me the game's heroine? Chills ran along my spine, causing me to shudder in the hot water.

♪♪♪

MY lesson days were scheduled for once a week on Thursdays at 5 p.m. Miss Ayumi was a young professional pianist, who participated in musical performances in addition to serving as a lecturer at a music university. She had won international music competitions in the past and expectations for her future as a pianist were high.

...Why has such an extraordinary person agreed to give piano lessons to a beginner? All of my doubts instantly dissipated the moment Mom handed me the Czerny music book. *It's finally going to happen! I'm going to play the piano!*

"Mommy, Daddy, thank you so much! I promise I won't quit halfway!"

"Okay. Now that you've started, make sure to do your best, Mashiro."

"Honestly, I don't know much about music, but you'll have recitals, right? I'll definitely come watch," Dad said.

I also need to do my best for my parents who kindly listened to my selfish request! Getting started at eight is kind of on the late side if you want to take a more professional path with the piano though. I'll need to eliminate the gap from this handicap with practice.

I returned to my room and pulled out my diary. I had already recorded the details from Kou's profile and events I thought I'd start to forget as the months and years passed. Anyone else reading it would probably be traumatized for life by what was essentially a stalking notebook. But the notes wouldn't be of much use if I really was in the remake version of the game.

My appearance and personality aren't of heroine quality as they're completely average, so I wonder if I can't somehow get the plot to flow the same way as the last game. Maybe I should ask Kon about it. She's such a pretty girl—the perfect match for my darling Kou.

Imagining the two of them side by side had me grinning like an idiot.

However, when I went to my lesson a little earlier than necessary on Thursday, Kon wasn't the only one waiting for me.

"U-Um?"

This is super awkward! For some reason, Kon and Kou had taken position on either side of me.

"What is it?"

"What?"

Their perfectly unified reply rattled both of my eardrums.

"Are Kon and Kou—I mean, Narita—friends?"

The last time I asked Sou about Kon he'd promptly said that he didn't know her, so I had naturally assumed his best friend Kou hadn't met her either.

"Heh. Just what could the answer be? What do you think, Mashiro?" Kou taunted, cocking his head with a bewitching smile. Had no one else been around, I would've rolled around on the floor with glee.

"Why are you teasing her? Isn't she asking because she doesn't know?" Kon interjected. She seemed upset since I entered the drawing room.

A frown clouded her beautiful face as she glowered at Kou over my head. Kou took her glare easily and grinned back at her, unruffled. Even his devious smile was cool.

What's going on here?

"You're seriously in the way here, Kou. I was waiting for this chance to have a long chat with Mashiro!"

"And that's exactly why you should've told me what you were going to talk about in the first place. Then I wouldn't have had to come all the way to Ayumi's."

I have no idea what they're talking about. The fact that Kou referred to Miss Ayumi as just Ayumi was surprising.

"...You know Miss Ayumi as well, Narita?"

"You've had nothing but questions for me today, Mashiro. All right. I'll answer your questions, so you have to answer mine too. You good with that?" The sexy air intermingled with his beguiling voice took my breath away and put me under a spell.

...Ack! Is this some kinda hypnotism? I'm dealing with an eight-year-old boy here. He's only a child. Get a hold of yourself, Mashiro! I nodded as I tried to calm myself.

Kou's gentle expression went sharp; his piercingly cold, callous gaze cut right through me. "What are you scheming? Not only did you go after Sou, you got close to Kon. What are you after?" he spat in a low, biting voice filled with hate.

His unexpected accusations made me go numb.

...Is he...suspicious...of me? Scheming? Does wanting to see his love events happen in the future count as a scheme?

"Kou!"

Kon angrily jumped to her feet just as Miss Ayumi's soft voice called in to the room, "Mashiro, you can come in now."

"TODAY will be your first lesson, so why don't we practice moving your fingers in a way we call piano fingering?"

Miss Ayumi adjusted the bench height for me and sat beside me. A delicate fragrance wafted from her.

Is she wearing Bvlgari's Eau De Toilette?

Her beautiful fingers slid across the keys as if they were slowly stroking them. I carefully imitated the way she touched the keys.

"Oh, Mashiro, is this really your first time playing the piano?" I nodded. "Did you happen to practice the music book songs already?" Miss Ayumi asked.

"Yes. I didn't know which song we were going to start from, so I went in order and practiced just the first five."

Miss Ayumi's mouth fell open. It's impressive that a beautiful person remains beautiful no matter how inelegant of an expression they make.

"I had originally planned for today's lesson to be on practicing with just your right hand, then your left, and to tie it up by slowly using both hands, but…"

"I wasn't sure if I had the right tempo down because I don't have a metronome at home, but I should be able to at least get it to sound like how it's written in the music book."

As I slowly played through the first song I had memorized, Miss Ayumi's cheeks flushed, as if she were deeply moved.

"Incredible! You must have practiced a lot!" She collected herself and peered at my face. "Mashiro, are you possibly thinking about becoming a professional pianist in the future?"

"No, not that far… It's just my dream to attend Seio Academy's Music Department. That's why…"

I was aware that I was hoping for something far beyond my ability and station in life. My last few words trailed off into an inaudible whisper.

"I see. Okay, let's do our best together to make that happen! I'll teach you with the same goal of getting you admitted."

The look in Miss Ayumi's eyes changed and the air around her turned serious. She was entirely different from when I first entered the lesson room. I gulped and held my breath.

"First, let's begin with where to place your hands. You seem to have more than enough strength in your fingers, so you have a tendency to rely on them. Relax the palm of your hands more and—"

Miss Ayumi and I concentrated on the music book in front of us. Before long, the alarm went off. The sixty-minute lesson felt like a mere ten minutes.

"Will you let your mother know that I'll call her tonight? I teach my students who are aiming to get into music universities solfège on Saturdays, and I believe you should participate in it too, Mashiro."

"Yes. I'll tell her." I bowed and excused myself from the lesson room. *Phew. I-I'm beat… But it was so much fun!*

I had a clear objective to strive for until the next lesson, and I returned to the drawing room feeling like I was on cloud nine.

"Mashiro, you can just ignore anything Kou says," Kon whispered in my ear as she passed by to trade places with me, leaving me to watch her dainty back in confusion. The door quietly closed, resulting in me being alone with Kou in the room's extravagant space. Recalling his earlier attack, I planted myself on the sofa away from him.

"Are you waiting to be picked up, Mashiro?" Kou promptly asked, as if nothing had happened between us.

"…Yes."

This is only the second time I've met Kou, so why did he say those things to me? I wanted to think it through, but Kou's gaze unnerved me so much that I couldn't gather my thoughts. *Ugh…Mom, hurry and pick me up!*

"Hmm. Hey, I haven't heard your answer to my earlier questions."

I knew it. He's bringing it back up!

"I'm not scheming anything. I honestly don't have any weird thoughts. I'm r-really not after anything."

Although I eagerly tried to defend myself, his first question about why I was here was warranted, because my actions had been perfectly suspicious. I'd be guilty as charged if he pressed me about what motivated me to start learning the piano.

"I see. I understand now."

"…Phew. I'm glad—"

"Don't be. I'm saying I understand that it's pointless to ask you."

Why is he so angry?! Scary! He's way too scary! I seriously don't understand. What if, even though I haven't done anything wrong, he can't forgive the sheer fact

I exist? If that's the case, then I'm at such a loss on what to do that it's depressing.

"If you try anything funny with Sou or Kon, I'll never forgive you. Got it?" Kou growled, then elegantly stalked out of the drawing room.

What does he mean by that? Why does he have to threaten me?

The only thing I could take away from Kou's attitude was that he hated my guts.

◇◇◇

Heroine's Results
Target Character: Kou Narita
Second Event: Wariness
CLEAR
◇◇◇

♪♪♪

THE shock hit me that night when I crawled into bed. My mind had been overloaded by my first lesson and rejected further excitement until it sorted through the first bout of it.

Cold eyes. A guarded tone. Kou looked down on me with suspicion and contempt when all I did was smile away like an idiot.

That's right, he looked down on me. After concluding that I'm a suspicious girl following around his precious Sou and Kon, he tried to get rid of me. It took me a while, but I finally realized that fact.

Kou was scarred by something that happened in his childhood, a truth that's revealed at the end of the game once the heroine and Kou become intimate. I appeared to have strongly provoked his trauma.

"Ahaha… This sucks, Becchin." I hugged the teddy bear next to my pillow and squeezed my eyes shut.

I was so ecstatic to have met my dearest Kou that I'd gotten ahead of myself. I had foolishly regarded him as a character in a game. This might be *Hear My Heart*'s world, but it's also our reality.

It's not like I was thinking of something as preposterous as wanting to date him. I would've been happy in the distant position of being his friend's friend and getting to watch him from afar. But from the real life's Kou's perspective, I was nothing more than a creepy, wannabe stalker. It made sense that he'd think poorly of me.

Putting all my effort into studying in this world; desperately staring down sheet music in the past world in order to compose songs; from Kou's point of view, all that I had done was merely a nuisance.

"…Aah…" I started sobbing.

I'm embarrassed. Sad. Mortified.

Until I cried myself to sleep, every single one of Kou's words repeated on an endless loop in my head. It was easier to resent his cold-heartedness. I didn't want to think about how shameful I had been in getting ahead of myself and being all excited over him.

♪♪♪

THE next day: as I've always possessed a shameless personality, I got back on my feet with a change of heart.

It's true that I was acting like an idiot, but I still didn't deserve those mean accusations from someone who doesn't even know me. I'll round up the pieces of yesterday's me, the girl who was sobbing like her heart had been broken, and toss them out with the garbage!

Besides, when you really think about it, I wasn't even the one who had started things with Sou and Kon, right? Sure, my motives for attending piano lessons were impure, but coming across Kon was a total coincidence, and a good one at that.

From the start, I never even wanted anything from my dearest Kou. I was hoping that at the very least we could be acquaintances, but if even that will bother him, I'll back down.

But Kon is another story. I've miraculously found someone else who has been reincarnated. I won't let him stop us from being friends.

…Now that it's come to this, I'll do whatever it takes to get admitted to Seio Academy and beat him at his own game!

With that, I devoted myself to studying and learning the piano, even more rigorously than I had before.

♪♪♪

AFTER school on the day before my second piano lesson, I bumped into Sou yet again. Or more like I found him lying in wait for me. He was casually leaning against the wall right beside my elementary school's gate.

Eri's eyes sparkled when she exclaimed, "Look, that boy! Isn't he super cool?" She elbowed me in the side for my agreement.

"Mashiro! ...I'm glad I got to see you."

I tried to hide in Eri's shadow and stealthily sneak by, but sure enough, he spotted me and ran up to us.

Eri grinned and laughed, "I'll go home first! Bye-bye!" She waved and promptly left me behind.

"I'm sorry about last time. I was rude... Bye," I immediately apologized, expecting him to bring up the awkward fight we had over the piano.

I had decided to keep a distance from anyone involved with Kou. Sou wasn't any exception, which is why I tried to walk past him after apologizing, but—

"Wait! I heard from Kou that he said some horrible things to you, Mashiro." His words stopped me in my tracks. "I told him he has it all wrong. So don't let him get to you. He's not a bad guy, but a lot has happened to him..." None of this was his fault, but when he spoke to me he looked desperate.

Guilt hit me when I saw Sou's cheeks flushed with red. He was still young. The eighteen-year-old inside warned me not to act like a child.

"Whatever circumstances he has, I'm not so kind as to excuse someone I barely know for saying horrible things to me. So...I don't want to be around Narita at all. But..." I paused there. Sou intently stared at my mouth, waiting for what I had to say next.

Hah. It's no use. I can't push him away. I can't cut him out of my life; he looks tormented by the thought of it.

"If you promise not to tell Narita that we've met up to talk, I'll fold origami for you again. Are you okay with that?"

"...! Yeah, I'm okay with that. Thank you, Mashiro."

Sou's dramatic shift from tensed anxiety to a radiant smile was adorable. He fiercely activated my maternal instincts. One way or another, our relationship the past year essentially consisted of him seeking me out and me giving him attention in return. Getting attached was inevitable.

"You sound like an adult, Mashiro, which is so cool! You really are amazing," Sou said, his eyes sparkling.

I'm not amazing. I'd obviously talk like I'm older because I really am ten years older, I wanted to confess and repent. But I couldn't tell him. I couldn't reveal the truth to anyone besides Kon, not to my friends or my family. I'd seen characters in movies and dramas live out their lives while hiding their true identities, but I had never imagined that it would be such a heavy burden to bear.

♪♪♪

THE day after I'd made up with Sou, I headed to the drawing room with a heavy heart, only to find Kon waiting for me there alone.

"Thank goodness! You actually came!"

My apprehension melted at the smile on her face.

I wonder if she was bothered by the way Kou rudely treated me last week. I'm happy she's worried about me.

"Of course I'd come. Kou may have angrily demanded, 'Don't come near Kon!', but I'm not obligated to listen to him."

"So the event did play out as it's supposed to after I left. But wasn't it a huge shock for you? I can't stand Kou's initial events."

…Huh? Event? That was an event?

Kon lowered her eyebrows sympathetically when she saw my dumbfounded look. The kind understanding in her eyes threatened to bring back the tears I shed last night.

"Right, you know nothing about the remake version. That's why I wanted to tell you in advance, but Kou was standing guard over me… I'm sorry. I thought I might not be able to tell you everything today, so I summarized the main points in this notebook. You can ask me anything. If it's something I know, I'll answer it." She handed me a full-sized notebook with a cute cover.

"Thanks."

She even went through the effort of making me handwritten notes. Kon is such a good person.

"The most important thing you need to know now is that this world really is the remake version of the game. Kon Genda can't become the heroine. Kou and I are twins, after all."

…What?

Whaaaaaaaaaaat?!

"Mashiro, you can come in now," Miss Ayumi called.

Natsu

I placed the notebook in the lesson bag Mom made for me and hurried to my feet. Overly flustered, I nearly tripped. But despite my mental state, the moment I entered the soundproof room, the piano possessed me.

♪♪♪

MOM worriedly glanced at me through the rearview mirror after she picked me up in our Kei car. Apparently, my silence since I climbed into the back seat was concerning.

"...Did your lesson go poorly?"

"Nope. Lessons were okay. Miss Ayumi told me to keep up the good work."

Relieved to see me shake my head, Mom smiled and returned her attention to the road. "You're really working hard, aren't you, Mashiro? What was it—a solfège? Isn't that difficult too?"

"Yeah. The audiation part is definitely hard. All of it is a first for me and it takes complete concentration to keep up. But I'm okay. I'm doing it because I want to. You also have it hard, Mommy, since you have to drop me off and pick me up. I'll go by bicycle next year."

"It'll take you more than thirty minutes if you do that. Rely on us while you're still in elementary school."

"I'm doing it because I want to." My own words dropped to the pit of my stomach like a rock.

It's true that I started for Kou, but it's different now. I love seeing my effort build on my past efforts, resulting in new achievements. I love the sound of the piano and how easily it changes its color and sound, from gentle to sad with everything in between, depending on how you play it.

I love the piano.

Eating dinner as a family, taking a bath, studying. It feels incredible to complete what I set out to do for the day.

Honestly, I wanted to review and practice the parts Miss Ayumi advised me about today, but I gave up when I looked at the clock. I was only allowed to use the piano until 9 p.m. It was already close to ten.

I tidied up my desk and double-checked that everything was ready for school tomorrow before getting into bed. I squirmed into a comfortable position and gingerly opened Kon's notebook. It took a lot of courage to start reading it.

<u>Heroine: Mashiro Shimao</u>
Admitted to Seio Academy's High School Department under a piano scholarship. Despite constant bullying from high-handed rich kids, she has the strength to ingeniously get back at them.

I read that far and reflexively shut the notebook. *What the heck?! Why do I have to be constantly bullied? That sounds scary!* Taking deep breaths to calm myself, I reopened the notebook.

The heroine from the original game is the first character to appear in the remake version. On the selection screen, the player chooses if she will be Sou or Kou's little sister. Both characters have quite the sister complex. The system is set so that whoever becomes the original heroine's older brother is the current heroine's romanceable character. Clear the game once, and Rewind Mode becomes available. The player becomes capable of returning to where Mashiro and Kon meet to replay the game.

This is horrible. There's a limit to how much you can change something for the worse. Making the original heroine a side character while keeping the new heroine's romanceable characters the same as the last game is basically asking most of the original players not to play. Depending on the player, that'd be a deal-breaker.

Like, did a lot of fans write in saying, "I want to become the younger sister of the romanceable characters!" or something for them to come up with this nonsense?

Hm? …Hold on. Kon said that she's Kou's twin sister. Does that mean I'm stuck with Kou as my romanceable character?!

Screw that! I absolutely refuse to go along with this! You can't forget being humiliated just like that. Even a one-hundred-year love will instantly turn cold. And I never had enough love for him to withstand such scorn anyway. After all, I only fell for him because of his looks. They say it's easy to confuse fandom with love.

I wonder if it would've been easier if I'd found out about this sooner. Then I could've seen that "Look Down on the Heroine Event" in a positive light, knowing that our relationship was going to start off like cats and dogs.

…Nope. Unthinkable. Not possible. I couldn't care less about "darling" Kou.

Natsu

Actually, I rather not even get involved with him.
   Change in plans. Now that it's come to this, I'll break all of the event flags!

♪♪♪

ONE night sometime after my change in plans, Hanaka came into my room and handed me the wireless house phone.

"Mashiro, a friend's calling you."

The only friend I could think of who would call was Kon.

"Hello?"

"Good evening. This is Kon. Do you have time right now?"

"Yeah, we can talk. Thanks for the notebook! I read all of it."

"I'm glad you seem to be in a better mood than I thought you'd be in. This 'remake' is really only in name. Doesn't it seem like a completely different game now? I was worried that you might've been reeling in shock about Kou."

Kon's notebook contained all sorts of shocking facts written in beautiful strokes. From what it said, when Kon was four, her parents let her childless aunt and uncle adopt her—hence why her last name was different from Kou's.

Kou's hostility toward me was due to an incident where a girl who had a crush on him went mad with jealousy and stabbed Kon with scissors. Apparently, the girl who stabbed Kon didn't know that she and Kou were actually blood-related siblings. Fortunately, the injury hadn't threatened Kon's life, but it left Kou with traumatic mental scars.

Of course it would. The girl fell in love with him all on her own, to the point that she was boiling with jealousy over him. After an incident like that, anyone would be afraid of readily accepting affection.

…I mean, isn't that way too depressing of a past? It's taking it a step too far to severely injure the original heroine for the sake of giving the characters traumatic pasts.

"If I didn't have your notes, I probably would've lost heart halfway through. I'm really nothing but grateful to you, Kon," I replied, and heard Kon suddenly exhale through the receiver.

"You don't have to be. I'm happy to help. I was honestly feeling discouraged, and it was a relief to actually meet you."

Anyone would feel uneasy if they were suddenly reincarnated into a video game world. I'd been sickly obsessed with Kou though, so it had been relatively easier for me to accept it.

…It'd been an awfully powerful sickness. What a relief that I got over it.

"So I called you because I have a favor to ask of you today…" Kon trailed off, as if I wouldn't like what she had to say. I had a bad feeling about this.

"You aren't possibly going to ask me to participate in *that* event, are you?"

"Please! …I'm positive my encounter event with Tobi won't activate unless you're with me."

Tobi was a hidden character that only appeared in the remake version. Full name: Tobi Yamabuki. He's Seio Academy's principal and his route was meant for Kon. His name immediately gives away the fact that he's a main character. *Hear My Heart*'s developer seemed to have a thing for giving all of the main characters names related to colors. Case in point: the character for Kou means crimson while Sou's means blue; Kon's means navy while Mashiro's means pure white. And Tobi's characters indicate reddish-brown.

As you'd expect, Tobi being a hidden character meant he wouldn't appear until the second play-through. Basically, only once the original heroine and new heroine have met is it possible to encounter Tobi Yamabuki.

"The Young Money Tree" was the name of his encounter event. Tobi's route had such a vulgar storyline that it created mixed reception among players. Can you blame them? The name of his encounter event was sickening enough to convince me why.

From what I gathered from Kon, the half-Japanese Principal Tobi possesses dainty and refined features. He's prince-like with golden hair and blue eyes. And twenty-three years old. And Kon, who's attracted to this prince, is eight. Can you believe there's a fifteen-year age difference between her and the prince?

It seems like he's not the principal yet either. He just returned from studying abroad at Oxford University and has spent the past year working at a company owned by a relative of his.

He'll be thirty when we start attending Seio Academy… Is it all right for a relatively young thirty-year-old to be principal? His age would've been a fine match for

Kon in her previous life, but it's an awful combination now. It's not even comparable to how mismatched Kou and I are. What a pedophilic prince.

"I see… It's not like I don't understand how you feel, Kon… All right, if Miss Ayumi asks me to go, I'll say that I will, for you."

"Thank you! You've really made my day!"

I made a strained smile at Kon's enthusiastic voice. It felt like I was watching myself before I had gotten over Kou. Looks like the Tobi sickness packs quite a powerful punch too.

"But I don't feel anything for Kou anymore, so don't try to forcefully set us up, okay?"

I was perfectly fine cooperating with Kon's otome game agenda, but I didn't want to get involved in things past that.

Kon seemed to reluctantly hold her tongue at my emphasized statement, then answered, "Fine."

What was with that pause? I'm worried…

Kon and Prince Tobi's romance was completely separate from the remake heroine's storyline. In other words, it was meant to be a reward for players who had played the last game.

Once I succeed in getting Tobi's encounter event, I won't follow Hear My Heart's storyline any further.

In my last life, I didn't have any particular aspirations for the future. I hadn't hoped for much outside of my vague ideal to work at a company with good pay. But I've been blessed with a second chance, so I wanted to venture out with different activities this time around.

For the time being, my goal is definitely the piano. My life's turning point will be the Junior Music Competition that takes place during my second year of middle school.

The game's storyline advances with Mashiro Shimao winning first place in this competition. As per the story, she gets chosen for a scholarship to Seio Academy based on her achievements at this competition.

It's the perfect opportunity to receive an expensive education with waived tuition fees. I don't want to miss my chance. All right, I'm going to do whatever I can to achieve my dreams!

♪♪♪

THREE months later: at Miss Ayumi's discretion, Kon and I accompanied her to a fine arts theater. The plan for the day was to watch an opera held in the large auditorium. The program was *Madama Butterfly*, a performance that would be played by a famous orchestra from Europe.

To think the day would come when I would be able to appreciate Puccini's opera in person... Oh, the feelings.

I paid for the ticket with money I had saved from my New Year's allowance.

"You mustn't waste it on frivolous things!" My parents, who were usually strict about how I spent my money would remind me, but in this case they happily agreed to me purchasing a ticket.

The lobby was packed full of people. Miss Ayumi showed us to our seats before informing us that there were some people she needed to greet, and returned to the lobby. "You mustn't move from here at all," she warned us, worried, but our actual personalities belonged to a twenty-four-year-old and an eighteen-year-old. There was little chance of us getting lost.

"Say, aren't these great seats? Who is Miss Ayumi really? Isn't this too fancy?"

"Miss Ayumi is the second cousin of me and Kou. This opera's sponsor company is listed on the pamphlet, right? The managing director of that company is Miss Ayumi's father. I think she used her connections to secure these seats."

I knew Kou's family was wealthy. Kon had been adopted, but it sounded like her uncle's family was even wealthier. Sou also gave off the impression that he was from a rich family.

The number of rich people in Hear my Heart is insane! Maybe they set the remake's heroine to be from an average household to alleviate the overdone upper-class feel of the game. I'm perfectly satisfied with my family so I don't really care, but wouldn't it be nice to have other people from normal households? Time to seek out commoner friendships!

"Even Miss Ayumi is a rich kid, huh? I thought that might be the case because of how big her place is," I muttered.

Kon grinned. "The house where she holds piano lessons is her second home. Her father built the house specifically for her to use for piano practice. The Matsushima main house is elsewhere."

Without realizing it, I let out a huge sigh. Money accumulates where there's already money.

"That's why you didn't have to hold back. You should've just accepted Miss Ayumi's invitation."

"I couldn't do that! Opera tickets are pricey. You're related to her, so it's fine for you, but I'm just a student. It's not good to leech off of others."

"I invited you, so you don't have to worry about paying for the ticket," Miss Ayumi had offered when she first invited me.

But I didn't think it was right for her to pay for my share. It didn't sit right with me. I was more than grateful to her for getting us such good seats.

I squinted against the bright chandeliers and listened closely. The sounds of instruments tuning radiating from the orchestra pit made me unbearably excited. I went out of my way to come, so I let myself be completely caught up in the opera.

This is Kon's encounter event. It has nothing to do with me. With such carefree thoughts, I failed to confirm the details of the event. Never had I imagined that Kon's encounter event and my next Kou event would occur as a set.

CG4: Foyer (Kon & Tobi)

WHEN it comes to opera, the first thing that comes to mind is the booming, powerfully expressive voices of the magnificent singers, but I'm of the personal opinion that the pure splendor in the stage settings is just as awe-inspiring. *Madama Butterfly* heavily features the influence of Japonism, which had widespread popularity during the time the opera was written, so I just can't wait to see the costumes! What I'm saying is, just start the show already!

Burning with uncontainable excitement, I practically stared a hole through the red theater curtain.

Madama Butterfly—Puccini's famous opera—opens with US naval officer Pinkerton attempting to have his marriage with a local Japanese young woman brokered. Pinkerton is an extreme pleasure-seeker, living flippantly with, "You have to enjoy life to its fullest!" as his sole motto while he ogles and flirts with the kimono-clad geisha of Japan during his time stationed there.

That's where the heroine of the opera, Ciocio-san, known as Butterfly, appears on the scene. Ciocio-san is the daughter of a samurai—although their family has fallen—and she misinterprets the marriage with Pinkerton as genuine, going as far as to secretly convert to Christianity for him. Her uncle is infuriated when he discovers this, and has all of her relatives cut ties with her for good.

American consul Sharpless requests that Pinkerton not "pluck" the delicate wings of Ciocio-san's innocence, but instead of taking his words seriously, Pinkerton toasts, "to the day when I will have a real wedding and marry a real American bride." Meanwhile, Ciocio-san remains unaware of Pinkerton's true intentions, rejoicing in the happiness that had so unexpectedly befallen her.

Ciocio-san and Pinkerton's love duet, the highlight of the first act, was truly breathtaking. Their first night was full of love; Ciocio-san is entranced by the momentary bliss. Spellbound by the perfect harmony between the singers and the live orchestra, I closed my eyes.

"For me, you are now the eye of heaven. And I liked you from the first moment I set eyes on you."

Ciocio-san's words, shimmering with wholehearted adoration for her idolized Pinkerton, pierced through my heart. Even if I wanted to avoid it, her words were a mirror echo of my past self, who had fallen in love at first sight with Kou. I had felt the exact same way for him as she does for Pinkerton. Only my affections had been for a two-dimensional character, which is a little pathetic, but let's not go there.

The first act came to a close in less than an hour and the lights turned back on. I was tightly wringing my handkerchief with my hands, absorbed in my lingering emotions, when Kon lightly tapped me on the shoulder.

"Miss Ayumi asked if we'd like to get something to drink. Let's go, Mashiro."

The foyer, or the lobby of the theater, was where audience members could purchase drinks and snacks to enjoy during intermission. I had secretly looked up this information beforehand and thought it was so cool that they didn't just call it the snack area.

The encounter event with Tobi happens during this intermission. I wonder what kind of person he is. Musing on such lighthearted thoughts, I stood up from my seat.

♫♫♫

MISS Ayumi, clad in a champagne-gold suit that accentuated her curves, walking beside the bisque-doll-lookalike Kon, stood out in the middle of the foyer like brilliant diamonds. I, at the very least had my best dress on, but I was pretty sure I didn't look like anything more than their maid.

Miss Ayumi headed straight for the buffet and ordered juice. Since she knew exactly where she was going, I came to the conclusion that she frequents this theater. She also reserved seats for us after all. I could only sigh over how very smart and stylish she presented herself.

"How was it?" she asked for my impression.

I honestly answered, "I hate Pinkerton."

She giggled, her laughter chiming like delicate bells.

"I'm looking forward to the aria in the second act. I might cry at the end." Kon's answer was so cute that both Miss Ayumi and I grinned at her. We compared our opinions on the first act congenially and finished our juice.

"Why don't we head back to our seats now?" Miss Ayumi prompted.

As I began to stand, Kon suddenly grabbed my hand. Her face was dreadfully pale. Surprised, I followed the direction of her gaze.

I watched a couple enter the buffet together. A tall man escorted an equally tall woman. Kon's eyes were locked onto him. But rather than the dreamy-eyed bliss of a girl who had encountered the man of her dreams, she wore an expression of a woman who had detected her archenemy. I wasn't expecting that. The man casually waved at Miss Ayumi.

"It's been such a long time, Ayumi," he said in English.

His smooth, soft golden hair looked like thread spun from the finest silk. His long bangs were parted in the middle, with one side tucked behind his ear. A soft twinkle lit his blue eyes, and the tall bridge of his nose with the thin lips that followed was positioned in such an exquisite way, you'd think he'd been chiseled by the gods.

Androgynous and delicate features—this must be Prince Tobi.

"Tobi! It really has been a long time. When did you return to Japan?" Miss Ayumi replied in Japanese, out of consideration for us.

"Just recently. My sister's been wanting to see you, so you'll probably be contacted by her soon... You are accompanied by some very cute little ladies today, I see." Tobi caught on to the situation and switched to impeccable Japanese. His baritone voice tickled my ears in a terribly attractive way.

"These are my students. This is Kon. She's already won competitions and has a bright future ahead of her. And this is Mashiro. She's only recently started the piano, but she has an incredible knack for it. I brought them with me today, thinking that it might serve as a good learning opportunity."

"I see. Nice to meet you, Kon. And Mashiro as well. You'll need a strong rival if you're going to continue down the path of music. I'll be looking forward to seeing you two mature into pianists with promising futures." He spoke fluidly, as if he were reading from a script.

Despite meeting the object of her adoration, Kon acted the same as usual. If anything, she kept her cool, so that she was practically indifferent toward him. When I had first encountered my dearest Kou, I had been nothing but the embodiment of a creepy stalker.

Kon knows how the event's going to go, but you'd still think she'd have more of a reaction...

"I can't believe you went out of your way to attend the opera considering how busy you are. Something to do with work?" Miss Ayumi asked. Prince Tobi gave a slight nod, making his golden silk-like hair glitter under the lights.

"Well, you could say that. Actually, I still don't know how things will play out."

Maybe discussions of him potentially managing a music academy in the future have already come up. It was just a hunch, but it seemed probable from the way he was talking.

"All right, I have to go now. I've made a lady wait for me. Goodbye, adorable little pianists." Prince Tobi winked playfully at us and suavely turned on his heel.

He's got horribly pretentious mannerisms. Like an overrated movie star!

Kon stiffly stared at him as he elegantly escorted away the woman who had been waiting at a slight distance.

"Who was he, Miss Ayumi?"

I already knew who he was, but it'd be weird not to ask. Miss Ayumi brought her palm to her forehead.

"I'm sorry. I forgot to introduce him. He's the younger brother of my friend. His name is Tobi Yamabuki." She glanced down at us as we both nodded and tilted her head in mild confusion. "I see you aren't surprised. Isn't his name a fairly strange one?"

Kon adorably knit her eyebrows and answered, "Please don't try to get me to agree, Miss Ayumi." She pursed her lips.

Kon has a unique name too.

I accidentally laughed out loud. Kon elbowed me, but she was also laughing.

She doesn't seem to be bothered by Tobi's date. I thought her stiff expression was because of the woman he was with, but maybe I was wrong.

"Are you okay, Kon?"

"Why wouldn't I be?"

"Well…because Tobi was with another woman," I whispered, so Miss Ayumi wouldn't hear.

Surprise flickered across her face before her eyes narrowed. "It'd be weird for him not to have a girlfriend at his age with those looks. I'm not bothered at all by it."

"I see."

"I know how to capture him. I'm okay. Thanks."

If she says she's okay, I'm sure she is. Kon's words rang with confidence, naturally convincing me. *With this, the day's event is over.*

I let the tension drop from my shoulders—and couldn't believe my eyes when I entered the foyer.

"Kon! You came with Ayumi and without telling me?!"

Kou stood several feet away in a suit, looking in my direction. I immediately darted behind Miss Ayumi to hide, but it was useless; the corners of his eyes shot up at once when he recognized me. To be honest, it really hurts to be looked at with absolute disgust as if you're some kind of repulsive bug.

"…Oh. Am I seeing things? Or is that someone who shouldn't be here?"

"Are you referring to me?"

This isn't the time to be depressed. I scraped together a pittance of courage and took a step forward. *I have no choice but to confront him directly now.* I absolutely loathed the idea of secretly running away.

"Looks like you can take a hint. Good for you. I thought you'd already forgotten what I said before."

"I haven't forgotten, but I don't recall ever saying I'd follow your orders."

"…You grew a spine? Shameless leech."

My mind went blank at the insult and I froze. Miss Ayumi stepped forward to protect me—then, before anyone could stop her, she slapped Kou sharply across the cheek with her right hand, making a resounding smack.

"Stop that nonsense this instant, Kou. I heard about it from Kon. I can understand how you feel, but there is a limit to how rude you can be."

Miss Ayumi stood up for me! Not for Kou, who's related to her, but for me, someone who just recently became her student! The shock and waves of emotions at her actions rendered me speechless. Even Kon came to stand in front of me to criticize Kou.

"Didn't I make it clear? Mashiro is the most important person to me. Don't insult my friend with your egotistic assumptions."

Kon's dainty back went rigid with anger. *Why is she going so far to defend me when we haven't even known each other for that long?* The answer eluded me, and I continued to watch, dumbfounded.

Kou didn't even bring his hand to the cheek that had been slapped. He just returned Kon's gaze, intense and furious. His tiny cheek had turned bright-red. Like Sou, he was only an eight-year-old boy. I felt ashamed of swinging from sorrow to joy while taking an eight-year-old's temper at face value.

The Kou standing here isn't the Kou from the game. The reality of that obvious fact finally set in.

"Here. Run this under water and use it to cool down your cheek... I don't think you'll ever come to believe me, but I'll never hurt Kon. I promise." I pulled a handkerchief from my dress pocket and held it out to him.

I know he'll curtly refuse. But I can't leave him like this. His expression told me that the mental scars from Kon's incident were still painfully raw.

All of the girls who fell in love with him, without exception, couldn't accept Kon's existence. Apparently, the girl who stabbed Kon had been a student attending the same violin lessons as Kou. Kon bore scars from those injuries. How he must've kicked himself, regretting that he'd brought danger to his beloved little sister.

And without much time to get over that horrible incident, I suddenly appeared around all the people who mattered most to him. It was only natural that he'd be cautious around me when I hadn't hidden my affections for him.

"…Sorry," Kou said in a thin voice and took my handkerchief.

I didn't think he would apologize—I was genuinely shocked. Sympathy welled up in me for the crestfallen boy.

"Thanks… Why don't we make up and stay friends then?"

"We were never friends to begin with. How would we do that?"

Good point.

Heroine's Results
Target Character: Kou Narita
Event: We're like Cats and Dogs After All

Original Heroine's Results
Target Character: Tobi Yamabuki
Event: The Young Money Tree

CLEAR
◇◇◇

♪♪♪

WE returned to our seats enshrouded by an indescribable awkwardness just as the curtain opened on the second act. Miss Ayumi and Kon kept checking on me to see if I was okay after what happened.

Now that I think about it, Kon said that she can't stomach Kou's initial events. Is it possible what just happened was an event too? What'll happen if I succeed in getting all the flags for his route without realizing it? Will the events automatically update to match what I'm doing to fit the game's progression? A beautiful singing voice scooped me out of the pits of despair created by questions that lacked any answers.

They were singing the most famous aria of Act 2 and the entire opera, "One Fine Day We Shall See".

"Oh, Butterfly, my sweet dear little wife, I'll return with the roses in that happy season when the robin builds his nest." Pinkerton leaves Ciocio-san with honeyed promises to tide her over as he returns to his own country. Ciocio-san is abandoned and holds the child they conceived together while she endures poverty.

Wholeheartedly believing in her husband, Ciocio-san awaits Pinkerton's return.

"He likely won't return." Others try to convince her.

The aria she boldly sings in return contains one of the most stunning phrases.

"One fine day we'll see a wisp of smoke arising over the extreme verge of the sea's horizon, and afterwards the ship will appear. Then the white ship will enter the harbor, will thunder a salute. You see?"

Her clear soprano reverberated through my heart, making it shiver passionately. The raw potency of sheer beauty was entwined in her voice, her emotions, spilling out of her vulnerable, ardent devotion.

"And when he arrives—what will he say? He'll call, 'Butterfly!' from the distance. Not answering, I'll remain hidden, partly to tease, and partly so as not to die at the first meeting."

Tears plopped onto my lap, seeping into my dress. I quickly brought my handkerchief to my eyes. I had watched the DVD many times, but seeing it live was a totally different experience.

The opera transitioned to the scene where Pinkerton finally visits Japan again. He didn't return to get Madame Butterfly, but to break off their relationship. Of all things, he had the gall to come with his legal wife, who he had married back home. No matter how many times I'd seen this scene, it was hard to keep watching. Sharpless couldn't bring himself to inform Ciocio-san of the news.

I understand why. You can't tell her something like that.

Learning of his return, the jubilant Ciocio-san applies blush to her cheeks, now sunken from the poverty she's lived through, scatters flowers around her room, and awaits her husband's return.

Clenching my handkerchief in my hand, I fiercely blinked back tears.

And then the destined third act descended upon us. Finally hit with guilt after seeing that his pitiful, Japanese wife had been faithfully awaiting his return, Pinkerton runs away. Ciocio-san is informed of the atrocious, cruel truth. But she's the daughter of a samurai, and breaking down in front of another is dishonorable. Instead, she tells his new wife, "May you always be happy."

It's decided that Pinkerton will take their child. "If my only option is to return to being a disgraced geisha, then…"

Ciocio-san takes a dagger, a memento from her father, and commits suicide, ending the story.

I clapped until my hands hurt, words from the bottom of my heart resounding throughout my body. *The sweeter the man's words, the more he can't be trusted. If I were Ciocio-san, I would've chased that ingrate Pink to the ends of the earth and kicked his ass. Why not handle it the American way with a lawsuit?! And then get him to cough up huge reparation fees and buy me a house, so I can treasure my precious son and bring him up properly!*

There's no way I'd meekly accept an atrocious situation like that. If I'm going to use a dagger, it'll be for slitting your throat, Pinkerton!

I bet Puccini never stopped to consider that a hundred years later, the young women of Japan would be viciously imagining such disturbing things. Thinking about it in that way was kind of funny and helped ease my aching heart.

♪♪♪

AFTER the day at the opera, I was shaking in my boots, apprehensive about whatever could happen next, but time passed by peacefully without any noteworthy events. Like before, I occasionally ran into Sou on the footbridge, and I met Kon at piano lessons. I hadn't come across Kou again since the opera.

Piano lessons progressed smoothly; I was now in the final stages of learning to play Czerny's No. 30. I quickly finished off the Bayer I had been working on at the same time and plunged right into the sonatina. Sadly, Czerny's No. 50 was more difficult.

I had taken to stretching my fingers while taking my baths. I wanted my hands to grow big enough to smoothly bring out the full sound of the octaves. It was likely nothing more than a myth, but I'd heard that continuing to massage your fingers makes them slender, and I wanted to believe it'd have some small effect in helping them grow larger.

Miss Ayumi was remarkably astounded by how quick I improved and picked things up, but if this world was following a game's plot, then something like a "Heroine Handicap" could be at play. I didn't want to think that was the case, but considering my past life's inability to learn the ropes for anything, it wasn't that far-fetched.

I would've been discouraged if the success I was enjoying through days, months, and years of hard work was summed up as the game's achievements rather than my own merely because I had the role of the heroine.

Right now, my studies weren't progressing as well as I wanted them to. I needed to start solving problems at an even higher level to continue improving.

Having analyzed my current predicament, I took my older sister— who had to begin studying for university exams in the upcoming year anyway—to the bookstore.

"Hey, Mashiro? Can I go browse the magazines?"

"No. I almost fainted when I heard about your GPA. What was it—D minuses on all your mock exams?"

"Ehehe. But look at it this way: I still have time before April! I'll get serious once I become a senior."

"…Did you know that the vast majority of students who fail entrance exams and can't attend university that year are those who don't come up with any plans to study until the end of their second year? It's always the people who say they'll do it later that never get serious. EVER."

"Geh…."

I kept my voice low so we wouldn't disturb the other customers while reprimanding my irresponsible older sister. Hanaka followed me with teary eyes to the textbook section. The plan was to find good reference books and workbooks that would familiarize Hanaka with academic standards and to use them to further my own studies. Even Mom began to panic about how bad Hanaka's grades were and gave us money.

"Don't let your sister have it," she had insisted when she handed me the money. But she didn't have to remind me.

After comparing the options, I bought eight books. This time,

I was able to carefully screen the books for selection without getting interrupted. Hanaka, on the other hand, made a face like it was the end of the world on the way from the register, the heavy shopping bags drooping listlessly from her hands.

"Don't make that face. I'll also be working hard alongside you. Okay? You're the one who said you want to work with kindergartners in the future. Your efforts won't go to waste!"

The last sentence was actually a line that my older sister from my past life had often said to me. When I felt like I couldn't keep up in school, she said that line to encourage me, put her arm around my shoulder, and brought her head against mine with a small thump.

"Yeah. I know…"

My current sister was far older than me so my arm wouldn't reach around her shoulder if I tried. Instead, I linked arms with her and brought my head against her shoulder. She smiled happily.

She abruptly came to a stop as we were about to leave the bookstore. "Hey, Mashiro, look at that!" She pointed to the large book display at the cooking section near the entrance.

"Make it at Home This Year!" A pink sign in the shape of a heart featured that catchphrase in a colorfully decorated area.

"Do you wanna make Valentine's Day chocolate at home together this year? We'll make dad jump with joy."

Hanaka's ulterior motives were as clear as day. She was going to use me to make the chocolate so she could give it to the boyfriend she recently started dating.

"Together? You sure you mean that?"

"Why wouldn't I?! Come on? Pretty please? I'll study hard. I'll do my very best, so please!" She pressed her hands together in an impassioned plea.

Today, she had paired a fluffy short coat with a miniskirt and knee-high, high-heeled boots. Maybe it was because it was a school holiday, but she was also wearing light makeup, fake-eyelashes, topped off with flashy nails. At a glance, she looked like an average easygoing, modern high school girl, but there was no mistaking that she was also a girl in love.

"Sure, okay. I'll do it for you, Sis. Since I love you."

You should convey everything you want to say while you're still alive.

That was one of the lessons I took from my last life.

"Yay!" Hanaka frolicked over to the pink display in high spirits. I followed her with a strained smile. As we were contemplating which recipe books to buy, I suddenly felt like I was being watched. The stare was coming from the nearby store entrance.

"Oh…Sou?"

The instant our eyes met, Sou turned bright-red and immediately did an about-face right out of the store.

Huh. Didn't he just get here?

I learned the reason for Sou's odd behavior a month later.

♪♪♪

FEBRUARY fourteenth that year was bitingly cold, with snowflakes lightly drifting through the air. I left the house rubbing my sleepy eyes. I had been up late last night, struggling furiously to make the desserts, which had effectively cut my sleep time short.

Everything was fine until I stood next to my overly enthusiastic sister in the kitchen. Unfortunately, baking with someone who roughly estimates measurements and tosses things haphazardly together was a lethal blow to my patience.

First, she didn't measure out the amounts specified by the recipe. Then she tried to randomly add ingredients without any rhyme or reason. Naturally, she created a lump that tasted like something foreign to this universe.

At this rate, it'll never end, no matter how long we bake!

Stressed, I ordered Hanaka to take care of washing the dishes. Things went relatively smoothly after that. I should've done that from the start, but I'd made the mistake of relying on Hanaka since she adorably made fists and insisted, "I'll help too!" I'm a big softy when it comes to my sister.

For Dad and Hanaka's boyfriend, we made a cake using cream cheese, chocolate, and graham crackers—which was called a chocolate fondant cake. I was relieved it turned out quite well for my first time baking it.

"Delicious! Mashiro, you're amazing!" Hanaka was so delighted when she tasted my baking that even I had to smile. In this life and my last one, my older sisters were like sunflowers.

Natsu

I had plans with Eri and some of the other girls I was friends with in class to exchange Friendship Chocolate. As you can guess, that's chocolate you make or buy to give to people who are nothing more than friends. It's one of the types of chocolate you can give to people on Valentine's Day in Japan. Giving chocolate is more complicated than you'd think here.

I baked brownies for my friends and folded an origami rose bouquet for the first time in a while to go along with it. A large rose is simple, but the smaller you try to make them, the more difficult it gets. I folded miniature bouquets for five people and decorated the top of my wrapped brownies with it.

I'd been absorbed in my studies and piano every day, so it felt like I had finally taken a breather for the first time in ages. Of course, after baking and the origami, I also finished the assignments I planned to work on, which is why I was incredibly tired the following day.

I left the house and met up with Eri shortly.

"Morning, Mashiro. It'd be a royal pain in the you-know-what if Mr. Kumaja spotted us exchanging chocolate at school, so let's get it over with now." Eri pulled something wrapped out of the extra bag she had brought with her. It was a warped truffle, held in place with cling wrap and tied up with a cute pink ribbon.

"Yay! Friendship Chocolate! Thank you. I made some too!" I pulled the brownies out of my extra bag.

Eri appeared astonished by the chocolate I handed her. "Mashiron, you made this by yourself?"

"Yeah. I tried it too, so I can guarantee the taste."

"Wow! This is incredible! The roses are super cute too. It'd be a waste to eat it."

Eri's innocent delight over my chocolate made me happy too. It's a treat to see someone delighted by something you made yourself.

Nobuo Takemitsu was our homeroom teacher again this year. He had officially declared, "You can't bring unnecessary things to school!", but the majority of girls secretly distributed chocolate during breaks. Seeing the boys restlessly waiting to get theirs brought a smile to my face. Takkun, who I mentioned before, seemed to be the most popular boy this year too.

"Is it true you don't like anybody right now, Mashiron? You made such awesome chocolates—are you sure you don't want to give it to any boys?" Mako, a girl in my friend group, excitedly asked during lunch break.

"She can't give it to any boys. Mashiron's lover is the piano after all. Right?" Sawa teased, as I always turned down their invitations with, "I can't hang out after school because I have piano lessons."

"That's right. I won't give any chocolates to boys until I have someone I really like," I replied, and felt my heart twinge.

Will that day really come? I can't imagine it since I've never experienced real love before.

Everyone giggled, thinking that what I said was meant as a joke.

"Mashiron, are you going to take the entrance exams for private middle schools?" Tomo, a friend from the same study group, inquired.

I shook my head. "No. I'm going the public school route."

"You are? I thought that getting into Seio was your dream?"

I'd told them about my dream for the future when they all began to get suspicious about my sudden passion for the piano. "I thought you were a part of the exam student group all this time!" Everyone, aside from Tomo, clamored.

"Seio Academy only accepts kids from rich families for their elementary school department and only opens up public applications for middle school onward. Their tuition is stupidly high, not something my family can ever afford. What about you, Tomo? Are you going to try for a private school?"

"I wanted to try for one, but Mom said I can't. Sigh... you need money to make money."

"I totally get that."

Our school district's public middle schools were known for their low academic level, so Tomo, who's smart, was worried about her future. The others in our group, noticing that the conversation was heading toward the dreaded topic of school, quickly left us.

"But I'm kind of relieved to hear that you'll attend public school too."

"Same here. Tomo, let's make the best of it even after we start middle school!"

I had felt an awkward gap between me and my old friends since I regained my memories, but in exchanging friendship chocolates, I was able to have fun chatting with them again. Perhaps adapting to my immature body was slowly causing my mind to regress to a younger age.

♪♪♪

ON the way home, I parted ways with Eri, who left for her weekly penmanship lessons, and walked home by myself.

I wonder if the snow will pile up. I hope it does. I approached the footbridge, gazing at the fragments of white dancing out their short-lived lives, when light-blue hair caught my eye. It was Sou. He was leaning against the railing without a jacket, despite the freezing temperature.

"Hey! Why are you dressed like that?! What happened?!" I accidentally shouted.

Sou spun around. "Mashiro! I'm so glad you're here!"

His perfectly shaped cheeks were flushed from the cold. Bright-red colored the tip of his nose too. Maybe if you're born with a handsome face you get to look handsome no matter the situation, because Sou's looks remained unharmed by the frosty air. Had I been the one with the red cheeks and nose, it would've been quite unpleasant to look at.

"What are you glad for? Sheesh. You're dressed way too light! Just looking at you makes me cold!" I took off the scarf I was wearing and wrapped it around his neck. It was olive-brown, and I knitted it last winter. The fluffy knitted spheres I had attached to the ends were silly on Sou, but he'd have to deal with it for now.

"It's so warm… Thank you, Mashiro."

"The weather's been bad since morning, but you still forgot your coat at home?"

"The one I've been wearing the past year got too tight for me to wear anymore."

His frame definitely has gotten more defined, and he has more muscles now too, compared to when we first met. He must've also gotten a fair bit taller over the past year.

"You can't wear it anymore…?" Sou gave me a haunted smile—I gasped. It was the dry grin of someone who had given up on hope. Not an expression that an elementary school student should know how to make, much less use. "But, isn't it already February? Your mom won't get you a new one?"

Sou lightly shrugged when he saw the change in my expression. "Oh? You don't know yet, Mashiro? My current mom is the woman that my dad remarried. She doesn't like me very much because I look exactly like my real mom, who left us."

I snapped, "So what? That's enough of a reason not to get a new coat for a child?"

Sou's lips had turned blue and were trembling. He shrugged again instead of answering me.

"Isn't this abuse? She's not beating you or anything, right?" I prompted, just in case.

He snorted. "She wouldn't dare. That woman doesn't have the nerve to do it."

"You need to tell your dad. I'm sure he'd—" *Protect you, Sou.* The rest of my sentence was cut off by Sou's dry voice.

"Dad's in Germany. He hasn't returned home for years."

I had no idea how to respond. To me, parents were a positive force in their child's life who lived to love their children. For there to be parents out there who don't love their children was shocking to me. I was overwhelmed by the reality I had disregarded as being unrelated to me when I saw news stories about such parents. My eyes filled with tears.

"…Don't cry, Mashiro. I'm fine. Really. I thought it'd be okay if I just stuck it out, but I'll ask her to buy me a coat. If I ask for something, she'll do it. I think she's afraid of making Dad angry. She's just indifferent toward me. There's no violence. I promise," Sou said cheerfully, out of consideration for me.

"I'm not crying! …Snow got in my eyes."

Despite spending a good period of time together the past year, I knew nothing about him. He's rich and cool. I had thoughtlessly envied what he had, admiring what I saw on the surface.

When we'd talked about the piano before, I had thought, "Sou could never understand how I feel when he's so blessed that he can get anything he wants."

I wanted to punch myself for that now. I was so self-righteous despite knowing nothing about him! Wasn't I the one who was actually blessed?

"You should hurry home. If you stay here forever you'll catch pneumonia."

"Yeah. But I wanted to see you no matter what today, Mashiro." Sou's cheeks, that must have been frozen stiff, softened into a real, gentle smile.

He's waited all this time in the snow because he wanted to see me? Why's this boy so attached to me?! Is it because of the origami? Is he that in love with unique origami?!

"Fine, I got it. Then let's go to my place."

"...Your place?"

"You'll seriously get sick if we stand around chatting out in the cold like this. My house is nearby. ...Oh, wait, do you have to head back home right away or anything?" I came up with this suggestion on the spur of the moment because I couldn't bear to watch him freeze any longer. Sou's eyes immediately brightened.

Innocent, sincere, cute Sou. This doesn't match the image he has in Hear My Heart at all. His setting has him far colder, aloof, and as someone who put up a thick wall to protect himself. Maybe he was supposed to be different when he was younger. I don't know, I never looked up information on him.

The notes Kon gave me didn't mention Sou at all. This is the world where Kon has been reincarnated as Kou's little sister, so if the world spins along the same course as the game, maybe Sou has no connection to our future. If that's true, then I can interact with him however I want to.

"Nope! I'll go. I want to go!"

"Okay! Let's hurry then! We're gonna run there!"

I grabbed Sou's surprisingly large hand and ran as fast as my legs could go. His chilled hand felt like ice.

When we get back I'm going to unlock the door and turn on the heater. Oh, and I'll make the leftover brownies our snack.

Sou wordlessly ran with me, squeezing my hand back as he sniffled. I kept my eyes trained forward and pretended not to notice his tears.

CG 5: Valentine (Sou)

SOU'S pretty blue eyes grew wide when he saw me open the front door with a key. "Are you always home alone when you come back from school?"

"Yup, I am. My mom's working at her part right now. Oh, do you know what that is?"

He tilted his head with a hint of disbelief, as if he were saying not to insult his intelligence. I guess that was warranted. Even a rich kid would know what a part-time job is.

"I do know. It refers to the voice *part* or the instrument *part* on sheet music, right?"

"I'm not talking about that kind of part."

As I thought, he's just a wealthy boy enrolled in a music academy who doesn't know much about the outside world.

I offered him the rarely used, houseguest slippers and asked, "Since you're so shocked that I have a key to my house, does that mean you have help working at your place...?"

"Yeah, I do. Mrs. Mie is a live-in housekeeper, but the other two come in the morning and leave at night."

"...I see."

He has three people working at his house! Awesome!

Sou slipped his feet into the slippers I put out for him without batting an eye and followed me inside. His gaze curiously flitted around, like everything was new to him. As soon as we entered the living room, I flipped on the heater. It whirred to life and began blowing out hot air.

I dragged it near the couch I made Sou sit on and adjusted the angle so it pointed at him.

"Wait here until you warm up."

I ran upstairs and tossed my backpack in my room. Then I dashed back to the living room and exclaimed, "Oops, I forgot that we need to wash our hands and brush our teeth! Sou, come here."

He chuckled. "You don't need to be in such a rush. Take your time cleaning up."

I sighed with relief when I saw his complexion had regained a healthier color.

"I was just thinking that you might not want to be left alone in an unfamiliar house."

"Normally, I wouldn't. But I don't mind it here. I'm not sure why, but somehow it's really relaxing."

Relaxing? Our disordered and messy living room is?

Incapable of tossing stuff out, our parsimonious dad had decorated the walls with chintzy things like pictures of me and my sister and old drawings we'd doodled when we were younger. He even framed and hung up the very first original origami I had folded in kindergarten. It was kinda embarrassing; the wall screamed that our parents excessively doted on us.

"Is this you with your older sister?" Sou rose from the couch, pointing at a photograph.

I was six during the summer that picture was taken. Hanaka had been playing with the hose in the garden and was the first to get sopping wet. Afterward, she came over to hug me, when I'd been trying to watch from afar. The two of us were soaked and fooling around in the picture, looking smaller than we were now.

"Yeah. We're not close in age. We don't look much alike, do we? My sister has always been really cute. Now she's super pretty."

"You do look alike. You look just like her. You were cute when you were little too, Mashiro." Sou's pretty almond-shaped eyes were fondly fixed on the picture hanging on the wall.

"You think? I hope so. Ah, the washstand is this way."

Even I found that embarrassing to hear, so I hurried him away from the picture. The bathroom was freezing. We took turns using the stepstool to wash our hands and rinse our mouths before returning to the comfortable, toasty living room.

"Phew...I've finally defrosted. It's really cold out today."

"It sure is. I don't ever want to leave here," Sou replied. He must've endured the frigid cold for a really long time to say that.

"I know what you mean. You can wait until you warm up before leaving. If you're okay with my sister's old clothes, I can give you one of her coats. If I remember correctly, there's a black duffle coat she hasn't used before. I'll look for it in a bit."

"Why are you so nice, Mashiro?" Sou asked, while I stood in the kitchen preparing some hot chocolate for us with my back to him.

Am I being that nice that it's worth commenting on? I thought I was only doing what most people would...

"Are you only this nice to me? Or do you treat just anyone this way?"

I nearly dropped a cup at his unexpected questions. His voice sounded sweeter than the chocolate smelled, knocking me off guard. I was utterly unable to turn around in that moment.

"...I-I want to help people who are having a hard time. I might just be a busybody," I responded in a roundabout way. I finished making the hot chocolate and returned to the couch with it.

"I see." Sou was noticeably disappointed.

He fiercely flipped my maternal instincts on again. *He's too cute! I want to pat him on the head! But it's not smart to get friendlier than necessary with him. He's Kou's best friend, and Kou will inevitably get involved if I get too friendly with Sou. I want to live out the rest of my life without ever getting involved with Hear My Heart's events again. I absolutely refuse to get Kou's Happy End, not to mention the Bad Ends where I get expelled from Seio Academy. I want to live the life I choose to the fullest this time around.*

"Anyway, let's have a snack!" I put the hot chocolate and leftover brownies on the table and smiled at Sou. "This is the leftover dessert that I baked yesterday, if you want some. It might be too sweet to have with hot cocoa though."

I wish I had something else to serve him, but unfortunately we didn't have anything readily available. The instant he saw the brownies on top of the plate his face lit up.

"Yes! It's chocolate! I'm not big on sweets, but I'll definitely eat anything you bake, Mashiro!"

Crud! Today is Valentine's Day!

Natsu

I swiftly grabbed a hold of Sou's hand as he happily reached for the brownie. "You don't have to force yourself."

Actually, please don't do this!

I reached for the plate and attempted to reclaim the sole brownie. But Sou still wanted to eat it, and it turned into a struggle to claim it.

"I want to eat it!"

"Give it up!"

We were about evenly matched. We weren't going to get anywhere at this rate, so despite it not being proper, I snatched up the brownie with my bare hand, and brought it up to toss inside my own mouth.

NOM!

Of all things, Sou put his mouth around the brownie in my fingers! He gulped it down instantly and finished off the remnants by licking his bottom lips while looking straight into my eyes.

"Yup, delicious… This is really great. I made the right choice not to accept chocolate from anyone else."

I couldn't respond right away. My heart squeezed. I had underestimated the power of what one of only two romanceable characters could do to you!

Even if he's only nine, how could my heart not throb for him?!

As I was losing myself in a dreamy state—

"You didn't take me seriously, did you? You should learn your place."

A line I could imagine Kou saying cut through, bringing me back to Earth.

If what Kon said was correct, and Mashiro Shimao is this world's heroine, then my actions might have an effect on the future. I should be on Kou's route. I know that if I crush all his event flags, a normal end where I don't end up with anyone awaits me. But I can't predict how Sou will play into things.

How I should act with Kou is obvious, but I should also try not to get too involved with Sou either. Redo features like save and load are only available in games. Reality doesn't have a reset button. I sorted out my thoughts and slowly exhaled.

"By the way, Sou, didn't you have something you wanted to talk to me about?"

"Yeah," Sou muttered, his cheeks turning red as I repositioned myself away from him. "I saw you and your sister at the bookstore a while ago. I wondered what it was you were staring so intently at, and I realized it was a chocolate cookbook."

This is bad. The direction of this conversation is really dangerous! I have to change the topic somehow.

"You know what—"

"I wondered if you were gonna give someone a valentine. I got all worked up thinking about it. So I wanted to do whatever it took to see you today and confirm it with you."

"I didn't give a valentine to anyone," I flatly denied. That had been the truth until the last piece of brownie. "I only exchanged friendship chocolates. I don't really know how it feels to like or dislike someone."

"…Was that brownie also a friendship chocolate?" Sou's beautiful eyes wavered.

"You're a dear friend to me too, Sou."

His affections are probably from longing for a mother figure. I feel like he's seeking the love and affection he doesn't receive from his mother from me because

I'm relatively mature for our age. Therefore, his feelings will only stay this way for a limited time. After all, he'll eventually catch up to me in age.

A year has passed since I remembered my past life. If you asked whether my personality's matured from eighteen to nineteen, there can be no other answer but NO. Humans are peculiar creatures. Maybe we can't mature if our mind and body aren't on the same page.

"I see... If we're friends, will you be with me forever, Mashiro?"

I kept my eyes lowered and searched for words. I honestly didn't know what the right answer was.

"I can't promise you that I will, but I'll try." The answer I came up with after thinking it over was unclear and half-baked.

Sou opened and closed his mouth many times before giving a firm nod. "Even if you can't promise, I'm still happy to hear you'll try. Thank you."

The overly mature smile from a nine-year-old made me uneasy.

Was my answer just now really the best one? I have no way to confirm it even if I wanted to.

Without being able to see parameters or affection bars, I had no choice but to fumble my way through.

Heroine's Results
Target Character: Sou Shiroyama
Event: Let's Just Stay Friends
CLEAR

♪♪♪

SOU ended up staying at my house until late evening. Mom's eyes shone when she came home from her part-time job and found him settled on the couch.

"I'm home! ...Oh my! How cute!"

Please introduce yourself before you fawn over him, Mom.

Sou remained unfazed as Mom acted like a fan who had just spotted a famous idol walking around town. "How do you do? I'm Sou Shiroyama, a third grader at Seio Academy's Elementary School

Department. Mashiro has been a very good friend to me. Please forgive me for suddenly intruding on your home today." He smoothly stood and greeted Mom so formally that I was stunned.

Sou's refined manners made Mom's inelegant behavior all the more conspicuous. "Amazing... Um, I'm Mashiro's mother. It's nice to meet you."

Just what's amazing, Mom?

Sadly, I get how she feels all too well. I knew what I was in for in advance and have gotten used to him as of late, but Sou is a handsome boy who can't help but draw attention.

"I'll excuse myself soon. Is it all right for me to come over again?"

"Of course it's all right. Where do you live? It's late now. I'll drive you home."

Mom's comment reminded me that the sun sets early in winter and I promptly opened the curtain to reveal countless stars twinkling in the pitch-black sky. Sou tried to politely decline, only to be half-forced into the car by Mom with me tagging along. His directions were easy to follow and we arrived at the Shiroyama residence without incident.

My mouth fell open at the enormous mansion. It was larger than I had imagined. The gate looked as if it couldn't be opened without at least two people.

Sou really is the son of a wealthy family.

When he got out of the car, he turned back to me and emphasized, "Come play at my house next time. You're always welcome here, Mashiro."

"Thanks... But it makes me kind of nervous."

"Don't worry. That person's barely at home. Mrs. Mie is nice—I'm sure you'll come to like her too."

When he says, "that person", is he talking about his stepmom?

My heart ached for Sou, whose tone turned bitter every time he mentioned her. Wanting him to smile like usual, I cheerfully agreed.

"Okay. I'll come over your house sometime too."

"Score! It's a promise, Mashiro." He instantly beamed and kept looking back at me the whole way to his front door like he was reluctant to leave.

Mom had held her tongue in the car, but she enthusiastically blabbed about Sou during dinner, making life difficult for me. Dad was shaken, while Hanaka overreacted, turning Sou's visit into something more than what it was.

"He's just a friend," I obstinately insisted, to no avail, as Mom's grin never went away.

"He was very polite! And a staggeringly handsome young boy."

"You're so lucky, Mom. I wish I could've seen him too!"

"I told you we're just friends. Thanks for dinner!"

I left the three of them to gush about it among themselves and headed upstairs. Shutting my door replaced the sounds of their lively chatter with silence. I didn't hate my family for having fun debating whether I have a boyfriend or not, but it was unbearably embarrassing.

I wonder if Sou is eating dinner alone in a huge dining room. What was the name of his housekeeper again? Mrs. Mie? I hope she's with him at least.

♪♪♪

THE next day was a Thursday—my piano lesson day. The more I practiced, the more I could tell my fingers were moving the way I wanted them to. I had always been good with my hands, so maybe I was meant to play the piano. I was nervous before and during every lesson, but they were fulfilling more than anything else.

"Okay, that's the end of the lesson for today… You're improving tremendously all the time, Mashiro. I am so happy to see that as your teacher."

Miss Ayumi seldom openly complimented me. Her rare words of praise easily lifted my spirits. I frantically tried to keep my lips from curling into a smile and answered, "Thank you very much."

"You're probably going to start hating playing nothing but practice pieces. If there's a song you would like to play, why don't we take it on with your other pieces at the same time?" She stepped away from the grand piano and headed for the bookshelf lined with music books. "At your current level…let's see… 'Für Elise' or 'Blumenlied' would be a good choice."

"I want to try playing 'Blumenlied'."

"Für Elise" is a good song too, but melancholic music makes me feel slightly uneasy. I prefer bright, cheery songs with a pop to them.

"Good choice. You do have a preference for fun songs after all. All right, I'll have you buy new music books then. Why don't we take this opportunity to let you try all different kinds of songs? How about this book?"

The cover of the music book Miss Ayumi showed me was titled, *Sonatina and Czerny Combined Song Collection*. Not only did it have the sheet music for "Blumenlied", it contained many other famous piano songs as well.

"I love it! I'll do my best to learn all the songs!" I loudly answered her, future expectations skyrocketing. *I might become capable of playing famous songs!*

"The amazing thing about you, Mashiro, is that you aren't just talk. I'm of the belief that 'I'll do my best,' is a phrase that's easier said than done." She smiled as she held the new music book out to me. "Whenever you become discouraged despite all the efforts you put into reaching a goal, remember you can always try just a little bit harder. Innate talents don't mean much compared to experience that's acquired through diligent work and practice, especially if you let them go to waste. I know that all too well." Her words rang of her own personal experience.

I completely agree. The only people who deserve to cry over not having any talent are those who have worked so strenuously at something that just the thought of their schedule would make you faint. I've only just now set foot in the entrance to that journey. The future of my endeavors is faraway; I can only see a glimmer of light at the end of the tunnel. Even so, I have no choice but to head down this path... No, I want to go straight down this path.

I returned to the drawing room after my lesson to find Kon already waiting. She was sitting on the edge of the sofa, intently staring at the sheet music spread out on the table. Her fingers danced across her lap. Her side profile was sharp—her expression frighteningly serious. She was concentrating so much that she hadn't even noticed me coming into the room. I froze at the doorway like I had been struck by lightning.

Kon is the same as me. She's not aimlessly following the plot of Hear My Heart; she's genuinely facing the piano.

Kon and I are rivals.

"Kon? It's your turn."

Kon jerked her head up in surprise at Miss Ayumi's voice calling for her from the other room.

"Okay! …Oh, Mashiro. You're back already. Good work today." She smiled softly when our eyes met and excitedly gathered her sheet music from the table and then stood with it under her arm.

"…Kon!" Without meaning to, I shouted her name when she passed by me.

"Hm?"

I couldn't find the right words against her endlessly calm gaze.

"…Let's do our best to learn the piano," is all I managed to say in the end.

Kon looked me straight in the eyes and replied, "I absolutely won't lose to you, Mashiro."

♪♪♪

I was waiting in the drawing room for Mom to pick me up when Kou showed up—my first time seeing him since the opera.

This is the epitome of awkward and unpleasant.

"Hello."

Kou raised an eyebrow at my basic greeting. "Hi. Long time no see. Done with your lesson?" He acted open and unreserved.

Maybe I'm the only one who's bothered by what happened before?

"Yeah, I just finished. I'm going to wait here until my ride shows up."

"Not like I can tell you not to." Kou lightly shrugged and sat on the sofa.

The conversation trailed off, silence reigning between us.

…Are we going to continue occasionally running into each other? It's already depressing to just think about it, but I don't plan on stopping my lessons with Miss Ayumi.

I opened my newly bought music book to distract myself. *Let's see what other songs are in here.*

As I flipped through the pages, a gentle voice came from right beside me.

"You've already made it this far?"

I lifted my face and was promptly shocked. Kou had moved to the seat right next to me.

When did he get there?!

There's no way he hadn't noticed my overreaction to his closeness, but he pretended not to as he peered down at my music book.

"…Yeah. But I only just got to this book today," I answered him because it'd be weird not to. Kou looked up from the book and matched my gaze. My heart started racing on its own as he held me captive in his clear, deep eyes.

"…It hasn't even been a year since you started?"

"Yeah."

Kou put his long fingers to his finely chiseled chin and said nothing more.

He has a perfect gesture for everything, including thinking! How irritating.

"I make sure to respect people who work hard," he suddenly said.

Huh? What'd he just say? I doubted my ears. *If I didn't mishear him, he just said something along the lines of him respecting me.*

The corners of Kou's lips turned up when he saw me speechless. "But at your current pace, you'll never catch up to Kon. If you plan on taking part in music competitions in the future, I can only say you're wasting your time on a losing battle."

His tactic this time seems to be lifting me up and then tearing me down.

I stared at Kou's provocative smirk and quietly scoffed, "We don't know if it's a losing battle yet."

His expression hardened cruelly. I obstinately glowered back at him. Invisible sparks flew between us.

I absolutely won't be the one to look away.

"Mashiro, I've come to get you."

The door opened, a carefree voice calling for me the very moment I had just resolved not to look away.

It's Mom! I can't stand to see her gushing over Kou like she did with Sou!

I frantically hopped to my feet. "Thanks for coming. Let's go!" I stood in front of her, blocking her view of Kou, and tried to push her out of the drawing room.

"How cold, Mashiro. Isn't this your mother? Aren't you going to introduce me?" asked a bewitching voice behind me.

Mom's gaze shifted to the boy beside me and stopped. "Ooh?!" Apparently, she was loss for words, since she stood still, looking at him in wide-eyed awe.

"It's a pleasure to meet you. I am Kou Narita. I'm always deeply obliged to Mashiro for spending time with me."

What the heck is with these boys?! Is it a required subject at a rich kid school to be able to perfectly greet adults for the first time? Apologize to all the third-grade boys across the world!

Kou took a side-glance at me gritting my teeth to keep my temper in check, and smirked in amusement.

"I see... This girl never tells me anything. It's nice to meet you too. I'm Mashiro's mom. Are you learning to play the piano from Miss Matsushima as well?"

"Yes. My major is the violin, but piano is my minor, so I occasionally watch her lessons. Miss Ayumi is a relative of mine."

"Ooh." Overpowered by Kou's maturity, Mom was too impressed to say anything more intelligent than that.

"Oh, yes, I forgot about this." Kou deliberately moved his hand to his jacket pocket. "I borrowed this from Mashiro a while ago. I should have bought her a new one instead to be proper, but that would be rude if this is something she is attached to.... Thank you very much for all you did for me that time, *Mashiro*."

He pulled out a handkerchief. It was a normal gray checkered handkerchief—the one I lent him at the opera.

He had plenty of time to hand me my handkerchief while I was waiting for Mom. Why give it back now?

Not sure what his game was, I stared at him in confusion. He met my gaze in a leisurely manner, then casually winked. I blushed on a reflex, realizing what he was after once it was too late.

This guy wants to tease me in front of my mom.

"My, how courteous of you. You even ironed it. Thank you. ...Silly Mashiro, don't be shy. Be sure to thank him too."

I snatched the handkerchief from Kou's hand. "Thank you oh so very much! All right, let's go!"

I shoved my entranced mom's back away from Kou and out of the drawing room with all my might. I have no doubt that he cracked up laughing once we left. Naturally, the dinner table was livelier than usual that night.

"I wish I could've seen Mashiro turn bright-red too! So, who's your favorite boy? You can tell your big sister!" Hanaka exclaimed, jumping up and down.

"I keep telling you all that it's still too early for that!" Dad pouted.

I didn't have the energy to make excuses and trudged my way upstairs instead.

♪♪♪

SINCE that day, I vigilantly scanned the drawing room at Miss Ayumi's for Kou before entering. So far, we haven't crossed paths again.

I want to become a middle schooler already. Mom and Dad said I can commute to lessons by bicycle once I'm in middle school. I'll be able to go right into my lesson and leave immediately after without ever entering the drawing room.

I occasionally ran into Sou. He would come over to my house when I met him on the footbridge sometimes. I was relieved to see that he got his mother to buy him a proper coat after we'd discussed it. Concerned he wouldn't go through with it, I had him show me the tags and found out it was an Armani coat. Who knew they made kids' clothes?! I couldn't even guess how much it had cost.

The wealthy Sou continued to want my origami. I gave him my newest creation on that day too.

"…What is this one?"

"Jordan's Petra Ruins. It's where the Obelisk Tomb is located."

Having successfully created Angkor Wat with origami, I was now devoting my time to folding the world historic ruin series. Sou was speechless. I wanted to believe it was because of the degree of perfection in my design, but it's probably due to my selective mania for origami.

♪♪♪

MARCH came around. We successfully saw off the sixth graders at their graduation and the majority of school events came to a close. One night near the beginning of spring break, I received a phone call from Kon.

"…What? Seriously?"

"Don't want to? I won't force you to, but if you're interested I would love to go with you."

Kon had informed me there was going to be a classical music charity concert, "Anticipating Spring Festival", held next Sunday. Prince Tobi was going to be present.

"I heard a famous pianist who's visiting Japan for the first time is going to play at the concert. You know the violinist in the CD that I lent you? They're returning to Japan from New York for the first time in years for this concert as well. Your favorite, Paganini, is part of the program too, Mashiro."

"Really?! I want to listen to the performance! Aah, but Kon, you know…aren't you going with Kou? Won't that turn into an event for me?"

I finished checking all of Kou's events listed in Kon's notes and was afraid of activating his "Let Me Hear You Play Someday" event. According to her notes, it was a romantic event where after appreciating music together, Kou whispers, "Let me hear you play the piano in this same theater hall someday."

Honestly, I can't imagine the Kou I know using a pick-up line on me.

"Um…I'm actually not sure about that," Kon's voice fumbled through the receiver. "As long as I am Kou's little sister, this world should be following *Hear My Heart*'s Kou Route, but not enough events are triggering for that to be right."

"…Good point."

I flipped back several pages in the notebook and ran my finger along several events I had crossed out. Not a single one of the events leading up to the "Let Me Hear You Play Someday" event had occurred yet.

…What does this mean? Has Kou's route already been locked off to me? The Normal End I'm aiming for is the one where the heroine succeeds at the piano but is alone romantically. It might be a possible future if I continue normally down the path I'm on!

Instantly in a better mood, I confirmed the details with Kon.

"Hmm. I'm not sure about that… It might be…but it might not be. Aaah, why did I…" she mumbled the last part and fell silent.

Maybe she feels bad for me because she knows I already broke the flags that let me get his events and can never be with him now?

"That's it? All right. In that case, I want to go too! When should I give you the money for the tickets?"

"I received complimentary tickets, so you don't have to pay me. But, um, Kou is—"

"Don't worry about Kou. I think I've told you this before, but I don't have even an ounce of affection left for him. So the tickets are free? How lucky! I'm really looking forward to it!"

Kon giggled through the receiver. It was a gentle laugh someone uses with a small child they love.

Out of nowhere, and I mean it was really abrupt, my chest squeezed, my heart aching.

"Good grief... Silly...ka... Why are you grinning?" A nostalgic voice played in my ears.

Who is it? Who were they? I was on the verge of recalling something critically important when the faint light of recollection went out.

"Okay, let's meet in front of the fine arts theater. I have the tickets, so don't be late."

Kon's voice brought me back to reality from where I was engrossed in my thoughts. "...Hm? Ahh, okay. Thanks for the tickets. I'm looking forward to it!" I answered cheerfully and hung up the phone.

Once I hung up, I forgot what had been nagging at the back of my mind.

♪♪♪

THE following morning, I told my family that Kon had invited me to a concert. Hanaka suddenly turned serious as she munched on her roll.

"Mashiro is going out with Kon again, but it's too pathetic if she has to wear the same dress as the one she wore to the opera. Buy her a new dress, Mom."

"That's true. We always have her wear Hana's hand-me-downs."

Dad dejectedly hung his head. "I wish I had a bigger winter bonus."

"Hang on a minute!"

I didn't tell them about the concert in order to guilt them into buying me new clothes. Learning the piano was already a burden on my parents. They had never paid for lessons or anything similar for Hanaka before, but she always encouraged me instead of treating me with jealousy.

As long as the clothes are clean, I'm happy with hand-me-downs or whatever else.

"I don't need new clothes. Hanaka's hand-me-downs are still new and cute."

"I don't want you to settle." Oddly enough, Hanaka wouldn't back down. "I still have money left from my part-time job. Can I use that?"

She had worked a part-time job at a beach clubhouse over her summer break. I remember how she laughed about how she was able to kill two birds with one stone working there, since that's where she met her boyfriend.

"Hana… All right, Dad and I will pay half then. You two can pick out an outfit on Saturday."

"Yay! I love you, Mom! Mashiro, the bookstore and library are out of the question this Saturday, okay?" She winked at me. A lump formed in my throat.

She went to work while complaining about it every day. She should've used the money she had worked so hard for on herself.

Tears threatened to spill from the corner of my eyes, so I quickly returned to my food. "…Thank you, Hanaka," I finally managed to say.

Dad wiped away my tears for me.

♪♪♪

SATURDAY finally arrived. We rode the train to a department store located in the city. I told her I was fine shopping at the mall in front of the train station, but Hanaka wouldn't let the opportunity to buy something nicer pass by.

She had me try on all sorts of clothes like she was playing dress-up and I was the doll. By the time we managed to pick an outfit, I felt a little dizzy. Dress, strip, dress, strip. Toward the end, I wanted to wander the store in my underwear.

"You look stunning in that! You're very lucky to have a wonderful older sister who will pick out your clothes for you." The shop attendant smiled fondly at us.

Hanaka preened, "You really do look the best in this one!"

Cute. My older sister is too cute.

After we finished shopping, we took a break before leaving at the café located in the department store's basement. I made my way to a table with a juice in one hand. Once we sat down, I asked her the question I'd been dying to ask.

"Is your wallet okay, Sis? I was shocked when I saw the price. Was the pay that good at the beach clubhouse?"

"Nope. It was average wage. But I saved every penny," she proudly answered. "I only took the job because I wanted to buy something nice for you in the first place, since you're always working so hard. So spending it on you is all good with me. You worry too much about stuff like this, Mashiro. You should rely on others more often."

Hanaka is the same age I was when I died. Was I as thoughtful of my family as she is?

I loved my older sister. But I never treasured her the same way Hanaka treasures me. Instead, I had relied too much on her kindness.

That's why things ended the way they did…

Unable to hold them back, tears spilled out of my eyes. Hanaka was flustered when she saw me crying.

"Whoa. Don't cry, Mashiro. You'll make me cry too. I'm not wearing waterproof mascara today!"

Hanaka was so silly for worrying about her makeup first and foremost, that I laughed while crying.

"I'm sorry, Sis. Thank you. I mean it."

This time…this time for sure, I'll make her glad to have had me as her younger sister.

CG 6: Someday My Prince Will Come (Kon & Tobi)

SUNDAY began with a sunny morning—the ideal weather for a charity concert. As soon as I woke up, I opened the curtains to gaze at the clear blue sky.

Truth be told, I was terribly excited for the concert and the chance to wear my new dress. I had been so impatient for the day to come that I accidentally got up far earlier than intended.

…5:30 a.m. is way too early! We're not supposed to meet up until 1 p.m.

The concert started at two, but we wanted to purchase the limited edition concert goods beforehand.

"Let's go early and buy the concert booklet," Kon and I had agreed when we were deciding on the time to meet.

Wanting a glass of water, I tiptoed downstairs, careful not to wake my parents who were still asleep. I planned to study until breakfast. I was almost a fourth grader. Time continued to steadily progress, and I wanted my knowledge to increase with it.

I returned to my room, neatly made my bed, and sat down at my desk, taking out my workbook. It was the ultimate workbook that reviewed the major subjects for all three years of middle school. I remained at my desk as I solved problems.

How much time had passed? Hanaka lightly knocked on my door and stuck her head inside.

"Good morning, Mashiro! It's finally the day—geh! Wh-What're you doing so early in the morning?!"

"Morning, Sis. What do you mean 'what'? I'm studying—"

"STOPPPP!" Hanaka pulled at her hair, messing up her bedhead, and ran downstairs.

You didn't have to flee like it's the end of the world. It's not like I'm going to invite you to do homework with me.

♪♪♪

WE always ate breakfast late on Sundays at our house.

"Let Mom sleep in. She's always doing so much for us at home and working part-time. She deserves some rest," Dad would insist, so Sundays were the day Dad cooked for us. I wanted to help out too, but they wouldn't let me do more than wash the dishes.

It's too bad, since I could cook so many things for them. I was actually good at housework in my last life.

Hanaka, on the other hand, was forbidden from entering the kitchen. After all, her previous offenses included exploding eggs on the stove and toasting bread into charcoal lumps. When she washed the dishes, they always broke.

…It's surprising she managed to hold a part-time job.

At half-past ten, I ate brunch with my family, then decided to spend the remaining time practicing the piano. About an hour in, Hanaka popped her head into my room again.

"Shouldn't you get ready soon?"

"Yeah. I'll get changed now."

"I'll do your hair for you. Come to the bathroom after you're dressed!" Hanaka seemed thrilled, as if she were the one getting a makeover.

I removed the dainty collared, sleeveless dress from the hanger and slipped it over my head. A satin ribbon belt was affixed to the white dress' waist. An elegant purple border accentuated the skirt, adding a fashionable variation in color. A petticoat was attached underneath, making the skirt flare out in a bell shape. I felt like a princess as I spun and the skirt spread out. By itself, the dress was too cold, so I wore a fur bolero. My polished, black one-strap shoes had been waiting for me in the entranceway since last night.

When my parents saw my attire, they immediately fawned over me, chattering, "Cute!" and "You look amazing!" Dad even brought out the camera so that he could take rapid consecutive shots of me in the entranceway.

♪♪♪

THE area around the fine arts hall was abuzz with people. I waved goodbye to Mom and headed straight for where they were selling the concert booklets.

Is Kon here already?

As I began winding my way through the crowds, I heard someone call, "Mashiro!" A voice so familiar I knew who it was without looking.

I warily turned, as exactly who I expected leapt out of the crowd. *Is there any other elementary schooler out there who looks this good in a charcoal-gray suit? I'm not going to waste my time by asking what brand it is.*

"...Let me guess, you were invited here by Narita?"

"Good guess. I didn't plan on coming, but then I heard you'd be here, Mashiro. I'm glad I found you!" Sou flashed his usual innocent smile.

Running into romanceable characters at a concert the original heroine had invited you to—can I really chalk this up to coincidence?

I pushed back my uneasiness and giggled in return. "I see. Maybe our seats will be close too."

"Probably. Kou's little sister invited you, right? This will be my first time meeting her."

"Her name is Kon. She attends piano lessons with me."

"Heh... You're still playing the piano..." Sou murmured, his tone deeper than usual.

"Yeah. You might laugh, but I want to go as far as I can. I'm aiming for the stars as a pianist! Just kidding!" I joked. Sou frowned.

Did something bad happen to him with a piano? Come to think about it, he looked distraught when I told him I was getting one.

"Did I say something wrong?"

"...No, it's cool. You haven't done anything wrong, Mashiro." Sou smiled again and offered me his left hand. "I love your usual look, but you're super cute when you're all dressed up too. You'll let me escort you today, won't you, Princess Mashiro?"

GYAAAH! I want to scream and curl up in a ball on the floor! This boy is fearsome! What's with his lady-killer skills at nine years old?! His reputation as a romanceable character isn't just for show!

"…What *are* you talking about, Sou? Have you gone blind? Open your eyes and take a good look. What part of *this* girl is a princess?"

Kou and Kon had come over to us without me realizing it; I had been too ecstatic to notice them. Kou was wearing a black suit this time, with the first button on his shirt undone and his necktie tied loosely. Pulling off a rough look while appearing almost mockingly handsome is what Kou Narita was created for.

Kon wore a classic Burberry dress. I almost sighed in awe at her outfit, since it was flawless on a classic beauty like Kon.

"Huh? You're who's blind, Kou. Oh, is this your little sister?" Sou remarked, as he turned his attention to Kon.

"Yeah. She's my princess. Isn't the real thing pretty?" Kou wrapped his arm around Kon's shoulder, pulling her close with a proud smirk.

"What are you calling your sister? Don't be stupid," Kon mercilessly retorted, as she squirmed out of his grasp and pulled away from him. She walked right over to me, cheerily exclaiming, "Hello, Mashiro. You look really cute! Your dress looks lovely on you."

"Hello, Kon. Thank you for inviting me today. You look super cute too!" I happily replied, trying my best not to even glance at Kou.

"…You've got some nerve, Mashiro. Ignoring me?" Kou cut between us, irked.

You're the one who started this fight.

I gracefully covered my mouth and gave a sarcastic laugh. "I'm *so* sorry. I can only see the things I want to look at."

"Heh. Is that so? What convenient eyes you have. I want a pair too."

"Unfortunately, it's not something you can buy with money."

Kon glanced between our fake smiles as we spitefully bantered, then brought her hand to her forehead with a sigh. Sou was taken aback by us too.

"The booklets! Come on, we must hurry to buy them! Okay?" Kon reminded us, forcefully changing the topic for a temporary truce.

As a group of four, we purchased the booklets and entered the lobby just as it opened. Eyes followed us wherever we went.

"Hey, look at them."

"So cute!"

"I just want to pinch their cheeks!"

"I wish I had two good-looking boys escorting me to concerts when I was their age!"

Indeed, Kou and Sou attracted more attention than usual when they were dressed formally. But in contrast to Sou, who grimaced over being stared at like a piece of meat, Kou remained thoroughly unbothered.

His expression screams, "I'm used to being the center of attention." The king of arrogance.

Kon abruptly stopped walking. I followed her gaze and immediately understood why. Prince Tobi, clad in a pure-white suit, was escorting a gorgeous blonde in our direction. He looked frighteningly immaculate in a white suit, which could easily be tragically ruined with one wrong move. The blonde bombshell he accompanied stood over six feet tall—almost the same height as him.

Is she a model? Her waist is so tiny it looks like she'll snap in half.

"It's been a while. Do you remember me? Cute little pianists."

"Of course we do. Hello, Mr. Yamabuki," Kon replied with a smile.

She looked delighted on the surface, but a closer look revealed that she had clenched her hands tightly into fists, turning the knuckles white. Inundated with the tension she exuded, I held my breath.

"Glad to hear it. Truth be told, I've actually done a little research on you since we last met, Kon. I make it a priority to check on promising artists in advance." Prince Tobi smirked roguishly, his eyes fixed solely on Kon. Even Kou held his tongue.

"What an honor. As a matter of fact, I plan to attend Seio like my brother here for middle school and on."

"Huh? What are you talking—"

Kou's protest was interrupted by Tobi.

"*I think you made a good choice.* Very nice. I have even more to look forward to now," Tobi replied smoothly, half in English and half in Japanese.

Kon thrust her hand out in a stop gesture to Kou, who looked like he had something he wanted to say, then responded in fluent English to Tobi. "*A wise girl kisses, but doesn't love. Listens, but doesn't believe. And leaves before she is left.* Please do not be mistaken—it won't go as you plan if you wish to turn me into one of your pawns."

"Haha! This is great. Quite wonderful actually." Tobi flashed a gorgeous smile and continued in a honeyed voice, "Then I look forward to the day you'll become a lady I want to kiss."

"……" Kon's eyes narrowed as she bit her lower lip.

Tobi kissed the cheek of the beautiful lady next to him to prove his point, then sweetly added, "Until next time," and left.

From beginning until the end of that interaction, I was completely lost.

Was that aggressive, bloodthirsty exchange an event for the original heroine?

"What a smug jerk," Kou criticized hypocritically, oblivious of his own arrogance. Talk about the pot calling the kettle black. He furrowed his brow and peered at Kon beside him. "Are you serious about attending Seio? You know why we deliberately had you attend a different school from me, don't you?"

"Let's talk about it another time… I'm sorry for making you wait. Shall we go?" Kon urged us forward with an awkward smile, and quickly walked ahead of us to avoid further questioning.

"What did Genda say in English?" Sou grumbled beside me.

I couldn't tell him.

A wise girl kisses, but doesn't love. Listens, but doesn't believe. And leaves before she is left.

Kon had quoted a famous actress whose life had ended at the young age of thirty-six.

What kind of route does Tobi have?

Every fiber of my being wanted to ask, but I had a feeling she wouldn't tell me.

Original Heroine's Results
Target Character: Tobi Yamabuki
Encounter Event: Someday My Prince Will Come
CLEAR ERROR

♪♪♪

WE had four seats in a row. Just like the time at the opera, the seats were special. From our position slightly to the left of center stage, I clearly saw the pianist's hands move. Kon and I sat in the center, with Kou sitting to Kon's right and Sou sitting to my left.

"You're best friends, so why don't you sit together?" I had suggested, and was promptly dismissed.

"Why do I have to sit next to a guy when I'm trying to enjoy a concert? Can you get any more pathetic than that?"

I refuted Kou's argument in my head. *And it's not pathetic to sit by your little sister instead? Your sister complex is beyond creepy.*

"I'm happier sitting next to Mashiro."

Yup, I expected that response from Sou.

The seating order didn't matter once the curtain rose.

The first half was an ensemble concert composed with an abundant variation of ensembles, including a piano trio, string quartet, and a woodwind quintet. We loudly applauded the top-notch professionals' perfect harmony.

The thirty-minute intermission came next, so I chatted with Kon while flipping through the concert's booklet.

"They're on a whole other level! I knew they would be, but hearing them in person is so different from listening to recordings. I'm so glad I came. I'm really excited for the solos in the second half!"

"You can say that again. The organizers did a great job gathering this many talented musicians for a charity concert."

You could tell just by looking at the career information listed in booklet that they were all highly distinguished musicians.

Kou snorted and shrugged dramatically. "Why do you make it sound like you're unrelated to this, Kon? Your adoptive father and uncle is the organizer."

He smacked the back cover of the booklet with his finger, pointing to the name of a huge corporation known to everyone in Japan.

Wait, she's that Genda? From the Genda Group?! Wow! Kon is a real high-society young lady!

"You didn't have to go out of your way to point it out," Kon curtly retorted. Maybe she didn't like people talking about it.

"Then that would make the organizer both Kou and Kon's uncle?"

Remembering that Kon had been adopted by her uncle, I tried to mentally organize how they were all related.

"That's right. Our mother's older brother is the current president and our grandfather serves as the chairman of the Genda Group," Kon confirmed, indifferent.

"Neat."

Kon's world was too out of my league for me to really understand, but even I could recognize that it was amazing. Bisque doll-like looks, a wealthy family, and a skilled pianist. I could only sigh in front of the quintessential ideal girl, who had all three categories checked off.

Kon doesn't act prissy despite being rich—she's always nice and friendly. What's special isn't just her title, but her disposition.

For some reason, Kou grew irritated while quietly watching us. "Neat? That's all you have to say? …Wouldn't you normally feel inferior and envious?"

"Excuse me? Aren't you just overly prejudiced?" I accidentally threw back, annoyed by his unreasonable accusation.

Sou smiled happily. "Too bad, Kou. Mashiro isn't that kind of girl."

"Ha! We'll see about that." For how cocksure his retort was, Kou looked obviously perplexed.

Does he really not get why I don't envy Kon? I started to pity him a little for only knowing such a narrow set of values.

"You might not believe me, but I adore my current family. No matter how much money or power I could have with another, I'd want the one I have now. There's simply nothing for me to envy."

If someone offered me the chance to switch places with Kon, I'd say no.

Lost for words, Kou cast his eyes down.

His ears are red. Maybe he's ashamed of what he said. I sure hope he is, I thought.

Kon chimed in to smooth over the uncomfortable situation, "…You really do love your family, Mashiro."

"I do. I've got great parents, of course, but my older sister is the best! So I'm happy with things the way they are."

"…You have an older sister?"

"Yup. Her name is Hanaka. Isn't it a cute name? She's got a few screws loose, but she's incredibly kind and adorable!"

"…Is she now?" Kon said reticently, her eyes fixed on me. Sadness accompanied by contentment filled her peculiar gaze.

...Shoot! This wasn't the time or place to reveal my love for my older sister! This is a great chance to talk about music. I don't want to let it pass by. I want to ask about things I don't usually get to hear about.

"Sorry for talking about myself so much. Did you guys have a favorite song?"

Despite how abrupt my change in topic was, Kon complied, tilting her head to think it over. "They were all great, but if I have to pick just one, it would be Nielsen's woodwind quintet. Aren't they members of the Berlin Philharmonic Orchestra? They were the best part. Simply superb. Not only was the grain of their sound fully synced, the traits of each instrument added their own flair to the music. I wanted to hear more from them."

Back to himself, Kou joined the conversation. "Good point. As always, you've got great tastes, Kon. Haydn's 'The Lark' did it for me. It's a staple piece for a string quartet, but they were in such perfect harmony that it was worth listening to."

Makes sense that Kou, with his love of music in the major key, would select that piece.

"What about you, Sou?" I asked Sou, but he redirected the question back at me.

"How about you, Mashiro?"

"Hmm. I've never cared much for sad songs until now, but what is it, Trio el—"

"Rachmaninoff's 'Trio élégiaque' No. 1?" Sou kindly supplied, when I couldn't remember the song title.

"Yup, that's the one. It was really good. I want to play like that someday too."

The twinkling sound of the piano as it follows behind the primary melody sung between the violin and cello—I was enchanted by imagining myself lightly tapping the piano keys to bring out that beautiful sound.

"You like *that* one? It's a depressing song with ominous origins, ya know? If we're talking piano trios, Tchaikovsky's 'In Memory of a Great Artist' is much more suited for concerts in my opinion. Besides, Rachmaninoff's piano parts can't be played unless you're accomplished at the transcendental technique."

"Don't jump down her throat so much, Kou. I bet any song Mashiro plays will have a gentle quality. I want to hear you play someday," Sou quickly interjected, offsetting Kou's mean comments.

Sure, it's not possible for me now, but what's wrong with having big dreams? This guy really ticks me off.

"Will you accompany me on the cello when the time comes, Sou?"

"…Yeah, I'd love to. I'll have to work hard to get to that level too." Sou nodded.

Kou leaned forward, his expression brimming with his intent to tease. "Looks like you're one violin short of a trio?"

He annoys me to death, but I can't hate him. Is he upset about being left out of the loop? Seriously now. Kou is such a child… Wait, he is a child.

"If I asked you to, would you play with us?" I returned.

Taken aback by my reply, he stared at me, then grinned. "Sure—if you become skilled enough to win a music competition somewhere."

"Please remember what you just promised."

Hmph. I'll practice a ton and eventually catch up to you. I'm looking forward to seeing the look on your face when I do, Kou.

Kou appeared to be baffled by my villainess snickering.

"Hehe. Looks like you lost, Kou," Kon said with amusement, ending the conversation.

Just before the second half of the concert began, I decided to ask Kon about something that had been bothering me all along.

When the heroine of the game, essentially the player, continues to make the wrong choices, the game finishes with a Bad End. But what about reality? Will everything reset back to the title screen like a game? Or will this world end as we know it?

The burden's too great if I'm the one holding the reins of this world's fate. Kon was reborn into this world like I was, but she knows far more about it than I do. And she seems to be acting according to some unshakeable plan.

"Say, Kon, what do you think will happen if I don't take part in the music competition?" I asked, bringing my face next to hers to whisper into her ear.

"Nothing will happen. Nothing will change." She lightly shook her head.

Can she answer this confidently because she knows the future of this world? This confirms it—she's different from me. I feel like she knows why she's here.

"The world will continue to spin even if I don't attend Seio?"

"Of course it will. You don't even have to put effort into the piano.

You're free, Mashiro. You can live your life how you want to."

Kon's voice came out very thin and quiet. For some reason I couldn't put my finger on, I could tell she was fervently trying to obscure some iron resolution beneath her calm countenance. I recalled the moment she confronted Prince Tobi.

"…You're hiding something, aren't you? Kon."

"I am. But I swear to you that I'm not lying. I'm just not telling you everything… Believe me, Mashiro. You have the freedom to choose."

You have the freedom. *Mashiro* is free to choose.

With Kon's words seeped in her gentle yet heartrending tone echoing in my head, I could only nod back.

♪♪♪

I put aside my thoughts for the second half of the concert. I had only been friends with Kon for a short while, but I didn't think I could easily overturn what she had decided on.

I don't doubt she was telling the truth when she said she couldn't tell me. When the right time comes, I'll have her tell me everything. That's good enough for me.

I came to a clear decision and concentrated on the remainder of the concert. What I was looking forward to most was the male violinist performing last in the second half. He was Japanese, but he lived and worked in New York City. His parents and siblings were all musicians, making him a thoroughbred musician. Tears sprung to my eyes just by seeing him bring the violin under his chin.

I can't believe the day I can see him in person has come!

Sou quietly placed his hand on top of mine as I was deeply engrossed in listening to the violinist play.

…Um? Glancing at him from the corner of my eye, I saw him clearly sulking. He was so cute it vexed me. *I wish he would stop, because I can't focus on the song now.*

The final song began while I was preoccupied with Sou's hand. The first note swung my entire attention back to the performer—it had the frightening ability to capture people's hearts.

Paganini – Caprice No.24

Paganini composed this esoteric violin song, which only he could play, just to show off his technique. The song starts off with a bang. His dynamic and aggressive bowing was thrilling, setting my heart ablaze. The audience breathlessly waited in silence until the last note faded into the ceiling before bursting into ear-piercing applause. My soul trembled in awe at the rich music that had captivated an entire theater hall.

I clapped as hard as I could too.

Sou had pulled his hand away at some point without me noticing. It was now pressed against his lap.

♪♪♪

WE left the theater hall to find orange light spreading from the setting sun, so that the surrounding area was softly enshrouded. The plan was for Kon to drop me off at home.

She offered to Sou as well, "Would you like to join us, Shiroyama?"

"I would love to, but…sorry, I have other plans," he answered downcast, then grumbled, "I'd rather go with you guys instead."

He put a tiny box in my hand.

"Hm? What's this?"

"Open it later. It's a day late, but this is my return gift for the Valentine." He smiled bashfully and lifted his hand. "See you later, Mashiro. I'm happy I got to be with you today."

He gallantly walked away, leaving behind the overly sweet line in his wake. I watched him leave in blank amazement.

Kon diffidently asked, "Return gift? …Did you give Sou chocolate?"

"Huh? No—actually, I guess I did? Maybe?" I sputtered, too flustered by what had just transpired.

Kou smirked deviously. "You gave Sou some, but none to me?"

A load of nonsense from someone who didn't even want it!

"If we're still acquainted next year, I'll fulfill my obligation and give you obligatory chocolate."

"Yeah, you do that. Spare me the handmade crap. I prefer Pierre Hermé over Godiva."

"Ahaha. Not *funny*."

"I'm not kidding."

Kon burst into laughter at our warring words. "Wow, Kou, you've taken a real liking to Mashiro, haven't you?"

"Huh?" Kou's eyes went round, and he turned the tiniest bit red. "Don't be stupid. As if I would."

Why is he suddenly bashful?! This isn't a cliché where you tease the girl you like relentlessly, right?! My heart stirred at the inconceivable thought. To my horror, for but a mere instant, I felt just a little delighted. I wanted to hit myself for feeling that way.

♪♪♪

ON my lesson day just before spring break, I opened Miss Ayumi's front door with a spring in my step. The number of songs I could play were steadily increasing. Unbearable pleasure accompanied the results from my daily practice. With every step I took up the stairs, the charm attached to the handle of my lesson bag swayed and sparkled.

Sou's present to me had been a music note charm. An imitation diamond sparkled at the tip of the silver G clef charm. It seemed like it was meant to be worn as a necklace, but I normally didn't wear necklaces, so I clipped it to my lesson bag instead.

"Hi, Mashiro."

"Whoa."

The drawing room was already occupied. Kou reclined on the sofa with his long legs crossed and flipped through a music magazine. I was on Caution Level MAX toward him ever since he had acted strangely on the way home from the charity concert. I wanted to make things clear between us before he manipulated me further.

"Hey…"

Why did you act like that last time?

I should've come out and just asked him, but I couldn't find the right words. Kou arched a questioning eyebrow.

"What? You started to say something, so finish it. Also, you forgot to greet me."

"Hello. How are you? I can't believe you would, but is it possible you're interested in me, Narita?" Desperate to get it out, I said everything in one go.

"…Huh?" He stared at me as if he had been hit with a bolt out of the blue.

I guess it was a misunderstanding on my part. I want to dig a hole and bury myself in it.

"You've finally lost your mind… What kind of wild ideas are you possessed by this time? Give it to me straight." He furrowed his brow and smacked the cushion next to him. Apparently, that was his way of saying to sit next to him.

I stifled my embarrassment and reluctantly sat down. "Just the sense I got because your ears were red on the way back from the charity concert. You know, when Kon teased you about me? And what do you mean, 'this time'?! Don't make it sound like I'm someone who's always fantasizing!"

"That's not something the girl who drooled when she first saw me with an expression that screamed, 'I've met my destined prince!', can believably say."

Heat rose to my cheeks.

He's going to jab me with that?! Aaah, God, please erase my memories of this person this instant.

"I guarantee I wasn't drooling!"

"That's the part you want to deny? …Listen, Mashiro…" Kou leisurely switched the legs he had crossed. Then he put his arm on the back of the chair and gazed at me.

The gesture, which was unbefitting of his age, really worked for him. Maybe because of his maturity. I quickly shut my parted lips when I realized that I was almost caught in his spell again.

"I rarely get to see Kon. I was happy to see my little sister smile without worry for the first time in ages. My precious princess has been in the dumps lately and never smiles anymore."

Wow…this guy has a genuine sister complex. Will Kon be okay?

I scooted away from Kou on the sofa.

"You're a moron for mistaking that as affection for you, Mashiro."

He finally came right out and called me a moron. For all of that, his expression and tone were mind-bogglingly gentle. Flummoxed, I was stumped for words.

"And you were even foolishly honest enough to ask me directly. You really are stupid."

Kou stared at me as I held my silence, and chuckled. Our eyes met, and his handsome face shimmered as it filled all I could see. My heart incorrigibly throbbed. There's not much you can do about your preference for looks, especially when it comes to faces. I defiantly appreciated his face to my heart's content.

We held each other's gaze for who knows how long before the corner of Kou's eyes softened.

"…I can kind of understand why Sou fell in love with you."

"Huh?" I squeaked at his sudden conclusion.

Love, he says? Just what did he come to understand?!

"You didn't notice even though he was trying so hard to appeal to you? Are you oblivious? Or are you skilled at acting oblivious? …Or do you really not use your brain?" Kou tossed aside my confusion without a second thought, and touched the music note charm hanging from my lesson bag. "Wasn't this a present from Sou? He went all out on this one."

"What are you talking about? Are you implying this is really expensive?"

"Not telling. You'd probably force it back on Sou if I did," he goaded, letting go of the charm.

Is it possible the imitation diamond on the tip of the G clef is real…? How can it be? It's pretty big.

"Mashiro? Are you coming?" Miss Ayumi called for me, just as I went pale.

I jumped to my feet and hurried to the lesson room. Being upset right before my lesson caused me to continuously make mistakes, and a stern-faced Miss Ayumi had me work extra hard as a result.

I need to train myself mentally to zone things out better…

Instead of going back to the drawing room, I waited for Mom in the entryway.

"What's wrong? You seem down today," Mom asked when I got in the car.

"I didn't receive passing marks."

I only told her about my lesson results, without touching on the fact I might have received an exorbitantly expensive present from my friend.

"Aw. That's too bad, huh?" Mom patted my drooped head and comforted me, "We all have days like that. Just work twice as hard next time, okay?"

THE closing ceremony that ended the school year proceeded without a hitch, and spring break finally arrived. I was officially a fourth grader now.

I may have been reincarnated, but as my daily life was extremely ordinary, I occasionally found the whole concept strange. With that said, I fully believed this was a second chance that I had the good favor to receive. The only advantage I gained from retaining memories from my past life was the strong determination and resolve they filled me with. I wanted to live every day to its fullest without being conceited or impatient to grow up.

Before I started studying, I picked up Kon's notebook for the first time in a while because I wanted to check something. The notebook only contained in-depth details on Kou's route. There weren't any entries or details on Sou.

What Kou said to me in the drawing room stuck with me like a small bone lodged in my throat, constantly stabbing at me.

"You didn't notice even though Sou was trying so hard to appeal to you?"

Of course I had suspected it. I just hadn't thought about it seriously because I was scared. Recently, I had stopped caring about our mental age difference. I wasn't sure whether my young body was causing my mind to regress or if my memories were fading, but lately I hadn't been able to remember what my eighteen-year-old self was like. But that's not what I was scared of.

What role am I playing in this world that resembles Hear My Heart? Why was I reborn into this world? Without knowing any of the basic information, I'm too afraid to fall in love with a romanceable character. As I've thought from the start, the safest path is the Normal End.

I never played the Love Triangle Route, so I'm omitting it from my notes.

I took another look at the key points written at the beginning of her notebook. The Love Triangle Route didn't exist in the original game. They added it to the remake version.

What should I do if I activated the Love Triangle Route and increased how much Sou will get involved with me? I gave up on thinking and heaved a long sigh. *I can't know what Kon doesn't. Even if I did activate a new mode, as long as I keep my distance from both Kou and Sou, the flags marking their routes will break on their own.*

Tired of deliberating, that was the optimistic conclusion I came up with.

Several days later, *Hear My Heart* would demonstrate just how powerful its compelling force was on the world.

♪♪♪

HANAKA was the most worried about how I spent all my time holed up in my room studying and playing the piano once spring break began.

"Take a break now and then! Okay?"

"Okay...but I don't really need one, you know?"

"You've been keeping at it for too long without releasing your stress. I don't know why, but it feels like you're in a rush to live out your life... I'm worried about you." Hanaka lowered her eyebrows and tightened her jaw. She made this face when she was trying not to cry.

"All right. I've actually wanted to buy some new hair accessories. Want to go shopping with me?"

"For sure! Let's go!" She beamed the instant I suggested it.

We went shopping at the mall in front of the train station. Cosmetics stores, accessory stores, clothing stores, and shoe stores—Hanaka was a shopping monster who knew no fatigue. She dragged me around from store to store without a single break. I quickly grew sick of shopping and decided to wait for her in the mall bookstore.

"I'll come back for you at three. Whatever you do, don't leave this store, okay? You're a smart girl, so I know you won't go off with a stranger, but... Ugh, forget it. I can't do this. Let's go home."

"It's okay. Didn't you say you still had some things you wanted to shop for? I won't leave this store no matter what, so you can shop without worrying about me. I'm already in the fourth grade, you know?"

I waved to Hanaka as she kept glancing back before reluctantly leaving the store. I browsed the display stands. I didn't have any money to fund my study armament, so I passed on the reference book corner this time.

I guess I'll check out the new book releases and skim the popular series that got hardcovers.

With my love of bookstores, I explored the large store feeling like I was on cloud nine. Suddenly, a single book caught my eye. Out of curiosity, I reached out for it and was about to read the beginning when inappropriately high-pitched, flirtatious voices squealed behind me.

"Let us browse the store with you!"

"Pretty please? Don't you want us around?"

"We won't get in your way."

I'm not against people talking, but I wish they would try to keep their voices as quiet as possible in bookstores and libraries. Annoyed, I turned toward the fawning voices. My gaze landed on a group of several girls and a boy they were clustered around—Kou.

Kou had paired a cotton jacket with skinny jeans, rebelliously mismatched with engineer boots. It was a considerably casual outfit for him, but I'd bet all my money that everything he was wearing, from head to boots, were high-end brands.

...This isn't the time to be checking out his fashion sense! I have to hide while I still can!

Unfortunately, it was already too late.

"I'm sorry. I'm meeting up with a friend. Can you give us some time together?" Kou mentioned with a grin, when his eyes locked with mine.

Friend...? What friend? Where? He's not talking about the old man in golf clothes reading next to me, is he?

"Sorry for making you wait. What were you reading?" Kou dashingly swept his hair up as he leaned over to peer at the hardcover business book in my hands.

25 Methods to Manipulate Others, Taught by Former Ginza Proprietresses

"...Pft." Kou looked down and put his hand over his mouth, struggling to stifle his laughter.

It shouldn't matter what others like to read! Really!

Miffed, I returned the book to its shelf, and turned on my heel to leave. I could feel the bloodthirsty stares from his fangirls, who stood watching at a distance. Of all the people, the last I want to be hated for associating with is Kou.

"…Are you ignoring me?"

"Haven't you mistaken me for someone else?" I snarled, refusing to look at him, though he caught up to me. "You've had your fun, so please hurry up and go somewhere else."

"Why can't you just give it up and play along? You've got nothing better to do, yeah?"

There it is—he's looking down on me again with his arrogance. He should just come out and say he wants my help if that's what he's after. He really is an oresama. I won't let him get away with it.

"If you plan on imposing on someone's time, shouldn't you treat them with the appropriate attitude?" I indignantly glowered at him.

Kou sucked in his breath and held his tongue. He silently followed me to the bookstore exit.

Now then, how can I outsmart this guy?

He apologized right as I started plotting. "…Now that you mention it, I was rude. Sorry. Help me."

Wow! He apologized!

Astounded, I looked up at him. There were signs of panic in his distraught expression. He must actually have a hard time dealing with those kinds of girls. Thinking of his past trauma made me empathize with him just a little—and I mean only a little!

"Fine. Let's get out of here first then."

"…Thank you." The tension went out of him as if he were truly relieved.

He knows how to thank people. What a surprise.

I mentally insulted him, and kicked the fluffy feelings surging inside me to the curb.

CG 7: Shopping Mall (Kou)

"SO where are we going?"

"…Good question. If you've got time, wanna leave the mall? It'd be a pain if those girls tagged along. My chauffeur is waiting in the car parked in the basement garage, so just say where you want to go and I'll take you."

What did he even come to the mall to do? He's empty-handed and doesn't seem to have plans to meet anyone.

"…What? Something on my face?"

"Didn't you come here to do something? I have to meet up with my older sister, so I need to be back by three."

"You do? Want to have tea then?" Kou suggested, taking notice of the teahouse right outside the bookstore. The classy teahouse served tea by the teapot, which meant it was expensive.

"I don't have that kind of money on me."

"Huh? There's no way I'd make you pay," Kou said bluntly as if the thought disgusted him, and briskly walked inside the teahouse.

"Wait up!" I ran after him, protesting, "There's no reason for you to treat me."

"If you need a reason, we've got one. I invited you."

He did, but still…

He stared at me as I refused to move, then sighed and offered me his hand. "Don't sweat the small stuff, get over here. It's improper to stand around talking in front of a teahouse."

He took hold of my hand as if it were the most natural thing in the world, catching me off guard. Then he led me inside, where a waiter immediately appeared to show us to our seats. Kou's big hand was smooth and dry. He pulled out my chair for me and had me sit before he sat in the seat opposite of me. Only after I settled in to the comfortable sofa chair did I finally realize what had happened.

Where'd he learn to perfectly escort his date?!

I could see out across the clear blue sky from the sixth-story window, and came to the conclusion it was just the extraordinary circumstances that'd set my heart aflutter.

This is just the Suspension Bridge Effect, I told myself. *The heart palpitations from being nervous in unfamiliar circumstances are having a strange effect on my mind, making me mistake these feelings as love for Kou. Yup.*

"Got a preference?"

I was so shaken that I nearly blurted, "Anyone who's not an oresama type."

He's only asking me about tea, but I thought he'd read my mind for a second!

"I guess I'll go with the Darjeeling First Flush. Straight, please."

This should be the right time of year for it. I opened the menu to have the—anticipated—high prices leap out at me. *Ugh, my stomach hurts just thinking about it.*

Kou blinked, cocking his head. His long eyelashes cast a seductive shadow on his face. "Heh…your taste in tea's not half bad. I'll have the same."

Once we had placed our orders, Kou leaned back against the sofa without uttering another word, as if he were deep in thought.

What's up with him? It'd be a lie if I said I'm not curious, but I don't want him to shoot me down if I ask.

Bored, I picked up the napkin on the table in front of me and folded it into a rose on a whim. My mood improved seeing it come out pretty well despite the floppy paper.

"…Sou said you're an origami genius."

"He praises me too much. I just like origami."

"No, he doesn't. You're exceptional at it. That's beautifully done," Kou replied, his voice filled with awe as he closely examined my paper rose.

Was that how he really felt? Was he teasing me? I honestly couldn't tell.

The waiter brought our tea while I was still puzzling through his intentions. The gorgeously clear, golden liquid attracted my attention. I took my time enjoying it with my eyes before picking up the cup. The initial taste was refreshing…the aftertaste invigorating. It brought an inadvertent smile to my lips; the flowery fragrance tickled my nose.

Kou stared at me intently as I smiled to myself, then admitted, "…I was actually supposed to meet up with Kon here today."

I realized that he was answering my initial question. I waited for him to explain, but he sipped his tea without saying anything else.

"Was she suddenly unable to come? Did something happen?" I asked, curious of the answer. Kou frowned painfully.

"Yeah. Seems like she's not feeling well. It happens occasionally. She has these chronic fits where she coughs nonstop and develops a fever."

"She does?! I-Is she okay? Has she been seen by a doctor or—"

That was the first I had heard of her having a chronic illness—I nearly fell out of my chair. Kou lightly shook his head.

"Of course she has. She's had all sorts of tests done, but they can't find anything clearly wrong."

"I see... But that's really concerning, not knowing the cause."

Kon's gentle smile crossed my mind.

A spasmodic cough and fever? Is this a trait they added to the original heroine? A chronic illness on top of her getting stabbed as a child…the remake version is too cruel to the original heroine.

I furrowed my brow as Kou muttered, "I think it might be my fault."

"Your fault?"

"…Yeah. Kon sustained a serious injury because of me. It might be a side effect from that. The doctors say it's unrelated, but Kon never even caught a cold until she got hurt."

Kon had said she regained memories of her past life due to the shock she underwent from being stabbed. Something about this didn't sit right with me.

Is there a connection between her being reincarnated and her poor health?

"Sorry for bringing up depressing stuff. I didn't plan to talk to you about it." Kou forced a smile.

I waved him off. "I already heard about it from Kon, so it's not surprising."

His eyes grew round at my words. "Kon told you herself? For real?"

"Yeah... What happened to Kon was such a tragedy for the both of you, Narita."

I'd be exposed if he asked me why she had told me about it. I definitely couldn't let him know that it had been a part of her explanation on the remake's plot.

Kou fixed his stare on me, scrutinizing me for clues. He didn't look away even once after my vague reply. There wasn't much difference between his behavior and a detective in the process of searching for a criminal.

"…You're surprisingly close friends with Kon."

"Yeah, we are close. We get along like normal friends do… Why?"

"Nah. It's nothing. I shouldn't have said anything if Kon trusts you," he answered coolly, and poured a second cup of tea.

He had buried his unease and loneliness to don his public mask in an instant.

It kills me to admit it, but he's really cool. I can't believe he's only nine. The same goes for Sou too, but maybe the two of them have been granted a special gift as romanceable characters.

"It's too bad you didn't get to see Kon. It'll probably be an inconvenience for her if I call while she's sick in bed, so can you tell her I hope she feels better soon?"

"…Yeah." The corners of his eyes softened as he gave a soft smile.

I'm under the strong belief that he's a cunning boy.

"Looks like it's almost time for you to go," he informed me. He had remembered that I said I was meeting up with my sister at three.

"Sorry that I need to leave first. Thank you for the tea. It was delicious."

"You're the one who saved me. Join me for tea again sometime so we can take our time."

Sometime—I had mixed feelings about that. I wished he wouldn't speak to me so kindly.

It's been two years since we met, enough time to prove I'm not some sort of dangerous stalker. He seems to have let his guard down too. I should probably forgive and forget how he treated me at first, but I don't want to end up hating myself and crying from shame because of another pitiful misunderstanding.

For better or worse, dear Kou has too much influence over my heart.

Heroine's Results
Target Character: Kou Narita
Event: First Flush Tea with You
CLEAR

♪♪♪

AROUND the time spring break was about to end, I brought my friends from school home for the first time since I had regained memories of my past life. I'd been friends with Eri, who lived in the same school district and always walked to school with me, since kindergarten. I became friends with Mako, Sawa, and Tomo when we ended up in the same classes two years in a row.

"We're gonna be fourth graders soon, huh? I hope we all end up in the same class!"

"Me too! You know how we'll have the summer camp field trip this summer? They said we can make our own groups of five for it! If we all get into the same class, let's be in the same group."

"I heard that Mr. Kumaja won't let kids be in the same group as their friends. We're going to be forced to draw lots instead."

"Seriously? That sucks. I want a different homeroom teacher."

I placed juice and cookies on the tiny tea table and joined the conversation. "What about Miss Micchan? She seems nice."

The five of us were crammed into a 108 square-foot room, making things all the more rowdy. They had all pestered me, insisting, "We want to see Mashiron's room," so I gave in and led them from the living room to my bedroom. The first thing I did was evacuate Becchin to a safe spot in my closet. It wasn't very mature, but I didn't want anyone touching him. Becchin was my oasis and mine alone.

"Oh, thanks for the snacks."

"Miss Micchan is young and cute. I like her too."

"But I heard she gives out a buttload of homework."

Everyone snacked on cookies while chattering away about school. Over time, the instances where I felt strange being surrounded by these girls who giggled at the smallest things had decreased. Lately, I'd been feeling fully satisfied by my elementary schooler life.

After a while, Eri's attention turned to the upright piano. "Oh yeah! Since we're here, I want to hear Mashiron play the piano!"

"Me too!"

The others unanimously agreed. They were curious since I was the only one in our group learning to play the piano.

"Sure, I'll play." I wiped my hands off on a wet towel and opened the lid of the upright piano, and quickly warmed up by lightly tapping the keys. "What should I play?"

"Wow! This is kinda cool!" Sawa exclaimed, her eyes lighting up as she pressed her hands together.

"Hey, why don't you play *the* song? You know, SAZE's new song. The theme song to the *Love You* movie?"

"I love that song too! It aired on TV yesterday."

The girls only had eyes for IdRev until recently. Their interest had switched to idols it seems. SAZE is a popular four-member group of attractive sixteen-year-old boys that's currently selling off the shelves. And their new song was for *Love You*, short for a manga titled, *I Love Me for Loving You*. Great naming sense, right? The TV drama adaptation had been a huge hit, warranting a movie adaptation.

Mako secretly showed me the manga at school one day, but I was put off by its bizarre plot about a boy who had only a few years left to live falling in love with a girl with an equally short time left to live.

"I don't have the sheet music for it. You guys okay with me playing it by ear?"

"I don't care as long as you play it!"

"Please!" Mako, a huge *Love You* fan, begged.

I had a gist of how it sounded because Hanaka had been singing it in the bathroom a lot lately. Thanks to attending the solfège every Saturday, I had developed an ear for music.

The original song is probably in D minor.

As I attempted the general melody with my right hand, the girls simultaneously shouted, "That's it! That's it!"

My left hand's chord progression was pretty random. D stands for the *re* sound. Normally, songs in the major key have *re-fa-sharp-la* as their basis, but *Love You*'s theme song is in the minor key and uses a *re-fa-la* triad instead. Adding seven short *do* notes to it transforms it into a D minor 7-tone. A chord sequences including a diminished triad with a subtonic 7-tone mixed with *re-fa-la-flat-ti* gives it a cooler sound.

Put simply, piano chord progressions follow general rules, so you just need to pick a chord that'll fit the melody for your right hand. I studied chord progressions in-depth in my prior life in order to clear the composition part in *Hear My Heart*. In the end, I didn't stand a chance on the game's exams with my stopgap knowledge.

Everyone sung along to my piano, so I felt like I'd become a kindergarten teacher. I was freed at last once they sang the song enough times to satisfy themselves.

"Whoa, what is this?! Mashiron, are you solving these super-duper hard problems?!" Tomo had discovered my high school level workbook while I was closing the piano lid.

"It's my sister's. I just borrowed it to see what it's like."

"You did? Wow…the pages are full of notes. Your sister must be really smart, Mashiron!"

"Ehehe…" I had no choice but to laugh it off.

Their sudden visit to my room turned out to be mentally exhausting in more ways than one.

♪♪♪

THUS, spring break ended, and the new school term started. I was glad our group of five was placed into the same class, but our joy was soured when we found Mr. Kumaja was our homeroom teacher yet again. What a weird coincidence, getting the same homeroom teacher three years in a row.

"Oh, Shimao. Let's have another good year together!" Mr. Kumaja smiled broadly and smacked me on the back. "You've got a tendency to work yourself too hard. Relax more! I'll listen to any worries you might have. You can feel free to tell me anything."

"Th-Thank you very much."

Apparently, he had the impression I'm a student who worries too much. I'd hate it if he said something like, "That girl is a little strange, so I'll be carefully watching over her until she graduates!" to the other teachers.

My encounters with Sou on the footbridge were as frequent as always.

"I want to go over your house today, Mashiro… Can I?"

"I need to study and practice the piano, so I won't be able to play. Won't you be bored?"

"I'm okay with that. I'll behave and not interrupt you."

When he begged me with those puppy-dog eyes, I had no choice but to give in and bring him home with me.

I know I'm gradually building a relationship between us. Is it okay to continue like this? Sou is so happy to come home with me, I end up letting it go every time.

"Go ahead and practice on the piano. I'll stay here."

Sou made the suggestion so as not to distract me, but I had qualms about leaving my guest and going upstairs alone. At the same time, I didn't think it was smart to bring Sou into my bedroom, so I decided to study in the living room on the days he came over.

"You're really smart, Mashiro." His eyes widened when he took a peek at the workbook I was solving. He actually looks his age when he makes that face, it's cute.

"I'm studying because I'm not smart."

No matter whether it's a quick wit or a good intuition, I completely lack any innate talents or genius. I'm content with working hard. Although, compared to my prior life, I'm actually seeing real results from my efforts this time. Here, if I work hard at something, I get good at it. Maybe that's my gift.

"It doesn't seem that way to me." Sou grinned, taking my answer as me being humble. It's as if he wanted to brag, "Isn't my Mashiro amazing?"

How long can I continue to outrun him? Sometimes, I feel flooded with anxiety. How will I appear in his eyes once we're the same age?

Since he had nothing to do after he finished his homework, I lent him one of my origami books. Only the sounds of my mechanical pencil writing across the page and Sou folding paper filled the quiet living room. He seemed completely at home with his knees curled up on the couch as he focused on making origami. Even without talking, the mood between us was always warm. It made me painfully aware of the fact that he was lonely at home.

♪♪♪

I occasionally encountered Kou too. *Encounter* was the perfect word for him. He had stopped showing up in the drawing room at my piano lessons, yet for some reason I bumped into him every once in a while when I went out. And I rarely went anywhere outside of my usual triangle of school, home, and Miss Ayumi's house. Nevertheless, I had a high encounter rate with Kou.

On one of those days, I was out running an errand for Mom, who had lamented, "Oh no, we're out of miso!" She had apologized when I agreed to go for her, "I'm sorry. You were in the middle of playing the piano too."

"It's totally okay! I'll be back in a flash."

Pedaling for ten minutes by bicycle from my house would bring me to an average-sized supermarket. There's a convenience store closer to my house, but those tend to be more expensive.

"The sun's about to set. Will you be okay? Come straight back home without taking any detours, okay?"

"Got it! I'm off then!"

I had grown from 4'2" to 4'7". My hand-me-downs had taken on more mature designs as well. That day I was wearing a three-quarter sleeve, off-shoulder jersey along with short-shorts. I slid on knee-high boots and straddled my bicycle.

On my way home after shopping, a friendly young man in a suit called out to me, "Can you spare a moment of your time? Do you live around here?"

"Yes, I do… What do you want?" I stopped peddling, but didn't get off my bike. It'd be bad if he was a pervert. I answered him in a dubious tone while keeping my distance, and received a wide grin from the man. His amiable smile eased my wariness a tad.

"Oh, thank goodness. I'm in a bit of a jam because I can't find my customer's house. The address should be around here too…" He rummaged through his briefcase and pulled out a folded map.

He appeared to be a salesman making runs in the area. It was hard not to stare at the mass of sweat building on his forehead. I sympathized with him and got off my bike.

"The place is called Crescent Moon Apartments."

"Oh, if that's what you're looking for…"

That apartment complex was close to where Sawa lived. It was in the opposite direction of the supermarket. There were a lot of residential buildings in the area, which complicated the roads. It'd be hard for a person to find what they were looking for on their first time there. I concentrated on the map in his hand, looking for where Crescent Moon Apartments were located with him, when—

"Mashiro!" A loud voice yelled my name, nearly making me jump out of my boots. "…What do you need from her?"

It was Kou. Did he run here? His bangs were all over the place. He grabbed my arm and pushed me behind his back.

"You okay?" he asked in a quiet voice.

I'm so shocked my heart nearly stopped! Because of you!

"Eh? What?! No, no! I'm not anyone suspicious!" Deducing the situation, the young man hastily pulled a business card out of his inner chest pocket. "I'm Saito from Tozaki Homes. I wasn't sure where one of my customers live, so I was just asking this girl for directions."

The poor guy was a complete mess. Kou glanced at the business card, turned around, and shouted at the large black sedan parked a slight distance away, "Mizusawa!"

A man in his late-twenties, who had been waiting beside the car, rushed over to us. He was a man with an imposing and gallant appearance, dressed fashionably in an impeccable dark-gray suit that didn't even have a string loose.

"This is Saito with Tozaki Homes. He seems to be looking for an apartment building. Give him a ride to it. I'll walk her home. Pick me up when I call you."

"As you wish." Mizusawa, the chauffeur, bowed without asking for an explanation.

"What? No, you don't have to go that far for me!"

"Please allow Master Kou to impart this kindness to you." Mizusawa brought Saito, who was flustered and trying to excuse himself, back to the sedan with him.

"...Listen, Mashiro..." Kou turned toward me as I absently watched the turn of events from beginning to end, and put his hands on his hips. He had finally let go of my hand when he did. The feel of his large hands lingered like sparks on mine. "Don't approach strange men at this hour; especially in those clothes."

For some reason, he began to lecture me. It took me a while, but I caught onto what had happened. Kou happened to see me while he was driving by and decided that I was being harassed by a suspicious man.

I looked down at my clothing. What was the big deal about showing my legs between the short-shorts and boots? It was the normal look.

"At this hour? It's not even much past five. And this is a normal outfit. What's his name—Saito? I pity him for being made out as a pervert."

"I won't listen to any backtalk. Anyway, be careful. C'mon, let's get you home."

I'd expect no less from an oresama. He won't listen to what I have to say.

...But he was probably worried about me.

Flyaway hairs stuck out, curling in different directions away from his usually perfectly groomed short hair. He must've gotten out of the car to run to my side. Kou despised seeing the people around him get hurt, after all.

"I apologize for causing you trouble. I'll be careful from now on." I pushed my bike to catch up alongside Kou and concluded with, "Sorry."

"...As long as you get it. Despite your appearance to the contrary, you are a girl. The world is full of guys with weird tastes you gotta be careful of."

That was so close to a heartthrob line, but the "Despite your appearance to the contrary" and "weird tastes" utterly ruined it.

"Okey-dokey-smokey."

"Drop the sarcasm."

"Okay."

Illuminated by the setting sun, our walking shadows stretched out from us across the sidewalk. There hadn't been much of a difference in our height when we had met, but before I knew it, Kou had grown a great deal taller. His sturdy, reliable back had protected me.

Thinking about all of that made me want to cry.

♪♪♪

THE seasons changed, and with it came the rainy period of early summer, bringing endless days of poor weather. Mom was in a tough position because the laundry could no longer be hung outside to dry. Lately, Clothes Rack the First and Clothes Rack the Second had been taking up the entire living room. The racks were packed full of hangers and bath towels tossed on it to dry. Even without opening the curtains, the only thing visible from outside our windows were the towels' opaque flower designs, which meant it was simply unthinkable to have guests over.

Sou was disappointed he couldn't come over. I suffered from my own form of grief over the lackluster sound coming from my piano.

"I'm sorry, Aine. Let's try to work through this."

Pianos are instruments made from wood, so humidity is their worst enemy. It might sound like a myth, but it really does affect the sound quality. For exactly that reason, I wanted a dehumidifier, but it was unobtainable with an elementary schooler's allowance.

I was in the middle of practicing Sonatine and Czerny's No. 50 on

Aine and was almost finished with both pieces. Quite some time ago, I had received a perfect score on "Blumenlied" and had since purchased a music book collection that included my next pieces, "A Maiden's Prayer" and "Venetianisches Gondellied". Miss Ayumi decided to have me skip Burgmüller and added music books from Chopin and Bach to my practice list instead.

Next year there will be a piano recital.

"I primarily teach children who aspire to attend music universities, so I don't hold a recital every year. We always end up prioritizing competitions. It's difficult to adjust the schedule to fit everyone, and I have various concerts of my own... This isn't fair to your parents though."

"That's not true! There's no need to go out of your way for us." I vehemently shook my head at Miss Ayumi's apologetic expression.

She was already busy as it was, and I didn't want to add to her workload. Her next performance was set for a large concert, conceptualized as a "Recital Contest for Young Pianists". I was super excited to hear that she'd be performing alongside a famous Japanese orchestra.

"I'm really looking forward to your concert, Miss Ayumi! My current goal is to get even better for next year's recital!"

"Haha. Then I'll need to start thinking up a good program for the recital now. You improve very fast, Mashiro. I look forward to seeing where you'll go from here."

The room seemed to light up whenever she smiled. At times like this, it really became apparent that she was related to the attractive twins. Maybe this is what's called having a presence about you.

"Um...I've been wondering this for a while, but why did you decide to teach me?" I inquired on an impulse when I was halfway out of the lesson room after packing away my music.

I once asked Mom the same question.

"I heard a famous pianist had opened up lessons in the neighboring town, so I gave her call since it wouldn't hurt to try. She immediately agreed. I wonder if she did because she gets good income from having a lot of students," Mom had answered.

She didn't seem to know that Miss Ayumi had no need to take on students to earn money. As it was, only five students received lessons from her, including Kon and me.

"To tell you the truth, Kon asked me to. She said, 'If you get a phone call from someone named Shimao, please agree to teach her for me. She's an incredibly talented girl.' Aren't you friends with Kon, Mashiro? The girl seldom asks anyone for anything, but she requested it as if her life depended on it, so I felt rather pressured to accept."

Those words came as a shock.

...Kon put in a good word for me? This is the first I'm hearing of it. That means she was certain of my existence before we'd met. She knew I would take up piano according to the game's plot. But she seemed unnaturally excited when we first met. It doesn't make sense.

I felt like I was overlooking something and it bothered me.

"It didn't take long for me to learn everything she said about you was true. You're a child gifted with a talent for working hard, and I believe you can aim for the top because of it." Miss Ayumi smiled softly and took both my hands in hers. "I'd guess you play about four hours a day. Yes? You are doing your very best at practice. You spend even more time over the weekends, no? Make sure you properly massage your fingers before and after practice to avoid damaging the tendons."

Her slender, beautiful hands covered mine gently, like they were handling the most valuable treasure in the world. The doubts I had about Kon became insignificant. I'm glad I met Miss Ayumi. I'm glad Kon made the necessary arrangements for me.

"I will." Overwhelmed with emotion, it took everything I had to manage that reply.

I left the lesson room and entered the drawing room, where Kon had already arrived. She was wearing a black short-sleeved dress, and half her hair was tied up with a red ribbon. Her music sheets were spread out, picturesque like a model young lady.

"Hi, Kon."

"Mashiro! Hi." She was delighted to see me. "I planned on coming earlier today, but I was late... Aaah, it's so miserable having no time to chat with you."

The way she flattened her lips in a straight line was so adorable, I instinctively felt like I had to pay someone just for looking. No wonder Kou had developed a sister complex with such a cute little sister.

"You'll be attending Miss Ayumi's concert too, right? Want to go shopping together beforehand? I was thinking it'd be nice to get a present for her."

It was standard to give flowers after a concert, but I had a hunch Miss Ayumi would receive more than enough flowers to fill her house, so I wanted to get her something different. A bouquet that could be purchased with an elementary schooler's pocket money would easily disappear in the sea of expensive flowers. My original plan had been to shop and buy her something by myself, but I wanted to cheer up Kon because she seemed disappointed. Besides, I'd wanted to become better friends from the moment I discovered that we had both been reborn into this world.

Now that I think about it, Kon never talks about her past life. How did she clear the impossible Hear My Heart? What kind of life did she live? There's so much I want to ask her. Maybe I can ask her during our shopping date.

"Really? Are you sure? That'd make me so happy...no, I'm really happy!" Kon was more pleased than I had thought she'd be, taking me by surprise. "Is it okay if I call you tomorrow? Let's decide where and when to meet then."

"Let me be the one to call you sometimes. You always call me first, Kon."

The cost of calling a landline for hours can't be cheap.

"Hehe. Don't let that bother you. You really are considerate, Mashiro."

I've heard someone say the same thing to me before. It feels very nostalgic for some reason.

"...You really are considerate...ka... One might even say you're too serious."

What is this? What the heck is it? My heart aches so much. Like it's being squeezed out of my chest. Who was it? Who was the one who said those words to me?

Fog instantly clouded my mind, baffling me.

"Kon? You can come in now."

Miss Ayumi's voice rang in the distance. It cleanly popped the swelling balloon of memories, swinging my mind back to reality. Stabbing, searing pain shot through my temples.

"...Mashiro? Are you all right?"

Kon's worry-filled eyes were right in front of my face when I came to.

"Ah...yeah. I'm fine, just fine. I zoned out is all."

"As long as you're okay... Don't overwork yourself." Kon reluctantly glanced back at me as she entered the lesson room.

I climbed into the back of Mom's car when she arrived, and the instant I squinted at the setting sunlight, the reason for my pain struck me.

Memories of my past life are fading.

It was terrifying to realize that only memories related to *Hear My Heart* remained vivid, while the rest of them were practically missing.

That's weird. Where did I used to live? What was my house like? What school did I attend? Who were my best friends? What are the names of my mom, dad, and older sister? What did they look like?

...What's my name?

"...!"

Horrified, I covered my face with both hands.

Why? Since when? I remembered everything so clearly when I first regained my memories too!

"Mashiro? Do you not feel well? Carsick? I'll crack open the windows."

I couldn't answer the questions that came from the driver's seat.

I love Mom so much. But now I can't remember my other mom who I loved just as much. I have the feeling she was a kind woman. No, that's not a memory, but what I hope is true.

I ran to my room as soon as the car pulled up in the driveway and dove onto my bed, clinging to Becchin and pulling him against my chest.

"No way...not this...anything but this...I don't want this to happen!"

I was engulfed by a profound, agonizing sense of loss. I couldn't even remember what I had forgotten anymore, but sadness and loneliness consumed me. Tears burst out, tumbling haphazardly down my cheeks. Stifling my sobs, I buried my face in Becchin's plush stomach and cried my heart out.

I'm sorry, everyone. I'm going to forget everything.

The vestiges of memories I had desperately tried to hold onto splintered into a thousand tiny pieces and melted away like snow. *I'd finally regained my memories from that life, but now I can't even remember them properly? It's not fair. How little respect must I have to so easily forget the family... the family I'd left behind by dying?*

The abundance of happy memories I should've had of my family disappeared as if they had never existed in the first place. Then even the memory of grieving and crying over their loss vanished without a trace.

Interlude: Promise (Kon)

"ARE you all right, my lady?"

I lightly shook my head to reassure the servant who had anxiously watched me cough spasmodically. "No worries. This is my usual fit."

I don't have poor health or a weak body. Occasionally, I start coughing, and develop a fever afterward. When the symptoms first appeared, my panicked parents brought me to many hospitals to undergo countless medical tests. In the end, they never managed to locate the cause. The doctors were at their wits' end, but I alone know the reason.

"…This is a warning."

A warning not to forget.

I remembered every word the man had said when he appeared that day, his blond hair fluttering in the wind.

There's no way I'd forget.

…ka…

In my heart, I quietly called out the name of the child I had known—the child who's no longer with me.

Hey, won't you smile? Live out your life and find your happiness this time. I'll take any path, even to hell and back, for that to happen.

♪♪♪

I suddenly awake in the dead of night to find a beautiful blond man standing beside my pillow.

"What? …My time limit shouldn't be up for a while."

His unearthly, dazzling crystal-blue eyes flash in the dim bedroom.

"I'm aware of that. I simply came to warn you, *Kon.*"

Looks like he has something to say. That's unusual.

I sit up, clicking on the lamp placed on the end table beside my bed. Even after exposing him to light, his presence remains the same, unwavering and real.

"Speak then."

"Mashiro's memories of her former life have been deleted."

"...Come again?"

My half-asleep brain instantly slams into consciousness. I squeeze the sheets I had been clenching tighter, wrinkling the silk.

"Why?! You promised not to get involved with her, didn't you?!" I lash out. He nods, still in good humor.

"I did. But *you* broke our deal first. You didn't clear the event like you were supposed to, throwing all sorts of errors into the world."

"...Mashiro is free. But you aren't, Kon."

I hadn't forgotten our deal. But I wasn't able to follow through with it.

The moment the spitting image of this man—Tobi—had been before me, my insides twisted. I had committed a fatal mistake by failing to act out my role as a smitten young maiden.

"Now what are you going to do, Kon? One of your wishes has disappeared." The man snickers gleefully.

Although he told me off for breaking our deal, he has reasons for welcoming my deviation.

Mashiro's memories of her last life are lost. I'll never have the chance to make her remember who I am.

"...What of it? It was a trivial wish."

"Ohh? I hope you really mean that. Otherwise, you are far too..."

Pitiful.

Chuckling mockingly, the man disappears like smoke.

I don't think I can sleep again tonight.

CG 8: Error (Kon)

KON and I decided to go shopping right after we finished our solfège on Saturday. A new cosmetic brand had opened a branch store in the mall where I went shopping with Hanaka over spring break.

Miss Ayumi keeps her nails short to keep from scratching the piano keys, but sometimes they're decorated with nail art. Maybe a gift card for a manicure or nail care goods would be a good present.

Aside from Kon and I, there's one middle schooler and two high schoolers who attend the solfège at 10 a.m. on Saturdays. The first thing we do is audiate, which is where we try to mentally distinguish the pitches of a musical piece.

Miss Ayumi plays a passage with sixteen bars with her right hand, and we write down the notes we catch by ear on music paper for her to check over. Kids with perfect pitch can supposedly catch the correct note right off the bat, but unfortunately I don't have that gift. So I write out the entire rhythm starting from la and then fill in the melody designated by the key; later adding in the chord.

At first, I couldn't get the hang of it, and the sound of everyone's pencils flying across the paper faster than I could conjure any answers brought tears to my eyes. The polytonal audiation Miss Ayumi adds with her left hand are still too difficult for me, but I'm gradually improving.

Once we finished audiating, we moved on to practice sight-reading and sight-singing, where we would read and perform a musical piece or notation that we hadn't seen before. Miss Ayumi hands us sheet music she prepared in advance and then she has us quietly read it before attempting to sing the piece aloud exactly as it was written.

Listening to other people sing doesn't do anything for you, so we waited in another room for her to call us up individually. Don't underestimate the pure level of intimidation radiating from Miss Ayumi when she judges you, sitting on a Victorian chair with her legs crossed. I was so nervous my first time that my voice trembled, creating an incoherent melody.

The solfège tested our ability to concentrate, and I was dead by the time it was over. Apparently, the two high school students also attend music grammar classes in the afternoon. They thoroughly drilled in harmonics and counterpoint music with the hopes of attending a music university or studying overseas. They also undergo training where they listen to music CDs and explain in their own words about the structure each song had been composed with and the expressions used.

Trying to make it in the music world is excruciatingly difficult. You can't become a professional with halfhearted conviction.

♪♪♪

MISS AYUMI allowed us to wait in the drawing room until the Genda family car came to pick us up. The two high schoolers spread out their lunches on the table to eat before their afternoon classes. They weren't the kind of lunches I was familiar with; they were miniature multi-tiered food boxes filled with quality food a five-star hotel would serve.

Is that spiny lobster I see?

Kanako Sakuragiwa and Aoi Sugitani—even their names sounded elegant—both attended Seio Academy's High School Department. The way they presented themselves and behaved was eerily similar. They were mild-mannered Japanese beauties and the spitting image of a "Yamato Nadeshiko"—women who embody the feminine virtues of traditional Japan. Kanako had long hair, and Aoi wore hers in a bob. This is a secret, but I use their hairstyles to tell them apart.

"You got a late start but are already so good at the piano, Mashiro! You're amazing!"

"I thought the same thing. You're both still in the fourth grade, am I right? I can already feel the pressure from you two."

I was a bundle of nerves whenever the two women I respected

spoke to me. "I'm not amazing at all! You're the amazing ones… I really admire your talents! Are you planning on attending Seio University?"

Kanako put down her chopsticks, tilting her head. I didn't mind if she answered me while eating, but she was determined not to speak with food in her mouth.

"Hmm. If I can advance far enough in September's music competition, I would like to apply for the Conservatoire's preregistration."

Conservatoire, or the Paris Conservatory, was a prestigious national music college in Paris.

That's Kanako for you! As expected of a skilled pianist who's won every single major domestic music competition. Only the pampered daughter of a wealthy, prestigious family can so easily mention studying abroad and not worry about costs.

"Are you planning to attend the Conservatoire as well, Aoi?" Kon asked.

Aoi smiled softly. "No. I plan on entering the university affiliated with my high school. I'm done with music competitions. I hate to disappoint Miss Ayumi, but I've given up on becoming a professional pianist. I want to become a piano teacher students can take lessons from without feeling pressured, so I'm planning on studying for that. After all, I believe there are people who want to learn how to play the piano even in adulthood."

Miss Aoi's Piano Class, huh? Sounds like fun! People have different objectives for the future even when attending a music university, I earnestly thought.

"Is it true that you'll be transferring to Seio for middle school, Kon? If I'm not wrong, you're currently—"

Kon nodded as the topic switched to her. "I'm attending Sencho Girl's Academy. But I want to switch to a school with a music-focused curriculum."

Sencho Girl's Academy is a famous private school for daughters of the superrich and powerful. All students are required to live in the dorms. The dorm's historical value and magnificent architecture is said to be the epitome of high-society's aspirations. Apparently, there's even an architectural style named after it: the Sencho Style.

"Wait, that means you currently live in a dorm, Kon?!" I blurted, getting a laugh out of both Kanako and Aoi.

"That's just like you, Mashiro. You're more surprised by the fact she's staying in a dorm than the actual name of the school."

"Hehe, you really are adorable."

Even Kon grinned at me. "I do. But I always go home for the weekends. They're surprisingly lenient as long as you inform them that you'll be spending the night elsewhere."

"Interesting. Dorm life, huh? I wonder what that's like. I've always wanted to try it once."

Considering it's a Sencho dorm, I bet the cafeteria food is beyond extravagant. As I daydreamed about having French cuisine for lunch, the Genda chauffeur arrived.

Or at least I thought it was going to be the Genda chauffeur, but we got Mr. Mizusawa instead.

"U-Um?"

If I'm not wrong, Mr. Mizusawa is Kou's exclusive chauffeur...

"Why are you here, Mizusawa? I requested Nonaga." Suspicious, Kon furrowed her brow.

"Master Kou insisted on coming as well. His school friend, Master Shiroyama, is in the car with him," Mr. Mizusawa explained, giving us a sympathetic look.

"For heaven's sake! He called Dad and asked about my plans again!" Kon huffed.

Not just Kou, but Sou's also coming? This shouldn't be a Hear My Heart event. Kon never included anything like this in her notes. What in the world is going on?

"My sincerest apologies, Lady Kon. I tried to raise my concerns about him tagging along, but—"

"I've no doubt my stupid older brother found some way to rope you in. What do you want to do, Mashiro? Should we take the train?"

Her suggestion to leave Kou behind appealed to me, but I could understand his desire to spend time with his precious little sister. His forlorn expression at the teahouse crossed my mind, leaving me stumped on how to reply.

Sou will be disappointed too. I haven't been able to hang out with him lately.

"I'm fine with us all going together. We can drag them around for tons of tedious shopping until they're bored out of their minds," I offered jokingly. Relief eased the worried lines in Kon's face.

...Even if we traveled by train, it's obvious they'd still follow us anyway, I added inside my head. *You can't underestimate Kou's sister complex.*

"In any case, I can't believe we're going to all be gathered in one place again… I wonder if this is what they call the butterfly effect," Kon quietly muttered.

The butterfly effect is a phenomenon in the chaos theory where, "a minute localized change in a complex system can result in large effects elsewhere." Kon seemed distressed things weren't progressing the way they were written in her notes.

"This isn't an event, is it?" I whispered as we slipped on our shoes in the entryway.

"I don't know. This event didn't exist in the remake version I played… Maybe I'm overthinking things, but it feels like someone's trying to stop us from being alone together. Doesn't it?"

Such a thought had never occurred to me, but now that she mentioned it, it rang true. Kou was at Miss Ayumi's for my first piano lesson—as if he had been there to ruin my chance to speak with Kon alone.

I had so much I wanted to ask her today, but we can't get into the nitty-gritty details with the boys around.

"I wanted to hear all about your past life too, Mashiro," Kon muttered as she laced her elegant leather shoes. Her lustrous brown hair spilled over the side of her face, hiding her expression.

Sadness steeped her every word, so I deliberately responded with pep, "Me too! I wanted to ask you all sorts of things about your past life. For some reason, I can't recall anything aside from the fact that I was obsessed with *Hear My Heart*. Everything else comes up blank. The only thing I really remember is that I was in high school. I hope to eventually remember my family and friends."

"…I see." She finished tying her shoes, jumped to her feet, and looked me straight in the eyes. Kon's expression took me by surprise— she was on the verge of tears. Her squared jaw took the air from my lungs. The core of my brain went numb.

Wait a minute? I know this expression; it's the same as—

"Actually, me too. I remember how old I was, but that's about it," she added in a tearful voice.

Maybe it's painful for her not to remember.

"Well, we might've had a horrible life! Who knows, maybe not remembering is for the better," I suggested quickly in hopes of cheering her up.

She squeezed her eyes shut and mumbled, "…Perhaps."

♪♪♪

MISS AYUMI'S house was fully equipped with a huge parking space. Normally I'd find Mom's compact Kei car parked there, but a Rolls-Royce Phantom waited for us instead. The back seat window quietly rolled down, and Kou stuck his head out from the lounge seat.

"Good work today, you two. Don't just stand there; jump in. Aren't you hungry?"

Sou politely got out of the car to greet us. "I came when I heard Mashiro was going. Sit next to me, Mashiro!"

I couldn't close my gaping mouth.

Where the heck do they plan to go in this unreasonably large, expensive, limousine-like car? A garden tea party at some mansion? There's no way this car can park in the mall's tiny parking garage. Are they idiots? My family could pay off all the loans and mortgages on our house and buy a vacation home on top of that if we sold a car like this.

"...Kon, can I go home?"

"I can only offer you my sympathies." Kon put her hand to her head.

Original Heroine's Results
Corresponding Event Not Found.
New Friendship Event: Remember Me
CLEAR

♪♪♪

LIKE most people, I never thought I'd get the chance to ride in a Rolls-Royce Phantom. The car was spacious inside to say the least. Luxurious leather seats with a lustrous wooden interior design—I could only sigh in awe. Beethoven's Violin Sonata played the moment the car smoothly drove off. The speakers and amp were really something else. The highest-quality sound enveloped me, reverberating in my soul.

Kou gazed at my face and chuckled. "You're cute, Mashiro."

I only heard that as sarcasm. What part of me was cute when my mouth had been hanging open since I climbed into the car?

I flattened my lips and snorted. "…I'm sure my peasantry is on full display. You've got horrible taste if you think that's cute."

"I think so too," Kou retorted, undaunted. He gracefully switched the legs he had crossed as he spoke to Kon, "Now then, what should we do for lunch? You good with the usual spot?"

"Don't ask me, ask Mashiro. You got away with this because she's kind, but this was incredibly thoughtless of you."

"Sorry. I thought it was a good opportunity since we couldn't meet up last time."

Kon bristled with anger. Even Kou looked uncomfortable. There was something fresh about seeing him that way. Actually, I'll be frank, it was *refreshing*.

"…Are you mad too, Mashiro?" Sou worriedly peered at my face. Peeking up at me with those imploring, teary eyes was such a cheap trick! "…I'm sorry I crashed your plans with Genda. But I haven't gotten to see you at all lately."

He was right. Days of bad weather had continued without an end in sight, preventing us from meeting up on the footbridge, and even when we managed to bump into each other, I couldn't invite him over. I still couldn't have anyone over with the living room occupied by laundry.

"I'm not mad. But don't do it again."

"I won't. Thanks, Mashiro." Sou's face lit up, and he smiled like I made him the happiest boy in the world.

His puppy-dog personality was running at full throttle today. He was supposed to grow up to be a mega oresama, but I couldn't find even a trace of that personality in him. I was beginning to worry that I've somehow been distorting how he was supposed to be.

"I was planning on having lunch at the mall. Where do you usually go to eat?" I asked, bringing us back on topic. Kon mentioned the name of an expensive hotel restaurant.

Wow. That's not the kinda place four fourth graders should go to for lunch.

"That's fine. Sou and I are good with anything. We just need to head to the mall for now, yeah?"

Mr. Mizusawa, hearing what Kou had said, turned on the blinker. We arrived at our destination in no time.

Once the train station was in sight, Kou addressed Mr. Mizusawa, "You can drop us off here."

"Yes, sir."

With perfect precision, Mr. Mizusawa spun the wheel and skillfully maneuvered the car into the narrow adjacent parking space. Pedestrians on the sidewalk turned to stare at us. Sou helped me out of the car, under the gaze of all those eyes. Kon excitedly stepped up next to me.

"Your clothes are always so cute, Mashiro. Do you pick them out yourself?"

I was wearing a three-quarters sleeve polka dot tunic over my shorts. I glanced down at my casual outfit, to my mules that laced up to my ankles, tied off with cute little ribbons, and cocked my head.

I'm wearing normal clothes though. The only thing I can say about my outfit is that it's not something you should wear in a Rolls-Royce.

"Nope. Most of what I wear are my sister's hand-me-downs. You know how I have a sister who's nine years older than me?"

"...Yeah. You said she's really nice."

"Yup, she is! But, you know, I'm almost as tall as her now. Once I catch up we'll probably buy clothes we can share."

Hanaka, who had stopped growing at five feet, envied my steady growth that's almost surpassed her as of late.

"You can already wear that outfit? Lucky you. You've got long legs too, Mashiro. Not fair!" she had grumbled just this morning.

"Sounds like fun to share clothes with your sister."

"Doesn't it?! Strange as it sounds, my sister is much cuter than I am when she wears the same clothes."

"You're cute too, Mashiro. You're super cute no matter what you wear," Sou insisted with a dead serious face.

I can't help but worry for this boy's future. What do I do if he becomes a male host at this rate?

"I don't dislike your outfit either, Mashiro. It's got this pep and cheerful feel going for it."

Kou's questionable compliment set my mind at ease. There's something uncomfortable about having your appearance praised by people who are much better looking than you after all.

♪♪♪

WE decided to have lunch at a Japanese restaurant—all because Kou insisted it would be better to eat somewhere expensive and quiet.

I love Japanese food, but my wallet is going to take a hit.

I was giving the menu a hard look over when Kou noticed and made a shrugging motion, "Worried about prices again? Take a hint and let me treat you without making a big fuss over it."

"I don't want to! Letting you treat me that one time still bothers me, Narita."

"You can call me Kou. It's kinda gross having you call me by my last name."

"Excuse me?!" I blurted.

Sou was the first to jump into the conversation, clearly unhappy with the idea of me calling Kou by his first name. "Mashiro can call you whatever she wants. Actually, it's best if she calls you by your last name forever. Also, what's this about you treating her? I never heard about that."

"You have nothing to do with what happens between me and Mashiro, Sou."

"…Cut the crap." Sou turned hostile.

Kon loudly sighed, making no attempt to hide her annoyance at them.

When did they start fighting over me?

I carefully observed Kou. When our eyes met, he sent a roguish wink my way. No matter how I looked at it, he had entered full teasing mode. Now his teasing target had switched from me to Sou.

"I'll start calling you Kou then. Also, Sou, I happened to bump into Kou once before and he treated me to tea. I'll pay for myself today," I explained, trying to mediate between them, but it only added fuel to the fire.

"…What are you after, Kou? You said you weren't the least bit interested in Mashiro before." Dissatisfied with my answer, Sou questioned Kou further.

They must've talked about me when I wasn't around. The "not the least bit interested" part stings. And I was starting to think we'd finally become friends. This is why I hate complicated relationships.

Kou glanced from me to Sou then flashed a confident smile. "I didn't think things would end up this amusing at the time. Sorry, Sou."

"Don't get involved with Mashiro if you're just doing it for your entertainment. All you really want is a toy to kill time with, don't you?"

The joking expression vanished from Kou's face at Sou's retort. The air around him seemed to drop a few degrees.

"I don't want to hear that from you, Sou. Aren't you looking to her as a replacement for a certain someone too?"

It was Sou's mask that fell this time. They glared at each other, neither backing down. "...Take it back."

"Well, well. What should I do?"

Kon's hand suddenly froze on her after-dinner teacup, startled by the explosive mood.

They're not fighting over me. They're jabbing at each other's past traumas using what only they know as close friends. My presence is nothing but a trigger. They're welcome to fight, but I wish they'd choose the right time and place for it.

"Thank you for the meal." I slapped my hands together and stood from my seat. "Kon, ready to go? Boys, if you want to fight, do it somewhere else. Honestly, it's unpleasant having to deal with you," I stated bluntly, giving them the evil eye.

They awkwardly looked down.

On top of interrupting my time with Kon, they started a fight in the middle of a delicious meal. Who do they think they are?!

"...I'm sorry, Mashiro."

"My bad."

They apologized without making excuses. They must've regretted getting too carried away with their argument. Even Kou looked remorseful. I couldn't stay angry for long when they looked so despondent.

"Don't let it happen again. Both of you are my friends! Neither of you is better than the other."

"...I understand," Sou meekly acknowledged.

Kou, on the other hand, flashed me a brilliant smile. "Mashiro, you've really got a different side to you."

"What are you talking about now?"

"You usually don't seem any different from a homely train wreck, but then you occasionally say or do something really mature. I want to get to know you even better. That's what it means."

If anyone other than my dearest Kou had said that to me, I would've punched them in the face. It's seriously not fair for him to have such a good-looking face. I wanted to shout, "A handsome face isn't a free pass. Take this slugger!" But I couldn't punch that face, unfortunately.

"And that's the side of you that really pisses me off, Kou. The cocky, confident side of you that screams, 'I know everything.'"

Sou voiced my exact feelings.

♪♪♪

WE settled on buying Miss Ayumi a fruit-scented hand cream and bath salts. Both containers had exceptionally stylish designs.

I hope this makes Miss Ayumi happy.

"I want to buy the best present I can get within my budget," I'd requested.

And Kon happily went along with me. I learned that no matter how wealthy her family was, her money sense was in line with mine. It was relieving to see her pick up two products with only a 100-yen difference to seriously consider if the price was worth it.

Sou and Kou were drained by the end of the day after we dragged them around shopping for hours. They probably didn't think it'd take long to pick out a gift. I felt bad for them, but they got what they deserved.

"Mashiro, I had so much fun today! Thank you," Kon called as she stuck her head out the Rolls-Royce window and waved. Her beaming smile brought a smile to my face too.

Kon really is friendly and cute. A lot happened, but I had fun too. Aside from dealing with the boys, being with Kon was very relaxing.

Later, when Mom went to take the trash out, she was interrogated by the neighborhood housewives.

"What kind of friends does your daughter Mashiro have?!"

No doubt it was the fault of that ridiculously impressive car.

♪♪♪

THE damp and chilly days of summer ran their course, bringing about the blazingly merciless sun. I borrowed Hanaka's sunblock and lathered it all over as a precaution every day. I'd heard how important protecting against ultraviolet rays from an early age was. Cursed with a plain face, I wanted to at least keep my skin healthy.

"Mashrion, it's so hoooot."

Eri, that's not a proper greeting. But I understand how you feel.

My backpack squished my sweaty T-shirt against my back in the grossest way.

"Morning, Eri. Let's fight through this. Just a little longer and it'll be summer break."

"We've got the summer school camp thing to attend first. Any hope for our destination to change to the beach? I want to swim. I need water! Water!" Eri sounded like a *kappa*—a mythical water creature that's obsessed with the water.

The summer school camp, which was meant to be a way for students to experience school in the great outdoors, was going to be a one-night, two-day bus trip right before the start of summer break. Students get in groups to share a cottage, make curry, orienteer, and enjoy a campfire together at night.

I don't want to go either. I hate that I won't be able to play the piano the entire duration of the trip.

♫♫♫

THE first thing I did when I got home from school each day was flip on the TV. I'd developed an aversion to the overly silent living room. Being home alone brought me unsettling anxiety and loneliness.

A talk show happened to be on that particular day. They entered a segment about a music festival occurring this weekend, so I picked up the remote control to turn up the volume while I folded laundry. The special concert, the centerpiece of the music festival, was titled, "A Midsummer Night's Dream ~Recital Contest for Young Pianists~" and they were widely advertising it.

That's the concert Miss Ayumi is going to perform in.

Rows of big corporations filled the sponsor list. Sou's family name was also listed among the names. I'd recently found out that his family's business is a top instrument crafter, currently fighting for the number-one spot in Japan. Naturally, I had heard of Shiroyama Instruments before, and my Aine was a Shiroyama Piano. But never in my wildest dreams had I imagined that it was the same Shiroyama as Sou's last name.

Since Sou's dad had taken over as the president of the Shiroyama Group, he had expanded it to focus on doing business in Europe. From what I heard, Sou's dad was in Germany for that reason. Sou's uncle, the executive vice president, was managing the Japan branch. This weekend's concert doubled as the official debut of a new Shiroyama piano model.

"The orchestra will play on Saturday. And Sunday will see the performance of the orchestra along with a pianist recital contest, making this an irresistible festival for classical music enthusiasts. I've heard that there won't be many same-day tickets on sale, but there will be some nonetheless. Why not make your way there for a fantastic musical experience?"

I watched the female newscaster cheerfully end the segment and shut off the TV. I quickly finished my homework, then played the piano until seven. After dinner, I took a bath and played the piano some more until nine. Once I finished that, I studied before going to bed. I woke up early the next morning and began my morning study session, which was always insufficient.

Occasionally, I found myself anxious that merely living out my life in a set pattern wasn't going to be good enough to achieve my goals.

Am I working hard enough? Will I get admitted to Seio Academy?

As the years passed, my desire to walk down the path of a pianist grew increasingly serious.

I like the piano. I love it. I'm not satisfied settling for just being good. I want to make it my profession.

Before getting into bed that night, I opened the music festival pamphlet I'd received at my last piano lesson. The first thing I did was search for Miss Ayumi's name.

Ayumi Matsushima — Performing: Tchaikovsky's Piano Concerto No. 1-1

She was going to perform an outstandingly famous grand musical prelude. The symphonic performance begins with the horn. Contrasting the descending horn, the piano ascends the octave, so that the musical introduction strikes with intense impact. It's superbly dramatic. The euphoria from switching from minor to major key accompanied by the sensational theme is simply marvelous.

Of all the piano concertos, this was one of my favorites. A male pianist played the piano part in the CD I owned. The powerful touch born from his blessed physique was full of dynamic appeal.

I wonder how Miss Ayumi will play the song. This will be my first time hearing her play the piano for real. Even the short pieces she plays as an example during lessons have an intoxicating sound that easily entrances me. I'm really looking forward to it. I hope Sunday comes soon.

I set aside the pamphlet and opened the window to let air blow into the room, usually closed off to the world whenever I practiced the piano. The midsummer's wind that slipped in through the window screen was lukewarm but still better than leaving my room stagnant.

It's been a while since we last went out as a family.

Miss Ayumi gave me four complimentary tickets to her concert. Complimentary tickets don't have prices on them. Mom had accepted them with carefree gratitude, until she opened the newspaper, spotted the ad where the prices were listed, and screamed.

"M-Mashiro! Did you know the front row seats to your teacher's concert cost 28,000 yen?!"

"It makes sense that they would, because the pianists will be accompanied by a full orchestra."

"There's tickets for four of us, so…um…it'd cost over 110,000 yen altogether?!"

"It is a lot of money when you put it that way. But Miss Ayumi's family is one of the sponsors, so I don't think she paid for those tickets out of pocket."

"Why are you so calm about this, Mashiro?! Honey!"

I had to pacify my parents about the ticket price just this past week. Dad nearly fainted when he heard the name of the company Miss Ayumi's father directs. I no longer felt like I could tell them Kon and Kou were children of the Genda Group and Narita Group respectively, while Sou was next in line to inherit the Shiroyama Group.

The world of classical music is like a plaything to the rich and powerful. I wonder what will happen at next year's recital. I hope I don't have to sell tickets. How much will they charge for our tickets? What should I do about my clothes for that day? There was no end to my worries once I started thinking. *I can't burden my parents more than I already have. Am I aspiring to go down a path beyond my means?*

My worries about the future gave in to the sleepiness tugging at me.

CG 9: A Song to Play Someday (Sou)

THE long-awaited Sunday arrived at last. I slipped on my favorite dress Hanaka had bought for me. Due to the heat, I didn't wear a cardigan or petticoat this time. Hanaka curled my hair for me with a curling iron, braided it on the sides for a mature feel, plucked my eyebrows into a smooth, clean line, and gave my eyelashes some oomph with an eyelash curler. She went all-out on my hair and makeup, like a professional beautician, before she finally released me.

"All done! How is it? What do you think?" I appeared as the spitting image of my sister in the mirror. "You're super cute! DAD! Come take a pic! Quickly!"

Hanaka, who usually wore gaudy clothes and accessories, donned a refined pale-pink dress for the day. Elegant French sleeves and a ribbon at her neck completed the classic look. Her outfit, combined with her pink hair, made her look like a flower fairy.

"You're both the cutest girls on the planet!" Dad exclaimed, clapping his hands together excitedly before running off to get the camera. The entire family was thrilled to attend a classical music concert together.

"Hey, since we're all dressed up anyway, let's take a picture as a family," Hanaka suggested.

I agreed. Dad wore a suit every day to work, but the last time I saw Mom dressed up was at my school entrance ceremony. We cleaned up the living room table, then sat close to each other as a family on the couch. Dad looked through the camera's finder to adjust its angle, pressed the self-timer switch, and rushed back to the couch.

"How many seconds until the shutter snaps?"

"I think it's set to ten seconds…"

"Too fast!"

"Come on, guys, look forward—ah."

CLICK.

The shutter went off while we were still in disarray. Our usual crazy, smiling selves were displayed clearly on the digital camera screen Dad showed us. No one was facing the camera.

"What should we do? Retake it?" Dad asked.

Hanaka beamed, shaking her head. "Nope, this is good. It captures the real us. It's the best."

A twinge in my heart went off at her sentimental comment.

I feel like something similar happened in the past… The memory's on the tip of my tongue, but it's blocked by some sort of boulder, and I can't remember.

I clenched my chest at the frustrating déjà vu.

♪♪♪

THE theater parking still had open spots because we left the house early. Our domestic car was snugly parked in the lot, which was otherwise full of luxury cars. Dad's favorite car was ten years old, but it hadn't lost its shine. As someone who took care of his things, Dad always used his day off to wash his car.

Behind Hanaka and me, our parents walked side by side, holding hands. This was our family's formation whenever we went out together.

"Oh, isn't that boy Sou?" Mom asked. I looked to where she pointed. *She's right.*

It was a rare sight; Kon and Sou were standing in front of the theater together.

"Is that Mashiro's boyfriend who keeps coming over? Okay, it's time for this big sister to introduce herself!"

"Then, as your father, I should—"

"Dad, Mom, you guys go on inside ahead of us!" I hastily interrupted, stopping Dad.

Who knows what a doting father might blather? I had huge qualms about letting my entire family meet and greet Sou all at once. Sou would probably feel unnecessarily hurt if he knew I felt this way.

"How cute! Mashiro's being shy! Why don't we meet at our seats then? Here's your tickets. The place is crowded, so be careful not to get lost."

"Aye, aye!" Hanaka answered with gusto, taking the tickets from Mom and naturally passing them over to me. I secured them in my purse, which I zipped shut.

Our parents gave us a wry smile.

"Hana, you always rely on Mashiro for everything."

"I'm scared of what'll happen if I accidentally lose them. Mashiro's good with these things, so I can relax when she's in charge," Hanaka bragged.

"You're right. Mashiro is good with these things," Dad agreed, serious.

My doting family members are at it again today.

♪♪♪

"KON! Sou!" I called out as I walked over to them. They turned around at the same time.

Kon looked like a tiny actress, elegantly dressed in a knee-length pearl-white dress, paired with high-heel sandals. Sou was wearing a light-gray summer suit, with a chic polka dot necktie fastened at his neck. Moreover, he had his hair partially waxed back. I had to blink several times at his dazzlingly handsome appearance.

"It's Mashiro!"

"Mashiro!"

Their expressions blossomed into wide smiles when they saw me, clearly taking Hanaka by surprise. She managed to pull herself together, then greeted them with a formal expression I seldom saw from her.

"Hello. I'm Mashiro's older sister Hanaka. Thank you for being such good friends with my little sister."

"I'm Sou Shiroyama. I'm the one who has received so much from our friendship."

"…I attend piano lessons with Mashiro. I'm Kon Genda. It's a pleasure to meet you today."

That's strange. Is it just me or does Kon seem tense? Is something wrong? Does she not feel well?

"Kon—"

"Thank you for being Mashiro's friend! I hope you'll continue to hang out with my gauche little sister!" Before I could get a word in edgewise, Hanaka regained her usual peppiness and playfully winked.

She was in the best of moods to have had a chance to use one of her newly learned exam vocabulary words—gauche. It was cute how self-satisfied she was with that.

"I also hope we can continue to be friends," Sou smoothly replied, unaffected by the abrupt wink that had been sent his way.

Kon quickly bowed her head, the color draining from her face.

"You guys got to meet up here, so I'm sure you have lots to talk about. Want me to head in first?"

"I have the tickets on me. Let's go together. Can we chat more during intermission?" I asked, saying the first half to Hanaka and the second to my friends.

"I would love to, but…" Sou glanced at Hanaka.

He must be worried he'd be interrupting my time with my family. That thoughtful side of him is unbearably cute!

Kon's sudden melancholy concerned me, so I took it upon myself to insist that it was okay even though I came with my family.

"We're lucky to have met up so fast! I want to chat some more. With you too, Kon!"

"Yeah. I want to talk to you as well, Mashiro." Kon raised her head, finally smiling again.

"Let's meet at the intermission area on the first floor then."

We said temporary goodbyes and went our separate ways after we decided the details of when and where to meet. Kon's gaze had been locked on Hanaka, not me, the entire time.

♪♪♪

MY family went wild over the extraordinary box seats.

"Amazing!" My parents mouthed.

"Right?!" Hanaka exclaimed—with hand gestures alone.

The concert hadn't even started yet—they could've talked aloud. They probably had researched classical music concert etiquette in advance, since the entire time we were waiting for the lights to shut off, my usually talkative family stayed quiet. How precious and heartwarming could they be?

Before long, the lights dimmed, and the hall grew quiet as if someone had turned down the dial on the audience's chatter. The conductor walked onto the stage, stopping in front of the assembled orchestra members, followed by the soloist. After a round of booming applause, the performance began.

The twinkling sound of the grand piano met the orchestra's grand music, without ever backing down. Even I knew I watched them perform with pure envy on my face.

I want to sit there someday. I bit the inside of my cheek, willing my intense desire back into my chest.

The young man serving as the first solo pianist appeared from the stage wing and played Mozart's Piano Concerto No.21—Kou's favorite concerto. The piano's sublime arpeggio stood out beautifully. It was a masterful performance supported by genuine musical technique.

I'm curious what Kou thought of it.

Miss Ayumi was the second pianist. A thirty-minute intermission would take place after her performance, followed by another two pianists. The survey attached inside the concert program had a section where you can write down who you believed was the best pianist.

Obviously, Miss Ayumi is the best performer! Regardless of how much I believed in my piano teacher, I still felt sick to my stomach with anxiety for her. *Good luck, Miss Ayumi!*

I looked to my right to find Hanaka with a serious face, squeezing her hands tightly together on her lap. Just by appearing on the stage in a deep crimson long dress, Miss Ayumi took the audience's breath away.

She's normally very pretty, but she's on a completely different level today!

Miss Ayumi sat in front of the piano and nodded to the conductor. One second later and the horn loudly burst out, followed by the powerful yet gentle chimes of the piano. I was covered in goose bumps after the first note. A series of sounds combining both strength and elegance delineated a world rich in expression.

I'm being taught by such an amazing pianist?

I was numbed to the core. Just as I was enraptured by the delicate sound of the piano, which spread forth like ripples on a pond, a gorgeous high-pitched tenor swiftly cut through the air. It was sharp, but not ear-piercing. Until the very end, the piano resounded serenely. I spent a dreamlike forty minutes holding a handkerchief to my unconscious tears.

Lights turned on to signal the intermission. My parents leaned against their seats motionless, like their souls had been stolen.

"I was moved to tears! I clapped too hard and now my hands are killing me!" Hanaka declared pitifully, massaging her bright-red hands.

"...Wow. All I can say is just wow. I'm deeply impressed," Dad commented.

"Me too... I want to hear this song again. Do you have the CD, Mashiro?" Mom asked me.

"I do! I'll lend it to you."

All three of them had become instant captives of Miss Ayumi's music after hearing her play for the first time.

The power of music is awe-inspiring. I hope I can entrance everyone with my music someday too.

"I'm going to see my friends for a bit!" I announced, scooting out of my seat.

"All right. Be back five minutes before it starts."

I restlessly left the theater hall.

Amazing! Amazing! Amazing! I want to hurry and share my impressions with Kon!

I rushed to the lobby where we were supposed to meet up and found Sou sitting alone on a sofa in the intermission area.

"Oh? Where's Kon?"

"She suddenly felt sick and Kou dragged her home. I wonder if it was an asthma attack. She had a terrible cough. She insisted she would go home after she saw you, but Kou wouldn't hear it."

"What?! Is she okay...? Now that I think about it, she looked pale."

"Did she? Sorry. I only have eyes for you, Mashiro, so I didn't notice."

I thought he'd say something like that. I won't be shocked anymore. Sou's just an honest boy. Yup.

"Are you here alone, Sou?"

"No, I'm with my grandmother. Along with my current mom and the cousin on her side of the family. They're annoyingly loud about every little thing. To be honest, I really didn't want to come, so I'm all the more glad to see you."

"I see. How old is your cousin?"

"The same age as us. She usually lives in England, but she happens to be back in Japan right now. She's crazy domineering and cocky."

"You shouldn't speak ill of others when they aren't around."

"Sorry... I won't say any more, so let me recharge a little. May I?" Sou looked imploringly at me.

Maybe he really is mentally worn out.

"Fine... Here."

What Sou's recharging meant was holding hands. I held out my right hand. He happily placed his hand on top of mine and squeezed. As his primary instrument is the cello, his palm and fingers were large and tough. We were just holding hands, but my heart hopelessly beat out of my chest.

"You have a different feel to you today, Mashiro."

"Maybe it's my hairstyle? My sister did it for me."

"She did? You're always cute, Mashiro, but you look so mature today I feel like I need to hurry and catch up to you." He lowered his long eyelashes and knocked his forehead against my shoulder. We were still holding hands, which made the whole situation embarrassing.

"Um...have you recharged enough now?"

Although we were sitting in a corner with few people, it wasn't like no one was around at all. The gray-haired elderly woman sitting on the sofa across from us smiled fondly in our direction. Heat rushed to my cheeks.

"Just a little longer... Mashiro, you want to become a pianist too, right?" he suddenly asked in a tormented tone that took me by surprise. He had his forehead pressed against my shoulder, rendering it impossible to see his face.

What does he mean by "too"? Is he talking about Kon?

"I wonder if you'll also eventually come to only care about the piano and see me as nothing more than a hindrance."

"...Excuse me?! That'd never happen!"

Where did that come from?!

He startled me so much that I accidentally shouted. I quickly bit my tongue and lowered my voice. "There's nothing more important in the world than the people who are living and there for you. What good comes of playing the piano in isolation? It hurts my feelings to hear that from someone I consider a dear friend."

Sou lifted his head and stared at me, dumbfounded.

"Don't say it again. I love the piano and want to get better at it, but it can't even be compared to you, Sou. Don't hold yourself to such low standards."

"I'm…dear to you?" he mumbled as if he were questioning himself. His eyes wavered. Tears brimmed, threatening to spill over.

I came to my senses and rushed to apologize. "I'm sorry. I went too far… I'm really sorry."

What am I getting so worked up about? Maybe hearing Miss Ayumi's passionate piano made me emotional.

Sou shook his head, wiping the corner of his eyes with his sleeve. "It's okay. I said something weird. I should've known better. You're you, Mashiro. Also…thanks."

"What do you mean I'm me?"

"It means that I really do love you, Mashiro," Sou declared with a mischievous smile. He continued, "I know that I'm just a friend to you and that's okay."

I think Sou is cute and I don't want to see him hurt. But I didn't think my protective feelings were the same as having a romantic interest in someone.

"You left out the dear part," I answered with a deliberate pout. Sou laughed aloud.

Heroine's Results
Target Character: Sou Shiroyama
Event: I'm Happy as Long as You're Here
CLEAR

♪♪♪

THE music festival ended as a huge success. Miss Ayumi had won the most votes on the survey. Worried about Kon going home early, I called her the next day. She informed me then about Miss Ayumi winning.

"Isn't it incredible that Miss Ayumi won hands down?! I wish I could've listened to her performance when I felt better."

"Yeah, it is incredible! Do you often have these attacks, Kon? I wonder what causes them... It must be painful."

"I'm okay. It doesn't happen that often."

I was relieved Kon sounded much happier than before on the other side of the phone.

I expressed my excitement to Miss Ayumi during my next lesson, "Congratulations! I thought you were the very best, Miss Ayumi!"

She smiled bashfully and responded, "Part of that is due to the assistance of the orchestra and the song."

Tchaikovsky's Piano Concerto is certainly a popular piece, but I think that's exactly why classical music fans, who are well-versed in the song, listen and compare between different pianists.

I brought the present I'd chosen with Kon backstage once the concert ended. As one of Miss Ayumi's students, I received a special backstage pass. Despite being surrounded by mountains of bouquets and large fancy presents, Miss Ayumi was extremely pleased with the small present I gave her. I couldn't help but grin when I saw the hand cream was placed front and center on the shelf in her lesson room. Even after the hand cream was long used up, our present continued to forever decorate that spot on her shelf.

♪♪♪

AT last, the summer school camp neared. My concerns about not being able to play the piano during our time away still hadn't been resolved.

Determined to find a solution, I bravely entered the teacher's lounge after school. Mr. Kumaja was right there when I went inside. He sat cross-legged on his swivel chair, zealously writing in the class journal. The towel he'd had around his neck during the day was wrapped around his forehead—possibly to keep sweat from dripping onto his paperwork. Any other person doing such a thing might've been frowned upon, but the look strangely suited him.

"Excuse me, Mr. Kumaja? Do you have a minute?" I inquired.

He immediately turned around while closing the journal and squarely faced me. "Sure thing. What's wrong? Rare for you to drop by."

"Um, I wanted to talk to you about the summer school camp..."

I began by recounting to him how I'd been studying the piano all this time and how I was serious about becoming skilled enough to go professional. He didn't rush me and responded back in a friendly way that made it easy to keep talking.

"Not touching the piano for two days is very problematic for me. My dad looked up our accommodations and their website stated that there's a piano in the main lodge…"

The schedule I received from school stated that we had free time from 7 p.m. until 9 p.m. I earnestly requested permission to play the piano at the main lodge during that time.

"Hmm," Mr. Kumaja murmured, straightening his lips as he held his silence for a time.

Music places heavy demands on routine daily practice on its musicians. They even say, "One day of rest sets you back three days." Letting your fingers become slow and sluggish means you'll have to devote time to repeating the basics over and over again just to return to your prior skill level.

Mr. Kumaja shook his head at my continued attempts to bring the gravity of the situation to his attention. "I understand what you want. I also understand that this is a very important problem to you, Shimao. You love the piano, don't you? But as your teacher, I believe it's important to take time away from the piano and studying sometimes. Why not chat and play with your friends and enjoy what you can do only during camp? I'm certain it won't have a negative effect on your future, Shimao."

"…But—"

"Obviously, I won't force it on you. It's not that there's anything wrong with being alone. But I can't give only you permission to use the piano. Other kids might want to play too. As a teacher, I can't give special treatment to students based on how serious they appear to be about something."

"…Okay. I understand."

It's no use. He won't try to understand how it is for me. I have a hunch that I lived a carefree elementary school life like the one Mr. Kumaja is advocating for in my past life. And I'd done so in this life until I regained my memories.

But I'll never make it in time if I live carefree. The piano isn't forgiving. I understood what he was trying to tell me, but I couldn't agree.

I've actually lived more than eighteen years. So it's too late for me now, Mr. Kumaja.

Frustration ran rampant inside me. I changed my sneakers at the shoe rack and ran off into the fierce glare of the sun outside.

I wish I was a Seio Academy student! Who knows if schools for the rich and the wealthy have summer school camps, but I'm sure even if they did, they'd have music practice be a part of it. Instead of closing the gap between me and Seio's students, it's only going to grow wider like this.

With my narrow-minded perspective as a child, my fate appeared decided for me. At the time, I'm pretty sure I looked as if the world had ended. I hadn't even noticed that a black sedan had pulled up alongside me on the road back to my house.

"...Mashiro? I knew it—it is you."

Startled, I raised my gaze from the road and looked around. My eyes locked with Kou's in the back seat.

Why is he here?!

Taken by complete surprise, I tripped.

"Oi, oi. You okay?" Kou got out of the sedan he directed to park on the side of the road.

What is with his timing?! I nearly bashed my face into the guardrail because of him!

"I'm not okay!"

"That's your fault for going around with your head in the clouds. You need to pay attention when you walk." His words, which would've normally never bothered me, felt like an arrow to my heart.

Yes, I just always have my head in the clouds. Sorry I'm not attentive 24/7.

"It's none of your business, Kou. Leave me alone!" I spat, shooting him a glare before I turned to walk away.

Unfortunately for me, Kou yanked on my arm to stop me from leaving. The momentum sent me falling backward. And just like that, I was in his arms. My heart hammered as his arm wrapped around my waist to catch me. Without batting an eye, he promptly helped me stand on my own again.

Wow, how strong must he be to catch and right me so easily? Is he really a kid?

"Y-You scared me!"

"Sorry. I pulled harder than I thought... What's wrong? Did something happen?"

Worry filled his puzzled eyes—or maybe not. *Yup, I don't think so. Just my imagination at work. He must be plotting to tease me once I tell him what happened.*

"Nothing's wrong."

"Hah…you really hate me. And yet you once looked at me with a twinkle in your eye."

"And whose fault do you think it is that changed?! Who?!" I retorted back at his snide remark.

It's overbearingly hot as it is. This argument is zapping the rest of my energy. I'll ignore him and go home.

I swiftly turned on my heel to leave when he called out to me, amusement coloring his voice. "The grand piano at my house is a Bösendorfer. Did you know that?"

A B-Bösendorfer?!

I cared more about the piano than the abrupt change in topic, hands down. I swallowed hard. Austrian piano makers don't manufacture their pianos in large numbers, so very few circulate Japan's domestic marketplace. Naturally, I'd never played on one, much less seen one.

"If you tell me what's going on with you, I'll let you play on it as much as you want… Now then, what'll it be? Unlike Sou, I'm not patient."

"P-Please let me come over!" I faced Kou, bowing my head.

I had tossed my ounce of pride in the gutter. Who wouldn't? I mean, it's a Bösendorfer! They're called Vienna's treasure for a reason!

The corner of Kou's lip turned up in a triumphant smirk. He's the devil, I tell you! He lures you in with his honeyed words and his bewitching handsomeness to corrupt his prey.

"Get in then. Mizusawa, give Mashiro's house a ring later. Tell them we'll bring her home before dark."

"Yes, sir."

Scary! He agreed promptly without asking for a reason! Also, why do you know my house phone number, Mr. Mizusawa…?

♪♪♪

THE Narita estate was a different style of stately manor than Shiroyama's. The sheer fact that it had a circular driveway in the front cast doubt in my mind. Was this really a person's house and not a hotel? A fountain sat in the center of the circular driveway, further accentuating its aesthetic. The garage was laughably long, completely horizontal. Luxury foreign automobiles must've been lined up in a perfect row inside.

"Welcome home, Young Master." A middle-aged man in a butler's attire greeted Kou with a refined baritone voice from where he waited in front of the grand entrance.

Y-Young Master?!

Laughter caught in my throat. Kou stared down at me with my shaking shoulders, his handsome face twisting.

"Don't laugh. Also, Tanomiya, I told you to stop calling me that."

"My sincerest apologies, Master Kou." The butler lightly sidestepped Kou's snappy reply and tilted his head when he saw me. "Oh. Now this is rare. To think you would bring home a lady other than Lady Kon."

"Don't comment on unnecessary things. We'll be in the music room on the second-story for a while. Bring tea and snacks whenever it's convenient for you."

"Yes, sir."

I bowed back to the butler when he bowed to me. "How do you do? My name is Mashiro Shimao. I attend the same piano lessons as Kon. I apologize for my sudden visit today." I gave my best attempt at a formal greeting.

"…I am Tanomiya. Thank you very much for your polite greeting." Mr. Tanomiya looked surprised for but a moment before his eyes softened, and he returned my greeting.

"Let's go." Kou grabbed my arm and briskly walked off with me in tow.

I feel like he's always dragging me around. He's not going to put a collar and leash on me eventually, right?

On our way up the grand spiral staircase to the second floor, Kou whispered, "It's been a while since I last saw Tanomiya caught off guard."

"He did look surprised. Was my greeting off?"

"No… It's probably because there hasn't been anyone else like you around me before. You're the first kid to go out of their way to introduce themselves to the help, Mashiro."

"I thought it was normal to introduce yourself to the people of the house when you go over to a friend's place. Isn't this just a case of 'birds of a feather flock together?'" I purposefully goaded him.

"Could be."

Keeping his face pointed straight ahead, Kou gave a lonely smile. This expression occasionally crossed his face—it was the face of someone who'd given up on everything and felt alone in the world. And each time I witnessed it, I found myself without words to offer him.

I want Kou to keep his haughtiness on at all times. I hate being tormented by these indescribable feelings.

"This is it."

We finally arrived at a room after he'd led me down a wide hallway with thick, plush carpet floors. We came to a halt in front of a thick door similar to the one I took piano lessons in, and Kou pushed down hard on the door lever.

Oh yeah, he said he was taking me to the music room.

As I stepped into the room, I was hit with approximately 800 square feet devoted to a magnificent grand piano and walls covered in violins.

What is this room?! It's awesome! I feel like I'm in a music store!

"Fwaaaaah," a sound of awe that didn't resemble a word in the slightest spilled from my lips.

"Haha! …Mashiro, your mouth is hanging open."

I was so mesmerized by the room before me that I didn't even mind Kou laughing at me. The jet-black Bösendorfer reflected the lights, glamorously sparkling under them.

"Can I touch it? Can I?"

I walked up to the semi-concert Bösendorfer, then looked over my shoulder to Kou. Semi-concert grand pianos are what schools and churches use. Full-concert pianos are bigger, the largest size piano on the market. And full-concert Bösendorfer's are over 2 meters long, hitting 2.90 meters at their biggest size—that's close to ten feet!

My current strength wouldn't even be able to begin to draw the sound out of those pianos. Even if I managed to make it play a note, the sound from a piano meant for huge theater halls would be painful in a room this size.

"Yes, yes. Wait a second." He smiled wryly and set his hand on the piano to open its lid.

Propping open the lid gives you a louder, more resonant sound than when the lid is down, but it's monstrously heavy.

W-Will he be okay?

As I was worrying, Kou simply propped the lid open, his face unruffled, and secured the lid prop into the cup.

"W-Wow… Oh yeah, Kou? How tall are you now?"

"Me? Let me think…about 5'3"?"

"Seriously…?"

That'd make him five inches taller than me. His arms look thin, but he was able to prop up the heavy piano lid, so he must really have muscles. How the heck is he a ten-year-old?

"Why do you look repulsed? Isn't this where you fall for me?"

"I don't want to fall for an elementary schooler like you, Kou."

"You don't want to, huh? …You really are intriguing, Mashiro."

For some reason, Kou was in the best of moods.

Maybe he's not a legit oresama, but a secret masochist… That's even scarier.

"Let's leave the idle prattle at that. Take a seat and show me what you've got." Kou snatched a folding chair from a corner of the room, then placed it a moderate distance away from the piano and leisurely took his seat.

Sucks for you if your plan is to put the pressure on me! I'm used to worse from Miss Ayumi's lessons.

I adjusted the bench's height and sat in front of the piano. Lightly placing my fingers on the keyboard, I tested the *do* key first. A gorgeous sound dispersed into the air. The sound faded softly, leaving behind a slight reverberation. It was a little slower compared to the quick rising sound of a Steinway. In exchange, its sound was deeper. Brahms or Beethoven would have better compatibility with this piano than Chopin, which relied on a lighter touch.

I warmed up my fingers with several musical scales, then moved my hands back to the first position on the keyboard.

Mr. Bösen, please accompany me for a short while, I whispered to the piano in my mind.

Brahms - 16 Waltzes, op. 39, No. 15 in A-flat Major

I chose the song I happened to be learning. It's a short song that has reappeared countless times with its sweet theme rearranged. While it's shorter than two minutes, I'm fond of the flowery tune.

Augh, I knew it! The keys are heavy! The parts where I can make my Aine beautifully reverberate at home aren't sounding the same way.

I marginally dropped the tempo and altered the strength I put into my touch. I played the song till the end, careful never to go too rough or wild with it. Quietly, I moved my fingers off the keyboard, reveling in the lingering sound.

Heavy, but unbelievably wonderful! I want to play it again once I'm an adult who can use its full potential. Crisp applause brought me back to reality. *Oh yeah, I forgot Kou was here.*

"…You're pretty good, Mashiro." Kou lowered his hands, his eyes piercing me with a challenging glimmer.

Is that astonishment and doubt I see in his eyes?

"Thanks. 'But it's like chalk and cheese compared to Kon,' is what comes next, right?" I beat him to the punch line I thought he might go for.

His lips curved up like a bow. "At present, yeah… Who are you?"

He had once asked me the same question in the drawing room at Miss Ayumi's house. But the nuance was completely different between then and now. Kou was genuinely interested this time.

Has he started to sense the inconsistencies between my appearance and personality?

I truly didn't know how I'd explain it. It'd be absurd to think he would buy a foolish story about me being reincarnated from another world. But I felt like I had to answer him sincerely this time.

"I really do love the piano. I love Kon even more. At least trust me on that much. There's no way I'd ever harm Kon."

She's my sole reincarnation buddy after all.

Kou thoughtfully pondered over my offered treaty in what seemed like a long pause, before the tension finally let out of his shoulders. "Is that so? All right. …Say, Mashiro, can you sight-read?"

"Hm? Well, if it's an easy piece."

Where'd that come from? I cocked my head.

He stood and pulled out one particular sheet music from the built-in bookcase. "I'll give you an hour. The rough sound will be good enough, so try picking up the sound from this."

The sheet music he handed me was Fritz Kreisler's "Love's Sorrow". The song's meant to be played as a duet between a piano and violin. I flipped through the pages of music, skimming it.

Doesn't seem to require techniques that are too difficult, but this is impossible to pick up in an hour! What'd he expect?!

"It's still too soon for me to play this."

Kou picked up the red pen sitting on the piano's sheet music stand and began writing on the sheet music. He erased the difficult notes and changed it to a simpler arrangement. Before long, the sheet music was covered in red.

"How about this?"

"...I could make do with this."

I kept my astonishment to myself. Without thoroughly sound knowledge of music, it would be impossible to mimic what Kou just did. He'd left all the important passages that would ruin the song if removed, and arranged them to a level easier to play.

And in mere minutes at that! He didn't check a single note on the piano.

"I'd just get in the way if I'm here, so I'll leave for a bit. You've only got an hour, Mashiro."

Just as he reminded me, there was a dull knock on the door.

"Come in," Kou called to the reserved knock.

Mr. Tanomiya entered the room carrying a tray with drinks and snacks.

Iced tea with sliced oranges and cookies! I instinctively gulped.

"...You're more interested in food than pretty things, huh, Mashiro?"

Ugh. Was I that obvious?

I grudgingly turned to glare at him and was taken aback by his expression. It wasn't the perfect smile he kept up for appearances, but the gentle expression he only showed to Kon that he wore as he lightly chuckled at me. My heart squeezed and noisily hammered.

Stop it. Don't get attached.

I balled my hands and tried to wrestle a grip on my wavering heart.

"You can take a break, but make sure to practice."

"Okey-dokey."

"Drop the sarcasm."

"Okay!"

After our trademark exchange, Kou and Mr. Tanomiya left the music room. Without a second's delay, I snatched up one of the cookies placed on the table. They were crunchy scrumptiousness. The mellow buttery flavor filled my mouth. I was thirsty too, so I picked up the large glass of iced tea. Ice cubes clattered together as I brought the straw to my lips with a smile.

What is this drink?! It's insanely delicious! Taking advantage of the fact no one was watching, I downed it with a few huge gulps and let out an unladylike sigh. *Phew! I've been revived! All right! Time to read the sheet music.*

I thoroughly wiped my hands on the wet towel they had considerately provided and went ahead and wiped my mouth with it too. Kou would laugh his head off if I had crumbs left on my lips.

"Love's Sorrow"—also known as *Liebesleid*—is one of the three short pieces for the violin and piano written by Kreisler and is a pair with "Love's Joy" (*Liebesfreud*). It was my first time seeing the sheet music, but I had heard it on CD before. The song is played in A minor. A heartrending violin melody accompanies the piano rhythm, reminiscent of a folkdance.

I started by skipping over the difficult parts to get the overall gist, then returned to refine the smaller details. I had no idea what Kou had in mind, but the most important thing to remember when two instruments come together is, "never stop playing halfway through." Even if you're off, you must push through as to not stop the entire performance.

Around the time I thought, *I think I have the overall feel for it,* I decided to measure my tempo. I grabbed the metronome then froze. The tempo instructions read, "Tempo di Landler".

What's Landler?

With no way to look it up, I decided to mimic the speed I'd heard on the CD version of the song. Kou returned around the time I was able to play through the whole song without tripping up.

"How'd it go?"

"I'm a long way from not making any mistakes, but I can play to a certain level… Oh yeah, what does this mean?"

I was getting to my feet to show him the sheet music, when he gestured for me not to stand, coming over to stand right beside me instead. He had to bend over and lean his face close to mine to see it. I didn't want to be nervous, but my body tensed automatically.

"Landler is a folkdance that used to be popular in south Germany. See the poco meno mosso instructions in the C part? Just play the vibrato a little slower than the waltz."

"R-Really? I see now. Thanks," I stammered quickly, hoping he wouldn't catch wind of my pounding heart. "Let's play it now then."

"Already? Let's try comparing and matching each other first. I'll play first. Start by listening and then catch up to where I'm at in the song."

So he wasn't trying to test my sight-reading ability. Turns out he just wanted to form an ensemble together. And this is coming from the person who said he wouldn't play alongside me until I won a competition when we were at that concert a while ago.

Kou is acting kinda strange today.

Noticing my fishy stare, Kou turned toward me while he prepped his violin. "What? You nervous? Or have you fallen for me?"

"As if! I'll never fall for you again!"

"That's admitting you've fallen for me once before," he laughed as he skillfully finished tuning his violin.

It's almost like he's happy to have someone tell him they don't like him.

"Sorry for the wait. I'm going to start now."

He straightened his back and brought the violin under his chin. That act alone was enough to warrant a painting. I sucked in my breath and stared at him, fixated. He was practically the younger version of my beloved Kou from the Performance CGs in *Hear My Heart*. My feelings from that time rushed back, bringing tears with them.

I loved him. I really loved him like an idiot.

He gently placed the bow against the strings and slowly started playing. As a violinist himself, Kreisler had composed songs that were especially appealing for the violin. In order to perfectly play "Love's Sorrow", the violinist has to have the techniques of position change, vibrato, and harmonics mastered to a certain level. The most complicated part in this piece is the high position harmonics that are required for the last note.

Kou hit the note without issue, but sliding six positions from C to A should've been quite the challenge.

Honestly, he's amazingly skilled. He should be able to play even more difficult pieces. His performance had been enough to convince me of that. I waited for him to lower his violin before clapping.

Kou pretentiously bowed back. "Thanks. Did you catch the gist of it? It's already late, so let's play together once and end it at that."

Oh gosh, I only get one chance at it?! I can't fail then.

No, I don't want to fail. Kou's violin was breathtakingly wonderful. I want to bring out his sound without dragging him down.

Heart pounding, I put my hands on the keyboard and waited for his signal. I matched my breathing to the first note and began to play the piano part. The graceful, soft violin beautifully sung with sorrow.

Aaah…it's no use. Far from complimenting his perfect phrasing, I'm ruining it!

The violin's final note faded, silence returning to the room.

I'll apologize before he's gets the chance to criticize me!

"I was all over the place! Sorry!" I jumped from the bench, vigorously bowing my head.

Even so, Kou said nothing. Not expecting that, I timidly lifted my head. For some reason, he was staring back at me with a baffled look.

"…Kou?"

"Ah, sorry… You're right. You were all over the place." He flashed his usual snarky grin and shrugged.

Weird. What was that look just now?

"I was. I want to challenge it again! Can I borrow this sheet music? I also want to try my hand at the original song without the changes."

"You can have it. It's probably not enough to thank you for playing with me though."

How generous! Simpleminded, I was jumping for joy just at receiving sheet music. I held the sheet music to my chest, thanking him profusely.

"…You're back to normal when you're like this…" he muttered with a bitter expression.

"Hm? What?" I asked, sensing he was bashing me again, but he only shook his head.

"Never mind."

The entire way home in the car driven by Mr. Mizusawa, all I could hear was the "Love's Sorrow" sung by Kou's violin.

CG 10: Mountain Road (Kou & Sou)

THANKS to Kou letting me play the Bösendorfer at his house, my gloomy frustration over summer camp lightened.

Mr. Kumaja is right. He can't give special treatment to one student.

I heaved my overstuffed Boston bag onto my shoulder and left the house.

"Morning, Mashiron!" Eri, who'd been overcome by the killer heat until recently, greeted me with a broad smile.

Why was she in such a good mood, you ask? Because she ended up in the same group as Majima—the boy she's always had a crush on. Majima, with his thin silver-rimmed glasses, is a boy who's smart and athletic. His slightly longer hair stands out among the many boys sporting buzz cuts. He has a gentle disposition, which means he's a gentleman to the girls, further upping his popularity in school.

"Is that the newest Branberry?"

"Ehehe, you can tell? I pestered Mom to buy it for me."

Ignorant as I was about fashion trends, I noticed it right off the bat. Branberry is a brand that boasts of overwhelming popularity with elementary school girls. The bright-red puffy short sleeves were the center point of the look Eri was wearing, paired with a light-blue mini flare skirt and leggings. The summer school camp guidebook stated, "Skirts are prohibited," but her outfit might be overlooked since it includes leggings underneath.

"It looks perfect on you, Eri."

"Ehehe. I hope Majima likes this outfit too."

She's too cute!

Five large buses were already at our meeting place.

"Good morning, Mashiro."

"What the heck do you have in your bag, Shimao?!"

Kids from my group who had already arrived started talking to me when I got to Group 2's bus. Tomo greeted me first. She's one of the five girls from our usual friend group. Hirato had been the one who was surprised by my bag. He's a sports boy who's a part of the regional soccer club and always makes a stupid ruckus in class.

"Seriously. We should just ask Shimao for a spare if we're missing somethin', because it looks like she has everything with her," Kinose playfully teased me.

His good-looks meant he shared popularity with Takkun as the most handsome boy at Tada Elementary School. Though, as someone who's friends with Kou and Sou, my opinion of him ends at, "Yeah, I guess he's got a pretty face?" But he seems to be extremely popular with the other girls.

They say he resembles the main vocalist from the super popular boy band SAZE. As I don't watch TV, I'll never get what the big deal is. Anyway, I was supposed to spend the two-day, one-night summer camp curriculum with these four.

I'm fine being with Tomo, who's always serious, but the two boys worry me...

Don't cause any problems for me, I thought as I greeted them, "Let's have a good time together."

We were supposed to sit with our group members on the bus. Naturally, I thought I was going to sit next to Tomo.

"Here, take the window seat, Shimao." Before I could do anything, Kinose pushed me into the window seat of his row then sat beside me.

"Um, I was planning on sitting with Tomo—"

"Miyano's sitting with Hirato."

When was that decided?

Mr. Kumaja climbed into the front of the bus while I remained dumbfounded by what had just happened.

"Okay! Quiet down, guys! I have an important announcement now!"

While Mr. Kumaja repeated the basic things we needed to watch out for and do, I observed Kinose beside me. He grinned every time our eyes met. I wasn't sure if he really looked like he was from a boy band, but I could tell he was a skilled lady-killer.

He's got what it takes to be a playboy, I mentally noted.

Kinose had thoroughly marked me and stuck next to me during orienteering. Orienteering was supposed to be a simple game where you used hints written on the map to search for checkpoints, and whoever made it to the goal first would win, but for some reason Tomo and Hirato stayed way behind us the entire time.

I slapped down every flirtatious attempt from Kinose, but what'd I expect from a popular guy—he just wouldn't back down. He continued to carefully solve the hints and collect checkpoint stamps along the way, so I had no choice but to cooperate.

I finally got to regroup with Tomo when we stopped for a bathroom break.

"Hey! Tomo, help me out here!"

"How can I? My hands are tied. Hirata blocked me every time I tried to go to you!"

What the heck? Kinose must've blackmailed him into helping.

"He said, 'Kinose has always had a crush on Mashiro. Help him out too.' ...What are you going to do?"

"Haah..." I sighed, barely holding back my desire to add, "What a pain."

Please don't involve me in elementary school love affairs!

We made curry for lunch. Kinose stayed beside me the entire time I made *taketonbo*—a simple helicopter-like bamboo toy—for the evening. He neither said nor did anything—he just grinned at me like a boy in love every time our eyes met.

He also went overboard praising the curry I'd been in charge of making, exclaiming, "This is super delish! So you can even cook, Mashiro!"

"Even? It's not like I'm good at a bunch of stuff."

"How are you not? You're smart and a great piano player, right? I've always thought you were awesome."

Is that what this is all about? Elementary school boys have a soft spot for motherly girls who can do anything. Sou's the same way. Ahaha...

Dinner was an all-you-can-eat buffet in the lodge's cafeteria. Finally freed from having to travel with our group, I heaved a big sigh of relief. I met up with Eri and the girls, and they began to question me about

Kinose.

"…What? Did it become a rumor already?"

"A school-wide one. People are saying it looks like Kinose and Mashiro are gonna start dating," Eri answered, her eyes sparkling.

Huh?!

My tea went down the wrong pipe. Mako, who sat beside me, rubbed my back for me as I choked and sputtered.

"No way! Not happening!"

"Awww. Why not?"

Everyone complained that I was being no fun. The girls from other classes who happened to be sitting nearby joined in with similar complaints.

Since when had they been listening?!

"He hasn't confessed his feelings to you yet?"

"I won't give him the chance," I declared on the spot.

"Meanie, Mashiro!"

"Poor Kinose!"

They then proceeded to guilt trip me.

♪♪♪

WE were supposed to bathe after dinner. Mr. Kumaja called me as I was returning to the bungalow to get my change of clothes.

"Shimao, there's a phone call for you from home."

"There is?!"

Did something happen?

Mr. Kumaja frantically shook his hand when he saw the color drain from my face. "Don't worry, there's nothing wrong. It seems like they forgot to tell you something. They said it's not a big deal, but it could have to do with them coming to pick you up, so you should call them back."

I unfolded the note he handed me.

Hm? Was this the number to Mom or Dad's cell phone?

I had Tomo go back first and ran to the main lodge under the dimly bright sky. I put coins into the payphone and dialed the phone number on the paper.

"Hello? This is Mizusawa."

This was Kou's doing! I considered silently hanging up, but changed my mind since, knowing the red demon, he probably wouldn't give up so easily. I held my other hand to my head as I weakly spoke into the mouthpiece.

"...Hello. This is Shimao."

"Hello, Lady Mashiro. I sincerely apologize for the hassle."

"Don't."

"I shall hand the phone over to Master Kou now." Mr. Mizusawa's quiet voice was laced with blatant exhaustion.

You've got your hands full babysitting a capricious young master. I feel your pain, I mentally put my hands together in prayer for him.

"Hi, Mashiro? I hope you're having a good time at summer camp."

"Get to the point already. I've wasted my money on this call."

"Oh, I forgot public phones cost money. I heard about your situation today from Kon. Sounds like you were ready to break down bawling about having to take a break from playing the piano? Why didn't you say anything yesterday? I would've done whatever necessary to help you."

If I remember correctly, I did complain to Kon about the piano a while back. Kou understands my drive and fixation for the piano—I'm incredibly happy to know that. He probably understands because he's the same as me. He acquired the legitimate technique and ability to express himself through music after slow and steady hard work.

"Not like anything will change by telling you... But, thanks anyways for caring."

"Who's to say we can't change things?" Kou replied mysteriously and chuckled. "What time are you free? ...Okay, got it. I'll send Mizusawa over to pick you up around that time. Wait in front of your bungalow."

"Huh?! What are you planning?"

"You don't want to waste your money on the phone, right? I'm hanging up."

...He actually hung up.

I still have no idea what he wants. I endured my impulse to fall to my knees, deciding to take my bath in the time slot it was listed for on our schedule. Running to the lodge made me all sweaty.

The large public bath was spacious, clean, and had just the right temperature hot water. Afterwards, I put my wet hair up in a bun and changed into a summer dress instead of pajamas. The linen sleeveless dress was comfortable and cool, perfect for use during the hot summer months. I left the bathhouse with Tomo, deeply inhaling the outside air.

"Phew…feels so nice. The air in the mountains is different after all. It's refreshing."

"It sure is! I think it feels even cooler than it should because we just got out of the bath."

While I was having a fun chat with Tomo on the way back, we came across Kinose and Hirato close to our bungalow. I couldn't help but be on edge after this afternoon.

"Oh, I'm glad we met up! Hey, do you have plans for free time?" Kinose asked.

"Sorry, I do," I instantly replied.

Was saying that too harsh? But I just can't stand this awkwardness.
Hirato, quit grinning this instant!

"…Do you possibly have plans…with someone else?"

Blegh. Don't corner me with that look, like a dog someone left out in the rain. Honestly, I have my hands full enough with Sou being the puppy-dog type! I don't need another one!

"…Lady Shimao."

Had it been good timing or bad timing? I don't know, but Mr. Mizusawa suddenly appeared behind me, dressed in a suit as always. He stood out more than usual in an area filled with nothing but bungalows and elementary school kids.

"I have come to pick you up."

Is this what Kou was talking about?! I have no idea where we're going, but this is a lifesaver right now!

"…I'm going to leave for a bit. I'll be back in time for the campfire."

"Huh? Sh-Shimao?!"

"My friends are here. Please find a good excuse if the teachers ask about me," I whispered to Tomo.

She nodded automatically. I waved to her and followed Mr. Mizusawa. We passed through the backwoods road and onto a wide logging road. Two boys were standing beside the black sedan parked on the side of the road.

"Mashiro!"

"Good evening, Mashiro."

One boy was Kou. Believe it or not, the other was Sou. They both flashed me brilliant smiles and held out their hands to me, as if they were saying, "Come to us." Their game-like pose was dizzying.

Is this also a coincidence and not an event? Is the world I'm living in really following Kou's route? I wondered about the absent Kon as I clenched the front of my dress.

Heroine's Results
Target Character: Sou Shiroyama & Kou Narita
Event: Midsummer Plunder
Entered Love Triangle Route

♫♫♫

A veil of darkness began to enshroud the corners of the sky. The mountain temperature suddenly dropped, covering my exposed shoulders with icy air.

"Aren't you cold in those clothes, Mashiro? Your hair's wet too," Sou asked, concern coloring his voice. Mr. Mizusawa grabbed a fluffy bath towel from the trunk and held it out to me.

"Please use this if you like."

"Th-Thank you very much."

I accepted it without hesitation, spreading it over my head. I undid my bun and ran the towel from the top of my head to the ends, in order to squeeze the water out.

"I just got out of the bath and didn't have a chance to return to my bungalow. I wish I'd brought a sweater or something to wear over my dress. I was in a rush because of how abrupt a certain someone sprung this on me," I explained, emphasizing my displeasure at the sudden turn of events, while shooting Kou a nasty look. He snorted at me.

"You're cute for getting flustered over a small surprise like this."

"What surprised me was your overbearingness, Kou."

I glanced down at my watch to check the time. Two hours exactly until the campfire was going to start.

"Sorry, I don't have much time. Can you hurry up and tell me what you want? It won't be pretty if my teachers find out I'm missing."

"Don't worry. Our destination is right over there." Kou angled his chin in the direction of a large chalk-white building. "That's our company's employee recreational facility. There's a fully tuned grand piano there. Catch my drift?"

"What?! …A-Are you insinuating…I can practice on the piano?"

"I told you I could change things for you." Triumph glimmered in his eyes.

As much as I don't want to, I have to take my hat off to him on this one. Going out of his way to arrange things for me was enough to move me to figurative tears.

"Thank you! Wow, I'm so, so happy! Really happy!"

Sou stared at me as if I was shining, then turned to glower at Kou. "You seriously piss me off."

"My bad?"

I'm going to ignore their nonsensical argument.

"How much time will it take to get there?" I asked Mr. Mizusawa. He glanced at his watch.

"Getting there by car should take less than five minutes. What time would you like me to return you to your bungalow at?"

Free time ended at nine. For the hour before lights out at ten, each group was supposed to gather around the campfire and discuss the events of the day and how they could have performed better. The teachers were currently busy preparing for the campfire. We had been instructed to spend our free time in the main lodge's recreation room or in our bungalows, but it wasn't as if the teachers were going to go around checking on everyone or taking roll call.

"It really is nearby, huh? I want to be back before 9:10 p.m. You good with that too, Kou? Thank you so much for this opportunity!"

"It'll be a hectic few hours, but there's no way around it. Ready to get going?"

Mr. Mizusawa promptly opened the backdoor for us. Kou climbed in first, then me, with Sou last. Impressed by the springiness of the wide leather seats, I comfortably leaned back. My sneakers hovered above the floor.

"Here, would you like to wear this? It'd be bad if you caught a cold." Sou took off his navy-blue, short-sleeve hoodie and handed it to me. The inside of the car was definitely warmer than the outside chill, but I was still cold.

"Oh…is it okay for me to borrow it?"

"Of course it is. Sorry if it's a little sweaty."

I decided to gratefully accept his offer, putting my arms through the big sleeves, which fell past my shoulders. *Sou really is a boy too*, I mused.

A faint flowery scent wafted from the hoodie once I put it on. *It's not even close to smelling sweaty.*

"I'll be sure to wash it before returning it."

The soft material was making me nervous. *This has got to be expensive. I have to be careful not to dirty it.*

"Don't worry about it. It's too big for you, huh, Mashiro. Wow, you look so cute."

"Um? Th-Thanks?"

Sou seemed to have a thing for me wearing the baggy hoodie, and his frank compliment brought an unintentional blush to my cheeks.

"Sorry to interrupt you guys, but we're here."

At Kou's announcement, I looked outside the window. The car had arrived in front of the recreational facility's large entrance.

I squinted against the bright outdoor lighting as I entered the desolate recreational facility. The inside was brightly lit too, despite us being the only ones there.

"You're not going to tell me you opened the building just for me, right?" I apprehensively asked, worried that had been the case.

"Don't get any weird ideas. It's a weekday. It's just a little before the employees are supposed to open the facility," Kou easily dismissed my question and showed me the way to the multipurpose room. The instant my eye caught sight of the grand piano at the center of the room, I could think of nothing else.

"Wow...! This will actually be my first time touching a Shiroyama piano! This is so exciting!"

Shiroyama's a popular domestic piano maker that's famous for their genuine sound and softer high-pitch notes. Both the keyboard lid and housing lid were already open. I lovingly stroked the pure-white keys, then looked back at the three men.

"I don't have much time, so is it okay if I start playing right away?"

"Sure. Should we leave the room?"

"I don't mind if you stay. Either way works for me."

Kou, who had spent yesterday with me while I played the piano, wasn't surprised by my request, but Sou's eyes went round.

"You're going to play now? Even though we only just got here?"

"Yeah. That's what I came here for."

My head was filled with thoughts about how I could make the most of my practice time. *I wonder if I can play for about an hour and a half. That's not much compared to my usual practice time, but it's something at least, and that's better than nothing.*

I lightly massaged and stretched my fingers before going into the major scales. Once I was able to smoothly glide my fingers across the keys, I tried my hand at playing a few Czerny lesson songs I had memorized. I repeatedly played the parts I felt were off, checking them over and over again.

CLAP! CLAP!

The crisp, booming sound brought me back to Earth and in the direction where Kou and Sou were. They had stayed after all. Kou had been the one clapping. Sou was fixedly staring at me, his face stiff.

"You have thirty minutes left. Just listening to practice pieces isn't enough for me. Can you play a real song for us?"

"A real song…?"

"You can do that much, right? Or are you only capable of playing the Brahms' piece from yesterday?"

Kou's provocation offended me.

I'm not at a level to play for people with an ear for music, but I can't back down after he challenged me like that. I earnestly searched for a song among my limited repertoire that would suit a Shiroyama piano. *Bach doesn't seem like a good fit. What about Chopin? …Yeah, I think Chopin will do!*

As I mulled over what piece to select, Sou suddenly broke his silence, "Kou, what's this about Brahms' yesterday?"

"Oh, I didn't tell you? I coincidentally ran into Mashiro on the way home from school yesterday and invited her over my house. She played the piano the entire time, so there's nothing for you to worry about, Sou."

Sou glared at Kou's confident smirk and folded his arms. "Don't lead Mashiro around by the nose. Didn't I tell you to kill time with someone else?"

"And I believe I told you that you have no right to tell me what to do, Sou."

…They're at it again.

I turned back to the piano and hit the D-flat black key. The boys, who had been about to fight, stopped yammering. Keep your mouth shut while an instrument is being played—my heart warmed with approval over the training they must have received.

I'll be honest and admit it now, I love them both. I care for them deeply as precious comrades who are walking the same path of music.

Before the sound of the note I hit faded away, I quickly played the rest of the melody.

Chopin – Waltz No. 6 in D-Flat Major, Op. 64, No. 1, "Minute"

The tempo instructions read *Molto vivace*—very lively. The way the graceful trills form the centerpiece of this song fits my image of Sou. I lightly hit the keys, as if my fingers bounced with every note. Perhaps it was because I had an audience, but my fingers moved smoother and faster than usual. The song was a perfect match for the Shiroyama piano, which reverberated with breathtaking sound. Whenever I thought I had hit a key too hard, the piano softened the high notes, flawlessly supporting my lead.

I played another Chopin piece next.

Chopin – Waltz No.7 in C-sharp Minor Op.64, No.2

The sweet melody that followed the heartrending theme of the first half fit my image of Kou. I tried playing the notes romantically racing up to the twinkling high-note peak, then dramatically shook up the tempo for the low notes appearing halfway through the song. Once I had finished playing the two songs in a row, I lifted my fingers from the keyboard.

"Nice. Very nice," Kou honestly praised me, applauding.

Now that's rare.

Sou wordlessly stood and slowly walked over to me.

What's wrong?

From the bench, I looked up at him when he came to stand beside me.

Why do you look so sad? I instinctively reached for him; I grabbed and squeezed the hem of his T-shirt. The always upbeat Sou felt terribly ephemeral, and I grew worried that he would fade away into the night at any moment.

"…You were great. Really great. Can I request another song?"

"If it's one I can play."

"Chopin's Nocturne Op.9-2."

"Ah, I can play that."

Nocturne Op.9-2 is one of the few songs among Chopin's music collection that isn't too difficult to play. It's a famous enough song that basically everyone must have heard it at least once in their life. I faced the keyboard again. Sou took several steps back and waited for me to start.

The grace notes of the melody played by my right hand were supported by the relaxed chord played by my left. This romantic song instructs the performer to play *espressivo*—to play expressively—but I wasn't fond of playing emotionally. Instead of using grandiose pauses, I went for a smooth, yet singsong sweetness.

A song that makes you think of the night, huh? It really is the perfect song for my current situation.

The last note hung in the air before softly melting away. Sou gave me a big round of applause this time. His face had regained its color, and he looked much better than before I played.

"I've heard that song many times, but this is the first time I liked it. Appreciation for a song varies depending on the person who plays it, huh? I guess that should be obvious, but I finally really understand it. Any song Mashiro plays will become a kind song to me."

What a killer line! This has definitely got to be an event now! Was Nocturne the flag?! I never saw any of Sou's events in the original Hear My Heart, so I have no proof that this is an event, but his lines and gaze are sweeter than honey right now!

"U-Um—"

"I agree. It was something else. You've got a thing for Chopin."

Even Kou had words of praise for me.

I'm going to go insane with him also being kind to me today!

Hesitant to say anything, I kept quiet.

"I have a request I want you to play as well, but it looks like our time is about up. I'll save it for something to enjoy next time."

"…Next time? You're going to continue bothering Mashiro?" Sou started the fight with Kou again.

"Why shouldn't I? It's one thing if Mashiro's unhappy about it, but you have no say in this, Sou."

I wish they would quit using me as an excuse to fight. As I was trying to come up with a way to stop them, the multipurpose room door swung open.

"Lady Shimao, it is time to go."

"Thank you, Mr. Mizusawa."

You have perfect timing as always!

I carefully closed the keyboard lid and stood up straight.

"You are both equally important and dear friends to me. You're neither less nor more than that. And my feelings will never change," is all I said before I turned to leave with Mr. Mizusawa.

"You hear that? You're a dear friend, Sou."

"Good for you too, Kou. Looks like you've been removed from your status as her arch nemesis. Congratulations."

They're still going at it. That must be the way they communicate. I'll leave them to it.

♪♪♪

I returned ten minutes before the campfire started as planned. I'd expect no less of Mr. Mizusawa to transport me without a minute's delay. Moreover, he had taken my hand and walked me back to where he picked me up because the mountain trail was dangerous after nightfall.

There's something lovely about an adult man who does everything perfectly.

"How old are you, Mr. Mizusawa?"

"Me? I will turn twenty-nine this year."

Twenty-nine! I knew he was a mature adult. Being surrounded by mischievous elementary schoolers on a daily basis makes me think I'd much rather fall in love with someone like Mr. Mizusawa if anyone at all. Rather than an oresama or the puppy-dog type, normal really is the best! I mean it!

Despite my determination to not get involved with *Hear My Heart's* storyline, it was unsettling that my life seemed to be teeming with events. Being with Sou and Kou kept me constantly busy, fielding a racing heart or hurt feelings. Even just being friends made me feel that way.

Will I lose everything if we become romantically involved? I don't want to be at the mercy of uncontrollable feelings. I only want to continue down the path of music in peace.

♪♪♪

I ran back to where the students were supposed to meet for the campfire, and luckily Tomo and the girls spotted me first.

"Welcome back, Mashiron!"

"I'm back! Sorry about that, Tomo! Did Mr. Kumaja say anything?"

"Nope. It's all good. I was playing cards with Eri and the girls in our room. Teachers never checked on us."

That was a load off my shoulders. *I'm convinced Mr. Kumaja would've blown his top if I told him I went off to play the piano without permission. He's super scary when he's angry!*

"Welcome back. So you know the guy in the suit?" Kinose asked, suddenly materializing out of nowhere.

"Yup. He's my friend's...older brother! They happened to be visiting a recreational facility up north, so they let me borrow the piano to practice for a bit."

Obviously, I couldn't inform them that Mr. Mizusawa's a chauffeur. The conversation would've gotten annoyingly complicated. Instead, I told them the rest of the truth and hoped that was good enough.

"I see. Is that friend...a boy?"

"Huh?! Y-Yeah."

How could he tell? I didn't say anything that'd give away my friend's gender, right?

My face apparently gave away my confusion, since Kinose cocked his head and supplied, "That hoodie. I take it you borrowed it from your guy friend?"

Oh no! I forgot I have Sou's hoodie on!

"Please don't tell the teachers."

He smirked at my request. "Of course I'll keep it secret from the teachers. I'd feel bad if you got railed on, Shimao," he replied smoothly.

Oh, he's not jealous. Phew, what a relief. He might claim he has feelings for me, but it looks like they were just casual.

"Thanks! That's a huge help!"

He proceeded to drop the bomb right after I let down my guard.

"No problem. You'll spend free time during lunch tomorrow with me, won't you?"

So that's what he was after! What a schemer! Why am I surrounded by elementary school kids who act nothing like their age?!

I reluctantly answered, "Fine," hanging my head.

Following the agreement, I watched the campfire with him and spent the whole next day playing together, and somehow by the end of it I'd been so tired on the bus home that I ended up falling asleep on Kinose's shoulder. I became painfully aware of the fact he wasn't a bad kid. But that wasn't enough of a reason to fall for him.

"I had fun on the trip with you, Shimao!" Kinose came over before leaving with his parents who came to pick him up, while I was still waiting for my dad.

"It was fun. Sorry about the bus! I'm sure my head was heavy."

"Nah, not at all. I got lucky to see your sleeping face, y'know?" he playfully teased. I dryly laughed in return.

Are sweet pick-up lines the standard fare for modern elementary school boys these days or what? Is this an otome game thing? The elementary school boys I previously knew were more interested in fishing for guppies in the creeks than girls.

"I think I like you, Shimao. Will you be my friend?" Kinose finally confessed, just as we were about to part ways.

This boy was skilled. He made his confession ambiguous by adding a phrase like, "I think" to the beginning, then had deftly added the hard to turn down yet not too forceful, "let's be friends" line. He put me in a situation where the only answer possible was yes.

"I thought we were already friends," I countered as a last resort.

"Woohoo! Can I call you Mashiro?"

I see what his plan was. He was executing a multi-tiered attack, shooting another request after an initial, forced positive response.

It took everything I had to manage an indifferent reply, "Sure, if you want to."

I'm dead exhausted and I just want to hurry home to study already. I don't care anymore.

"You can call me by my first name too."

"Goodbye, Kinose."

You think I'd fall for that?

I grinned and waved goodbye. My group of friends, who watched my war of volleying exchanges with Kinose from a safe distance, let out disappointed sighs. With their fascination of romance, it must've been an unsatisfactory conclusion for them.

"What a waste. What don't you like about Kinose?" Mako badgered me with a pout after Kinose left.

I promptly answered, "His age."

"Whaaat?! Then what age is your type?"

"…Around twenty-nine," I stated. Eri gasped. Girlish screams erupted around me.

Aaagh! I was joking!

♪♪♪

THE day after the summer school camp was a public holiday. Just as I feared, I discovered my piano skills had dulled a little. Normally, I would practice for four hours on weekdays and eight on my days off. Merely taking a single day off seemed to set me back months. I wanted to cry at this cruel reality.

If the short summer school camp made me regress this much, what's going to happen during the longer school trips?

There are pianists out there who dislike practice, going as far as to publicly announce that they practice for less than one hour every day. But that's something only the chosen can boast about. As I lacked any innate talents myself, my only option for getting better was to practice, practice, practice.

Half-crying, I rehabilitated the strength and maneuverability of my fingers with scales and arpeggios. Taking care not to stiffen the back of my hand into a rigid position, I loosely spread my entire palm. While I had strong fingers, my left hand's ring finger and pinky finger remained the weakest no matter how much I tried to toughen them. I repeated the scales as many times as necessary so that all my fingers hit the keys with the same power, bringing out sounds of equal volume. Next, I focused on the accent. Then the staccato. Finally, I upped the tempo speed.

KNOCK! KNOCK!

Someone knocked on my door after I'd been practicing the basics for about two hours.

"Mashiro, you have a call from Kon." Hanaka worriedly looked in my eyes as she handed me the phone. "There's no need to panic and rush, Mashiro. Don't worry. You'll get the hang of it again in no time."

Hanaka understood the reason I didn't want to go to camp.

"Yeah…sorry, Sis. Weren't you studying? Sorry for being so loud."

"I'm fine! Don't worry about me. Check this out. It's what I use when I'm studying." She lifted the headphones dangling around her neck and grinned.

She had downloaded a CD called, "Classical Music to Make You Smarter" onto her cell phone. She was trying her best to do well on her entrance exams in her own way. Talking to my cheerfully optimistic sister always improved my mood and gave me courage. Feeling better, I unmuted the phone.

"Hello? Kon?"

"Oh, Mashiro, hello… Sorry about Kou. You wouldn't believe how shocked I was to hear that he went as far as crashing your summer school camp. I've been feeling really bad about how my slip of tongue brought that disaster on you."

Judging from what Kon said, Kou went back to the Genda estate and reported everything he had done from the beginning to the end.

"Don't be sorry! It actually turned out to be a real lifesaver for me! All thanks to you, Kon," I exclaimed, voicing my real feelings on the matter and heard her sigh with relief.

"I'm glad to hear it. I also heard from Kou that you went to the Narita estate, Mashiro?"

"Ah. Yeah. About three days ago? We happened to bump into each other after school and he invited me over. He let me play the Bösendorfer!"

"He did? Hehe. Bösen is on the heavy side, but it has a great sound… Sooo, I was thinking…" She trailed off, as if the rest was hard for her to say. After a pause, she continued with determination, "Would you like to come over to my place? All I have is a Bechstein, but it's fun to play and compare the sound."

"Oh my gosh! Can I?!" I accidentally shouted.

I always admired the Bechstein and dreamed of playing on it at least once in my life.

"Of course you can! …So, our moms have been saying they want to meet you, Mashiro. They're a little on the strange side, but they're really friendly… Would you like to meet them?"

By "our moms", is she talking about the mother who gave birth to her and Kou, along with the older sister-in-law who adopted Kon?

Seriously?!

"Oh no, did I make some sorta bad impression at Kou's house…?"

I did everything I could to behave properly and politely, but I'm nothing more than a commoner when it comes down to it. I haven't a clue about manners so there's a chance I screwed up somewhere without realizing it. Maybe they're going to take the roundabout way of telling me off. Was it wrong of me to chat the ear off the young maid I spotted on my way out? How could I not have? She was a maid! A real maid! I was excited!

"What? No, that's not it at all! If I had to say why, it's the complete opposite of what you're thinking—A-Anyway, I won't let it take up too much of your time! I'll shoo them away as quick as I can. …Also, there's something I want to tell you about Sou," Kon's voice faltered, indicating it was a serious matter that was difficult to bring up over the phone.

Now that I think about it, I've never had the chance to talk alone with Kon for long. Someone has always interfered with us until now. This might be a good chance for us to chat.

"Sure. When should I come over?"

I think there was a book on manners somewhere in the house. I don't want Kon's moms to hate me. I'll be sure to be prepared this time.

"Really?! Um, how about the first Sunday in August?"

I didn't even have to check my calendar. Like spring break, I hadn't made any plans for summer.

"Okay."

"Hehe. An instant reply?" Kon happily giggled. "I'll come to get you at ten in the morning. Tell your mom you'll be having lunch at my place, Mashiro," she insisted, before hanging up.

Curiously enough, hearing Kon's voice had warmed my heart. It was the same feeling I had whenever I talked to Hanaka. I spoke with both today, which meant the healing effect was doubled!

All right! The rest of today's practice is gonna be a blast!

I skipped back over to Aine.

CG 11: NOT FOUND (Kon)

THE first quarter came to a close with straight A's on my report card. My parents praised me like crazy at dinner after seeing it, giving me complicated feelings about it. An undeniable sense of guilt for cheating at life, as I had already done it once, rose restlessly inside me.

Would I be able to take pride in my efforts after passing the age of my death in my last life?

Hanaka joined in, rejoicing as if it were her own report card. "Amazing! You're so amazing! You're working so hard, Mashiro!"

"How's your report card look, Hana?"

"Please don't ask," Hanaka moped, instantly losing all the pep in her voice.

"Studying isn't everything and results aren't everything," Dad comforted.

"That's right. Both Mashiro and Hana are doing their best! Our girls are both amazing!" Mom loudly declared, getting a laugh out of everyone.

STAB!

A sudden stabbing pain shot through my head—I grimaced. *Here it is again. Lately, I've been getting sharp pains in my head much more often. I haven't told anyone yet because it immediately goes away... A sudden, sharp stab, and then it's gone. But it's inevitably followed by extreme, debilitating sadness.*

A normal fun dinner with my family—there shouldn't have been anything depressing about the situation, but I had an incessant desire to sob. I felt like I was looking through thick glass at a scene I wouldn't get back for all eternity.

"Mashiro? Not going to eat your food?"

"...No, I'll eat!"

Mom made my favorite *omurice* and Hanaka's favorite tofu and tomato salad. She cooked them as a special reward for working hard all quarter. Somehow, I managed to suck back the tears threatening to gush out and picked my spoon up.

♪♪♪

THE Sunday I planned to visit Kon finally arrived. Mom left first thing in the morning to buy macarons at a famous patisserie in front of the train station for me to bring as a gift.

"I heard they taste great, but I wonder if Kon's family will like them," Mom wondered aloud, a little worried about her choice.

"I'm sure they will! Thank you!" I cheerfully reassured her as I buckled my sandals.

I pulled out the most formal dress from Hanaka's hand-me-downs for the occasion—a black short-sleeve dress with a collar, and paired it with matching black polka-dot wooden sandals and a basket-style bag. I went out the front door with the box of macarons we had chilling in the fridge until the last minute. A young man I hadn't met before stood beside the Benz parked in front of my house.

"Lady Shimao, I am Nonaga, the chauffeur who will drive you around today. Please don't hesitate to let me know if you have any requests."

"Thank you for going through the trouble of picking me up!"

His polite greeting made me nervous. Mr. Nonaga smiled kindly as I awkwardly nodded. From what I heard, he was Kon's exclusive chauffeur. He was slightly younger than Mr. Mizusawa. His low, husky voice, along with his well-proportioned, tall figure was attractive.

He opened the back door for me, and I clumsily climbed inside. I still couldn't get used to being escorted. Kou's house was about a twenty-minute drive from mine, but Kon's was farther.

Mr. Nonaga noticed me fidgeting with my bag in the back seat through the rearview mirror and offered, "Shall I put on some music? The CDs Lady Kon usually listens to are already in the CD player if you are interested."

"Oh. Please do put it on then."

I'm sure they're classical music CDs. I wonder if it'll be piano music or—

I attentively honed my ears with excitement for what was going to click on, only to have my jaw drop at the song that played over the speakers.

Is this a SAZE album? I was floored to hear the twin vocalists singing a song filled with cheesy catchphrases in their sweet voices. *Whoa. I didn't think this would be what Kon usually listened to!*

"Does Kon like boy bands?"

"She does have quite the fondness for them. Not only this group, but also…"

I dumbly made attentive noises back while Mr. Nonaga listed off the various idol groups.

Kon has the same exact tastes as Hanaka! I can't believe she has more in common with my older sister than me…

I imagined the two of them screaming at the top of their lungs while waving fans decorated with their favorite idol at a concert, and grinned like an idiot.

♪♪♪

BOTH Sou and Kou's mansions had been breathtaking, but Kon's home was on a whole other level.

Even if someone had told me, "This is Kenrokuen—one of the three most beautiful gardens in Japan," I would've nodded along without a doubt because of how extravagant this sprawling garden and Japanese-style mansion was.

You could play Castle Hide-and-Seek here! Where you slide open all the sliding doors down a long hallway to find someone, making huge banging noises along the way!

I continued to imagine silly things as I got out of the car. I set foot inside the foyer, which was about the size of my house's entire second-story.

Is this a hotel lobby?

"Mashiro! Thank you for coming over!" Kon was waiting for me, dressed in a cool silk gauze kimono.

The smell of incense in the air paired with the image of a beautiful girl dressed traditionally in a kimono before me—it was as if I had wandered into another realm.

"Thank you for inviting me, Kon. This is a small token of my appreciation, but I hope you'll enjoy it."

Kon smiled broadly when I handed her the macarons in a similar fashion as I had seen demonstrated in commercials that advertised giving gifts at the end of the year.

"Wow! Are these macarons from Miyahori? I love their macarons. Let's have them together later."

Good job, Mom! I mentally shot my mom a thumbs-up. She'd be so happy to hear that her present had been a huge hit later.

Kon must've been happier with it than I thought, because she seemed to be brimming with excitement. "Come in! Come in! Let's go to my room first. I'll introduce you to my mothers during lunch."

"Please excuse my intrusion," I commented formally.

Kon turned to the maid-like lady standing back awaiting commands and directed, "Put these in the fridge to keep them cool. Tell Mother it's a present from Mashiro," as she handed her the wrapped macarons.

Kon usually calls them her "moms" over the phone, but it looks like she says "mother" at home.

"Why are you laughing?"

"No reason. I was just thinking you were acting really cute."

Kon's mouth fell slightly open at my honest reply. Her eyes went round like saucers, and she stared right at me. I was startled by her dramatic reaction.

"Wh-What's wrong?" I asked nervously.

She tightly squeezed her eyes shut and lowered her head, enduring something powerful that was beyond me. By the time she raised her face again, her gentle expression had returned.

"…Someone very dear and precious to me had often said that… I'm sorry. Hearing it just hit me really hard with nostalgia."

I wasn't sure how to respond; she had referred to the person in the past tense. Sadness seeped from every word she said.

"Umm…I'm sorry?"

"Hehe. You really are a nice girl, Mashiro… Come on, let's go! My room is this way!"

Beckoned by her slender white hand, I followed her deeper into the mansion. Kon's room was western-style, instead of the Japanese-style you might expect. The room connected to hers was where she kept the piano and it had completely soundproof floors. The entire mansion had been built with Japanese architecture, so I was surprised her room didn't match the rest of the house.

"I had them renovate it," she told me when I asked her why.

Now that she mentions it, the room does look renovated.

Seeing me restlessly fidget, she showed me straight to the piano. In the dead center of the spacious practice room sat the Bechstein in all its glory. And a radiant crown logo was emblazoned in the lustrous black body!

"You're an open book, Mashiro. I can see your eyes sparkling. You can touch it as much as you want."

"Thanks! Um, is it possible to get you to play for me, Kon?"

While we were students under the same piano teacher, Miss Ayumi's lessons were taken individually. So despite the fact that years had passed since we'd met, I'd never heard Kon play the piano before.

She regretfully shook her head. "Sorry, I'm wearing a kimono today. I won't be able to step on the pedals."

"Ah, that's true. Good point. Sorry about that. Then I'll play for you instead."

Please take care of me! I whispered to Bechstein in my heart as I settled on the bench in front of it. Kon and I were of similar height, so I didn't have to adjust the bench.

I briefly warmed up my fingers, then put my hands on the keyboard. Unlike the Bösendorfer, the Bechstein let out a quick and clear sound. Yet, the sound wasn't shallow or lacking in the slightest way. It had a rich softness to it. The easiest way to explain it is that it has a clear sound, purely unmuddled.

A song by Ravel or Debussy would sound really beautiful on this piano.

I decided what I wanted to play and adjusted my hands on the keyboard to match the correct position.

Ravel – Sonatine, No. 2, "Mouvement de Menuet"

This was one of my current practice pieces I'd been struggling with, unsure how to delineate the unique rhythm from the harmony. The song doesn't require a particularly complex technique, but I'd had a hard time memorizing it since the exact melody was difficult to grasp. Apparently, people say this song is the masterpiece of all piano minuets. It carefully strings the notes together with a slower tempo.

I know it's weird to say this when I was the one playing, but I was thoroughly astonished by the brilliance of the grace note's trill. As one would expect, the sound was completely on another level of beauty compared to my Aine.

Although I played through the song without any critical mistakes, there's a reason why Ravel has been compared to a sorcerer, conjurer, and illusionist—I found myself unable to bring out the beauty of his piece.

Grr! How vexing! I need to practice more!

I returned Kon's warm applause with a strained smile. "Ravel is tough! I should be playing it exactly as the music is written, but the sound doesn't come out pretty at all. I wonder how I need to play it."

"Hmm. It's true it varies from person to person on what's easy and what's hard. Did you know Kou complimented how good you are with Brahms?"

"Well, Ravel's definitely one of the composers I have a harder time with. But I love listening to his 'Bolero' and 'Pavane for a Dead Princess'… If I was better, I'd be able to master it. I just suck is all. There's no other explanation for it."

Kon had a mixed look in her eyes as she watched me angst. "… You plan on going down the path of a professional pianist, don't you? I could tell by listening to you play. Casual interest and effort alone would never have brought you this far. You're serious about the piano, aren't you?"

"I am. I don't know how far I can go with it though. But I really love playing the piano."

"I see."

I followed Kon back into the other room. Inside, a simple double bed was pushed against the wall, and a lounge suite rested on top of the Persian carpet, across from a fancy, natural-wood study desk. Overall, the room emanated maturity. Only the school backpack hanging off the side of the desk attested to Kon's current age.

We sat facing each other on the lounge suite, sipping the iced green tea the maid had brought without us realizing. The nice and cool, quiet room almost made the outside heat and noise a distant memory.

"By the way, what is it that you said you wanted to talk about over the phone?" I asked, suddenly remembering.

Kon sat up straight and gazed straight into my eyes. "This applies to the remake version of the game, but as long as I'm Kou's little sister, you normally shouldn't be able to activate even a single event with Sou."

"...Really?"

Considering how attached Sou is to me, I have a hard time believing I haven't triggered any events with him.

Kon appeared to be of the same mind, agreeing, "I think what's happening is weird too."

What's going on then?

She knitted her brow and continued reluctantly, "At first I was wondering if you had gone off course from *Hear My Heart*'s plot. But later on, I remembered there's a bad end... It occurs when you open Kou's route, but only ever talk to Sou and compose nothing but songs in the minor key, rapidly increasing Sou's affection. Halfway through, Sou snaps, 'Don't play around with me!' The game ends with...Sou Confinement End. I've been worried senseless lately, thinking what if something that outrageous could happen in reality..."

What the heck? That's insanely scary. Confinement End? As in he's going to lock me up and keep me as a pet or something?! If it actually happened, I'd have a heart attack from the sheer incongruity with his current personality. This goes way beyond the bounds of what people call Gap Moe—feeling excited over drastic changes in characters' personalities.

"Wh-What should I do, Kon?! Um, it's okay for me to think of you as the remake version's support character, right? Like the ones who give you hints to get to the good endings? Please tell me if there are any events I need to avoid!"

I need to avoid the Confinement End at all costs!

I looked imploringly to Kon, who answered my gaze seriously. "Should this world flow along the game's course, a girl named Midori Misaka will be a student at Seio with us. She should be of great help to you... I've said this before too, but you are free to live as you want, Mashiro. You don't need to be manipulated by *Hear My Heart*.

"As long as you quit the piano, you won't have to take part in the competitions or attend Seio. You might be able to live out your life without meeting misfortune. No, maybe you could just play piano as a hobby instead of professionally, and that'd do it…" Kon desperately suggested, tears in her eyes.

If she's reacting like this, it must be a horrifying Bad End. Chills crawled along my spine. I still couldn't choose to quit the piano, even after knowing that.

"I don't want to quit the piano. I want to study music at Seio."

"…No matter what?"

"No matter what," I asserted.

Kon flattened her lips. After a long pause, she reluctantly nodded. "To be honest, I've become attached to Kou too, and a piece of me still hopes that you and he will become a great couple. But, at the same time, I don't want you to come to Seio. The risks are too great. I want you to live out an enjoyable life in a world unrelated to *Hear My Heart*… But telling you this will only make things harder for you."

I found her sincere plea a little surprising. I never imagined she cared so deeply for me. Kon, more than I'd ever thought or gave her credit for, had given great consideration to my path in life.

"No, I'm glad you told me. I'm super lucky to have someone like you, Kon. You care about me like family when our only connection is that we were both reincarnated into this world."

May she hear the sincerity in my words as I heard it in hers, I prayed as I answered her.

She shook her head, tearfully smiling at me. "I'm the one who's glad. Because, Mashiro, you are—" She abruptly stopped, cringing. Her gaze moved to the empty space beside me. "…Don't touch her," she muttered.

The fierce gleam in Kon's eyes was sharply aimed at the space next to me.

♪♪♪

◇◇◇

Original Heroine's Results
Event: ???
Corresponding Event Not Found.

Error messages fill the game menu floating in the air. The man shrugs casually, and heads for his contractee. She had incorrigibly violated the rules again. Across from his contractee sits the girl set as the world's heroine.

"It's a pleasure to meet you, Mashiro," the man greets, knowing she can't hear him, then sits down beside her.

The contractee immediately notices him. The *despair* he's anticipated from her is instead replaced with waves of fury.

"...You're the one who messed up, Kon. You mustn't pull yourself out of your own role," he states, testing her. He pretends to wrap his hands around the heroine's neck. Fear seeps into his contractee's emotions.

The man takes a deep breath, relishing in her sweet, sweet fear.

◇◇◇

♪♪♪

A maid came to inform us that lunch was ready, so we made our way back through the maze-like hallways. Breathtaking paintings reminiscent of Kanō Eitoku's famous *Birds and Flowers of the Four Seasons* decorated the *fusuma*—traditional sliding doors in Japanese homes. I couldn't pass by them without being wholly captivated by their beauty.

"I thought this was a house we could play Castle Hide-and-Seek in, and it looks like I was right."

"Haha. I like the sound of that. Once we're older, let's wear *uchikake*—you know, the bridal robe with trailing skirts you wear over your kimono? And have a serious game full of acting out the castle part!"

"Then you'll be Iesada Tokugawa's lawful wife, Tenshouin, and I'll be one of the maids who came with you from Satsusama, Kon."

"What? No, you'll play as Imperial Princess Kazunomiya, Mashiro."

"That's too big of a role for me!"

We giggled as we walked the halls. Eventually, Kon stopped in front of a door.

"Mother, it's Kon."

"Please come in," came a gentle alto voice from the other side of the fusuma.

Kon gracefully lowered to her knees, then elegantly slid the fusuma open. I quickly followed suit, sitting formally on my knees as decorum dictated in this situation.

"Thank you for coming. Please come in!"

"Please pardon our intrusion."

You're not supposed to step on the cracks between the tatami mats, I think... Gah, trying to walk without stepping on them is harder than I thought! I proceeded into the room with small, controlled steps. I perched on the edge of the *zabuton*—a flat floor cushion used in rooms with tatami mats—and bowed formally, while pressing three fingers of each hand to the floor.

"Thank you very much for honoring me with your invitation today. I am Mashiro Shimao."

"My, oh, my! What a courteous young lady! How do you do? I am Kon's mother, Chisako."

"I am Kou's mother, Sakurako. It seems like our children are always spending time with you. Thank you for being their friend."

The two women sitting on the other side of the low table amiably introduced themselves. Miss Chisako had orange hair and jet-black eyes, a contemporary beauty with drop-dead gorgeous facial features. Miss Sakurako, on the other hand, had red hair and dark-brown eyes. Kou shared her hair color, while Kon had her eyes. Her amorous lips and beguiling gaze closely resembled Kou's.

Miss Chisako was dressed in a silk gauze kimono. I think it was made by Nishijin Textile. The silk double-woven obi adorned with Japanese iris brought the piece together in a refined and refreshing manner. Meanwhile, Miss Sakurako had tied off her summer pongee with a light-beige silk-woven obi. Both looked like they had been made to wear their clothes, and the effusive high-class aura they radiated overwhelmed me.

"I am the one who is grateful for their friendship."

Mostly just Kon's friendship, I added in my heart. *When I think about it carefully, Kou has helped me out a lot too, but his kindness lacks sincerity in one way or the other.*

"Come now, there's no need to be so formal with us! Our Kou, who seldom compliments others, has said you're a very interesting girl, and Kon's always going on about Mashiro this and Mashiro that. That's why we've always wanted to get the chance to speak with you," Miss

Sakurako exclaimed, happily putting her hands together.

Miss Chisako nodded along. "I'm very delighted for this chance to meet you today. I would love to chat about everything right now, but why don't we have lunch first?" At her command, the help started carrying plates of food into the room. "I heard from Kon that you aren't picky, so we left the menu to the head chef's choice. Are you all right with that?"

…*Head chef?!* I mentally did a double take as my full attention was seized by the incoming traditional Japanese meal, which was brought in by courses, steadily crowding the table. Before I could answer, my stomach did—with a loud growl. Kon burst out laughing. *Gah, how embarrassing!*

"I see you're hungry, Mashiro."

"You don't have to say it aloud! I-I'm sorry!"

"Don't worry about it. I'm glad that the food appears to suit your tastes. Eat as much as you like."

Sakurako Narita and Chisako Genda were sisters-in-law. Yet, they got along so well, you'd assume they were blood related.

A dish of horse mackerel and tomato topped with a plum and basil relish was served as the starter, followed by appetizers consisting of grilled mushroom and bacon, and miso-dressed shrimp with green beans. Conger eel soup was next, followed by sashimi, *chawanmushi* (savory steamed egg custard with chicken, mushrooms, etc.), grilled sesame seed *Kamonasu* eggplant, and deep-fried foods.

At first, I had sighed over the splendor of the food arrangements and the grandness of the plating, but halfway through I was sighing from the pain in my gut. I glanced at Kon beside me and saw her trying to loosen her obi. At least it wasn't just me! Each dish was small and elegant, but there were an endless number of dishes to eat!

"…You see, Kou was born with a natural talent, so my husband took advantage of the opportunity and had him do all sorts of things. To make matters worse, when Kou succeeded at the tasks his father set for him, my husband acted as if it were only natural for him to succeed and wouldn't praise him at all. My boy often cried over the way his father treated him as a child. Taking pity on him, my mother along with our relatives started spoiling Kou rotten, further twisting his personality in a weird direction…"

Before I realized it, they were talking about Kou's childhood.

Huh. Since when did we start talking about Kou? I was so intent on the food that I wasn't listening. I tried to imagine tiny Kou sobbing. I couldn't help myself from giving a small giggle.

"Whether it was horseback riding, chess, or fencing, he immediately mastered anything his father had him learn. He became an expert without having to put much effort into it, so he looks down on the rest of the world."

I randomly responded with, "Is that so?" and "Wow, that's amazing", while doing my best to down the food in front of me.

It was then that Miss Sakurako frowned and inquired, "You aren't being manipulated and bothered by him, are you, Mashiro?"

I almost accidentally nodded along and agreed. I pried my eyes away from the cool, grilled *onigiri chazuke*, frantically shaking my head.

"He hasn't seriously tried to do anything that I would really hate. How should I put it? He uses discretion. I'm always impressed by the way he knows just when to back off." I was trying to back him up with that comment, but Kon burst out laughing again.

"Haha! Mashiro! You really are funny!"

Miss Sakurako and Miss Chisako held handkerchiefs over their mouths, their shoulders trembling with mirth. But I mean, it's not like I was going to tell an outright lie just because his mom was present. My remark was genuine, the best words of praise I had for him.

"Please continue to be good friends with our children, okay?" Miss Sakurako smiled kindly at me as I took many short breaths in attempts to quell my stuffed stomach after finishing off the grapefruit gelatin served for dessert. She was such a gentle and warm woman, that it was hard to believe she was Kou's mom.

Miss Chisako enthusiastically insisted, "Please do come and play at our house anytime you like."

I honestly couldn't understand why it had been so difficult for Kon to ask me to meet her mothers over the phone. They were incredibly friendly and sensible women. They acted neither pompous nor egotistic about their upper-class status. Rather, they were so much like college girls, you wouldn't believe that they had children in elementary school.

After lunch, Kon and I returned to her room, where she let me use her piano again.

"I love songs written for the piano, but I also really love opera music," I mused.

"In that case, I'll play a simple arrangement and you can sing it," she offered.

Kon had changed into a cool striped dress after returning to her room, as her obi had been too tight to bear any longer. She took a seat in front of her Bechstein and placed her fingers on the keyboard. From the very first phrase, I realized she was playing "One Fine Day We Shall See" from *Madama Butterfly*.

Oh yeah, I forgot that we went to see it together last year. It's kind of embarrassing to sing, but since there's no one but Kon here, I guess it's okay!

"Un bel dì, vedremo."

I tried singing the Italian lyrics, which I had completely memorized after watching the opera on DVD too many times to count. Kon's musical accompaniment on the piano was so perfect it was hard to believe she arranged the piece herself. Spellbound by the magnificent piano, I sung at the top of my lungs. Kon laughed aloud when I tried to sing with vibrato like the opera. I endured my desire to laugh with her and sang till the end. My singing had turned the song into a questionably cheerful aria.

"Hey, Kon, why can you play the piano part like a pro?!"

"That's my line. Who sings in Italian?! My stomach hurts! You even added vibrato to it!"

We rolled on the floor with laughter. After we regained our composure, I swapped places with Kon and played the theme song from *Love You* for her, because of her love for SAZE.

"How did you know that I'm a fan?! Nonaga ratted me out!" Kon initially panicked, but she started singing along before I had even finished the first chorus. She's too cute.

"Why did we meet?
We are so close to farewell
Or should I believe in the future?
That we will surely meet again?"

I couldn't stop laughing at the way Kon enthusiastically sang the high point of the song. She sang the song three times through before giggling too.

"I'm surprised you can play this song, Mashiro."

"Some of my friends are obsessed with *Love You*. They requested that I play it for them over spring break."

"Cool! Now that I think about it, the second movie is supposed to be playing in theaters soon."

Surprised, I looked at Kon. "Didn't the first movie end with both the hero and heroine taking their final breaths at the same time in the hospital?"

I remembered how worked up Mako had been when she recounted every bit of the movie's storyline and how she had bawled throughout it.

"It did, but in the second movie, their lives were somehow barely saved and they're both in comas, but they're healthy and all lovey-dovey in their merged dreams."

"What the heck?!"

The chaotic storyline was only getting crazier. Kon still intended to see it on the opening day though.

"How could I not go when the leading man is played by the cool Misaki?!"

"That's one of SAZE's lead vocalists, right? Oh yeah, by the way, there's a boy in my school who's rumored to be a Misaki lookalike."

"For real?! I want to see him!"

Kon felt more intimate and relatable when she was fangirling. I couldn't help seeing her the same way I saw Hanaka, though their appearances were polar opposites.

"He's nowhere near as cool looking as Kou. You'll be disappointed when you see him."

"Kou's my older brother. I've never looked at him that way."

Kon was so adorable when she puffed out her cheeks like a hamster, that I nearly swooned. I think Kou's sister complex is partly her fault too.

♪♪♪

ONE afternoon, several days after I visited the Genda estate, a large package arrived at my house.

"Thank you for a magical time together. We picked this out because we want to see you wear it, Mashiro ♪ We're certain you'll look like a doll in it ☆ With love from Chisako & Sakurako ♡"

Dad and Mom screamed upon seeing what the odd, overly enthusiastic card was attached to—a kimono

Is it normal to send a kimono as thanks for coming over?! Now I understand why Kon had been so reluctant on the phone!

Dad rang up the Genda household to insist that we couldn't accept a gift this expensive, but through a long conversation, they somehow convinced him to take it.

"They apologized for it not being completely made-to-order, because they used their daughter's measurements instead of Mashiro's..." Dad relayed, as he hung up the phone. He seemed out of it for a while afterward.

Is that what they should be apologizing about?!

Mom and I stared off into the distance.

♪♪♪

HAVING been set on full alert against *Hear My Heart*'s plot progress due to Kon, I was practically let down by how peaceful my summer break went by. During the mornings, I concentrated on playing the piano. Once lunch came around, I absently watched TV while snacking on the food Mom made me.

The laundry dries really fast, and I have to bring it inside before it's too late. Let your mind wander just a little, and the bath towels will become so starchy that they'll be rough enough to scrape the skin off the person using them! Be vigilant against overdrying!

I squinted against the blistering sun as I went out, dashed back inside the living room with the laundry, and proceeded to fold clothes while basking in the lukewarm air blown from the fan. Ironing in the summertime without AC was a form of torture.

After I finished all my chores, I showered, changed, and peddled my bicycle ten-minutes to the nearest library. Libraries, where you can use air-conditioned study rooms for free, were my greatest ally. I'd study there until five, then return home just as Mom was getting back from work.

"Oh, you went to the library again?"

"Yup. It's cool there. Hanaka's not home yet?"

"She's probably playing around before coming home again. She's working hard by taking the summer crash course at her cram school, so we'll have to overlook her occasional breaks," Mom replied, rolling her eyes. I laughed with her, then headed back upstairs.

Hanaka laid spread out across the table during dinner like a zombie.

"Hey, Hana! That's poor manners!"

"But…if I move even a little I feel like all the knowledge I've crammed into my head will fly away." Hanaka pushed herself upright and buried her head in her hands. I moved behind her to rub her shoulders. Paying attention to lectures in the same position for hours caused the tension to seep from her shoulders down her back. "Phew. Thanks, Mashiro! You're the best!"

Mom said nothing more while Hanaka blissfully sighed. Dad stared enviously at her receiving a massage, so I rubbed his shoulders after dinner too. With fingers strengthened by folding origami and playing the piano, I could press all the right pressure points.

"It feels so nice!" Dad rejoiced a little too much.

I need to rub Mom's shoulders before bed too.

From there, I practiced on the piano again until nine. I became capable of playing Ravel to a certain point, but I still hadn't gotten perfect marks for his piece yet. Even though I flew through the Chopin and Bach pieces I was learning at the same time with flying colors, I just couldn't do the same with Ravel.

"Your sound is coming out monotone and thin," Miss Ayumi pointed out. The inability to get away with simply performing a song how it's written on paper is part of the profundity of classical music.

Since summer break began, I hadn't come across Kou or Sou once. Seio was on the semester system, so their classes had already been in session since the middle of August. Whether they were just too busy or I had managed to break all the flags necessary to score events with them was a mystery, but either way, not running into them made my days peaceful.

To begin with, we're living in two completely different worlds. I'm sure time will continue to add a gradual distance between us.

One more week and summer break would be over. Once I was back in school, I wouldn't have time to think about them anymore.

♪♪♪

HAD I jinxed myself by getting emotional or had an event triggered on its own? I'll never know, but on my way back from the library, I heard a short honk behind me.

This has happened before.

I squeezed my breaks, got off my bike, then slowly turned around. A familiar Rolls-Royce decelerated, parking swiftly on the side of the road.

Kon? Or is it…

I swallowed the lump in my throat, waiting for the back seat window to roll down.

"Hi, Mashiro. Did you go to library again today?"

The instant I spotted a lock of red hair, I knew who it was. I was startled by the fact part of me felt relieved to see him. And I was reeling at the fact part of me was *happy* to see him.

No, no, no. Mashiro, get a hold of yourself! You're confused!

"Hello. Did you ask Kon about me again?" I retorted with deliberate snark, determinedly denying the feelings in my heart.

The corners around Kou's eyes softened as he made a gentle smile. "Bingo. I thought I might get to see you."

The worst part of this is that even though I know he's only putting on a show, my heart still flutters at these kinds of lines. I feel lonely without seeing him, but actually meeting him is just as bad. My feelings become all messy and I can't keep my cool.

"Aren't you on your way home from school, Kou? Be safe on your way home. Bye," I said in one breath, gave him a short smile, and waved goodbye.

Staying longer than necessary won't do me any good. I'm happy as long as I know he's doing well.

Kou hopped out of his car just as I put my foot on the pedal. Then he used his long legs to nimbly step over the guardrail and block my path.

"Isn't that a little too much, considering that we haven't seen each other in a while?" he growled in a low voice.

I cringed. "…Yes, I'm sorry."

I awkwardly got off my bicycle and faced him again. He swept his bangs back, staring at me with indecipherable eyes.

"Didn't you say that Sou and I are 'important and dear friends' to you during the summer camp? Does not seeing someone for a short span of time make your definition of 'important and dear' change?"

He hit me where it hurt, rendering me incapable of answering. The phrase "double standard" came to mind, where you treat something completely different depending on the time and place for your own benefit. I was undeniably using a double standard.

My desire to live a life unrelated to *Hear My Heart*. My desire to treasure Kou and Sou as wonderful friends on the same path to music. These desires couldn't coexist, but both occupied my mind and heart with the same gravity.

Observing my silent struggle, Kou let out a sigh. "Well, let's forget about that for now. I heard Mom had a kimono custom-made for you. Since you have it, why not wear it this weekend and come see the fireworks with me?" He lightly changed the topic.

I had plans this weekend. Mixed feelings of disappointment and relief filled me as I shook my head.

"Sorry, I have plans to see a movie with Kon after the solfège on Saturday, and I promised my school friends that I'd go to the pool with them on Sunday."

"Hmm. Guess that's that then. By the way, what pool?"

"The nearby community pool. I doubt you've been there before, Kou."

I'm glad Kou backed down so fast.
Relieved, I teased him.

"You're right, I haven't."

"Right? I just tried to imagine you at a public pool, and it was so out of place I had to laugh."

"Hey, that's not true." So he said, but he must've also imagined himself there, because he chuckled. Amid the evening sunlight, dyed in a gradient of colors, the gentle breeze lightly tossed his dazzling red hair.

"Ah, but, I guess it would be impossible for me. I have issues being in crowded places with an unspecified number of people," he agreed, reversing his position.

That's what I thought. Many families bring their young kids with them, and the pool was always crowded. I couldn't imagine Kou, who had been brought up as a wealthy young master, ever setting foot in an old public pool you couldn't call pretty even if you wanted to be nice.

"Thank you for inviting me out. I hope you'll do it again sometime."

"…You're suddenly being nice and honest." His eyes went round, like he hadn't expected that out of me.

He ticked me off by the way he implied he didn't want me to be nice. He was a genius at getting under my skin.

"You condemn me when I'm cold to you. But you're upset when I'm nice. What attitude must I take to satisfy you, Kou?" I demanded, ready to start a fight.

A complicated expression crossed his face. "Good point… I wonder what it is that I want. I guess I want to be the one to make a pass at you, but I don't want you to make a pass at me?"

What the heck?!

"Excuse me?!"

"I know, it's confusing and selfish. I agree. But I can't believe I actually told you how I feel just now. You're welcome to be angry at me, Mashiro."

"…Haah." I sighed, utterly exhausted.

What's wrong with this kid? Even if I want to be angry, I can't. He defanged me with his last few lines.

Kou, who never revealed how he truly felt, had expressed his true feelings for the first time—at least that's how it felt to me.

CG 12: Pool (Kou & Sou)

THE Sunday I had plans with my school friends arrived. The moment I woke up, I opened the curtains to check if it was sunny outside.

Yes! It's perfect weather!

Typically my family went to an amusement park during summer break, but we canceled our plans this year due to Hanaka's university entrance exams. In other words, I hadn't left the house even once over break. It wasn't a big deal to me since I love studying and playing the piano, but I was honestly getting sick of my routine between home and the library.

"Mashiro, please tell me I'm wrong, but I'm guessing that you're planning on wearing your school swimsuit?"

I nodded affirmatively in response to Hanaka's question. "I am, because the one I wore last year is too small for me now."

"You can't go in that! Don't you have one of my swimsuits I haven't used much?"

Yes, I did have a bathing suit that would fit me among her hand-me-downs. But it was a two-piece bikini—the type where the shoulder straps tie around the neck in a big ribbon. The design was cute, but the problem laid in the fact that it would reveal my entire stomach. If you were being friendly, you could say I'm slender. Being frank though, it was too much of a leap for me to take when I have no waistline or curves.

"Why not take both with you? You'll feel comfortable with your choice if your friends are all wearing their school bathing suits too. And if not, you'll have an alternative," Mom suggested, which convinced me to bring both.

She's right. I'd hate to be the only one wearing the school required bathing suit.

I added the pink bathing suit to my cherry-design waterproof bag I'd prepared the night before and left the house. We were going to meet at bicycle parking in front of the community pool. I tucked my tiny wallet, which held the 200 yen entry fee along with some extra cash for snacks, in my shorts' back pocket and hopped onto my bicycle. Bright sunlight shone down from the clear blue sky and reflected off my handlebar.

This is going to be a fun day! Humming a cheery tune, I pedaled my bike ahead.

Everything had been going well, as we were able to successfully meet up at the bicycle lot, but...the five of us froze in front of the pool reception desk.

"The Pool is Closed in the Morning for the Community Swim Meet."

Eri flicked the massive sign hanging over the reception desk. "What the heck! How were we supposed to know?!"

"I wonder if they sent out a notice to the neighborhood association... What do you guys want to do? Should we come back again in the afternoon?"

"I can't. I'm going to my grandma's. I'm only free for the morning."

"Me too. My mom's forcing me to finish the rest of my summer homework this afternoon."

Everyone had their afternoon booked with other plans.

"Then I guess we'll give up on the pool today."

Waiting around in front of the closed pool forever wasn't going to do anything for us, Tomo pointed out, so we decided to go our separate ways for the day.

"You didn't get to go to the pool even once this summer, Mashiron," Sawa said gloomily.

I put my hands together in an apologetic gesture for failing to hang out with them as I exclaimed, "Sorry!" I felt really bad for turning them down until today despite their many invitations.

Noticing I seemed to be unusually lackluster, Mako offered a reassuring smile. "We'll be sure to come together next year! And let's avoid waiting until the last Sunday next time!"

Having gone out of my way to get ready for going out somewhere,

I didn't feel like just returning home. So I notified Eri, who would've walked home with me otherwise, "I'm going to the bookstore before I go home," and saw my friends off.

In contrast to the excitement I felt parking my bike, depression loomed over me as I pulled my bike out of its parking spot. Since I had been hyped for it for days, I found myself unable to shake the desire to swim.

"Tch!" I grumbled, kicking a stone.

Then I heard someone shout, "Mashiro!"

"Sou?!"

The boy with light-blue hair running toward me from the parking lot was undeniably Sou.

Did he grow a little taller again? His broad smile feels nostalgic now. I'm happy to see him! The same joy I'd felt when I saw Kou welled up in me for Sou as well.

"Wow! Long time no see!"

"Yeah! I finally get to see you again! I've wanted to hang out with you again for what feels like ages," Sou greeted me, happiness flooding his voice.

...Gah. Why must he always be so cute? I don't want to believe this honest kid has the potential to lock me up in the future.

"You can't swim in this pool, right? Come with us to somewhere better!"

Can't swim in the pool? Us? It finally occurred to me to ask why Sou was here.

"Um, did you hear about my plans from Kou?"

"Yup. He said you were going to the community pool today, Mashiro. When he looked into it, he saw they're booked through the morning, and he thought you might have some free time."

"...Does that mean Kou is here too?"

"Yeah. He mentioned that he was just going to drop by to see how things turn out, so I had him take me along for the ride."

So that's what happened. What were they planning to do if my friends had still been around? This is Kou we're talking about. I bet he would've just invited everyone along.

"By somewhere better, you're talking about a pool, right? I'll say I'm happy and leave it at that. I really wanted to swim today."

"Haha. Yeah, you looked like it," Sou agreed, taking my hand. "You can come back for your bicycle later. Go ahead and lock it for now... Let's go, Mashiro!"

I almost swooned from his beaming smile, which was more dazzling than the blazing sun.

♫♫♫

THEY had come in a Saab cabriolet—a soft-top convertible. Not only were they using a shiny foreign automobile, they had the top down too. And inside sat the kind of people who attract attention wherever they go, making us even more conspicuous than usual. Kou sat in the passenger seat, wearing a cool white linen shirt and beige shorts. Naturally, the first two buttons on his shirt were undone. Irrational rage simmered inside me at his relaxed yet calculated summer style.

Why the heck do his looks have to match my preferences to a T?!

"Morning, Mashiro."

"Good morning, Lady Shimao."

"Good morning, Kou, Mr. Mizusawa. I look forward to spending the day with you."

I had a buttload of things I wanted to say to Kou, but I refrained, as Mr. Mizuawa was present. I quickly bowed my head and climbed into the back seat. Sou sat down beside me.

"Let's get going." At Kou's cue, the car pulled out of the lot.

I didn't ask where we were headed. A little later, I realized I hadn't thought to ask because I trusted him, which frustrated me in a way I can't explain.

No matter how much I try to be on guard with them, it's pointless. Somewhere in the depths of my heart I want to be involved with them. What if these feelings only exist because of Hear My Heart's power and pull on this world? That would be so unbearably cruel.

♫♫♫

I found my first time riding in a convertible surprisingly comfortable and enjoyable. To say the least, the wind felt amazing racing through the car. I gave up on feeling embarrassed by the stares coming from the sidewalks each time we stopped at traffic signals—not like I could do anything to stop them.

"If I'd known we were going to meet up today, I would've brought your hoodie. Sorry for holding on to it for so long."

"It's fine with me. I'm the one who's sorry for not contacting you sooner. Kou wouldn't budge on wanting to surprise you."

I had the sneaking feeling that Sou, just like myself, was often subject to Kou's manipulations.

I leaned in toward his charmingly shaped ear to whisper, "You've got it rough, being stuck with a friend like him."

Sou's cheeks flushed.

"I can hear you, Mashiro. What? Do you want me to tease you that badly? Just say so and I'll happily oblige you."

He has the ears of the devil too!

♪♪♪

OUR destination turned out to be a members-only gym. Apparently, they have a pool in their building as well. As soon as we set foot in the gigantic glass building, the receptionist bowed to Kou. We walked down a plush carpet hallway to a glass elevator, also ridiculously humongous, which we took up to the highest floor. I glanced curiously around the gym when we finally arrived.

"Not many people here."

"Only a select few can enter. Obviously, it'd be mostly empty."

Is he trying to boast about the fact that he's one of the select few? Exasperated, I looked up to check Kou's expression. But to my surprise, it was completely different from what I had expected. He had an icy, dead look in his eyes—I flinched.

Why do you look so lonely, like you're the only one in the world? You should be acting more proud and boastful like the child you are!

"The women's changing room is over there. Come down to the bottom pool after you change."

"Okey-dokey-smokey."

"What was that?"

"Okay!"

Sou observed our usual banter and muttered disappointedly, "For all you say about each other, you get along real well."

Just what did he see to make him think that?

"C'mon. Wipe the stupid look off your face and go get changed already." Kou gave my shoulder a shove when I continued to stand there with my mouth agape at Sou's remark.

What part of us gets along real well?! Did you see what he just did?! This guy just pushed me! And he even said my face is stupid!

Sou gave a dry laugh as I pointed at Kou, wordlessly flapping my lips in protest. Kou mercilessly bent back my finger.

What's going on? Since we met up and chatted yesterday, Kou has lost all reservation toward me. And I might actually like it?

A grin naturally came over my face. There was a hop in my step as I headed to the changing room.

♪♪♪

IN a room too luxurious to call a changing room, I changed into Hanaka's bikini. I had no idea how much Kou would torment me if I came out wearing the school bathing suit, and I didn't want to find out. Boy was I lucky that Hanaka had advised me to take the bikini! I shoved my vinyl bag—which didn't belong in a fancy place like this—in the locker and tied my hair up in a high ponytail. Tucking my towel under my arm, I raced down to the lower level. Kou and Sou were already swimming in the empty, 170-foot long pool.

"Mashiro! We're over here!" Sou was absolutely dazzling as he waved at me, shaking the water out of his wet hair.

Yup, he's a boy. Of course he wouldn't have a shirt on. Right.

Their slender yet well-defined, muscular physiques forced me to be conscious of our gender differences. Much to my dismay, I already had to see boys my age half-naked on a regular basis during swimming classes at school. Nevertheless, I was unable to look straight at the two of them, my heart hammering away.

"Are you embarrassed?" Kou swam right over to me, coyly rested his arms on top of the pool coping, then looked up at me with flirtatious eyes. The increased appeal from his soaked hair was dizzying.

You guys are on another level!

"What're you saying? I'm not embarrassed!" I snapped and sat down on the edge of the pool. I carefully lowered my feet into the water. It was neither too hot nor too cold, but the perfect temperature.

"Did you warm up already, Mashiro?" Sou caught up to Kou and lined up beside him, placing his arms on the coping as well, so that he was looking up at me from the same position.

"Yup, I did."

"Then I can do this." He reached out and grabbed my arm, then pulled me into the pool.

SPLASH! Water shot into the air as my entire body was suddenly engulfed by the warm water.

"Sou!"

"Sorry, I couldn't wait any longer." Water droplets from the splash had sprinkled his face. I couldn't stop myself from smiling back at his innocent laugh.

"You really like her don't you, Sou," Kou stated while wiping his face, having been equally drenched from the splash.

"Yeah, you can say that again," Sou seemed to boast.

My heart ached at how his expression looked so hopelessly happy over being able to like someone.

He must have wanted an older or younger sister at some point. Someone he could love, who would love him back unconditionally.

"Even though Mashiro doesn't see you as anything more than a friend?"

"I told her I'm happy being friends as long as that means I get to stay with her. Didn't I, Mashiro?"

"Y-Yeah."

Sou hadn't backed down in the slightest, even when Kou prodded further. Sou really didn't hope for anything in return for his affections.

Maybe even if I don't fall in love with him, he won't break down like in the game's bad end if I continue to treasure him as a friend.

"I see." Kou appeared unsatisfied with Sou's answer but swiftly ended the conversation with, "Well, whatever. We're here now, let's enjoy ourselves."

♪♪♪

WE hit a beach ball around, and I cheered the boys on as they dived off the diving board—unexpectedly, we had a fun time playing games in the pool together. Honestly, I didn't think we *could* have so much fun, which made the experience twice as sweet.

"Wow! Wow! You guys can even do a perfect dive! I totally can't dive from that height. Maybe I could do it if someone pushed me off, but I rather not... Wait, don't get any funny ideas! Please don't push me off, okay?!"

Kou and Sou were taking turns diving off the thirty-foot high diving board with perfect form. Exhilarated, I cheered for them loudly and clapped. I guess I looked silly, because they exchanged looks before laughing at me.

"Sorry, I got a little too excited," I apologized.

"Nah. I just thought you were cute for showing your excitement. Right, Sou?"

"Yeah. You're super cute. It makes me want to give you even more of a thrill."

Sou was one thing, but I felt like Kou was making fun of me. Yet the entire time we played together, as hard as it is to believe, he refrained from mocking me or jabbing us with sarcastic remarks. His boyish, innocent laughter made him appear far more childlike than ever before. I loved seeing him this way.

"Let's compete, Kou," Sou dared.

"How rare, you're challenging me. Of course I'll take you on."

"Time us, Mashiro!" Sou handed me a stopwatch he borrowed from the lifeguard. "Here you go. Be sure to cheer me on," he insisted sincerely, gazing deep into my eyes.

I almost nodded on a reflex, but I felt the urge to glance at Kou's reaction. Noticing my gaze, Kou arched an eyebrow and held up his hands—a gesture to go ahead.

"Good luck, Sou! Make Kou lose!" I had to say after seeing Kou brimming with confidence.

"You've got it!" Sou ruffled my hair and dived into the pool.

"Ready! Go!"

They simultaneously kicked off the pool wall at my signal. Their gorgeous front crawls captivated me as I followed them along the poolside. They touched the wall on the other side of the pool—170-feet from where they started—at the same exact time. I glanced at the watch to see it had just hit twenty-nine seconds.

...Isn't this an insanely fast time?

"How did we do?"

I showed Sou the stopwatch when he removed his goggles, panting. "You arrived at the same time. At twenty-nine seconds exactly! What are you guys?! Is there nothing you can't do? You're ridiculously awesome!"

They ignored my excited gushing to exchange looks, their shoulders heaving with heavy breathing.

"...It's unusual for you to take something seriously," Kou marveled.

"You're the only person I never want to lose to."

"Heh... Haha! Things have gotten interesting for the first time in a long time."

What are they even talking about? ...Now that I think about it, Miss Sakurako did say that Kou has lost interest in everything because he can easily master anything. Maybe he's happy that he tied with Sou?

Sou let out an irritated sigh as he glanced between us—from me, who was confused, to Kou, who was brimming with confidence.

Heroine's Results
Target Character: Sou Shiroyama & Kou Narita
Event: I'm Serious Now
CLEAR

♪♪♪

THEN came the start of Fall Quarter. As soon as it began, the months seemed to fly by—maybe because there were so many school events taking up my time. Students had to participate in everything, from the Sports Festival to the Choir Festival to the fall field trip. Had my past life been this hectic too?

Kinose became a member of the Sports Festival committee and outran everyone in our grade's relay race. All I can say is that boys who run fast are popular in elementary school.

"Want to run with me?" he invited me. I politely turned him down as everyone around us booed.

His cool eyes and straight nose did make him look just like SAZE's vocalist, I realized. I have no doubt that he'll be even more popular once he's in high school. Nevertheless, my heart wouldn't move even a millimeter for him. Yet my fall field trip ended up being with him too.

My most vivid memory of the whole excursion was my intense desire to cram as much beach sand into Hirata's irritating grin as possible because of the way he watched us with that stupid look on his face.

I was rapidly improving on the piano. Miss Ayumi gave me passing marks on Ravel's "Sonatine", so I moved on to practicing his "Alborada del Gracioso". Kon was amazed to hear the news.

"Already?! Isn't it too hard?"

"Yeah. My sheet music's covered in black from all the notes Miss Ayumi scribbled on it for me. I'm tearfully crawling through it."

"After you finished the Sonatine you should've moved on to the Sonata. If we're going by music theory, you wouldn't be challenging this piece for a while…"

According to Miss Ayumi, I had mastered enough technique to tackle the Sonata next. "I want you to solidify your foundation by practicing songs by Chopin and Bach while taking on progressively more difficult songs at the same time. It's all right if it takes time to master. Let's work hard at it together!" she had encouraged.

It was true that I seemed to have a natural skill and deft fingers, as I could quickly master fast passages and complex finger movements. I found reading sheet music harder than anything else. Even if I painstakingly crammed the sheet music into my head so that I could play a song, I still had a long way to go in order to master it.

"To begin, you must perform the song accurately, exactly as it's written. You're free to come up with your own interpretation *after* you can play the song precisely as the composer intends, without any mistakes!" was Miss Ayumi's policy.

"Mashiro, don't you find the recital's program insufficient for you?" she inquired at my last lesson.

Kon, Miss Ayumi, and I were supposed to take turns playing Beethoven's Grande Sonata "Pathétique" relay-style in the recital. I was responsible for the second movement, which undeniably required less technique than the songs I was currently learning.

In contrast to my lessons, Miss Ayumi had instructed me, "Don't just play the song as it's written at the recital. I want you to show everyone your interpretation, Mashiro."

Maybe playing a song below my current skill level will allow me to bring out my interpretation of the song's theme more fully? I'm always being strictly ordered not to ignore the musical directions, but now I'm suddenly told to interpret it my way. Classical music requires as much concentration as Zen Buddhism.

♪♪♪

ON the first Friday of October, Sou came over to my house after school. A cool breeze slipped in through the cracked window, lightly tossing his silky hair. We were spending our time like we always did, with him passionately folding origami next to me while I studied my books.

"Oh yeah, I have fall break starting next week," Sou brought up, abruptly looking at me.

Fall break?

"That's a thing? How long is it?"

"Ten days… Dad wants me to visit him, so I have to spend it in Germany."

Germany in the fall, huh? Judging by Germany's latitude, its position kinda lines up with Hokkaido on the world map. I bet it's far chillier than here.

Despite the calendar's announcement that we had entered October, many days of scorching heat still lay ahead for the other islands of Japan. These were the days where I'd wear long sleeve shirts, just to find myself overheating and unable to make it through the day. I envied Sou's luck as I pulled at my T-shirt, fanning cool air down my chest.

"Lucky! Germany has all four seasons like Japan, so I bet the fall colors are pretty over there right now. I want to visit someday to see it for myself."

Sou's gentle smile disappeared into a grave expression. "I'm sure it'd be a lot more fun if you were with me, Mashiro."

"Think so? Show me around when we're older!" I answered thoughtlessly. Sou gave an ambiguous nod in return.

He returned his attention to the paper he had been in the middle of folding after that. Sou didn't normally talk much, but he was especially quiet today. When it was time to leave, he wouldn't let go of my hand.

"What's wrong? You're not acting like yourself today."

"...Mashiro, I..."

"Yeah?"

"I don't like my current mom very much. And I just attend school for the sake of attending it."

"...Yeah."

"I think I like playing the cello, but..."

"Sou?"

His hand quivered around mine. With his eyes locked on the entryway tile, he murmured, "Why am I still a child?"

"What?"

I couldn't follow the sudden change in topic. His expression immediately softened when he saw that I was baffled. "Sorry. Even I forgot what I was talking about... See ya later, Mashiro. Look forward to the souvenirs I'll bring you back from Germany."

He quietly released my hand and turned away.

He seems to be really worried about something, but his thoughts on it aren't organized yet. I hope he'll confide in me someday.

That's what I was thinking as I watched him leave.

♪♪♪

NOVEMBER was when it finally began to feel like fall. The leaves of the crape myrtle planted in our small garden had turned red. This was my favorite season. The air was crisp and clean. The sky appeared endless. Accomplishing the goals I set each day made ten days go by in no time. Sou came back before I even had the chance to miss him. He sent me a ton of souvenirs too. My entire family rejoiced over the Lindt chocolates and the Leysieffer *Baumkuchen*. Naturally, Mom and Hanaka are extremely fond of sweets, but even Dad has an unexpected sweet tooth.

"My whole family was absolutely raving about your presents! Thank you so much for sending us stuff!" I thanked Sou again when he came over my house.

The soft yellow light filtering through the lace curtains alluringly lit Sou's hair with a glow while he sat on the couch. He'd grown much bigger; he could no longer sit with his legs curled under him.

"What about you, Mashiro?"

"I was obviously the happiest of all!"

"Haha. That's obvious?"

Taken in by Sou's pure smile, I smiled widely in return. I listened with great interest to his tales of sightseeing and experiences with the food in Germany. He seemed so crestfallen before he went on the trip that it was a relief to see him come back with refreshed spirits.

"Oh, right, right." His eyes sparkled as he rummaged through his schoolbag. "This is another present for you, Mashiro."

He pulled out a music book. Mendelssohn's "*Song Without Words, Op. 109*", a duet composed for the cello and piano. The piano's sweet melody is lifted higher by the cello's gentle sound, a combination so enchanting that it's one of my favorite songs.

"Thank you! I love this song! …Does that mean—"

"Yup. If you're interested, would you like to play this song with me?"

When I recounted about how I'd played a duet with Kou over the summer, Sou had requested, "Play a duet with me sometime too." This was the perfect chance; I had always wanted to hear Sou play since the very first day we met.

"You don't even need to ask! It's my pleasure!" I instantly exclaimed, hugging the music book to my chest.

Sou made a small relieved smile at my answer. "Thank goodness. I was kinda worried about how I'd handle it if you turned me down. But don't get your hopes up too high. Unlike Kou, with all his ensemble experience, I've barely played with a piano before."

"You haven't?"

Kou and Sou may be attending the elementary school department, but they're still students at Seio Academy, which specializes in music education. I had assumed they had courses and other projects where they formed an ensemble with multiple instruments.

"Yeah. We're required to form an ensemble, but I always got stuck with Kou for it," Sou explained.

He sounded so disgusted that I couldn't stop myself from laughing. "Kou would sulk if he saw the face you're making."

"Well he's such a pain. Just because he's amazing, he thinks it's fine to demand a ridiculously high level from others. He's normally friendly, but man does he become a different monster when it comes to music. He absolutely refuses to compromise. That's why he refuses to partner with the girls in our class. No matter how much they badger him, he just apologizes with a fake smile and sidesteps them."

Really? I'm surprised he played with me at his house then.

"Let's stop talking about Kou. When can we play together?" I asked, interrupting Sou's envious ranting by patting him on the head as I turned my attention to the calendar. A flower sticker was stuck on December 23rd. Kon had invited me to the Narita estate for a Christmas party on that day.

"Why does the party have to be held at the Narita estate?"

Kon had shrugged at my question and defended her choice, "Because it's supposed to be a Christmas party, you know? Holding it at a Japanese-style manor will spoil the mood!"

When she put it that way, I kind of had to agree. Her Japanese-style manor would definitely clash with a Christmas tree and Christmas lights.

"It's a tradition for Kou and me to each perform a song at the party every year. I want to hear you play the piano too, Mashiro."

"That sounds wonderful!"

"Doesn't it? Hehe. Okay, it's decided then. Our moms are looking forward to seeing you again, Mashiro."

I had casually accepted her request to play a song at the party, but I hadn't decided what to play yet.

I know! Participating as a duet with Sou could be fun! We had so much fun hanging out at the pool together last summer. The four of us could have a blast together if Sou tags along to the Christmas party too.

I quickly explained the situation to Sou and tried inviting him, "What do you think? We'll have to get permission from Kon and Kou of course, but I'm sure they'd want you to come."

"A Christmas party at Kou's?" Sou pursed his pretty lips, considering it for a moment before nodding. "...Okay. I'll tell Kou. Let's practice together at my house on the days you're free."

"That's a good idea. I'll master the piano part completely before December then. Let's perfect it together! Pinky promise!"

I held out my pinky finger. The frown lifted from his face and he wrapped his pinky finger around mine.

"Finger chopped off, ten thousand punches," I sang, "whoever lies has to swallow—a thousand needles would hurt, so what should we make the punishment instead?"

"What kind of pinky promise is that?" Sou cracked up, then flashed a grin like he just thought up a great idea. "If you lie, you can never leave me."

"That's worse than a thousand needles!" I refuted, shooting him down.

"Tch." He puffed out his cheeks in a pout.

I was all smiles whenever I was around Sou's kindness. I never even stopped to think about his potential feelings in suggesting that punishment.

♪♪♪

AT last, it was December. The winds had taken on a biting chill. It became unbearable to walk to and from school without a warm scarf. As always, I took a triangle trip from home to school to Miss Ayumi's. The only difference was that one time Kou kidnapped me after school to take me to have tea again, this time at the Narita estate.

His butler, Mr. Tanomiya, welcomed me with open arms. "I am glad to see you again."

"Yes, I'm here again!"

He might've only greeted me to be polite, but it made me feel special.

Kou groaned and made a face. "Is it just me or do you treat him completely different from how you treat me?"

"Well, Mr. Tanomiya is nice."

"Aren't I nice too?"

"Shall we have a long discussion on the definition of 'nice?'"

In witnessing our bickering up-close and personal, Mr. Tanomiya seemed astonished, his voice tinged with awe as he commented, "Master Kou truly favors Lady Shimao."

Just what had he seen to come to that conclusion? I'll never know.

I followed Kou to the second-story. This time he brought me to the parlor instead of the music room. A maid promptly served us warm black tea. It was milk tea, brewed with Assam Autumn Nal harvest leaves, and it had a delicious sweetness to it.

After we shared what was going on in our lives lately, Kou suddenly switched topics. "Oh yeah, I heard you told Sou about the party on the twenty-third?"

"Yeah, I did. It just came up in the flow of the conversation. Should I not have told him?"

"What kinda conversation was that? Well, it's better he knows now rather than hearing him complain about it later."

"Right? I plan to play Mendelssohn's 'Song Without Words' with Sou. Look forward to it."

Kou carefully assessed my face as he slowly returned his teacup to the saucer resting on the table. Then he gracefully stood and moved to the seat directly next to mine.

"Hey, Mashiro…"

…He's close!

I scooted away, but he closed the distance just as fast. And he kept doing it—he chased me all the way to the sofa's armrest before leaning in close enough for me to notice how long and beautiful his eyelashes were.

"Wh-What?!"

The alarm bells blared in my head—Kou reached for a lock of my hair and flashed the most stunning smile.

"Did you know that you're the only girl I have ever invited to my house?" he asked alluringly.

"Ah, is that so?" I answered robotically.

"You're the only one I want to make music with too." He kissed the lock of hair he held and lowered his eyes, wrenching my heart. "Yet no matter how much time passes, you continue to treat me coldly, Mashiro. Even though you sound so happy whenever you talk about Sou. Don't you think you're being cruel?"

"I don't. Because this is what you want, Kou." I remained resolute.

I was fully aware that he was playing a game with me. *This guy has a completely screwed-up personality.* If I took his pick-up lines at face value and wholeheartedly replied that I felt the same way, he had every intention of pulling the rug out from under me with a line like, "Just kidding! Did you actually think I was seriously trying to flirt with you?"

"If I fell in love with you, rather than being satisfied, you'd be disappointed."

"…You're smart, Mashiro."

"You've got a horrible personality, Kou."

"Yeah. I'm aware of it." Kou pulled back from me, looking more pleased than I'd ever seen him before.

His twisted personality is not to be underestimated. He's nothing like the kind and friendly Miss Sakurako. Maybe he takes after his dad.

I tried to imagine Kou's dad, who I hadn't met yet. Instantly, a good-looking man wielding a sexy face as a weapon with a sharp tongue to dish out cynicism and capricious whims came to mind in the same second.

Please let him be out of town for work during the party on the twenty-third! Naturally, I'd be no match for a powered-up adult version of Kou.

♪♪♪

ON the first Sunday in December, I had Mom drive me to the Shiroyama estate. As I was about to ring the doorbell with my frozen fingers and a homemade roll cake dangling in a bag from my wrist, the double doors suddenly opened.

That scared me! Do they have security cameras—they must have security cameras.

"Welcome, Mashiro!" Sou, dressed in a light-beige sweater and jeans, joyfully welcomed me.

"Hello, Sou. Here's my thanks for inviting me over. Sorry that it's homemade, but would you like to eat it together later?"

He took the bag from me, opened it for a quick peep inside, and grinned widely. "Score! I'm crazy about your homemade roll cakes!"

"I made sure to cut back on the sugar for you."

"Thanks. Hurry inside! Isn't it cold?"

I happily accepted his offer and set foot inside the unduly spacious marble entranceway. An antique wooden bench was placed against the wall right in the entranceway, so I sat down to unzip my long boots. The heating made even the marble floors hot. I took off my coat and scarf and hung them over my arm. Today Hanaka lent me a white knit dress. It had short sleeves with fur around the collar. It was a bit of a mature design, but its overall fluffiness made it super cute.

"Your outfit today is really nice too. You look great," Sou complimented me right off the bat, and I felt happiness spread through me.

"I borrowed it from my sister. I'll let her know you think it's pretty... Oh yeah, is it okay for me not to greet the people of the house?"

"Yeah. The help normally commute and are off today, and Mrs. Mie is working in the kitchen. Oh, but I think she'll come by to bring us tea later."

"...I see."

I was trying to ask about his mom, but Sou only mentioned the help. Unwilling to push further, I let him show me the way to estate's east wing. As soon as I entered Sou's exclusive soundproof practice room, my eyes locked on the grand piano. The gorgeously polished, mirror surface of the piano had been painted meticulously to bring out the details and texture of the mahogany wood it had been crafted from. Its stunning design took my breath away.

What brand is it?

I searched for an inscription but couldn't find one.

"It's a beautiful piano. What company made it?" I asked, looking over at Sou. He shrugged, the expression wiped from his face.

"It's a Shiroyama piano Father had custom-made for the woman who gave birth to me. It's the only one in the whole world, so he never put in the company inscription. He said Mother begged him for the piano instead of an engagement ring."

"I see! How romantic!"

Sou's birth mother also played the piano. What a lovely anecdote! She wanted a piano that could be her partner forever in place of a ring she wouldn't be able to wear when playing.

Spellbound by the piano's history, I turned to face it again, when Sou quietly asked behind me, "...Do you want a piano that badly too, Mashiro?"

"I do. It's not realistic, but a girl can dream. I mean, you can't wear rings while you play the piano. So I can understand why she would want a piano, which she would touch more than anything else, instead. Playing a song on the piano for your beloved, who custom crafted its every detail for you and you alone is the epitome of love! Love, I tell you!"

"...If only that were true," Sou replied with a self-derisive edge.

All I had ever heard about the woman who had given birth to him was that she left them when he was still very young. I'd been hesitating for the longest time about whether it would be okay to ask him the details about what had happened. I felt like if I let this chance pass, I'd never be able to ask him again.

I spun around and daringly ventured, "Was your mom a pianist,

Sou?"

He tilted his head ever so slightly before answering me with complete indifference. "Yeah. I haven't told you yet? Have you ever heard the name Risa Morikawa before?"

What did he just say?! I wonder if there's anyone out there who's learned to play the piano without knowing the name Risa Morikawa—she's that famous.

Risa Morikawa had been a female pianist, the first Japanese citizen and youngest person overall to win the Tchaikovsky International Music Competition. They say she had been in great demand for TV shows, domestic and international music concerts, and festivals until she retired some ten-odd years ago. The many music records she'd left behind were still popular to this day. Once you heard her passionate yet ephemeral performance, you could never forget it.

"I've not only heard of her—I own all her albums!"

Sou's lip curled up and he muttered, "I see. That woman is my birth mother. I'm the reason Risa Morikawa retired, Mashiro."

His declaration was so shocking that my brain couldn't process it correctly.

"Wh-What? …But I heard she retired because she hurt her hand—"

"After she gave birth to me, her health failed and she had to undergo medical treatment for nearly two years. She became mentally unstable when she could no longer play the piano as she used to. In the end, she was so desperate that she tried to escape the medical facility by climbing up a fence and took a huge fall. That's how she severely damaged both hands. Those are the injuries that ended her life as a pianist. She resents Father and me to this day for stealing away the piano, which she cared about more than her own life," he explained in a single breath.

His heartbreaking past that I could've never imagined was like a sheer bolt from the blue—it rendered me utterly speechless.

…I see…so that's why…Sou doesn't like the piano. It must've always been painful to listen to the piano that took his mother from him. The face he'd made when I first told him that I was learning to play the piano… His behavior at Miss Ayumi's piano concert… It all makes sense now.

The memories of Sou's actions and words came back like a torrent one after another, filling in the missing pieces.

"I'm sorry… I may not have known, but I've been incredibly insensitive…" I finally managed to get out, and I lowered my head deeply to him. I couldn't think of any other way to apologize.

"Don't apologize! I didn't tell you because I wanted your sympathy, Mashiro!" he shouted as if a dam had burst—he grabbed both my shoulders, lifted my chin, and threw his arms around my back in a tight embrace. Held in Sou's large arms—he was two heads taller than me—I was stunned.

In that position, the words he had shouted slowly permeated throughout my very being. He told me not to apologize. That he didn't need my sympathy.

"Mashiro... Mashiro." He repeated my name over and over again, desperately, in a tearful voice. With my cheek pressed against his chest, I felt the strength leave my body.

Sou is lonely. He's unbearably lonely.

"Please... Mashiro...please be the one who won't leave me. Don't go anywhere." His hoarse plea rang like it was squeezed out from the farthest depths of a bottomless abyss.

CG 13: Scars (Sou)

AFTER burying his face in my shoulder and holding me close for some time, Sou bashfully released me. He took the handkerchief I held out to him and rubbed the corners of his eyes as he let out a single sigh.

"I'm so lame. Sorry...for suddenly doing that to you."

"You surprised me, but I'm not bothered by it." I laughed for his sake, but it didn't lift his crestfallen face. I put my hands on my hips to change the glum mood. "Kou would be so mad at me if he found out. He'd tell me off like, 'What're you doing? You're the worst of the worst crawling this Earth for making Sou cry!'"

"Nah, I'd definitely be the one he'd tease."

I arched an eyebrow and tried to mimic Kou's voice, "Ha! You were able to make *that* Sou cry? What in the world did you do, *Mashiro*?"

Sou burst out into uncontrollable laughter. "How did you do that?! You sound just like him, it's scary!"

"Right? He's made so many sarcastic comments to me that I've become capable of flawlessly copying him. Like now, if he saw us wasting time here he'd say, 'Why don't you hurry up and start the ensemble already? I'm not made up of free time, unlike *some* people.'"

"He'd totally say that! Crud! I'll definitely laugh in his face when I see him tomorrow!"

His carefree laughter set my mind at ease. I earnestly hoped Sou would find happiness in his life. I couldn't do much for him, but at the very least, I was willing to mimic Kou whenever he needed it.

"I'll be sick to my stomach if we perform bad enough to warrant

Kou's torment, so are you ready to start practice?" Sou suggested, after taking several deep breaths to settle his feelings.

"Okay! Let's do this!"

♪♪♪

I took the opportunity to get acquainted with the piano while Sou set up his cello, playing several short practice pieces to warm up. His mother's piano possessed a welcoming, clear sound that cast doubt on the fact it hadn't been played in ages. I could tell it was being tuned.

Who maintains the piano? Sou's dad? Or his second wife? Either way is sad. Whoever does it must be filled with mixed feelings.

When I stopped practicing to stretch my arms, I noticed small objects decorating the bay window.

Ah…is that origami? Oh, they're the ones I folded!

Origami versions of a grand piano, the Tour De France monument, the Luxor Obelisk, and the Leaning Tower of Pisa, which was held upright by a small support pole, sat on the windowsill.

How ironic that the very first origami I gave Sou to cheer him up when we first met had been a piano of all things. While it was a total coincidence, I feel bad about it now.

Noticing where I was looking, Sou turned red and mumbled, "I was gonna move them somewhere else, but forgot."

"Why move them?"

"I didn't want to repulse you. Don't you find it creepy that on top of keeping them all, I'm using them as decorations?"

"Not at all. I'm very happy about it!"

I'm convinced I would've become much more obsessed with origami had I not encountered the piano. That's how much I love origami. Even now, I'll start folding paper when I feel suffocated by piano practice or my studies. Having someone keep, moreover display the creations I put my whole heart into, is the ultimate compliment to me as an origamist.

Sou seemed relieved. "You don't know how glad I am to hear you say that… Sorry, I want to tune, would you mind playing the A note for me?"

"You've got it."

He placed the cello between his legs and sat down. I pressed the A key as I tilted my head to take in the sound of his tuning.

"I see you don't use a tuning meter," I commented.

"Hm? Yeah, it's faster to match it by ear. Didn't Kou tune the same way too?"

Most string instruments have to tune all five musical intervals across their four strings, using the A string as their base to tune the other three. Sou methodically checked the sound as he turned the tuning pegs, then drew his bow with just the right amount of strength across the strings with a trained hand. A beautiful double-stop filled the room.

I quietly observed the exchange between Sou and his cello. He treated his cello with loving care.

I'm so glad. He wasn't lying when he told me he loves the cello.

"All right, I'm ready. If you don't mind, I want check how you play the piano part first, Mashiro."

"Okay. Let me know if the tempo is off."

Lied ohne Worte D-dur, Op.109.
Song Without Words in D-major, Op. 109.

"…Does this work for you?"

"Did you really start playing the piano only recently?"

"Yeah. Oh, but it'll be my third year playing soon."

"Nah, you're way beyond a third year… I get why Kou wanted to play with you," Sou clarified quietly with admiration, then picked up his bow. "I got the feel for it, so let's get started."

If we were performing at a concert, the piano would be situated behind the cello or to its side, but because it was only practice, we sat facing each other. At my signal, we played the song from the beginning. The first note Sou drew out of the cello sent goose bumps rippling down my arms.

He's skilled! And the sound has depth!

His cello softly sang a sweet melody as if it were whispering to someone precious. The song's velvet-like resonance echoes throughout your eardrums for the first half, before launching into a sorrowful melody. Not wanting to lose to his sound, I sent my fingers dancing across the keyboard, my left hand playing the gentle notes, my right hand calling forth the high-pitched tenor.

And then the song circled back to its original theme. Following Sou's cue, I slowed down the tempo to let the notes linger slightly.

We need to practice this part together more.

Sou took the lead at the end, making it easier to match our breathing. After the last note, I removed my hands from the keyboard to madly applaud.

"That was an incredibly beautiful and gentle performance! Sou, your cello's really something!"

"Thanks. I think it's because of you, Mashiro. The feeling of my sound was different from usual."

"That's not true. It's all your skill, Sou!" I passionately insisted.

Sou gave a wry smile. "You really are soft on me, Mashiro."

"Huh? No, I'm not."

"Nah, you absolutely are. At the end of the day, you never push me away and you're always encouraging me." He sorrowfully lowered his eyes while stroking his cello.

"Is there something wrong with that?"

Is he warning that I'm stepping past the realm of friendship? I think it's natural for friends to encourage each other. You don't have to be romantically involved to care about someone.

"...No, to me it's great! By the way, we went off-key halfway through. Want to play it together again?"

"I had the same thought. Do you mind giving the signals until I get used to it?"

"Sure, let's do that."

We continued to practice for a while afterward, until a light knock on the door distracted us.

"It's probably Mrs. Mie."

Sou propped his cello up and went to get the door, turning the heavy and noisy doorknob to pull it open. But it wasn't Mrs. Mie standing there. A tall, slender, beautiful woman entered the room, followed by a middle-aged woman. The beautiful woman wore a classy silver suit—she appeared to have returned from an outing. Her lustrous raven-black hair further amplified her bewitching beauty.

"...Mother."

"I thought I was imagining things, hearing the piano... You have a friend over?"

"I do."

"Will you introduce me?"

Panicking, I jumped to my feet and hurried over to them. Sou was standing rock-still and glaring at her, evidently shaken by her unexpected appearance.

No good will come of waiting for him to introduce me at this rate.

I opened my mouth to introduce myself, when—

"Oh my. What do we have here? A pianist with pink hair and olive-brown eyes. I wonder where I've seen that before, hmm? She looks just like a certain someone we know."

"Mashiro doesn't look anything like her." Sou moved in front of me, hiding me from sight. "Don't lump her in with that woman!"

"What are you getting all riled up for? If she's such a precious little friend of yours, you should at least have the common decency to introduce her to me, no?" Her singsong soprano voice lacked any inkling of emotion. Her flat, lifeless gaze instilled chilling fear in me.

Before I knew it, I gripped the back of Sou's sweater.

Heroine's Results

Target Character: Sou Shiroyama

Event: First Time Making Music Together

CLEAR

◇◇◇

We weren't going to get anywhere at this rate, so Sou reluctantly introduced me, "This is Mashiro Shimao."

"You have a fine name. I am Reimi Shiroyama, Sou's stepmother." Miss Reimi sidestepped Sou to stand next to me. I quickly dropped my hands and turned to face her.

"It is a pleasure to meet you, Miss Reimi. Sou is always such a wonderful friend to me."

Miss Reimi carefully studied me as I dropped my head in a polite gesture. I saw her glossy red lips curl. She was as stunningly beautiful as her name suggested, with the characters for "graceful beauty", but her smile never reached her eyes.

"I see. Then I assume you are his classmate from Seio."

"No, I attend Tada Elementary."

"Tada? Was there a school called that around here?"

Was she genuinely ignorant of the district's major public school's name, or was she just being grossly sarcastic?

As I hesitated, unsure of how I should answer her, Sou grabbed my arm and pulled me to him. Then he proceeded to hold my hand defiantly in his. His handsome side-profile was stiff and tense.

"Jumping straight to investigating my friend? It doesn't matter who she is or where she's from. She has nothing to do with you."

"Unfortunately, to my great displeasure, it does have something to do with me. During my husband's absence, I must take full responsibility for your actions. Besides, wouldn't the little girl be just pitiful if she were under some dreadful misconceptions?"

"Misconceptions?" Sou repeated, wariness clouding his features.

Miss Reimi turned her hawk-like eyes on me. "For example—oh and this is a good example—she might mistakenly believe you have *feelings* for her."

"That's not a misconception. After all, I *do* have feelings for Mashiro."

Sou's bold declaration startled me. Even Miss Reimi and the help were shocked.

"H-Hey, Sou!" I quietly warned, trying to shake his hand off. But I couldn't get free because he held my hand much tighter than I thought.

"I'm the one who has unrequited feelings for her. Satisfied now? Hurry and leave, would you?"

"…Miss Shimao, was it?" Miss Reimi blatantly ignored Sou and the door he was pointing at and spoke to me instead. "Sou already has his life partner chosen for him. Furthermore, he'll be moving to Germany once he graduates elementary school. You only have two years left together, but do enjoy them while you can."

"Ah…yes, ma'am."

Miss Reimi's words spun around my head.

What does she mean he has a life partner chosen for him? What's this about him going to Germany?!

"I won't accept it!"

"No one asked for your opinion. Grandmother and your father have both approved. Isn't it wrong of you not to make things very clear for her? …That my niece is your fiancée."

Wow. The Shiroyama family's really something else. They get their children engaged when they're still in elementary school. Too much had happened. My emotional defense instincts kicked in, disconnecting me from reality. *Now that I think about it, he did mention at Miss Ayumi's concert that his cousin on his mother's side of the family had come too.*

"Enough of this. Leave," Sou growled. He let go of my hand, headed straight for the door, and threw it open, glaring furiously at Miss Reimi.

"I suppose I have no reason to stay... I apologize for intruding on your time, Miss Shimao." She apologized indifferently, then turned on her silver heel.

From the beginning to the end, I couldn't read her. She didn't seem as angry or amused as her word choice had indicated. It was like she merely acted to fulfill her obligations. Sou remained staunchly silent until she left the room. Finally, the door quietly swung shut behind her, leaving the two of us and the help in the room.

"...Don't worry about me. I'm okay," I cheerfully reassured before Sou could say anything. "Some unknown kid came inside her home while she was away and randomly started to play with a priceless piano. I can understand why she would be upset."

"You haven't done anything wrong, Mashiro. That woman normally treats me as nothing more than air, but she chose now to pretend like she cares. You can forget everything she said. I'm sorry you had to see that," he apologized.

All I could say in return was, "It's okay. I'm okay."

Sou didn't tell me anything else about his fiancée or about moving to Germany after graduation. It's not like I could do anything even if I knew the details, but my heart took a hard blow when he didn't confide in me. I turned away from these complicated, selfish feelings and put a lid on them.

"Young Master," the help prompted, after waiting patiently for a break in our conversation.

So much had occurred in a short span of time. It was beyond what I could handle; I was at my limit. I couldn't find it in me to crack a joke about him being called "Young Master".

"Oh. I'm sorry, Mrs. Mie. You brought us drinks, didn't you? You can leave them on the table."

"All right. I have the roll cake Lady Shimao brought as well. What would you like to be done with it?"

"Let's eat it together. Okay, Mashiro?"

"Okay... Um, thank you."

This must be the live-in help, Mrs. Mie, who Sou always talks about. His attitude with her is completely different.

"Were you carrying the tray all this time? It must have been heavy for you," he said sympathetically.

"This tea cozy is adorable!" I exclaimed.

"I made it. It's a by-product of my love for sewing." Mrs. Mie organized the tea and cake neatly on the table before kindly adding, "I am delighted to find you are as lovely of a young lady as Young Master spoke of."

"I've also heard a lot about you. I'm glad we got the chance to meet."

"What an honor. Thank you."

Sou fondly watched us exchange smiles.

I'm glad he at least has someone compassionate around, with Mrs. Mie being here. Maybe Sou's honesty comes from the affection she shows him.

♪♪♪

"I'LL find a day that woman isn't home and let you know. You have to come over again sometime," Sou insisted as I left the Shiroyama estate.

I decided to take my leave after we finished having tea together. Sou wasn't pleased, but I couldn't play in good conscience with Miss Reimi around. If I were her, I wouldn't be happy with some weird kid I didn't know using the priceless piano that had been left behind by my husband's ex-wife.

I'd be better off not coming to his house again.

My legs nearly buckled when I saw Mom pull in to the driveway to pick me up. Without even realizing it, I had been incredibly nervous. Before getting into the back seat, I turned my head to gaze up at the mansion. How many houses like mine could fit into the space the Shiroyama mansion occupied?

"Welcome back, Mashiro. How was it? Did things go well?"

"Yeah, it went okay, I guess. Thanks for picking me up."

"You're welcome, sweetie. Are you okay if we stop by the supermarket on the way home? There's a special sale going on in the next hour."

"Of course we can."

I settled in to the seat and buckled in. My thrifty mom never failed to check the coupons and sales noted in the newspaper.

I wonder what's on sale today, I absentmindedly thought as I stared out the window. *The people at the Shiroyama estate probably don't use ads and sales to decide what they're going to buy for groceries.*

When it comes down to it, we really do live in different worlds.

♪♪♪

I didn't visit Sou's house again. It felt way too awkward, and besides, he was busy with his academy's finals. The number of times we met up on the footbridge decreased as well.

"I'm really stressed out because I never get to see you anymore!" he complained to me on the few days we coincidentally ran into each other.

"Now, now. We'll be entering winter break soon. We have the Christmas party on the twenty-third too."

"I know, but still… Are you going anywhere over the break, Mashiro?"

"I don't think we're doing anything as a family because my sister's entrance exams are right around the corner. I have plans to see a movie with friends from school."

"Nice. I wish I attended the same school as you."

Sou informed me he was going to spend his short winter break in Germany again. He said he'd rather go than be manipulated by Miss Reimi and her family. By Miss Reimi's family, he must've been including the girl who's supposed to be his fiancée.

Miss Reimi said his fiancée is her niece. She must be pretty with how gorgeous her aunt is. The kind of girl anyone would accept standing arm-in-arm with Sou.

No matter how much I wanted to deny it, realizing that I had to let go of my affectionate puppy-dog Sou someday made me feel hopelessly lonely.

♪♪♪

IT was the day of the Christmas party. Hanaka sat at the breakfast table on the verge of tears, because she had to attend a special course at her cram school.

"Mashiro, you're gonna change into that dress later, right? Leave your hair to me. I'll turn you into a princess!" It sucked watching her try to put on fake cheer for me.

"Don't you have to attend the special course for twelve hours today? Do your best. I'm sure it'll rapidly improve your knowledge! Because you get to study for twelve hours straight!" I gave her a thumbs-up, to which she pressed her own thumb against with a weak smile.

"Thanks, Mashiro. But I'm sure…I won't…return alive. Please… enjoy the Christmas party…in my…stead."

"Hanaka! Don't die!" I clung to her side when she dramatically collapsed on the table, pretending to sob over her death.

Mom's exasperated voice came from behind us, "Eat your food before it gets cold."

"Yes, Mother. Sorry." Excitement over the party was making me act crazy.

"I hafta hurry and face reality too." Hanaka sighed and ripped a chunk out of her bread.

I looked forward to the Christmas party for two explicit reasons. The first: getting to spend a nice long time with Kon. We saw each other at Miss Ayumi's on our lesson days, but we barely had any time to chat, always ending our encounters with little more than greetings and small talk.

To me, Kon is a best friend I can't live without. I'm constantly reminded of how glad I am that she's in this world with me. Part of that has to do with the fact that she's a friend who is also dead serious about the piano. To be sure, our connection as people reborn into this world is another huge factor. But there's something else. Being with Kon sets my heart at peace in a way nothing else does. Getting to spend a whole day with her was more than exciting.

The second reason for my anticipation was that I'd get to wear clothes that weren't hand-me-downs for the first time. I hadn't asked my parents to buy me new clothes. Our household expenses were already stretched at the best of times since we had to pay for Hanaka's cram school and off-campus tests. The new dress had actually been a present from the kindhearted mothers of my best friend.

"Sorry for making you come to the party on our whims☆ We're just dying to see what you'll look like in a dress~♪ And so, since we couldn't resist, we had one made for you! Your prince will come to pick you up on the day of the party. With love from Chisako & Sakurako ♡"

Why is it that they exude the image of calm, refined madams with soft demeanors in person, but when it comes to their cards they let loose and sound like schoolgirls having fun?

This time they sent me a long sleeveless dress. The large ribbon tied at the neck was light-beige, while the dress itself was a stunning aqua. It loosely spread outwards from the waist to the hem. Not only had they sent me a dress, but they also threw in a snow-white cashmere coat and silver satin pumps.

"We are more than looking forward to hearing Mashiro perform on the piano. The dress is merely a small token of our appreciation. You needn't be modest," Miss Chisako said over the phone, going as far as to call my parents to ensure we would accept it.

I hoped this wealthy celebrity mother would eventually come to realize that her "small tokens of appreciation" scared the socks off of commoners.

We were going to exchange Christmas presents in a game at the party.

"I can't buy expensive presents!" I freaked out when Kon told me.

To which she responded, "Of course not! We're in elementary school, silly."

I thought exchanging gifts with the rich and powerful meant buying things with a lot of digits in the price tag. I'm relieved it doesn't.

After much worrying and contemplation, I decided to knit a colorful scarf from cashmere silk yarn I'd splurged on. I chose light-beige and dark-caramel yarn to use as the base, with indigo, light-blue, and red yarn as the accents. This way I could include all the colors of everyone's names.

There was no guarantee Kon would receive it, so I came up with a design that wouldn't be too feminine. The front and back designs were complex, but they posed no trouble for me to knit. I weaved the knitting needle at a breakneck speed and completed the scarf in less than two days. Wrapping the scarf in nice wrapping paper and tying a ribbon around it resulted in a splendid gift.

They were going to pick me up at eleven. I had Hanaka do my hair before I changed into the dress. I put on colored lip gloss to finish my look and went downstairs to show my parents. Just like every other time, they made a fuss about how cute and pretty I supposedly was. Though I knew it was only the praise of doting parents, I couldn't help but feel happy to be complimented. Time passed as I was getting ready, and when the clock struck eleven, the doorbell promptly rang.

"Whoa, right on time. It's probably Mr. Mizusawa! I'll get it!"

"Wait, Mashiro. They're always looking after you, so we need to introduce ourselves as well. Come on, darling."

"Good point."

I slipped into my coat, reached for my lesson bag, which was stuffed with my present and the music book, then headed for the front door. Dad and Mom followed close behind. Careful not to rip my stockings, I slowly lowered my feet into the pumps. I opened the door—and couldn't believe my eyes.

"Hello, Mashiro."

It wasn't Mr. Mizusawa. Dressed in a black tuxedo and a black long coat, Kou stood handsomely in my doorway, holding a bouquet of roses. His long bangs were waxed back, so that he looked like anything other than an elementary school boy.

"I've come to pick you up, my princess."

Dad stared in blank amazement at the sight of Kou's sweet smile as he smoothly delivered a pretentious pick-up line as if it were only natural. Mom sighed wistfully behind me, sounding like a small girl who was watching Cinderella attend the ball for the first time.

"Your prince will come to pick you up on the day of the party."
By prince, they meant Kou?!

I was utterly petrified by the arrival of an unexpected prince.

CG 14: Secrets (Kon & Tobi)

"Y-YOU'RE K-Kou? I-I heard you were in the same grade as Mashiro…" Dad questioned, his voice full of surprise. He was so shocked he stuttered.

I understand how you feel. Meeting such a mature elementary school boy makes you feel uneasy!

"You must be Mashiro's father. I'm very pleased to meet you. My name is Kou Narita. Yes, I'm the same exact age as Mashiro. Your lovely daughter has been a wonderful friend to me."

It itches! His words are gonna give me hives! I fidgeted, wanting to stamp my feet in frustration. *His good-looks and fake act have climbed to new heights. They're a national treasure now.*

"I had the pleasure of meeting Mrs. Shimao once before at Miss Ayumi's piano lessons… Oh, yes, I forgot."

Kou dropped his gaze to the deep-crimson flower bouquet in his arms and suavely pulled a single rose from it. He carefully inserted the rose, which had the thorns taken off and a trimmed stem, in my hair. Instantly, the flowery aroma of the damask rose wafted from my hair, tickling my nose.

Wow, it smells even more wonderful than I thought it would. My face naturally softened into a smile. Kou stole a peek at my face, returning a tender smile.

"Looks like you've taken a liking to it. Doesn't it smell nice? This is my favorite flower."

Crimson Glory, right? …I know. I remember the smell. After all, when I saw that it was your favorite in the fanbook, I rushed to the florist to buy a bouquet.

"These flowers are for you, dear Mother. I realize it isn't quite Christmas yet, but have a merry Christmas." Kou reverently held the rose bouquet out to Mom.

Boy, the look on Mom's face when she accepted the massive bouquet with over fifty roses! Her cheeks flushed pink and her eyes lit up like a little girl's.

"Thank you! They're wonderful! I wonder how many years it has been since I last received a bouquet!"

"I'm sorry, sweetheart... I'm a husband who forgets to do things like that..."

I hadn't seen Mom this delighted in ages. Mom loves anything beautiful and she truly enjoys flowers as well. She won't buy them for herself because she's trying to keep to the household budget, but I should've used my allowance to at least buy her a single rose. She'll probably have to cheer Dad up later.

I turned to Kou and lowered my head. Right now, I wanted to take this chance to honestly thank him. "Thank you very much. For picking me up and for the flowers."

Surprise flickered across his face for but a moment before he smiled back and replied, "I'm happy to do something as small as this for you anytime."

From his deportment to his...everything else, he was a picture-perfect prince standing in my entryway.

Once we finished saying goodbye to my parents, we headed to the Benz parked outside my house.

I greeted Mr. Mizusawa, who waited in front of the backseat door. "Merry Christmas. Thank you for always picking me up and dropping me off. I'll be in your care again today."

"I will be sure that you travel to and from your destination with the utmost safety. And may I add, you're even more stunning than usual today."

"I am? Th-Thank you very much."

He complimented me in that deep, sexy voice! I'm thrilled, even if it was just flattery!

"C'mon, get in already. It's cold out here." Kou seemed irritated for some reason and dropped his prince act. He should be declared as a national treasure just for how fast he can switch attitudes. Kou quickly climbed into the car then held his hand out for me. "Come here. Be careful not to step on the hem of your dress and rip it."

"I won't!" I held up the sides of the dress with one hand and took his hand with my other, allowing him to guide me safely to my seat.

The thick aroma of roses still lingered in the car. I sniffed deeply, breathing in the smell, which got Kou laughing at me.

"Quit acting like a dog." His gaze was filled with tenderness as he said that, completely throwing me for a loop. It took a minute before I reacted, pursing my lips in mock annoyance at him.

He called me a dog!

♪♪♪

THE Narita estate came into view while Kou and I were exchanging playful banter in the back seat. Immediately, my attention was stolen by the fir tree placed in front of the water fountain. The huge tree and grandly decorated mansion were on par with the Christmas decorations used at amusement parks.

Kou exited the car first, then went around to open the door on my side. He's undeniably chivalrous at times like this. I placed my hand on his and lowered my feet on the pavement, careful not to let my dress drag.

"Thank you. Your Christmas tree is something else!"

Hearing the excitement in my voice, he smiled fondly at me. "I'm glad you like it." He proceeded to place his hand on the small of my back. "I think you'll be able to enjoy the beauty of the lights better on your way home. Let's go inside now. I would hate for you to catch a cold, Mashiro."

This is Kou, right? He wasn't abducted by aliens, was he?

"…You were just thinking rude things about me again."

"I wasn't. I was just wondering if you're the real Kou right now."

"…What do you mean by that? Sheesh. This is what I get for going out of my way to be nice to you…" he complained, but he escorted me like a gentlemen from beginning to end.

My eyes rounded in awe as we stepped inside. The entrance hall, parlor, and every other room that we passed through were impeccably decorated for Christmas, matching the holiday with red and green adornments. A man who appeared to be the doorman took my coat and purse. Then Kou led me to the parlor on the first floor, which was equipped with a real, roaring fireplace. The popping, crackling firewood further boosted the Christmas cheer.

"Mashiro is here!"

"My! *My!* My! What a doll! You look adorable!"

As soon as I entered the room, Miss Sakurako and Miss Chisako flew to surround me, as if they had been awaiting my arrival. Kou shot me a sympathetic grin and moved to the sofa near the window.

"Thank you very much for inviting me today. How can I ever thank you for going as far as giving me such a lovely dress too…"

"Whatever are you saying?! We are the ones who must thank you for heeding our selfish whims."

"Indeed. And I must say, you look spectacular in those clothes! We made the correct choice in ordering from that shop, Sakurako."

…Did Miss Chisako just say order? I sure hope they didn't go out of their way to custom-order this dress for me.

I had just managed to somehow get a smile on my twitching face when Kon and Sou joined us.

"It's not fair for you to hog Mashiro to yourselves, Mothers! We've also been waiting for her. I request you trade places with us soon."

"Hehe. My apologies, dear. I suppose we shall excuse ourselves for the time being then. We'll speak with you some more later, Mashiro." Miss Sakurako gave me a small hug and Miss Chisako squeezed my hands.

"I hope we will get more time to chat," I responded with a smile, feeling there was no better answer than that.

I could tell that they both sincerely liked me, but I couldn't understand why.

"Welcome, Mashiro. I'm sorry our mothers are so over the top. As you can see, they've been so excited lately. Especially Mother Chisako. She's always wanted another daughter to spoil, so she can't help spoiling you like you're her child too."

So that's the reason they spoil me.

"I don't mind at all! I have nothing but gratitude for how kind they always are to me. They even sent me this dress—oh! I just noticed, but your dress and mine are a matching pair!"

The large ribbon on Kon's dress was champagne gold; the dress itself was an eye-catching deep-crimson.

"They are. You'll be performing with Shiroyama, so your dress is light-blue. I'll be performing with Kou, so mine is a deep-crimson. Our mothers went and decided that on their own. But I was right to let them handle our dresses! Mashiro, you look amazing in this dress."

"That's what I was going to say about you! Kou must've fawned all over you—weren't you overwhelmed? I can just imagine him going, 'I'd expect no less of my princess. You're very beautiful, Kon.'" I showed off my Kou mimicry, surprising Kon and getting a loud laugh out of her.

Sou covered his mouth with this hand to restrain his laughter, but his shoulders were shaking. He was wearing a white tuxedo. The snow-white color brought out the blue of his hair. His authentic pretty boy appearance was enhanced even further.

"But you really are pretty. I wish I could've escorted you instead."

His straightforward compliment drew a silly grin out of me. "You look dashing today too, Sou! A tuxedo really suits you!"

"Really?! Yay!"

Yay? That's a ridiculously cute response!

Kou appeared with a drink in hand while the three of us were happily chatting away. "You seem to be enjoying yourselves a lot. I hope you weren't having fun badmouthing me."

"Oh dear, you overheard us?" I insinuated with a wide grin. He shrugged, dismissing my game.

"Apparently all of our guests haven't arrived yet. Let's talk on the sofa." He led us farther into the room.

"There's going to be other guests?" I clarified, curious.

His lips curled into a goading smirk. "We're putting on a musical performance. The more guests the better, wouldn't you say?"

"…What are you talking about? I haven't heard anything about this." Kon tilted her head, clearly suspicious of whatever Kou had up his sleeve.

"You haven't? Well you'll find out soon enough."

She groaned and wrinkled her nose—a supremely adorable gesture. As four, we snacked on the sweets that had been left out on the table, and were enjoying warm chai tea when we heard a loud surge of cheerful voices from the entrance hall.

"Sounds like our guests are here," Kou commented.

We all turned our attention to the entrance. Right on cue, the parlor's huge double doors swung open—I nearly gasped when I saw who it was.

"Hello, Kon, Mashiro. Thank you for inviting me today."

Miss Ayumi, Prince Tobi, and someone else I didn't know walked into the room.

"I'm glad to be graced by your presence once again, little pianists."

"Hello. How do you do? I'm Arisa Yamabuki."

The unfamiliar, beautiful woman with blue eyes and honey platinum-blond hair was Prince Tobi's older sister!

Miss Ayumi presented them to us with a smile, "I've introduced you girls to Tobi before. Arisa here is my best friend and Tobi's older sister."

"It's a pleasure to meet Ayumi's adorable students. Did you know that she's always talking my ear off about you two? I'm thrilled to meet you girls!" Miss Arisa flashed us a friendly smile as she held out her right hand.

Um, does she want to shake hands?

Noticing my hesitation, Kon stepped up to take the lead.

"It's nice to meet you. Thank you very much for coming today." Kon shook Miss Arisa's hand, then dropped into a graceful curtsy immediately after.

She went first so I could learn from her. I put out my hand as well, to be surprised by the strength Miss Arisa shook my hand with. After shaking our hands, Miss Arisa took a step back and let Prince Tobi have her spot.

"This marks our third time meeting. I suppose I can finally greet you this way?"

"This way?" Perplexed, I cocked my head.

"Haha. Your confused face is quite adorable too." Tobi lifted one of my hands in his, wrapped his other around my shoulder, then leaned over and pecked me on the cheek.

This guy just kissed me on the cheek!

Sheer shock made my voice catch in my throat. Maybe Kou thought I was going to punch Tobi for it, because he grabbed my right hand without a moment's delay. Or held it back, rather. Sou did the same thing to my left hand. Detained between two tall boys like a suspect about to be dragged off to the police, all I could do was wordlessly flap my lips. Meanwhile, Prince Tobi moved on to peck Kon on the cheek.

"You are in Japan right now, so please let this be the first and last time you greet us with a kiss."

Aaah, Kon, you are so cool!

"How regrettable. What misfortune has befallen me—to be faced with two of the most adorable angels on the planet but not have permission to kiss their cherubim cheeks." Prince Tobi sighed dramatically.

"You get off easy with your misfortunes all the time," Miss Arisa playfully teased, as he looked wistfully to the heavens.

Miss Ayumi swiftly added another quip, "Now this is a rare sight. To think a veteran player like you would get rejected here of all places."

"That's not true. Those who are dearest to me are always cold," Tobi responded, smiling.

Obviously he was joking, but there was something sad about what he had said. My eyes darted to Kon. She had a cold stare fixed on him.

I knew it. She doesn't have affection for him. The nagging feeling I had reared its ugly head again. Kon insisted that she wanted to do Prince Tobi's route and capture him. *Come to think of it, not once did she say that she liked or loved him. I simply interpreted it that way.*

But then why would she want to go down his route and win his affections if she doesn't care for him?

Sensing my eyes on her, Kon shifted her gaze, and our eyes met. When she looked back at me like this, her smile was heartrendingly radiant.

Hey, Kon? What is the secret you can't tell me?

Original Heroine's Results
Target Character: Tobi Yamabuki
Event: A Christmas Reunion
CLEAR

THE main venue for the party was the dance hall on the first floor of the east wing. I was beginning to learn that it was pointless to wonder about things like, "are dance halls normally included in houses these days?"

Miss Ayumi played a jaunty waltz on the Steinway grand piano set against the farthest wall of the room while Prince Tobi escorted young and beautiful women to a dance in turns. They did have the party take part in a dance hall, after all.

Tables full of food were positioned on both sides of the spacious hall. Several chefs wearing white hats waited at the tables. From the looks of it, they were cooking up hot omelets for people on the spot.

"Are you interested in the omelets? Let's have them make us some," Kon suggested. I took her up on it, and we headed straight for the omelet corner.

A young male chef masterfully whipped up a soft, fluffy, superbly shaped omelet. He topped it off with a savory cream sauce and a sprinkling of truffles. Not only did it look picture perfect, it tasted scrumptious too.

A Christmas tree—not quite as large as the one decorating the courtyard but still ten feet over my head—stood gorgeously decorated by the floor-to-ceiling window. Multicolored candies and countless candles hung from the tree. Remarkably, they used real candles to decorate the tree as opposed to strings of electric lights. Who knew that there were special candle holders for the occasion? Were they set up to prevent the tree from catching on fire?

I walked around visiting the different food tables with Kon and tried to eat a little bit of everything that looked delicious. Sou and Kou were relaxing on an ottoman enjoying their guy time. They were often on edge in front of me, so it was heartening to see them get along like regular best friends. No one was paying any attention to Kon and me.

Now's my chance!

I boldly prompted Kon, "Say, Kon, do you hate Prince Tobi?"

"...Do I look that way to you?" The pause before she answered lasted for but a second. She smiled slowly. "It's okay. Prince Tobi is a special reward for the player after they clear the game once. He doesn't have an affection meter or required parameters. He's an easy character to get as long as you fulfill his conditions."

"I see."

She had cleverly shifted her answer to something unrelated to my initial question. Before I could say anything else, she quickly continued, "Thank you for worrying about me. I can't tell you the details, but I plan on doing his route and winning him over. I only needed your help for his Encounter Event. The rest of his events will activate automatically now, so everything is okay."

My doubts and questions only increased. Kon refused to answer whether she liked or hated him and wouldn't tell me why she seemed so obsessed with trying to go through with his route in the first place. The only thing I knew for sure was that she had a good reason for it—the determination in her eyes said it all.

Please don't ask me anymore.

Her implicit message was clear, leaving me no choice but to back down.

♪♪♪

THE piano stopped and the music vanished from the hall. Dance time had come to an end. Miss Sakurako came over to us while we were chatting on the ottoman with the boys.

"If you kids are ready, would you like to honor us with your musical performance now?"

We had just been talking about it:

"It's almost time for us to perform. Are you ready, Mashiro?"

"Yeah, probably. Agh, I think I ate too much."

"…Mashiro. Your stomach is bloated."

"It is?!"

"Kou, don't tease her. It's okay. Your stomach isn't sticking out or anything."

"…I hope you lose all your hair someday, Kou."

That was the conversation we were having when Miss Sakurako approached us.

"Who's going first?" I asked.

"You're the guest, so you decide, Mashiro," Kou softly answered.

He was always teasing me to death, but he just had to be sly by occasionally acting like a gentleman when it mattered.

"Okay, we'll go first then. I'd lose all confidence and not be able to play if I had to go after hearing Kon's performance."

"Got it. Sou, I had my butler bring your cello to the side of the stage for you. Why don't you go get set up?"

"M'kay."

Miss Sakurako directed the maids, and the dance hall was tidied in record time. They put away the tables and carried in comfortable chairs that they situated in front of the piano.

"This is getting exciting. Have fun playing up there today, Mashiro," Miss Ayumi said encouragingly.

…Miss Ayumi, that's going to have the opposite effect on me! I honestly didn't think they were going to make this big of a deal out of our performance!

This was going to be my first time playing the piano in front of people I didn't know. Sou finished tuning and came over to me while my heart hammered.

"Hm? Are you a little nervous?"

"Not just a little—I'm very nervous! Sorry if I make any mistakes!" I looked up at him from the piano seat to see him smiling broadly down at me.

"There's something novel about hearing you talk about being nervous, Mashiro… You'll do just fine. Focus on my sound alone. Don't let anything else in." He scooped up my right hand and placed a kiss on my fingers.

"S-Sou?!"

"A charm so you can play like you always do," he stated, free from ulterior motives, then cracked a wide grin at me. I felt like burying my face in the piano.

"Heh. What a great knight you have there." Prince Tobi whistled.

Even Arisa chimed in, her hands clasped together, "Very nice! I love seeing cute moments like this!"

"Kou! If you don't put your best foot forward, Sou will steal Mashiro from right under your nose!" Miss Sakurako chided, slapping Kou's shoulder frantically as he sat beside her. He gave her a bitter smile.

"Mom, you're getting too worked up."

That was the first time I'd seen Kou truly uncomfortable. *He's no match for Miss Sakurako.* Realizing that refreshed me. *I almost always forget that he's still an elementary school boy too.*

Thanks to Sou and Kou, the tension left my locked shoulders. I placed my fingers on the keys and sent Sou the signal to start. Our sound melded together so harmoniously, you couldn't even compare it to the times we had practiced together. The lingering notes of his cello were the only sounds I heard as I played. We exchanged glances, chasing after each other's sound, as if we were having a secret conversation that only we could understand. The last note rose into the air before softly melting into silence. Sou lowered his bow, and the room exploded in applause.

…Aw, it's over. I wanted to play more.

I reluctantly got up from the piano. Then I walked over to Sou, who was putting away his cello, and expressed my gratitude. "Thank you, Sou. I had a blast playing with you!"

"I'm the one who should thank you. I never thought a day like this would come, where I could play alongside the piano and enjoy it. I believe it's because it was with you that I could play the way I did."

His words were colored with emotion, and I gratefully accepted them. I glanced over at Miss Ayumi, who smiled and mouthed, "Perfect score."

Kou and Kon were up next. I sat beside Sou as I waited for their performance to begin. They chose to play Mozart's Violin and Piano Sonata No. 18 in G-major.

I knew it'd be Mozart. After all, he's Kou's favorite composer.

Kou's colorful, peppy violin intermingled with Kon's delicate, graceful piano. I was mesmerized by how perfectly in-sync they were, in a way only twins could be. Kou's honest joy for being able to play with Kon's piano was conveyed through the sound of his violin. The cheerful melody and upbeat rhythm from playing in G-major was wondrous to the ear. Their song contrasted the song we had chosen; it was unmistakably an active piece.

When the song was over, Kou lowered his violin and dropped into a refined bow. Both Sou and I loudly clapped for them. Thus, our small concert came to a close.

"Both pairs were remarkable!"

"Thank you for a lovely time."

Miss Chisako and Miss Sakurako were more than delighted. Relieved, I stood from my seat.

I walked over to Kou and Kon to accept my defeat. "Wow, you guys were as amazing as I expected! You had me mesmerized."

"You flatter us too much!" Kon happily replied, "You and Sou were just as amazing." She threw her arms around me in a big hug, then put Kou on the spot by asking, "Didn't you think so too, Kou?"

"You could say that. It wasn't half bad… Anyway, where'd that change of heart come from, Sou?"

"What change of heart? I just matched my sound to Mashiro's piano." Sou shrugged with indifference.

"I'm surprised you can say that. Take our practice sessions just as serious then," Kou remarked, exasperated.

"Don't wanna. Takes too much effort," Sou grimaced.

It sounded like he normally performed with the bare minimum of effort required. I felt myself making a wry smile as I watched them, when Miss Sakurako interrupted, "Say, Kon? It seems Arisa and the others have plans after this. We're going to see them off. Chisako and I will be excusing ourselves here, but let Mashiro and the others enjoy themselves in the meantime."

"Okay." Kon nodded and left to see Prince Tobi, who was getting ready to leave near the door. "Thank you very much for coming today. Please visit again."

"I should be the one thanking you. I had a great time." Prince Tobi grinned.

Kon flashed a blinding smile in return. "I'll do my best to make sure you actually mean it when you say that next time."

"*It's all up to you…* See you next time, Kon," Prince Tobi imparted, half in English and half in Japanese. His words implied a deeper meaning than he let on, but he swiftly disappeared out the door.

♪♪♪

THE time we had left before I had to go home zoomed by. Fun times are always the shortest. The sky had darkened outside the windows, so we decided to exchange presents before leaving.

We sat in a circle passing presents around to the rhythm of "Rudolph the Red Nosed Reindeer," which Kon and I sang. The moment the song ended, we all opened the present in our hand. Sou received the present Kon had prepared. Inside the wrapping paper was a pair of Dents gloves. I nearly fainted when I saw them.

Dents gloves cost more than 10,000 yen! I underestimated what the wealthy thinks is "cheap"!

I received Sou's present. It was a music box crafted out of walnut wood that included two songs: Pachelbel's "Canon" and "La Campanella". Yet another pricey present. The sound quality was leaps and bounds beyond any normal music box you could buy in stores.

Kon received Kou's present, which was a remarkably adorable snow globe. Inside the crystal glass, finely detailed children were having a snowball fight around a grand church. I peered at it with Kon as she flipped it over. When she turned it upright, snowflakes floated softly onto the children.

The snow globe was a lovely Christmas-themed present with a price cheap enough the receiver wouldn't have to panic. To be honest, it seemed like Kou had the most common sense among the three of them.

That means the scarf I knitted ended up with Kou.

"Heh, this is stylish. What brand is it?" From the first glance, he already seemed pleased with the scarf, taking it in his hands to carefully examine every detail.

"I knitted it. So it's Mashiro Brand."

"…You're kidding."

"Why do I have to kid about something like that?"

"No way a kid like you can knit something of this level."

"What a way to get a compliment!"

Kon giggled while watching our childish bickering.

"I wish I could've gotten it," Sou muttered, envy coating his every word.

I suddenly got a great idea. "Then why don't you exchange gifts? You got Kon's present, right, Sou? I'm sure Kou would prefer Kon's present anyway."

"…Are you implying you're dissatisfied with Kon's choice?" Kou snarled at Sou, his mood instantly souring.

"I'm not. I'm really into what she picked out too, but Mashiro's scarf is special," Sou contended, holding firm.

I was certain Kou was going to give in. He should've lost interest in it the moment he learned that I knitted it.

"Why don't you give it to him? I'm sure you have plenty of better scarves than what I can make, Kou."

"Don't want to." Kou clenched the scarf I made and turned his face away.

Oh dear. He must be appalled by the fact that Sou was so willing to give away Kon's present.

"Look at what you did, Mashiro. Kou's pouting because you want to take away his present." Amusement shimmered in Kon's eyes as she poked fun at us.

That's not why he's upset!

"Please don't say weird stuff," I stated.

"Don't be ridiculous," Kou grumbled.

Our voices had overlapped in perfect sync.

♪♪♪

NEW Year's holiday came soon after, and I devoted myself to nothing but studying my books and practicing the piano at home. Miss Ayumi was out of Japan until the end of January because she was holding a concert in Vienna. Losing my twice-a-week lessons left me with an empty feeling.

Sou was away in Germany, while Kon and Kou were traveling Europe with Miss Sakurako. Not being able to see them over the break added to my loneliness.

I went to watch a movie with my usual group of friends from school for a day, but once evening rolled around, my desire to play the piano won out. It wasn't bad chatting with friends and riding our bicycles to the shopping center under the cloudy gray sky. It wasn't like I disliked Kinose or Hirata either. And of course, the movie was enjoyable. Plus, my parents had rejoiced when I left the house to hang out with my friends.

But I believe I was possessed by a dark, depressing anxiety for the future.

Should I really be having fun right now?

I have to work harder.

I want to become a scholarship student at Seio. Is that possible if I'm doing this? I want to hurry and catch up to where everyone else is.

I could only forget these incomprehensible feelings of impatience and unease when I drove myself into a corner by burying myself in work. My fretfulness became intolerable whenever I was left with free time. I constantly interrogated myself if I should be wasting my time away from the piano.

Mashiro Shimao: a girl with spotty memories of a past life. Despite remembering that I had been reincarnated from another world, I could barely recall anything about my old life. Some nights, I couldn't help feeling like I was being kept alive in this world for the sole purpose of functioning as *Hear My Heart*'s heroine.

What if my desire to be with Kon, Sou, and Kou, and even my dreams of becoming a pianist, were all just the by-product of game programming?

"Becchin, am I doing the right thing? Is it okay for me to live like this?" I rubbed my cheek against my teddy bear's plush stomach. His inanimate softness worsened my loneliness all the more.

It was at times like this that I always felt the indescribable need to see Kon.

♪♪♪

THE excessively long winter break gave way to winter quarter. It wasn't long before the day that would determine Hanaka's future had arrived.

"The weatherman said it's not supposed to snow today, but be careful out there, Sis."

"Yeah, I will be."

"You have more tests tomorrow. Come straight home after you finish today."

"I will... Hey, what's wrong with you? You're as pale as a ghost, Mashiro."

I clung to Hanaka as she ate breakfast, cooked specially to be high in DHA. For some reason, anxiousness overwhelmed me, and I was afraid to leave her.

"I want to come with you to the test center. I want to wait for you outside," I blurted out, sudden but quietly.

"You want to go that far?!" Hanaka exclaimed, gaping at me.

"Hanaka finally got serious about her tests, but it looks like her nervousness rubbed off on Mashiro instead," Mom commented.

Dad looked up from the newspaper to kindly reassure me, "She'll be fine, Mashiro. Even if she fails, it's not like she'll *die*—"

"STOP IT!" I screamed. My throat trembled with the shriek.

My entire family sucked in their breath.

Aaah. I finally realized why I was so worried about Hanaka. I died in my last life on my way home from the test center.

"Mashiro, why don't you take today off and get some rest? You've been pushing yourself too hard lately. I'm sure you're wearing yourself out." Mom walked away from the sink and over to me. She pressed her cold hand, a testament to the dishes she had just been washing, against my forehead.

"Hmm. Doesn't seem like you have a fever."

"But she looks sick. I'll be a-okay. Relax and wait for me at home. Have confidence in me! Okay?" Hanaka grinned, thudding her chest assuredly to put me at ease.

"Relax and wait for me at home. Have confidence in me!"

Hadn't I said those very same words to someone before? All I could remember was that they were someone very special to me, someone I had loved.

"Okay. I'll sleep in my room today. You've been studying so hard all this time, Sis, I'm positive you'll get a good score. Please be safe on your way there and back." Somehow, I managed a smile. Painfully reluctant, I stepped away from Hanaka.

"Okay! Let's go out to eat as a family after I finish the last of my tests tomorrow!"

"That's a great idea! We haven't eaten out in a while."

"I'm looking forward to it too," Dad said.

Everyone agreed unanimously and smiled. I laughed, forcing the twitching corners of my lips up into a smile in order not to cry in front of them, then returned to my room.

…What was I thinking and feeling the morning I had left home to take my tests? I desperately searched through the blank space of my recollection. Not even a speck of dust drifted from the shelf of emptied memories.

Immediately after getting into bed in my pajamas, tears spilled messily down my cheeks. I didn't even know why I was crying. I stifled my sobs by burying my face in my pillow and bawled until my tears dried up.

♪♪♪

THUS, time passed by. Hanaka successfully became a university student without dying. She hadn't been able to get into her first choice but was accepted by her second choice.

"If possible, I want to become a certified kindergarten teacher," she announced enthusiastically.

I'm surprised she was able to raise her grades that high. I felt impressed by my very own sister. Hanaka's amazing at looking after others and has fundamental nerves of steel, so she might even become a kindergarten principal someday.

I progressed to fifth grade as I welcomed my third spring since first regaining my memories.

By then, I stopped being a serious, moping heroine. Hanaka safely turned nineteen, and that was enough for me. I have confidence in how quick I get over things. I immediately switched my thought process, deciding to enjoy my current life instead. After all, nothing would come from obsessing over what I could no longer recall. Besides, it's not as if I were the only person who's anxious about the future. That's something everyone feels.

My primary goal was to make sure I didn't die a stupid accidental death. That was the most important thing to watch out for. I had already finished reviewing all five primary subjects at the high school senior level, so I changed my focus to keeping that knowledge updated and fresh.

And I had the piano. At any rate, I devoted everything I had to practice and aimed to win the middle school competition coming in a few years. I had to clear the recital coming up next month first, but it didn't worry me too much. I was confident after having three months to prepare. Naturally, I had perfected my solo piece, Beethoven's "Pathétique, Second Movement", while my duet piece with Kon was coming along nicely.

Why should I care if my existence in this world is at the behest of someone's schemes? I'll stubbornly live out my life my way and absolutely find happiness!

CG 15: ???

WE entered the month of May, bringing the day of the recital all that much closer. The recital was scheduled for the last Saturday of this month, and the venue was the Civic Auditorium of all places!

"D-Did you say the Civic Auditorium? Um, I suppose it'll be held in one of the smaller halls?"

Miss Ayumi smiled, shaking her head. "The small hall? Never. Of course it will be held in the biggest auditorium hall. I booked the whole place for this week and next weekend, so we can rehearse twice."

The biggest auditorium! I've heard it can fit over 1,500 people! How is that an okay place for holding a piano recital?!

It goes without saying, but I found myself unable to point this out to Miss Ayumi. All I could do was frantically mouth words without making a proper sound.

"The tickets have already sold out. What I want for you is to only focus on giving your best performance, Mashiro," Miss Ayumi comforted me, misunderstanding the reason for my nervousness.

Well, yeah, I was concerned about selling the tickets. But my head's blaring with the fact that I have to play in front of 1,500 people! …Wait a minute, did she say it's sold out?! It must be Miss Ayumi's fame that got people to buy tickets to hear her play, but this puts a tremendous amount of pressure on me!

What should I do if they boo me off the stage? …That shouldn't happen, right? They'll probably quietly leave the auditorium if they're dissatisfied. Aaah, that'd be crushing as well.

"Are you curious about the order we will be playing in? Let me give you the schedule now. Here you go." She handed me the program, which was printed in color on glossy paper.

"I'll do my best," I replied in a thin voice.

♪♪♪

I opened the program booklet as soon as I got home. The paper was firm and hard to rip. It'd be horrible if I cut my fingers on the edges, so I put on a pair of plastic cooking gloves from the kitchen before flipping through it.

The program lineup looked like this:

ACT 1

Beethoven – Piano Sonata No.8 "Pathétique"
1st Movement: KON GENDA / 2nd Movement: MASHIRO SHIMAO / 3rd Movement: AYUMI MATSUSHIMA

Chopin – Etude Op. 10, No. 12 "Revolutionary"
RINKO MIYASHITA

Brahms – "Intermezzo" Op. 118, No. 2
AOI SUGITANI

Bach – "Partita" No. 2, BWV 826
KANAKO SAKURAGIWA

ACT 2

Tchaikovsky – The Nutcracker Suite for Two Pianos
KON GENDA / MASHIRO SHIMAO

Mozart – Concerto No. 7 For 3 Pianos In F, K. 242

KANAKO SAKURAGIWA / AOI SUGITANI / RINKO
MIYASHITA

Liszt – Hungarian Rhapsody No.6
AYUMI MATSUSHIMA

FWMP! I shut the program booklet and let it fall on the table.

This program is something else. It's a lineup of famous yet easy to
listen to pieces.

The program showed me the full name of the middle school
student Miss Ayumi always referred to as Rin. Reading the performers'
profiles revealed that everyone but me had experience winning music
competitions. Only I stood out as the sole anomaly.

"Mashiro, why the long face? And what's with your hands?" Hanaka
asked as she hopped downstairs. She'd been more attentive to her
makeup than usual this time. Natural makeup, she'd informed me, takes
much longer than other styles.

"Hmm, it's nothing. Anyway, you've put a lot of effort into your look
today, Sis! Let me guess…you have a date?"

"Ha! Ha! Ha! You've done well to guess my secret!" She pulled her
smartphone out of her purse and showed me a picture. "This is Shinji
Mitsui, a fourth year at my university and my boyfriend! I'm going out
to eat with him now."

"…Which one is your boyfriend?"

On her screen was an overly enthusiastic college girl holding up a
double peace sign between two young guys.

*She should really quit playing to the trends whenever she takes pictures. She ruins
her naturally cute face.*

"Obviously it's the one you can just tell is in love with me with a
single glance!"

"Heh?"

"….Too much? Guess I went a little overboard. It's the guy wearing
the dark-blue cap."

*Oh yeah, that reminds me, she was all excited last month because she'd been
invited to a baseball game. Still though, it's only the beginning of May. She hasn't
even been in school for more than a month. I can't trust this guy, considering how fast*

he seduced a first-year student. Besides, he looks way too frivolous.

I snorted. "Are you really okay with a guy like this? You'll attract a bunch of creeps if you're not careful with your cute looks and personality, Sis."

"...Stupid doting little sister."

"Did you say something? Hm?"

"Nope. Notta. But please trust Shinji! And I'm not just saying that because his name means trust!"

"......"

"Wh-What's that judgmental look for? He looks like the shallow type, but he's super serious!"

"I see. What about this guy?"

I pointed to the other young man, who wore glasses and looked like the uptight kind of person who'd major in the sciences. Nothing about his looks stood out one way or another, but his eyes gave me the impression he was smart. He had a straight nose and thin lips. His black hair fell in layers past his ears, its edges cut evenly.

To be honest, I thought he was Hanaka's boyfriend at first glance.

"He's Shinji's friend, Tomoi Matsuda. He said he's aiming to become a teacher too. He's totally smart!"

Tomoi Matsuda?

...Tomoi?

The longer I stared at the picture, the more I felt like I had seen him somewhere before. Before long, the extreme surge of déjà vu shoved me into an intense case of halation—white flashed through my brain, sending a furious wave of pain crashing over—my head was going to split open.

"Aggh...."

"Mashiro? Mashiro!"

"Sor—I'm gonna barf..."

"Eeeh?! He's ugly enough to make you barf?!"

No. That's not it. It's just—

I couldn't collect my thoughts; my head felt like it was being sawed in half. I stumbled up the stairs to the second-story with a flustered Hanaka's support. Somehow, I was able to rip off the sweaty plastic gloves and chucked them on the floor.

"It's nice to meet you."

"I'm dating...moi... I thought you knew already..."

"Why didn't... tell me?!"

"You're wrong...I didn't..."

Disconnected fragments of a memory flashed before my eyes and shattered.

That was...that person was...

Hanaka frowned when she saw me collapse onto my bed. "Mashiro, have you been sick? You've been acting a little weird since New Year's break. Come on, let's take you to the hospital to get examined again."

Right after I regained my memories, my parents brought me to several different hospitals and doctors, worried about the sudden change in their young daughter. But not a single hospital could find anything wrong with me. It's wasn't like a tumor had formed in my brain.

I had the odd certainty that this searing pain indicated it had something to do with my past life.

...Why did I become so obsessed with Hear My Heart in the first place? Suddenly, that confusion raced across my mind.

An escape from reality.

A second chance at love.

Those key phrases clicked in place just as a violent wave of exhaustion rained down on me.

"Good night." Induced by a familiar sweet voice, I let go of my grip on reality.

◇◇◇

"IT'S still too soon for this," the man whispers, holding his hand over Mashiro's forehead as she sleeps.

This error should've never been possible normally. Kon's meager attempt at resistance seems to have opened multiple tiny seams across the world.

It's an absolute taboo for a heroine to learn the workings of the world she's in and how she got to be there. A heroine can act heroine-like because she doesn't know anything. She can live earnestly, bravely, and happily through ignorance.

In order to erase the burden of the heroine's painful memories, the man has to use even more powerful means this time to send her memories into oblivion. He rips Mashiro's past suffering from her, and it takes on an odd light, transforming into a round orb.

He holds the sparkling orb to his chest. Instantly bliss, pungent enough to numb, surges through him.

Aaah, you two are just so wonderful.

Hope. Joy. Desire. Trust. Dazzling pure emotions, accompanied by those that form under the surface, like the reflection in a mirror— despair, sadness, jealousy, anxiety. Every form of emotion he's ladled out of the girls have transformed into his provisions, his strength.

"Come. Won't you play with me some more?"

The man forcefully stomps out the new results card that had been about to bloom into fruition, cackling at the top of his lungs.

◇◇◇

I ended up sleeping like I was dead until the morning after passing out. I didn't even take a bath and I missed out on dinner. I didn't accomplish the piano and studying goals I had set either—that was the worst part.

Was I really that exhausted? I thought I was sleeping great thanks to the nice weather recently.

I leapt out of bed and glanced at the clock. It was a little past six. Strangely enough, the intense pain in my head was gone, as if it were never there in the first place. If anything, I felt better than ever.

I showered and went down to the living room just as Mom woke up.

"Good morning, Mom."

"Good morning." Mom, still dressed in her pajamas, wore a stiff expression. She gently held her hand against my forehead, then gingerly put pressure on different parts of my body. "Does it hurt here?"

"It doesn't."

"How about here?"

"Doesn't hurt there either."

We repeated this several dozen times before she finally removed her hands.

"I think you should take today off from school and go to the hospital with me."

"Why?"

"Why? Because you—" Mom's lips trembled. She suddenly pulled me into her arms. "I already took today off work. Please, Mashiro. Won't you let them examine you again? It's not normal to pass out from a headache."

"…Okay. I'll go."

When Dad awoke later, his face was also grim. "Please call my cell phone as soon as you know something," he told Mom.

I learned from them that Hanaka had canceled her date and stayed by my side the entire time after I passed out.

I feel bad.

Harboring an unbearable sense of guilt, I obediently followed Mom to the large hospital in the next town over. The doctors sent me around to all the different medical departments for a MRI, CAT scan, and various blood tests. We went first thing in the morning but ended up stuck at the hospital past two. They were unable to give us the results the same day, informing us we that we had to come back again in a few days.

Wow, how annoying.

The young doctor who questioned me had stubbornly demanded answers to things like, "Did you fall off the jungle-gym? From the stairs? From the slide? From the swing?"

How many things can you fall off of? Are elementary schoolers in constant danger of falling?

Obviously, I shook my head to all of it, but the doctor's eyes glimmered with doubt.

…I told you I haven't fallen off anything or into anything or onto anything!

I held Mom's hand as we returned to our car. Since it was such a large-scale medical facility, they were equipped with a massive garage for guest parking.

"You okay, Mom? You look tired."

"I'm okay. What about you, Mashiro? Holding up okay? I didn't think it would take this long."

"Yeah. But I'm starving."

"Me too! Want to stop somewhere to eat on our way home?"

"For sure!"

We swung our hands together, grinning at each other. I was really happy because I rarely got the chance to spend so much time with

Mom. But her lips turned down at the corners when she watched me hum a chipper tune.

"I'd be lost if something ever happened to you, Mashiro."

"Where did that come from?"

"Please don't die before we do."

"...Of course I won't!" I squeezed Mom's hand, hoping to dry the tears welling up in her eyes. I smiled broadly to show her that she didn't have to worry so much about me, my thoughts absently drifting back to my past life.

What was my mom like in my past life? Did she cry when she received word of my death?

♪♪♪

THE day after I went to the hospital, I was invited over to Kon's house after the weekly solfège. We were assigned to play "The Nutcracker Suite" as our recital duet piece. The song was originally written for the ballet, and it's famous enough that even people without an interest in classical music would've heard it at some point. The arrangement's a popular choice for two pianists to play on the same piano, but for the recital we were going to use two separate pianos, which massively increased the difficulty level.

Unlike when you're sitting directly next to each other, playing on two different pianos means that you can't signal the other pianist with your eyes or breathing. Incidentally, the person taking the treble and right hand part of the piano duet is called a primo, while the person playing the bass and left hand part is called the second. Kon would be the primo this time, with me as the second. Some people confuse the division by conflating primo with the principal melody and second with the accompanying melody, but that's not how it works.

A four-handed performance on two pianos requires the pianists to sit facing each other, obscured by their piano. They must have a strong grasp of the other pianist's habits in order to flawlessly sync their tempos. Using two pianos makes the musical expression far more dynamic.

Currently, believe it or not, there were three pianos lined up in Miss Ayumi's lesson room. Her other students were taking it up a level by playing three pianos at the same time.

I'm panicking enough as it is, just having to match my tempo to one other player! Their level is way beyond mine!

Kon and I had thoroughly memorized our individual parts already. We decided through discussion that all we had left to do was to fervently practice together until we nailed our tempo.

I came over her house today because she invited me to practice, so how did it turn into this?!

"Doesn't this piece have a lovely mature vibe to it?"

"It does! But they're still in elementary school—this design is too cute to toss aside either!"

After fully measuring Kon and me in our underwear, Miss Sakurako and Miss Chisako held various cloths against our chest and face to inspect how they would look on us. They weren't done even once they decided on a cloth to use—the ladies flipped through the design book the tailor had brought out, eagerly going through and shooting down the options.

"Mother, may we leave now? We don't want to lose our time to practice."

"Good point. Sorry for making you do this. We'll wait for a good time to have tea brought to you." Miss Chisako turned to me and apologized again, "Please forgive me for forcing you to accompany us when you merely came over to practice."

I nearly leapt from my seat. "D-Don't be sorry! I was happy to spend time with you both. B-But is it really all right to make me a dress too…?"

"Don't say that. We're doing this out of our selfish whims, so you should rather be angry at us for doing it! Tell us off for deciding everything without consulting you." Miss Sakurako gracefully covered her mouth with her hand, laughing like a lady.

Uh? Am I supposed to laugh with her here?! This is too difficult for me!

"Look forward to the dress we'll have ready for you on the day of the recital!"

I thanked the two enthusiastic, bubbly ladies and made my way out of the abundantly spacious, Japanese-style room. Even Kon was worn-out.

"…I really am sorry about my moms."

"No, don't be! I'm very happy they like me so much. I hope I can pay them back someday."

Kon looked relieved by my comment.

Our original goal, to practice, was going to be held in the soundproof room recently built in the annex building, instead of Kon's room. They had even gone as far as to buy two new pianos for us.

I knew it. The rich and powerful have no sense when it comes to money.

"Want to start by playing from the beginning to the end? Whenever there's a part that doesn't sound right to us, let's write it down on our sheet music."

"Okay!"

We played with the sheet music in front of us today just in case, so we could immediately fix any mistakes we made. Kanako and Aoi were going to serve as our page-turners at the recital. They weren't present for our practice session, so we practiced part by part, stopping at every section that sounded off. The quick tempo of the "Russian Dance (Trepak)" proved particularly difficult. We replayed it many times, fixing the pieces as we went along, but we were far from perfect.

"We just can't seem to match up, huh? Messing up at the cha-cha-kacha-cha-cha-cha part is incredibly irritating!"

"I totally agree. It's the highlight of the whole song. We have to be in perfect sync for it. Also, we need to watch out for the increasing tempo at the end."

"Yeah, yeah! That one too! I know! Why don't we use our voices while playing?" I suggested. Kon stuck her head around her piano to give me a confused look.

"Our voices? How would we do that?"

"Let's shout the signal by saying stuff like, 'here!' and 'now!' and let's sing the melody to the most important parts."

"Okay, I think I understand what you mean…that could work."

An absurd method indeed, but beggars can't be choosers. In any case, I wanted to match up as precisely as possible.

"Okay, let's start on Trepak first."

"Sure!"

In the end, the voicing method dramatically helped us improve our timing. Although I'm confident that anyone would've burst out laughing if they had watched us shouting, "Here!" and "There!". But we didn't really have any other choice, because we couldn't hear each other over the pianos without shouting at the top of our lungs. My voice was but a hoarse whisper by the evening when I bid goodbye to Miss Chisako and Miss Sakurako before going home.

♪♪♪

I received a phone call that night.

Did I forget something at the Genda estate?

Assuming the phone call was from Kon, I rushed to the wireless phone upstairs.

"Hello? This is Mashiro."

"Ah, Mashiro? It's Sou."

I was fairly surprised by the voice coming through the receiver. Sou hadn't called my house since that time we made plans for last year's Christmas concert.

"Sou? What's wrong? Did something happen?" I asked, concerned.

He paused for a minute, then struggled with telling me what he'd called for, before finally working up the nerve to say, "Hey...I got tickets to the amusement park from Mrs. Mie. Would you like to go with me?"

"To the amusement park?! I'm up for that!"

He just wanted to invite me to hang out? I worried for nothing!

"It's decided then. When are you free?"

"Hmm, all my days are buried with stuff related to the recital starting next weekend. Would it be too late to go next month?" I replied, having returned to my room to check the calendar.

"Can you do tomorrow?" he asked in return.

I didn't have any plans for tomorrow, which was a Sunday.

My only plan was to practice the piano all week during the Golden Week holiday. What should I do?

"I'm free. But the recital's coming up real soon. I was planning to practice."

"June is mostly rainy days. The weather's supposed to be great tomorrow... Can you really not make an exception this time?" His voice clearly betrayed his disappointment.

Aah! Don't get depressed!

"Is there something special about tomorrow?" I asked, curiosity getting the better of me. I felt like it was out of character for him to suddenly invite me out and push so hard to get me to agree.

"…Yeah, I guess you could say that… But it's not that big of a deal."

"Tell me. I'm curious now," I urged.

In a ghost of a voice he mumbled, "Birthday."

"What was that?"

"It's my birthday. So I thought it'd be great if I could spend it with you, Mashiro."

I froze for a good minute, the telephone tightly grasped in my hand.

His diffident voice broke through my silence, "Never mind. Sorry for putting you on the spot. Good luck with practice."

"Don't jump to conclusions! You didn't put me on the spot. That's not why I was quiet. I was just surprised, is all. Umm, I'll get my piano practice out of the way in the morning and leave my afternoon free for you. We can have fun until we drop!"

"…Are you really sure it's okay? You aren't forcing yourself to go?"

The depth of Sou's meekness made me want to cry. He was welcome to ask for more from me—we should have built up enough of a friendship for that, but he always retreated right away.

We decided on the place and time to meet, and I ended with, "Good night."

"Good night, Mashiro," he returned, his voice husky.

♪♪♪

THE following morning, I exerted myself not over the piano but the kitchen counter. It was his once-a-year birthday. We couldn't start the celebration without a present.

I had actually wanted to make him an extravagant lunch but didn't have enough ingredients to do so. After much contemplation, I decided to bake him icebox-style cookies with a batter made from cheese and basil. Sou wasn't fond of sweets that were too sugary—I thought he would be happier with this type.

While I waited for the cookies to finish baking, I used my special skill in origami to fold him a tiny dragon. Once I had finished folding the emerald-green dragon, I attached silver beads to its face as eyes. I chose this because emerald was May's birthstone, while dragons are said to bring good luck. I stuffed the cooled cookies in a decorative bag, then tied the dragon to the front of it with the ribbon I ran through the dragon.

Yes! It has the extravagant look I was going for!

I glanced at my watch, internally praising my good work and saw it had just hit noon. I gulped down the sandwiches I made on the side, then stood to leave just as Hanaka came downstairs.

"Good morning, Mashiro."

"You mean good afternoon! I made sandwiches—feel free to eat them when you feel like it."

"Thanks… Hold up! You aren't thinking of leaving now, are you?" I nodded. Hanaka's eyes grew larger than saucers. "Don't you have a date with Sou today?! You can't go in such a slapdash outfit! You can't! This is all wrong!"

"Huh? It's not a date—"

"Quit yapping and get movin'!" Hanaka dragged me upstairs to have me quickly change. The three-quarters sleeve dress with a printed design that she yanked out of her closet fell eight inches above my knees.

The mature design is wonderful, but aren't I showing too much leg?

"Don't you dare wear leggings or anything else underneath. You've got gorgeous legs, Mashiro. Show them off! It's only May, so you can go for the casual look by pairing it with western boots."

Next, she escorted me like a prisoner to the bathroom mirror. With awe-inspiring speed and mastery, she increased the volume of my eyelashes, painted my lips, and curled my hair.

"Okay, you're perfect now. You're super cute! Have a good time!" Hanaka flashed a satisfied smile and gave me a small push.

I dashed out the front door saying, "See you later!"

Dad's screams of, "Why is she so dressed up? Huh? She's going on a date?! Why didn't I hear about this sooner?!" leapt out the door behind me.

I walked five minutes to the main road from my house to find the Shiroyama car already waiting for me there. Sou was standing beside the car.

"Hi. Thanks for inviting me today."

"Thank you for coming when I asked for the impossible."

He opened the door for me, and I climbed into the back seat. I greeted the chauffeur, who nodded back. When I sat down, the hem of my dress inched up higher than I had expected.

My thighs are on full display!

Sou bashfully chuckled as he watched me struggle to yank down my dress. "Your outfit today is cute, Mashiro, but I'm not sure where I should look."

"My sister went all-out. Sorry." I grabbed a handkerchief from my purse and spread it over my lap.

Will this solve the problem? Disappointment was written all over Sou's face. *Do boys want to see a girl's thighs that badly? ...I'm sure he does. He's already eleven.*

To distract from my legs, I held out my present for him. "Here you go. Happy birthday!"

His eyes sparkled with glee, "For me? You sure?! You didn't need to get me anything though," but instantly dimmed as he concluded, "I knew I shouldn't have told you about it."

"It's nothing big. I just baked you some cookies. Oh, but they're freshly baked this morning, so I can guarantee their taste. Open it! Open it!" I insisted.

Sou's eyes rounded. "Freshly baked? I thought you said you were going to practice in the morning?"

"Hehe. I skipped practice to bake cookies. Don't tell Miss Ayumi on me, okay?"

He looked from the cookies in his hand to me, his eyes growing misty. "...It's impossible for me not to fall for you when you do stuff like this," his voice trailed off.

I didn't catch the last part. All I managed to hear was the, *it's impossible* part, so I reiterated, "Don't tell Miss Ayumi no matter what!"

He laughed a little, clenching the wrapped bag to his chest like a child who had received a treasure.

♪♪♪

WHEN we arrived at the amusement park it was bustling with people. I occasionally visited this amusement park with my family—the last time being two years ago—but it had completely changed since then. A ton of new rides had been added to the park.

"Wow! Where do you want to start?"

"I'm good with anything. This is my first time at an amusement park.

I'll leave the decisions up to you, Mashiro."

I wonder if he doesn't go places like this with his family… Of course he doesn't. All right, today big sis Mashiro is going to show him the amusement park ropes!

"Can you handle thrill rides? Like roller coasters?"

"Probably?"

"Then let's tackle the coasters first! And then we'll ride the relaxing ones, saving the Ferris wheel for last!"

"Sounds good. You look like you're really enjoying this, Mashiro."

"I am. I love amusement parks."

"I see! I'm glad you do." Sou blissfully smiled and said, "Let's go," and took my hand.

His hand, which was a whole size bigger than mine, set off the most complicated feelings inside of me.

This is what Hanaka wanted to happen though.

He attracted attention wherever we went.

"Is that boy a model?"

"Wow! He's so cute!"

Isn't he? He's a cutie, right? His personality is a hundred times cuter than his appearance too.

Filled with pride for my friend, I strut through the park with Sou. As you'd expect from a holiday week, every attraction had a long line. Whenever we had to wait in line, we played the word game *shiritori* to pass the time. *Shiritori* is a word game where you have to say a word starting with the consonant of the last syllable of the word given by the previous player. A recent trend in *shiritori* is to limit the words you can say to a specific theme. We daringly chose music as our limiting theme this time!

"I'll start then. To play with affect or emotion—Affettuoso."

"I get it. That's what we're going for? Then, making each note brief and detached—soffocato," I countered.

"Hm… a rapid, measured or unmeasured repetition of the same note—tremolo."

"L? Lamenting… Lamentando."

"Do? Sorrowfully…Dolente."

Sou's a Seio Academy student too. I was rather confident I could win at this theme, but it's hard to break the tie.

We heatedly tossed music words back and forth, making it our turn to get on the ride in no time. Heart beating wildly, I lowered the lap bar. The roller coaster train ascended the lift hill dramatically, and the climb started to slow more and more as we reached the acme of the structure.

All the noises stopped. Then I felt rumbling in my seat as gravity ripped the cars downward, the wind slapping me in the face along the way. The ear-piercing screams of all the thrill seekers behind and in front of me only boosted my excitement further, as my body shook from all the twisty turns and loops that yanked the cars every direction. Laughter erupted from me with the thrilling motion and the adrenaline rush.

By the time the cars returned to the station, we were both laughing our heads off. I hopped down the steps while trying to push my bangs down. I looked over my shoulder at Sou—he was still laughing.

"Aaah! That was fun!"

"I had fun too! It's so weird to laugh out of fear!"

"I know. It was more spectacular than I expected."

Sou swung my hand around with a lively expression. His elementary school boy-like gesture warmed my heart.

Why is it I feel deeply relieved to see him smile like this? It makes me wish he would smile and laugh this way all the time.

"Let's ride that one too, Mashiro!"

"Okay! Let's go!"

Laughing, we held hands and ran off toward the next ride. Then we shared a smoothie, and Sou waved at me from where he was watching as I rode the merry-go-round alone. Evening came while I was chasing Sou and trying to hit him for forcefully dragging me into the haunted house when I hadn't wanted to go.

"All we have left is the Ferris wheel."

"Yup."

The massive Ferris wheel also served as the amusement park's landmark and symbol. Whenever I came to this park, I always rode the Ferris wheel last. That way, everyone could enjoy the night scenery as they looked back on the fun day they'd had. I had every intention of ending my day at the amusement park with Sou the same way.

The four-person gondola slowly ascended into the air. Fascinated by the gradually shrinking amusement park, it took a while for me to notice the silence.

"…What's wrong? Tired?" I asked Sou, sitting beside me. He pointed outside without saying anything.

I followed the direction of his finger, turning my gaze toward the gondola next to ours. A couple was hugging inside. Flustered, I turned around to see a young man and woman making out inside the other gondola as well.

"Whoa! What are they doing?! …Is this couples' time on the Ferris wheel?"

"We were surrounded by couples while we were waiting in line too."

"We were?" I cocked my head, straining to remember.

Sou heaved a lengthy sigh. "Figures. That's the kind of person you are, Mashiro."

"What is that supposed to mean?"

"…It means I had my hopes up," he playfully whispered, pecking me on the cheek.

"Wh-Wh-What was that?!"

"A European-style greeting."

"Excuse me?!"

Don't mimic Prince Tobi!

"This is Japan!" I protested, my cheeks the color of ripe tomatoes. He innocently laughed as he apologized.

CG 16: Recital

ASIDE from the one day I hung out with Sou during the Golden Week holiday, I spent the rest of my days immersed in literally nothing but playing the piano until the day of the recital. It was a real struggle to perfectly sync my duet with Kon, and I nearly had a heart attack when we rehearsed in the largest auditorium hall with Miss Ayumi sitting in the audience seats, arms folded, scrutinizing our sound.

The dress Miss Chisako and Miss Sakurako had tailored for me was a snow white, long dress with a bare top, embroidered in gold. Pink rose corsages lined the bodice, and the airy bell-shaped skirt was puffed out by a petticoat. In contrast, Kon had a dark-blue version. The glamorous luster cloth was inlayed with Swarovski crystal beads. The mature design fit to her body's curves and had slits up the side to make it easier for her to step on the piano pedals.

The day before the recital, they raced to the venue with our finished dresses. They went absolutely wild in the waiting room as they had us change into the dresses, gushing as they took our pictures.

"We hired a beautician to handle your hair and makeup tomorrow too!"

I nearly fainted when I heard the name of the beautician Miss Chisako had hired.

Isn't that the famous beautician I sometimes see on TV? Isn't this going overboard for a recital?

Seeing me turn into a petrified statue, Miss Sakurako reassured me, "It's okay! We hired the beautician to handle Ayumi and all her students' hair and makeup. So you needn't worry about anyone being left out."

What part of this is okay? They're only making it even more of a big deal than it already is.

"Thank you for doing so much for us." I decided to thank them and leave it at that.

The dress and beautician had been amazing in and of themselves, but then they took it a step further by preparing another dress for the second act.

How much did they spend in total? I probably won't be able to pay them back unless I rise to become a really famous pianist...

As I was plotting how to get rich quick, Kon quietly warned, "Mashiro, you look like a scheming villain."

♪♪♪

WITHOUT further ado, the day of the recital arrived. The auditorium opened at 2 p.m. and we would begin at 2:30 p.m. We were supposed to bring our lunches for the meeting at 10 a.m. Seats were set aside for family members, so they could come closer to the starting time without having to deal with the ticket hassle. I rode with Kon to the auditorium in a Genda car driven by Mr. Nonaga.

"Mashiro, are you nervous?"

"Yeah. But now that we're this far along, I want to hurry up and finish my performance."

"I understand how you feel. To tell you the truth, I'm excited." We held each other's hands in the back seat. "Naturally, we'll kill it for our four-handed performance on the piano, but let's put our heart and soul into 'Pathétique' as well! I'll play with everything I have in the first movement before handing the reins over to you."

"You can count on me. I'll do my best to steer the song right where we want it. I doubt Miss Ayumi would hold her tongue if I got us off course, and I'd prefer to return from the auditorium alive."

"...Don't say stuff like that."

"...Okay, sorry."

Once we arrived at the auditorium, we held a detailed meeting about the recital, and then I rushed to down the tiny rice rolls Mom made for me. The bewildering hustle and bustle after that was really something else. Everyone changed into their formal dresses, and the beautician's staff styled our hair and makeup in an assembly-line, sending those who were finished first back to their individual anterooms. My hair was tightly curled, sprayed down with hairspray, and my face was powdered.

I confirmed that "Mashiro Shimao" was written on the nameplate before entering my anteroom. Then I stood in front of the full-length cheval mirror hanging on the wall, gazing at the girl as pretty as a princess reflected back at me.

"Whoa…I guess he's a famous beautician for a reason!" The beautiful girl's beguiling lips moved, mimicking my words. "This is amazing!"

Getting a full makeover is like a dream come true!

I twirled in front of the mirror and curtsied. Mesmerized by the mirror, I fooled around until I heard a light knock on the door. I glanced at the clock on the wall—it was a little before two.

It might be Mom and Dad! Feeling like I was on cloud nine, I threw the door open. I wanted to show off my temporary princess form, ready to boast about it.

"Yes, Dad—Wow!"

I instinctively shrunk back from the blur of pure-white roses thrust in front of my face as soon as I opened the door.

Wh-What's going on?!

Red and light-blue hair peeked out from behind the massive bouquets, which must've contained over a hundred roses.

"Hi there, Mashiro."

"We came!"

Kou, donning a dark-gray three-piece suit, and Sou, in his black three-button slender suit, entered the anteroom carrying a bouquet each. Both bouquets were made up of white roses, as though they had coordinated it beforehand.

"Thank you for going out of your way to see me! Are those for me?"

I've never seen so many roses before.

Spellbound by the overwhelming number of roses and the dreamy fragrance they emitted, I held out my hands to accept the bouquets. However, neither Kou nor Sou moved an inch. They gaped at me, astonished.

"…Wh-What's wrong?"

Maybe the flowers weren't for me?

Seeing them just stand there gave me a horrible sense of dread. I'd be a ridiculously pathetic person for misunderstanding if they had meant to bring the bouquets to Kon after seeing me. Slowly, I dropped my hands to my sides.

"Are you really Mashiro?"

Just when I thought they finally said something, it was just Kou making a silly sound of disbelief.

Is this his roundabout way of implying that they put too much lipstick on the pig?

"Yes, I'm your Mashiro. Do you have a problem with that?" I quipped back, my voice dripping with sarcasm.

It did the trick in bringing Kou back to his usual self. "Since when did you become mine? I wish you'd leave the joke at your makeover."

"Look who's being shy. You can confess the truth. Say it. 'I was charmed by your beauty.'"

"Ahahaha… That's not a funny joke."

But you laughed!

Sou placed his bouquet on the anteroom table and came back over to me. "You're always cute, but today you're especially beautiful. Hey, let me get a better look at you."

"Huh? Ah, um…thanks?"

Straightforward compliments make me hopelessly bashful. Sou's eyes softened lovingly as he smiled warmly at me.

"I really want to hug you, but I'll endure until your performance is over. It'd be a shame to mess up your pretty hair or perfect looks."

"No hugging! Touching is off-limits!" I emphasized.

"Tch. Stingy," he grumbled, pursing his lips.

Pulling such an adorable face is off-limits too!

Ever since the amusement park, Sou had increased how touchy-feely he was with me, so I was warily keeping my distance from him. My honest feelings were that I didn't want to fall in love with Kou—an oresama with a problematic, traumatic past—or Sou—who would charge headlong into a twisted Bad End if I took one wrong step. Besides, we were all still in elementary school. I thought it was too soon for us to think about love and romance.

"Had your fill?" Kou waited until my conversation with Sou petered off before handing me his bouquet. "Congratulations on your first official performance.”

“Wow! Thank you!”

The bouquet he handed me was a lot heavier than I expected. Gravity knocked me off balance, and Kou quickly supported me before I fell forward. Watching everything unfold from the sidelines, Sou bitterly frowned.

“That was a cheap trick, Kou.”

“For the guy who got to go alone with her to the amusement park, you seem to lack confidence.”

...This situation makes me feel like a toy two kids are arguing over, or like the son the two mothers fought over in “The Judgment of Solomon”.

“I’m looking forward to hearing how you’ll play ‘Pathétique’, but I’m especially excited for your four-handed piece with Kon,” Kou said with a radiant smile after he lifted the bouquet out of my hands and positioned it on the sofa.

Is that actually a warning not to drag Kon through the mud with me?

“Thanks. I’ll do my best,” I answered, my cheek twitching. He nodded encouragingly.

♫♫♫

AS the boys were leaving the anteroom, they passed my parents, who started a whole different kind of ruckus when they came in to see me.

“Is this some kinda magic?! You look like a different person, Mashiro!”

“You’re so beautiful, it’s almost like you aren’t Mashiro!”

Different person. Not you. Hearing those phrases repeated gradually gave me mixed feelings.

The results of my medical exams at the hospital returned last week with the good news that they hadn’t found anything abnormal with me. My parents, who had been gloomy up until they received the news, rebounded, doting on me more than ever before.

“You’re so pretty, I doubt you’re my own child!”

“No, darling, she looks just like you did in your younger years! She’s your spitting image!” Dad gushed.

“Oh, honey, don’t be silly,” Mom giggled, bashfully turning aside.

I wish you guys wouldn’t flirt in front of me.

"Where's Hanaka?"

"She came with Shinji and his best friend, and they went on ahead to their seats already. She said she wants to take a picture in the lobby after the recital ends."

I received five tickets in total from Miss Ayumi. Hanaka said something about wanting three tickets, and now I knew why. She came to my recital with the two guys she'd shown me on her smartphone.

◇◇◇

Heroine's Results
Target Character: Sou Shiroyama & Kou Narita
Event: Transformation into a Princess
CLEAR
◇◇◇

♪♪♪

THREE pianos were set up on the stage. Two of the pianos were lined up at the back of the stage, while the Steinway that was to be used during the first movement was moved to the stage's center. I watched from the stage wing as Kon stepped forward. The audience exploded into applause, louder than I had anticipated. Miss Ayumi wasn't lying when she said it was a full house. Kon gave a formal bow, then sat in front of the grand piano.

Beethoven – Piano Sonata No.8 "Pathétique", First Movement

Kon played the sonata-style, slow introductory theme, ringing out the defined stress sounds according to the forte instructions. Enthralled, I listened attentively to the rich sound of the solemn chord.

Where does she pull such energy from with her fragile body?

When I closed my eyes, the small girl in front of the piano vanished. I was submerged in her vigor and power, something you'd expect from an experienced male pianist in his prime. Beads of sound twinkled from the rapidly descending E-flat minor notes. Theme three featured an Alberti-type figuration for the bass, with delicate tremolo octaves. No matter what part you dissected, it was a dynamic, romantic performance that left nothing out.

...I don't want to lose. I tightly balled my hands into fists. *I don't want to lose to you, Kon. Someday, I want to stand by your side as your equal.*

Amid the thunderous applause, Kon returned backstage, slightly panting. I lifted my face and stepped out into the blinding lights.

Second Movement

The second movement exemplifies the expressive Adagio style, which was distinctive of many slow movements in the classical period, by instructing the player to play Adagio cantabile—slowly, as if singing. This piece, which begins with a theme featuring a songlike, rising tone sustained by a sixteenth note harmony, contrasts with the faster tempo of the first movement in various ways.

The famous *cantabile* melody is played three times, and I played the triplet rhythm that made up the predominant chord with a controlled, gentle hand. Rather than play the sweet, lyrical melody emotionally, I approached it with a style that gave an overall view of the piece. While imagining the bubbling sounds of a smoothly flowing brook, I put my heart into expressing the music as simple as possible, with no extra spins or additions.

I conscientiously struck out each note, letting the sounds linger and resonate with deep sound, without muddying their tone even once. Waiting until the final note faded, I slowly stood from the bench. At the very least, I had played how I wanted to play the song.

Relief at the sound of booming applause from the audience took the tension out of me. When I returned to the stage wing, it was Miss Ayumi's turn to take the stage. The momentary glimpse I caught of the stern look on her face as we passed by one another made me gasp. Her eyes were locked and focused on the piano and the piano alone.

Age doesn't matter. Teacher or student doesn't matter. We'll always be rivals vying for best performance whenever we play in front of an audience. Her expression had taught me that once and for all.

Third Movement

The final movement of the Rondo sonata presents a beautiful theme oozing with sorrow on top of the accompanying arpeggio. The instructed speed is allegro—fast. Following piano sonata basics, the main theme closely resembles the second theme of the *Allegro* of the first movement. There's a theory you leave an adagio in the center of the movement.

The splendor of Miss Ayumi's clear high notes was outstanding. Shimmering beads of sound danced into the air. The fluent primary melody vividly constructed the contour of the song's tune. The artistry of her reverberating, descending triplets was fantastically magnificent.

As Miss Ayumi returned to us, the loudest applause yet roared and boomed at her back. She finally relaxed into a smile when she saw Kon and me enthusiastically clapping.

"Go get ready for your four-handed performance, girls."

"Yes, Miss Ayumi."

I accompanied Kon back to the dressing room where the beauticians awaited us. I had to fight my desire to run back and listen to the other girls perform, so I could change and do the final checks for our two-piano performance. This was one of those times where I couldn't help but feel disappointed to be one of the performers.

The famous beautician along with his staff changed our outfit and hairstyle to something entirely different. Kon ditched the long dress for a bright-green cheongsam with cotton roses embroidered on it. A deep-crimson cheongsam with embroidery of Chinese phoenixes had been prepared for me as well. They were both sleeveless, long dresses with slits that reached above the knees. Why cheongsams? Supposedly, because among the songs included in the "Nutcracker Suite" there's one titled, "Chinese Dance".

I'd never get the chance to wear one of these if not for a time like this, I thought seriously. *I feel like I'm cosplaying.*

They touched up our makeup and added more flare to our eyes.

"Kon, the cheongsam looks like it was made to be worn by you!"

Her porcelain-like, silky smooth skin and smoky eye makeup intensified the stunning oriental beauty of the dress. By this point, her incomparable beauty reigned supreme.

Kon giggled as I fawned over her. "I could say the same for you, Mashiro! You're so cute, I could hug you!"

Kon transformed into the female version of Sou! And thanks to the handiwork of a famous beautician and his army of stylists, I had become 2,000 times cuter than normal. I looked in the mirror and was unable to find any signs of the original me. Modern advancement in hair and makeup techniques was terrifying.

♪♪♪

"MASHIRO."

"Hm?"

On our way back to the anteroom after changing, Kon abruptly stopped, staring intently at me, earnestness glimmering in her eyes.

"Your performance earlier was simply outstanding, Mashiro. You've convinced me that I can't play like you."

What's she saying out of the blue? That's my line.

I was going to say that aloud, but bit my tongue. Her expression reminded me of a string stretched taut. Even I could sense the dangerous level of tension that could cause her to snap.

"Miss Ayumi said, 'Mashiro possesses her own, unique world. Once she acquires the technique, skill, experience, and the knowledge necessary to fully express her world, she'll be able to go farther than any of us.'"

"Unlikely. She's overestimating me... Let's say what she said is true— it'd only be because I'm *Hear My Heart*'s remake version's heroine," I said humbly, feeling like it was far too great of a compliment for me.

She vehemently shook her head, brushing aside my answer. "You don't seriously believe that, do you? Just how much time do you think we've sunk into our practice? All the time other kids our age spend watching TV, playing, and chatting, we've been using wholeheartedly on the piano. I don't want to write off the accomplishments of our hard work with some clichéd reason like it's just because we're 'heroines'. Don't you feel the same way, Mashiro?" she argued passionately, her voice quivering.

She's right. I don't want to write off my accomplishments as merely the game's handiwork. The enthusiasm and passion we pour into the piano isn't some hackneyed cliché. My heart rejoices and races whenever my fingers dance across the keyboard. Despair darkens everything in front of me when I can't get the piano to sound the way it does in my head. I hate it. I want to quit. But the second after I have those thoughts, I miss it unbearably and want to go back to it.

"Yeah…you're right. We're sick. I know we are. We've got Piano Fever."

"Piano Fever, eh? …Yeah, you might very well be infected with it, Mashiro." Kon enviously closed her eyes and quietly continued, "I'm different. My piano is a means to an end. I'm positive that in the near future you'll become someone out of my reach, Mashiro." She bit her bottom lip. "But I can't lose. I absolutely can't lose to you until high school." Each word she spoke overflowed with indescribable anguish.

I had no words for her desperate attempt to motivate herself—her sentence was meant more for her than me.

Kon had a secret. Our current conversation told me her secret involved the piano. Honestly, I was frustrated. I wished she would open up and share the burden causing her to suffer. But I had a weird conviction that she would never tell me, no matter how much I pestered her about it. The secret she harbored was one she had pledged to take to the grave and see through until the end alone.

♪♪♪

KON'S anteroom was stuffed with a large assortment of flowers and bouquets.

"Wow! Now this is something else!"

"Most of them are from people related to my father. The room is too small for both us and the flowers. We won't be able to relax here. Can we discuss our plans for our performance in your anteroom?"

"Sure thing," I happily agreed to her request.

She grinned from ear to ear as soon as she spotted the bouquets from the boys in my room. "Are these from Kou and Sou?"

"Yup. What color were the flowers they gave you? I don't think navy-blue flowers exist, so did they go with pink?"

"I didn't get any flowers from them."

"You didn't?"

Sou's one thing, but is it even theoretically possible for Kou not to give flowers to his beloved little sister?

Stunned, I blinked repeatedly at her. She joyfully put her hands together.

"That Kou sure is smooth when he wants to be."

"I wonder what he's after this time."

Our voices had been perfectly in sync. We looked at each other in surprise before bursting out into laughter. Afterwards, we talked about how great it would be if our four-handed piano performance could be just as in sync while we double-checked each other's music. Around the time we finished our final checks, the announcer's voice came over the anteroom speakers, informing us that intermission was over.

It was time.

"See you on the stage."

"Yeah. Meet you on stage."

We high-fived, carefully adjusting the impact. I went to the left stage wing and Kon went to the right stage wing. Matching our timing to the announcement, we proceeded to our pianos, which had been set facing each other on the stage. The audience applauded wildly for us in our matching cheongsams.

I feel a great deal more comfortable now compared to the first performance. I want to enjoy myself to the fullest now that I'm here.

"Good luck," Aoi whispered encouragingly from where she sat as my page-turner.

"Thank you. I'm counting on you."

I nodded visibly and waited for Kon's signal.

Tchaikovsky – *The Nutcracker Suite* for Two Pianos

The score had been originally composed to be performed by an orchestra for the Nutcracker ballet. This musical suite is something Tchaikovsky rearranged for the piano. The following selection of eight pieces from the ballet score comprises *The Nutcracker Suite*: Miniature Overture, Marche, Dance of the Sugar Plum Fairy, Russian Dance (Trepak), Arabian Dance, Chinese Dance, Reed Flutes, and Waltz of the Flowers.

These songs are frequently played during the Christmas season in stores, lending to the assumption that practically everyone has heard them in passing at least once.

The opening cheerful melody is to be played rhythmically. The

Natsu

"Dance of the Sugar Plum Fairy" slows down the tempo and is to be played in a way that gives a sense of mystery. "Trepak" is a vigorous race across the keys. The mistakes I had been worried about were nonexistent, bringing an unintentional smile to my lips as I played.

Why is this so much fun?!

I could easily sense the audience's favorable reaction. Honing my senses to the max, I felt like I was playing with my back against Kon's. Our sound blended, syncing so flawlessly that Kanako later remarked, "The timing of your every breath was exactly the same. It scared me!"

Natsu

We flipped the toy box brimming with sparkling toys upside down, colorfully and vividly painting the auditorium with our music. The final piece, "Waltz of the Flowers", is to be played slowly and romantically. We rushed up the rippling arpeggio, beating out the jaunty waltz rhythm. I played the bass taking Kon's hand in mind, as if I were escorting her. She responded by bringing out the whirling, bouncy primary melody, like she was twirling under my raised hand.

We removed our hands from the keyboard simultaneously after letting out the final note, stood, and walked to the center of the stage to meet. Taking each other's hand, we bowed as the screams of "Bravo! Bravo!" shook the walls of the auditorium. Waves of people jumped to their feet to applaud us. Panting, Kon and I looked at each other, beaming with pure satisfaction. It was a feeling I had never felt before.

The other girl's "Concerto #7 For 3 Pianos" and Miss Ayumi's "Hungarian Rhapsody" were all breathtakingly phenomenal. Despite the fact that our performance was meant to be a recital, the calls for an encore were so unending that Miss Ayumi returned to the stage with a wry smile. She bowed to the audience and sat before the piano once again.

Completely under the assumption that she only planned on greeting the audience, we exchanged startled glances. The final song, not listed in any program, was Chopin's "Nocturne No. 8 Op. 27-2". Goose bumps rippled across my skin from the very first note. The enchanting droplets of sound resembled bubbles rising from the finest-quality champagne, pleasantly resonating throughout the auditorium. In the center of the bright stage, Miss Ayumi's porcelain hands elegantly flew across the keys.

Silence reigned over the audience. Everyone was so enraptured by her performance that they even forgot to breathe. The last, quiet notes gently swirled into the air before disappearing like melting snow. A Nocturne you wanted to listen to on repeat forever.

My first recital ended emotionally; I had been moved to tears.

♫♫♫

WE descended into the lobby to greet our friends and family who were in attendance. A crowd of people were waiting for us, quickly sectioning the performers into separate groups. Hanaka, who had spotted me first, ran over to me, handkerchief at the ready.

"Mashiro! You performed your very best! You made this sister of yours cry!"

"Ehehe. Thank you for coming," I giggled. Then I bowed to the two tall guys standing directly behind her. "Hello. I'm Mashiro Shimao. I've heard a lot about you from my older sister."

The guy with the short green hair was most likely her boyfriend. He flashed a friendly grin. His chill-guy persona screamed of his popularity with the ladies.

I'm guessing that's Tomoi beside him?

Tomoi looked like a serious guy with black hair and black eyes—a rarity in this world—as his defining feature. The cool one was undisputedly Shinji.

Sis, your sole interest in attractive guys has yet to change.

"Wow. What a reliable little sister we have right here. And a gorgeous one, at that!" he began. "Ah, I forgot to introduce myself. I'm Shinji Mitsui."

"I'm Tomoi Matsuda."

They casually introduced themselves.

Locking completely onto Shinji's flattery, Hanaka was all smiles as she gushed, "Isn't she? She's smart and a skilled pianist too! She's a little sister I can be really proud of!" She wrapped her arms around my shoulder while displaying her full doting-older-sister syndrome.

Happiness and bashfulness fought for supremacy over my emotions.

"Since we're here I want to take a picture with her. Can you do that for me?"

It wasn't Shinji who reached out to take Hanaka's smartphone, but Tomoi.

"I'll take the picture. Why don't the three of you get in it?"

"Wow, you'll do that for us? Thank you so much!" Hanaka showered him with her most radiant smile.

"No problem. I'm not doing much," Tomoi perfunctorily replied.

Something about his expression caught my eye.

Hm? Is it possible he likes…

Attentively observing their interaction, I watched him carefully take the picture, then, almost obnoxiously too carefully, return her smartphone as if it were a valuable crystal. He clearly had been extra cautious not to accidentally brush her fingers in the process.

"I think it came out well."

"Let me see... You're right! You're great at taking pictures, Tomoi!"

Tomoi gazed at my innocent older sister excitedly checking the screen like she was a goddess. While the two of them conversed about the picture, Shinji kicked up a conversation with me.

"When did you start playing the piano? You're really good at it."

I responded back with typical responses while I continued to observe Hanaka and Tomoi interact, careful not to be noticed. For some reason I couldn't put my thumb on, I felt hopelessly bothered by him.

"Mom and Dad said they'd wait for you in your anteroom. Tell me all the nitty-gritty details about today when you get home, okay?"

"Okay. Thanks. Shinji, thank you very much for the bouquet." I parted from them with the bouquet I'd received from Shinji resting across my arms.

It was a cute bouquet with large roses, rice flowers, and pale-yellow spray carnations, accented with eucalyptus leaves.

He's really shrewd.

As I was examining the bouquet, impressed by Shinji's choices, Kou and Sou came over to me.

"So this is where you were."

"Good work out there, Mashiro!"

I instantly knew they came by the sudden surge of chatter from the people around me. Their formal appearance today only furthered the envious glances I received.

"What did you guys think?" I asked.

"Eighty points."

"You were amazing!"

Kou and Sou replied simultaneously.

Sou seemed to be handing me flying marks, but I wasn't sure what the basis for Kou's grade was.

"Is eighty points good?" I questioned, uncertainty coloring my voice.

Kou stared at me and suddenly laughed. Lately, he had a tendency to look at me with the utmost gentleness in his eyes, as he was doing right now. I wish he would stop because it gave me the urge to ask him, "Did you eat some rotten food?"

"Just kidding. You get a hundred points."

"Then just compliment me from the get-go!" I had to retort.

He cracked up laughing at my frown. His grin was a boyish one. Unconsciously, my heart throbbed for him.

You'd be cute if you always showed that honest smile.

"You're leaving already? You look so cute though," Sou said, reluctant to part after I told him that my parents were waiting for me in the anteroom. He took both of my hands in his. "I wanted to take you out for Chinese food."

"That sounds good," Kou interjected.

"I wasn't inviting you," Sou snapped back.

I gently squeezed his hands back before softly letting go. "I don't want to make my parents wait too long. I'm heading home after I say goodbye to Miss Ayumi. Thank you for the flowers."

"...If you must." Sou hesitantly backed down. His disappointment, tinged with loneliness, squeezed my heart.

Why is he so attached to me? He's like a baby bird that I accidentally imprinted on. I wonder if I turned his attachment switch on the moment I handed him the origami grand piano on that footbridge.

"Let's hang out again, okay?" I stood up on my tiptoes to pat him on the head. He sheepishly smiled back at me.

"Spoiling him too much won't do Sou any good," Kou spat in exasperation, sounding like a dad.

♪♪♪

OVER summer break, I made a habit of going to Kon's house to play the piano. Miss Chisako constantly called to invite me over, insisting, "It'd be a shame to let the annex we built and the two pianos that we bought for the recital to go to waste, so please come over and practice whenever you have the time." At first, I modestly turned her down, but it was starting to feel like I was being rude for constantly refusing, so I gratefully accepted her kind offer.

The first day I went to her house for practice, Kon and I played a four-handed performance on the same piano. Miss Chisako requested that we wear the matching cheongsams from our recital for the small performance.

"You know how you did your four-handed performance on two pianos for the recital? I was deeply dismayed that I could only take pictures of you girls from different angles."

Apparently, Miss Chisako and Miss Sakurako had hired a cameraman, who set up a costly video camera and a digital camera with sniper-rifle-length lenses on it, in the middle of the auditorium.

"Oh, Mother! Did you make Mashiro succumb to your whims again just because you wanted to get a picture of the two of us together?" The corner of Kon's eyes sharply turned up.

"Now, now," I soothed her, "If she's pleased with something as easy as this, I'm happy to comply."

When I thought of everything her mothers did for me, letting them take a picture of me in the dress they had custom-made couldn't even begin to pay back the interest on my debt to them. Besides, getting to play alongside Kon was always a blissful time for me too. I smiled from where I sat in front of the piano at Miss Chisako, who was fussing happily over the camera angle. Donning the same matching dress from the recital, Kon seemed rather content sitting beside me, for all her complaining.

"Want to play from the 'Waltz of the Flowers' then?" Kon suggested.

That was Hanaka's favorite song. If she were here right now, she would be bouncing up and down alongside Miss Chisako.

"Sure. I still have it memorized, so I'm okay without the sheet music."

"I'm fine without it too. Let's start then."

We looked at each other's faces, inhaled, and dropped our fingers on the keyboard. The euphoria of being one that I had felt during the recital engulfed me once again. Kon's sound truly sparkled and dazzled. The joy I experienced playing alongside her was special; not even I could understand why warmth filled me whenever I was with her. She was simply an irreplaceable treasure to me.

♪♪♪

Natsu

HAVING cleared the immediate goal of performing well at the recital, I reset my sights on the music competition that was supposed to take place in three years. According to Kon's information, a large-scale piano competition for students was going to be put on in October of our second year in middle school.

Participants had to be in middle school or higher, and would be divided into middle school, high school, and university divisions. The winner of the university division would be given the special privilege of performing alongside the JNK Symphony.

Today marked the first time Kon and I would have an in-depth chat about the competition. There was a fireworks festival going on, so we finished our piano practice by early evening. Miss Sakurako was to join us later for dinner at a traditional Japanese restaurant situated on high ground with a clear view of the fireworks.

"You don't have to take me to dinner too—"

"Stop being modest! Accept our whims!"

After our routine debate, I gave in again as always.

"Why don't you just give up already?" Kon whispered to me.

Aaah, the size of the debt I want to repay after I make it big is growing with a snowball effect…

With Miss Chisako's help, I donned a high-quality, plain-woven hemp cloth kimono and sat on the spacious veranda facing the courtyard. Japanese morning glories decorated my obi, while Kon's had fireworks. The mid-August evening breeze had become cooler. We listened quietly to the evening cicadas chirp in the distance for some time.

"Something about the cicadas you hear at night makes me feel terribly lonely," Kon softly confessed.

"I agree. I wonder what this feeling is."

"…Maybe it's homesickness," she whispered, staring into the distant sky. "…want…to…" she continued as she pressed her hands together in prayer, her voice so tiny that it was barely a voice.

"Kon?"

"Hehe. It's nothing. Just a prayer!" The gloom vanished from her countenance. "We were going to talk about the music competition, right? Let me think. For the preliminaries, you must pick one song out of five categories. I believe the finals were from J.S. Bach's Sinfonias. In *Hear My Heart*, Mashiro chose Ravel's 'Pavane for a Dead Princess' as her free song."

"Ravel… I'm gonna have to practice hard to play his songs."

"You have three more years to go. You'll do fine if you keep at your current pace," Kon declared, giving me her stamp of approval.

I hope that's really the case.

I gazed up at the faraway sky, swinging my dangling, geta clad feet from where I sat on the veranda. The light seeping through the gaps of the trailing clouds dyed the area dark orange.

"You aren't going to enter this competition, Kon?"

"Nope. I won't. I'll be participating in Seio Academy's competition." Kon followed my lead and gazed out at the same sky, reaching her dainty white hands towards it. She shaded her eyes from the setting sun, then suddenly sighed. "I plan to win that competition and accomplish my goal without fail."

"…Can I ask what your goal is?" I timidly ventured.

She tilted her head, smiling self-derisively. "Kinda pointless for me to hide it now… I came to this world to take back someone very dear to me," she declared, then angled her chin away. She stayed perfectly still as though she were waiting for some kind of punishment to befall her.

Completely at a loss, I was left speechless.

I knew it. Kon knows why she's in this world. How come she knows when I don't? What in the world is going on?

Finally, she relaxed her entire body. She turned toward me with a piercing stare. "…I won't lose, Mashiro. I absolutely won't lose to you at Seio."

BZZZ-BRRZ-BZZZ

The evening cicadas' calls seemed to grow ten times louder, so that they were deafening.

CG 17: Fireworks (Kou & Tobi)

MISS Sakurako wasn't the only one awaiting us at the luxurious traditional Japanese restaurant on the hill. Believe it or not, even Kou and the Yamabuki siblings were there.

"Eh?! Why...?" Kon was uncharacteristically surprised. She seemed unaware there would be other guests joining us.

"Is this a game event?" I asked in a whisper. She vehemently shook her head.

"I don't know... But this event didn't exist in the game."

This has been bothering me for a while now, but I have the sneaking suspicion that our Hear My Heart knowledge and experience isn't very useful. I should've destroyed all the event flags a long time ago, yet I frequently encounter Kou and Sou. It's one thing for me not to know what's going on considering I've never played the remake version, but it's strange even Kon is unable to predict what's going to happen next.

"Maybe this is no longer the *Hear My Heart* we know," I offered.

Kon thoughtfully lowered her eyes, nodding. "Probably... Or it's possible you've entered the Love Triangle Route I didn't clear."

Love Triangle Route?!

Kon clearly frowned, while I was still reeling in shock. "I don't think that's what's happened, but I'm mentioning it as a possibility. I've heard balancing the affection parameters for the Love Triangle Route is near impossible, and there were no guides or information on it when I played. Isn't it too improbable for you to have coincidentally ended up on the route that no one has gotten before?"

"Yeah, you've got a good point there."

"Let's not worry about it too much. Okay?" she emphasized, sounding like she was trying to convince herself more than me.

Miss Chisako greeted us with an explanation for the extra members, "I thought it would be lonely with just us girls, so I extended an invitation to them as well. I haven't had the chance to see the Yamabuki siblings since last year's Christmas party."

You only feel lonely because you reserved the entire private VIP room...

"I thought this was meant to be a dinner party for the family. You should've just rented a smaller room," Kon grumbled under her breath.

"A smaller room? How could I do that when this room has the best view?" Miss Chisako defended, surprised Kon would suggest otherwise.

She prioritized the view over the price and size...

Kon and I exchanged secret glances and sighed together.

"I'm thrilled you invited me, Auntie. I love fireworks. I wish Ayumi could've come," Arisa said with a smile. She was wearing a short-sleeved cardigan dress. Prince Tobi also tactfully thanked Miss Chisako and Miss Sakurako for their invitation.

Prince Tobi wore a khaki summer jacket paired with white hemp pants and a loose necktie to accentuate the look. He exuded his trademark handsome young man aura as always.

As for Kou, he was smoothly pulling off a classic look in an *Ojiya-chijimi* long kimono. From the way he had tied his obi low around his waist, to his lightly tied-back hair, he modeled Japanese traditional clothing so well he seemed to walk right off the pages of a storybook. He was the epitome of everything I wanted in a man; his current outfit was a feast for my eyes.

Aaah, how vexing. It really ticks me off when I think about how incredibly cool he looks.

"*You look stunning!* A picture of perfection in a kimono," Prince Tobi praised, half in English and half in Japanese, as he walked over to Kon and me. Apparently he had attended our recital in May, because he started talking about it. "I've always held the opinion that Ayumi's recitals are not to be missed, but I was especially correct in my choice to go this last time. Kon, you mentioned that you'll be coming to Seio once you graduate, yes? Our family manages the academy."

"You do? I've been looking forward to attending after hearing about the academy from my brother," Kon replied sociably.

"The academy's prestige will rise with a student like you in attendance."

"Thank you very much. I hope I can live up to your expectations."

They smiled at each other—Tobi, the living embodiment of a prince, next to the girl whose beauty far exceeded the average beautiful girl. Although it should've been an enviously picture-perfect scene, I couldn't help but get the feeling they were sounding each other out.

Kon, your eyes aren't smiling at all…

I quietly took my leave and headed farther into the room at Miss Sakurako's suggestion. We had an unhindered view of the river from the room-length window, and we could even see people running around preparing to launch the fireworks.

Out of consideration for Prince Tobi and Arisa, who weren't used to sitting in the traditional seiza position—which involved sitting on the heels while kneeling with the tops of the soles lying flat on the floor—a rug was rolled out across the tatami mats, with a large table and chairs set on top.

Thank goodness! Now I don't have to worry about my legs going numb while we eat.

As I was inquisitively observing the scenery outside, Kou approached me from behind. "Good evening, Mashiro. You look surprisingly nice in a kimono," he remarked, making his usual gibe, when I turned around.

"Good evening, Kou. Your greeting had a gratuitous addition."

"You think so? I'm guessing the morning glory obi is Auntie's tastes." Kou leaned in ever so slightly and softly whispered, "It really suits you well. I'm sure Sou will be bitter about missing this." He brushed a stray hair behind my ear.

A single lock of hair had slipped from my traditional hairdo. Heat rushed to my cheeks at his gentle touch. *Wait a minute. His behavior toward me has been weird for a while now. Maybe he's still playing that game with me—the 'Fall Hard for Me' Game.* The thought, along with my own pathetic sense at naming things, sent chills running down my spine.

"Um, thanks… Anyway, you sure love to tease Sou. Not a very nice hobby you have there," I scolded.

"Sou's reactions are amusing. He's normally this aloof guy who acts indifferent toward everything that goes on around him. But when it comes to you, he turns serious and gets worked up like he's a totally different person," Kou replied, with the most pleased smile. Charming fiend.

I'm sure he teases him because they're close friends, but I wish he wouldn't use me as an excuse for his antics.

"You, on the other hand, have got a seriously bad personality. Anyway, don't go out of your way to tell Sou about tonight."

"Haha. Are you hinting that you want tonight to be just our little secret, Mashiro?" Kou put his hand on the sliding door frame right beside my face, placing his other hand on the other side of me simultaneously. Once I was trapped between his arms, he peered into my eyes. "I like that kind of play. It makes my heart race," he whispered suggestively.

His voice tickled my every preference—my heart nearly skipped a beat as a conditioned reflex—but I somehow held my ground. I'm firmly opposed to the way he tries to test and feel people out.

"You've gone too far with your game!" I slammed my hands against his chest, shoving him away with all my strength.

He moved back without much resistance. "What's wrong? Your cheeks are bright-red."

"This is why I'm saying you have a horrible personality and hobby to boot!" I complained as he feigned a shocked expression.

Kon, who came over to us while I hadn't been paying attention, sighed loudly. "Kou. Haven't I told you to quit bullying Mashiro?"

"Bully? Moi? Never! I'm just teasing her. C'mon, don't give me that scary stare-down." Kou deflected and patted his beloved little sister on the head.

Kon shook her head, prying his hand off. "Don't come running to me if you end up regretting it," she warned cryptically.

An abundance of food was carried out not long after. In the blink of an eye, fine dishes, exquisitely arranged in small bowls and flat plates, filled the large table, which was carved out of a single slab of Yakushima cedar. Prince Tobi and Miss Sakurako brought the Edo Kiriko cut glasses, filled with cold sake, to their lips. On the other hand, Arisa and Miss Chisako didn't drink alcohol.

BOOM! CRACKLE! POP! POP!

The sudden rumble of earthshaking booms nearly had me leaping out of my seat.

"It's started!"

Following Miss Sakurako's enthusiastic voice, I turned my attention to the open windows. Fireworks burst through the dark night, like fiery blooms among the stars, captivating me. They bloomed into brilliant lights and vivacious colors before fading, leaving a puff of smoke in their wake. Prince Tobi and Arisa whooped as Japan's representative firework, the chrysanthemum firework, exploded. It burst into a sphere of colored stars, transforming from crimson to blue and leaving a visible trail of golden sparks.

Without realizing it, I had been so entranced by the fireworks that my chopsticks were dangling from my fingers.

"Mashiro, that's bad manners," Kou pointed out from where he sat beside me.

"Ah, I'm sorry." I quickly returned my chopsticks to their holder.

"The way you genuinely listen to others when they point something out to you is seriously adorable." Kou smiled devilishly, gazing at me.

"How long are you going to keep testing me?" I demanded, unable to stop my curiosity.

Is it impossible for us to trust each other as normal friends?

"…I meant that as a real compliment though," he pouted, dissatisfaction coloring his features.

That was a lot like The Boy Who Cried Wolf, considering all his previous actions and words until now.

"I'll never come to love you, Kou. You can rest assured about that," I promised him wholeheartedly.

He pursed his lips, selfishly muttering, "I'm less happy about that now."

Heroine's Results
Target Character: Kou Narita
Event: During the Night of the Fireworks

Original Heroine's Results
Target Character: Tobi Yamabuki
New Event: Progress Observation
CLEAR

♫♫♫

THE hectic season had circled back around again; fall was truly, egregiously teeming with back-to-back school events. Athletic meets, choir lessons, and field trips mercilessly chiseled away at my stamina and emotional strength, draining me to a husk. Once, I'd accidentally fallen asleep in the drawing room before one of my Thursday piano lessons. It was horrible.

"Mashiro, you have bags under your eyes," is all the usually strict Miss Ayumi had said to me that day. I believe it's because I was sorely lacking the ability to concentrate, which made it pointless for her to give me detailed directions.

The "Sinfonia, No. 7" I had worked so hard to polish was filled with consecutive wrong notes. I had moved on to Bach's "Sinfonia", having completed his "Invention" long ago. Just a little more practice and I would be ready to take on "The Well-Tempered Clavier Collection". Unlike the other songs, it's distinct in its demand for the left hand to press down with a complex touch.

But I practiced so hard! Mortified, I secretly cried in the back seat of Mom's car when she drove me home.

Immediately after I got home, I threw open my music book and focused on practicing the parts I'd failed at during my lesson.

I need to make sure my left hand plays as well as my right. No, that's not it. I have to do that part again. Oh, that sounded right. I'll play it again so I don't forget how it felt.

Mom, who came to check on me, quietly left when she saw my hands dancing across the keyboard like I was possessed.

♫♫♫

WEEKDAYS, I practiced on Aine. On Saturdays after the solfège, I took my boxed lunch with me to Kon's and practiced on the grand piano in the Genda annex. So went my weekly routine. Gratitude wasn't even the beginning of what I felt toward Kon and the Genda family for allowing me to borrow their annex.

Kon's Papa, who I only met once, was a man of imposing stature and a calm demeanor. He spoke to me in his rich baritone voice, "Thank you for always being such good friends with Kon."

Then he patted me on the head as I nervously greeted him, thanking him for everything the Gendas did for me. Soon he disappeared like the wind. His schedule was booked to the last second of every day.

The final month of the second quarter finally arrived. I received an invitation to a Christmas party from Miss Sakurako while I was practicing on the Genda estate's grand piano. A maid usually brought me tea, so I was startled to see Miss Chisako appear with the tray that day.

Can I be frank? Carrying a food tray is not suitable for someone in a fancy dress.

"We were hoping you would come to the Christmas party this year. And we have a favor to ask of you. Both Sakurako and myself want to hear you play in an ensemble again!"

"You do? B-But there are only two weeks until the party."

If it were a solo performance, I could play Chopin's "Revolutionary Etude," which I recently received full marks on, but I don't think there's enough time to practice with someone else.

Kon knitted her eyebrows disapprovingly at Miss Chisako. "Mother, don't ask for the unreasonable."

Kon knew I had added experimenting with Ravel on top of my normal piano practice recently. She was being considerate of how hard it would be to force in ensemble practice on top of everything else I had on my plate.

I had already let Miss Ayumi know, "I want to participate in a music competition once while I'm in middle school."

After thoughtfully considering it, she'd answered, "All right. Since you are going to participate, let's aim for first place."

Thus, Miss Ayumi's Spartan training had increased tenfold, making me regret telling her so soon.

"But her ensemble last year was spectacular," Miss Chisako pleaded, "We want to hear it again. If you don't have enough time to practice, we'll settle for an easy song!"

We couldn't just halfheartedly toss together an easy song, especially when we would be performing in front of an audience. I strongly believe that no one who takes music seriously could settle for putting on a slapdash performance.

"Mother!" Sure enough, Kon's shapely eyebrow shot up under her bangs. I quickly placed my hand on her arm.

"Don't be mad. Christmas only comes once a year. I want to go all out too."

"...Mashiro..."

Miss Chisako, despondent after taking Kon's reprimands, instantly lit up. "Mashiro, thank you for listening to our whims! You're welcome to practice in the annex on weekdays too. Come Sundays as well. I've already informed Kou and Sou about the party. I'm positive they'll be delighted when they hear you've given the okay."

"You always do so much for me. I will do my very best to make sure you enjoy it as much as possible," I responded, smiling.

But I was depressed on the inside. *Why can't the ensemble be another four-handed performance with Kon? If Miss Chisako's already finished making the necessary arrangements with the boys, this could very well be an event. That'd explain why she's being pushier about this than normal.*

I was starting to get the feeling that no matter how much we resisted it, everything in our lives was bound to twist and distort in an attempt to follow *Hear My Heart*'s plot.

I can't even imagine what an ensemble involving the four of us would be like. That said, I think there'll be arguments over the pairing this time if I suggest forming duos like last year. Sou will absolutely insist on pairing with me, and assuming Kou's still playing his games, I can count on him trying to weasel his way in.

Ah, why don't Kon and I pair up, and Sou and Kou can pair up?!

...Yeah, that'd never happen.

Miss Chisako placed the tray on the table before leaving the annex. Kon poured me a cup of Guangxi tea. I filled it to the brim with milk, transforming it into milk tea. The tea itself lacked almost all bitterness, tinged instead with a natural sweetness that came from the flower's nectar. Its flavor profile took me by surprise as I rarely drank Chinese tea.

"This is really delicious and relaxing."

"I'm glad you like it. I always drink this tea in the winter... Sorry about Mother. I'm not trying to defend her actions, but this might be happening because of an event."

"Ah, you think so too? I thought it was weird for both Kou and Sou to be involved."

"Yeah… As long as you aren't moved from the heroine's role, like it or not, those two will probably always be there."

Kon's theory was that I could cut my connection to Kou and Sou if I stopped playing the piano.

She's probably right. Yet, despite knowing that, it's impossible for me to give up the piano.

"Yeah. But lately I've started to come to terms with it. Sou is a cutie, and I don't hate Kou either. I think I'd be more heartbroken if we suddenly stopped seeing each other altogether."

"For heaven's sake! You always let yourself get attached like that," Kon complained, puffing out her cheeks.

Her intimate remark was heartening, but an eerie sense of déjà vu overcame me.

Have we had this conversation before?

"I'll stop worrying about it then, if you're fine with things this way, Mashiro!" she cheerfully declared, ending the topic there.

After we finished enjoying the warm tea, we immediately started discussing the ensemble. Together, we scoured the plethora of sheet music lining the shelves in the annex.

"Balancing the sound with two pianos, a violin, and cello is too difficult. That said, we don't have time to rearrange a song either."

"If you don't mind, why don't the three of you form a trio instead? Don't you think something by Brahms would fit the party atmosphere with its floweriness?"

"Hmm, but what about you then?"

"I'll get permission to do a solo. I think our mothers want to hear your ensemble rather than mine. They're taking advantage of your kindness to go overboard, like they're your groupies. They're so pushy!"

I pacified Kon's resurgence of fury, then started searching for sheet music for a piano trio.

"Oh, maybe I'll go with this: Brahms' Piano Trio No.1, Op. 8, First Movement."

"Geh. Mashiro! Are you viciously trying to drive yourself up a wall?!"

"…Good point. Is it too much? I love this song though."

In contrast to its exceedingly high difficulty level, the song is flowery and bright. The piano, violin, and cello all compete for dominance without giving ground, upping the bar for one another as the song progresses.

"I love Mendelssohn's Piano Trio too, but it's hardcore. Aah, so many options, so little time to choose!"

"Go with the first one. I adore the third movement."

"Oh, me too!"

Despite passionately discussing our favorite Piano Trios while picking out the sheet music, I wasn't getting anywhere with a decision. In the end, I decided to choose after I'd heard Kou and Sou's opinion. Kon pulled out her smartphone and called Kou on the spot. Kou was able to get ahold of Sou, and we arranged to meet up at the Genda estate at one in the afternoon on Sunday.

♪♪♪

UNDER the cloudy sky that threatened to snow at any moment, I buried my face in my scarf and walked up to the Genda estate's gate. The magnificent Japanese cypress gate unlocked the instant I pressed the intercom, swinging open without a sound.

At a passing glance, the Genda estate looked like a traditional Japanese-style mansion that was probably under the cultural heritage society's protection, but beneath its exterior hid a high-tech home with modern security. I trudged straight for the annex without stopping by the main house. It was five minutes before the time we had agreed to meet up, but Kou and Sou were already there.

"Hello, Sou. It's been a while, Kou."

Sou came over my house about once a week after school, but I hadn't seen Kou since summer break. The fireworks' festival had been the last time we met up.

Kou looked up at me from where he leisurely relaxed on the sofa. "Long time no see… Did you lose some weight?" He frowned slightly.

I've been so busy this fall and haven't really had much of an appetite either. I don't think I've lost enough weight to warrant attention though.

"I understand the piano is important to you, but take care of yourself too," he continued, unusually upfront with his thoughts.

What's wrong with him? Should I be worried?!

He sighed at my stiff expression. "When will you stop giving me that look?"

"You reap what you sow, Kou," Kon bluntly chimed in. Kou fell silent.

I sat down beside Sou and peered over at the sheet music he was flipping through. "Oh, is this Chopin's Piano Trio?"

"Yeah. It's only ten minutes long. I brought it from home thinking it might be a good option."

Closer inspection revealed the margins were covered in notes. They were neat notes but clearly indicated that this sheet music belonged to someone who had used it.

If it's been used before in the Shiroyama house, that'd mean…

I carefully inspected Sou's face. He slyly inclined his head.

"Don't want used sheet music? This is one Mom left behind."

"Don't be ridiculous! Please give me the honor of looking through it!"

"Haha! Suddenly sounding formal over something like this is just like you, Mashiro."

"Because it's sheet music with notes by *the* world's Morikawa! …Ah, sorry."

"No worries. I'm happier if you don't change how you act for me." Sou smiled brightly, laying the sheet music on top of my open hand with a fwump.

Excited, I ignored everything else and started paging through the score from the beginning. His mother's interpretations were written by the tempo instructions, along the motif, and in the margins. Notes like "Don't rush too much" and "Watch out for the left hand" filled the white spaces.

Wow! This is so relatable! Even a pianist of Risa Morikawa's caliber practiced while noting her mistakes so she could improve through trial and error. I have to work even harder!

Kou, who had taken up a position on the sofa directly opposite of the table, suddenly butted in, "I don't believe it. Sou, did you actually tell Mashiro about Risa?"

"I did. Quite a while ago. Wasn't it around this time last year when we discussed it?"

"Hm? …Yeah, that sounds about right." I studied Kou's face, curious as to why he seemed so shocked. "Is it that surprising he told me?"

Without answering me, Kou eyed Sou provokingly, "...You're really serious, Sou." Undaunted, Sou returned his gaze.

"I've been saying as much for a long time now."

"Midori Misaka, was it? What do you plan to do about your fiancée, hm?"

My heart leapt out of my chest at the name Kou had mentioned.

So Sou's fiancée is named Midori Misaka... Hang on? Isn't that—

Kon immediately caught on and forced her way into the boys' conversation. "Sou, your fiancée is named Midori Misaka?"

"Huh? ...Yeah. She's a cousin on my stepmother's side."

"No way. How can that be? Because she's supposed to..." Kon trailed off, her eyes as wide as saucers.

...She's supposed to be my support character.

"Should this world flow along the game's course, a girl named Midori Misaka will be a student at Seio with us. She should be of great help to you..."

Recalling what Kon told me before only added to my confusion.

The girl who is supposed to be my support character is Sou's fiancée?

"Kon, what's gotten into you all of a sudden? You okay?" Kou asked.

"...I'm sorry. It's nothing." She took a deep breath, relaxing her tensed shoulders. "I was just a little surprised because I've heard her name before."

"Probably because she's the heir to the Misaka Conglomerate. Does she attend the same school as you?"

Sou jumped in to answer, "No. Midori lives in England most of the time. She rarely returns to Japan... Besides, as I've told you both, our engagement was an arbitrary decision by our parents and grandparents—neither of us wants it," he spat, not even trying to hide his disgust.

"That's not the problem here," Kou retorted with a stern face. "I'm saying you have to take your parents' decision seriously. What if Mashiro gets serious about you when she's older? She'll be the one who gets hurt. Don't lead her on under false pretenses."

"Since when have I been leading Mashiro on? I could say the same exact thing to you."

Before I realized it, they were both standing combatively, the mood explosive.

I stepped between them, trying to stop them from taking it too far. "Stop! I'm fully aware Sou has a fiancée and I'm fine with it. I won't get serious about him romantically, and I don't feel like I'm being led on. By either of you. Anyway, forget that stuff and pick a song already! Okay? We don't have time. We won't make it in time for the party if we don't hurry."

"She's right. You're only wasting time debating. We don't know what will happen in the future," Kon backed me up, assertively ending the argument for the day. Kou shook his head as he sat back down and sighed. Sou fell silent, biting his cheek.

...Anyway, that surprised me. I didn't think Kou would speak so defensively on my behalf. He might've only said it to provoke Sou, but I was touched by his sincerity. But I feel like Sou's naïve attachment to me is only growing stronger. I love him as a friend and want him to be happy... These aren't romantic feelings.

"I'm not lying," Sou stated.

"I won't get serious about him." My words had been an unintentional knife in Sou's heart.

"I'm sorry. I didn't mean it that way," I frantically apologized.

His lips sorrowfully formed the ghost of a smile. "I'm sorry too. I don't want to put you on the spot either, Mashiro."

My guilt only grew worse whenever we spoke about it. If I wasn't willing to return his feelings, I should've put distance between us. While my mind understood that was the right thing to do, I struggled to enact it in reality.

"Please...Mashiro...please be the one who won't leave me. Don't go anywhere."

I had been a hopeless case from that moment. I couldn't forget his expression when he'd made that plea.

We ended up deciding to perform Chopin's "Piano Trio Op.8 in G minor, First Movement". This particular trio isn't performed often for concerts, but I'm fond of the way it was composed. Although it has a few of the grace notes Chopin is known for, the classical, conversational duet between the theme and antiphon is beautiful.

Kon made copies of the different instrumental parts for us, and we went straight into practice. The boys, having brought their instruments, quickly finished tuning, and jumped right into rehearsing their parts. Kon volunteered to be my page-turner, to which I gratefully accepted.

Thanks to having listened to the CD countless times, I had a good idea of the harmonic and melodic progression. I roughly practiced the sound while confirming Miss Morikawa's notes. Somewhere in my head, I registered the vague sounds of the violin and cello. The spacious annex allowed us to practice without distracting each other. Amid the sounds of three different instruments playing at once, we concentrated on our individual sounds alone.

♪♪♪

THE following Sunday, we decided to test out what we sounded like together for the first time. I was grateful that Kon tagged along to assist in checking our sound balance.

"Don't drag us down, Mashiro."

"And don't screw up the high-notes, Kou."

Sou sighed as he watched our standoff, sparks flying between our threatening chuckles and snide smiles. "You both better not rush ahead with the song just to compete with each other."

As you'd expect from the tempo instruction Allegro con fuoco—to perform quickly in a fiery manner—the song is dominated by a dramatic melody. In the beginning, the violin plays the principal melody and the piano repeats the same theme, as if it's chasing after the violin. The cello steadily supports the back-and-forth argument between the two instruments.

I thought it went rather well for our first time playing together, but I missed two notes.

Hmm, this is pretty difficult. I thought I was skilled at Chopin's songs, but I think I'm too soft in differentiating the sound of the principal melody from the background melody. Striking the keyboard with fiery passion for the entire song gives it an overdone image, and that's where I'm stuck.

"Sorry, can we go again? I want to drop the tempo slightly and double-check the lesser notes."

"Sure. You good with that, Sou?"

"I'm ready anytime."

We engrossed ourselves in perfecting the trio, with Kon pointing out the sections we needed to improve.

"...Why don't you guys stop here for today? If you practice the parts you need to fix individually, I'm sure you'll be able to match each other better next week," Kon pronounced authoritatively. Thus our practice for the day came to a close.

The short hand of the clock was already past the four. I nodded and eased my stiff fingers. Sending my fingers flying across the keyboard to match the instructions for a fiery playing style for an extended period of time caused my muscles to ache; the palm of my hand spasmed at random. As I was massaging my fingers at the joint, beginning with the thumb, Kou came over to the piano after putting away his violin.

"You'll only end up hurting yourself by pressing that hard."

"Huh?"

"I'll show you the way it's done. Here, lend me your hand."

"It's fine. I'll do it myself."

Kou snatched my hand and began massaging it with his long fingers. He must've been used to doing it for Kon because he was skilled. He knew all the right spots to hit. His hands were unbelievably kind and warm, in contrast to his usual snark. To be frank, it felt heavenly.

"Thanks...but why?"

Why are you doing so much for me?

Tactfully picking up on the unasked question, Kou quietly answered, "To thank you—for playing along with our moms' selfish whims when you're so busy. Besides..." he continued in a husky whisper, "I love your sound, Mashiro."

Unsure of how to respond, I pretended like I hadn't heard him. After all, a compliment like that was bound to move my heart. If he had purposefully said it, knowing what power his words had over me, it would be nothing but sly.

Interlude: A Certain Woman's Confession (???)

I had a sister who was a year younger than me. Her name was Rika. With only a year's difference between us, we'd been raised like twins. My adorable little sister who fumbled over my name, Hana, as a toddler, grew up in the blink of an eye, then breathed her last breath five years ago.

   ...I killed her.

   The sweet girl who waited at the end of the road in front of our house for me to come back from kindergarten, because I started attending school a year before her.

   The kind girl who quietly let me lean on her shoulder to cry when I experienced my first heartbreak in middle school.

   ...I killed her.

   It can be said that a single, incredibly stupid push is all it takes for one's situation to drastically deteriorate, like a single domino toppling over the entire row. My situation had been exactly like that.

   For some reason, I wasn't able to tell Rika about my boyfriend, who was two years older than me, who I started dating when I began high school. Had I been afraid of making her feel left out? Or had I just been shy? For whatever trivial reason forgotten to me now, I hid my boyfriend's existence from my little sister.

   Being the stupidly optimistic person I was, I never considered the possibility they would run into each other somewhere without me knowing. By the time I had learned that, "Anything can happen in life," it was too late.

Rika had fallen in love with my boyfriend. My wise little sister had seen right through Tomoi's plain appearance, to his hidden sincerity and earnestness.

"Is Tomoi your friend, Hana?"

When she had asked me that question, I should've answered, "No, he's my boyfriend." But in my panic, I chose to dodge the question instead.

"He is. He's an upperclassman I get along very well with," I explained, then added for insurance, "He seems to have feelings for someone else."

"Hmm," she mumbled, "I wonder what kind of person he likes." And sighed.

For the first time in my life, I had lied to my little sister, "Beats me." I tried to push through with the lie to make it seem real with a vague smile.

Rika was only sixteen. I decided to convince myself she would eventually fall in love with someone else.

I had betrayed my only sister in the cruelest, most backhanded way.

♪♪♪

ONE year later: Rika confessed her feelings to Tomoi.

My little sister's heated, unrequited love was shattered in an instant by Tomoi's honesty. "I'm dating Hanaka. I thought you already knew, Rika."

As she possessed a straightforward disposition, Rika came directly to me. "Why didn't you tell me?!" she demanded.

"You've got it wrong. I'm not like that with Tomoi." I continued to dodge the issue, despite my lies crumbling down around me. In that moment, I not only betrayed my sister but my boyfriend as well.

I don't want to hurt my precious little Rika. No, that's not it. I don't want to hurt myself, I thought.

Rika quietly stared at her cowardly older sister for a long time. And then she said, "I'm sorry. I cornered you into this, Hana." She laughed, her expression contorting from the sadness she was suppressing.

My legs trembled; I was unbearably ashamed of my heartlessness. "Sorry. I'm so sorry," I apologized emptily, over and over again, through my tears. Rika smiled softly and forgave me.

Even though it had been my sister's first broken heart, I had gone as far as to steal her chance to cry.

A while later, Rika became obsessed with a certain game—a love simulation game where you can fall in love with fictional boys. I didn't know how to help her.

"Focus your time and energy on real life over some stupid game," I snapped at her once, not sure how else to handle her obsession.

She should have retorted, "What gives you the right to say that?!"

She should have told me off, "And who's fault do you think it is that I'm like this?!"

"Ehehe. I can't stop. He's so cool!" She'd made a dorky grin, looking at me with kind eyes.

I had long since cut off contact with Tomoi. He constantly messaged me, saying we should meet up to have a serious talk about what had happened, but I always turned him down with, "Sorry. I can't do this anymore."

I had loved him. I had been hopelessly in love with him, but my immature choices made a mess of everything.

And then that fateful day came. It was dreadfully cold out. Worried about Rika, who'd gone to take her university entrance exams, I left to meet her on her way back home. She was slowly walking down the sidewalk on the opposite side of a major road.

Slightly hesitating about whether I should call out to her from across the road, I ended up deciding to cross the intersection to meet her instead. I planned on jumping out at her from behind to give her a great big scare.

"Wah! Hana!" Rika would surely look at me with wide eyes before slipping into that dorky smile of hers. I wanted to see that smile.

Annoyed by how slow the signal was, I impatiently pounded the button, then ran across the street when the light finally turned green.

Just a little farther. Just a little more, and I'd be there. The moment I opened my mouth to shout her name—

Rika's back suddenly vanished as though a magic spell had been cast on her.

Confused about what had just happened, I was left standing there, paralyzed with horror. The woman who had been standing next to Rika shrieked in the loudest voice, carrying over a street full of pedestrians.

"Oh my God!"

"A girl fell in!"

"Someone! Call an ambulance!"

Rika? Where's Rika?

Step by step, I advanced like I was walking through fog. Before long, the open abyss of a manhole filled my eyes.

I don't remember much of what had happened afterward. I think I screamed and bawled all day long. I also feel like I hadn't said a single word at all. I repeatedly cursed myself; I should have never crossed the intersection using the pedestrian crosswalk. I should've called out to her from across the street and stopped her. My sister would still be with me if I'd only reached out to her.

They say she hadn't noticed the manhole at her feet because she was gazing at the poster in the game store window. The information was confirmed by the testimony of the woman who had been walking directly behind her.

As soon as I found out, I went back there to confirm it. Tears blurred my vision the very instant that I recognized the stupid poster in the window. The words I saw through the flood of tears formed the title of the love simulation game Rika had been obsessed with. The very game I suspected she would've never gotten so obsessed with had things not gone the way they had with Tomoi.

Tubes were connected all over Rika's body when the doctors had pronounced, "There is a very slim chance of her ever regaining consciousness." Apparently, there was massive damage and swelling in her brain from the impact when she hit the bottom of the manhole.

Dad and Mom had begged to keep her alive, pleading, "As long as there is any chance at all, please let us take it."

But I knew better.

This was my punishment.

Of course it was. I *killed* her.

Rika won't come back until I redeem myself by atoning for my sins. So I decided to take her back, no matter what I had to do.

I've no doubt that by that time I had already...gone **_insane_**.

CG 18: NOT FOUND (Kon)

TIME passed until it was the day of the party. Miss Sakurako and Miss Chisako sent me another dress this year. I pulled out the "What I Owe Them When I Grow up" note to record the date and items I had received.

I'll pay them back a little at a time when I'm old enough to get a job. I couldn't accept it emotionally otherwise. Dad and Mom got that faraway look in their eyes again when they saw the humongous box arrive.

This year, Sou came to pick me up in the Narita family car. Upon seeing Sou in his black tuxedo paired with a charcoal-gray tail jacket, Dad muttered, "Why is Mashiro surrounded by kids like this…"

"Your dress last year was pretty too, but this year's is extra gorgeous."

"Thank you. You look cool too, Sou. You look more grown-up than usual. Maybe it's because of your different hairstyle," I commented in return.

Sou smiled bashfully, red rushing up his ears. "I'm the happiest when you compliment me, Mashiro."

Relief always surged through me whenever I saw his cheerful expressions.

We headed to the Narita estate as we chuckled and giggled over inside jokes. The gigantic Christmas tree was enshrined in the same spot in front of the mansion as it had been last year.

"This tree is awesome! I saw them light it up on my way home last year. I still can't forget how stunning it was!"

"…Mashiro." Sou squeezed my left hand as I was gazing up at the towering tree. "Is it okay if we take a detour when I send you home?"

"Sure. Need to do something?"

"Yeah… Why don't we go inside now? Your hand is freezing." He opened the front door and led me inside.

We headed straight for the dance hall, the gorgeously decorated mansion interior dazzling me. Everyone had already gathered. I spotted Prince Tobi among the guests— yup, I thought he'd be here.

"Mashiro!" Kon, donning the same organdy sleeveless dress as me but in a different color, excitedly ran over to us. The cream-colored dress, which flared out at the giant ribbon on her waist, was a perfect match for her. My dark-purple dress shared the same design again. On both, the pale-pink tulle overlapped like petals.

"Thanks for inviting me! I'm dying to hear your performance, Kon."

"Thank you for coming. I'm also super excited to hear you play!"

Kou was chatting with a red-haired man deeper in the room. The handsome man looked like his older body double, like a much more polished version of Kou.

"Kon, is that man—"

"Yes, our father," Kon confirmed. "He's going in to work late tonight because he wanted to hear us perform. Both the husband and wife are really self-indulgent," she complained, pursing her lips.

Miss Sakurako's a beautiful woman and their father's a handsome man—it's no wonder Kou and Kon ended up with show-stopping looks. It all made sense now.

Kou, finally noticing our presence, came over to us, followed by his papa.

His papa greeted me first, "Hi there. You're Mashiro? I've heard much about you. Thank you for coming to our home today." His voice was a honey-sweet baritone, and I was trapped in his deep violet eyes, numbing me to the core.

He was unbelievably stunning up-close.

"H-Hello. I'm very grateful for all you and your family have done for me. Thank you very much for always going out of your way to have dresses and kimonos custom-made for me."

"Haha," he chuckled.

I ran off my thanks nervously, as if it had been the most critical moment in my life, and dipped my head. Kou's papa softly patted me on the head, drawing a sigh out of me with his flawless touch.

"No worries. Sakurako does it because she loves to. But I understand how my wife feels now. You're an adorable young lady who deserves to be pampered," he said with a grin.

I was paralyzed on the spot. *H-He's cool! Oh no! My heart is pounding out of my chest!*

"What're you taking him seriously for? Obviously it's just flattery," Kou interrupted, scowling at my fangirling.

He's right! That was dangerous! I nearly fell in love! Because unlike a certain someone, he's terribly kind, exudes a magnanimous air, and his looks are spot on with my tastes!

"You must be lacking in confidence if you're talking like that, Kou," his papa teased.

"Zip it. You've finished greeting her. Hurry back to Mom." Kou forcefully shooed his papa away, then sighed. "You're drooling again, Mashiro," he warned after we watched his Papa leave.

Quickly, I wiped my mouth. "There's no drool!"

"I'm saying that you were dreamily staring so hard you practically did."

I was that obvious? ...I need to watch out next time.

After we ate a buffet-style lunch, the time to perform arrived. Kon came to get me while I was enjoying after-dinner tea with Miss Ayumi and the other ladies. I followed her to the piano.

"Oh no, Kon. I think I'm more nervous now than at the recital."

"Probably because it's an ensemble. It's difficult to perfectly match up your sound. But you'll be just fine, Mashiro!"

It was really reassuring to have Kon right beside me as a page-turner. Now several times more relaxed, I flexed my fingers and decided to warm them up first. Once I finished, I let the A note ring out so Kou and Sou could begin tuning as they sat with their instruments out.

Before long, the sound of tuning came to a stop, and with instruments at the ready, they turned their eyes to me. Nodding, I visibly exhaled to signal them.

Chopin – Piano Trio Op.8 in G minor, First Movement

The melody of the violin was sorrowfully delicate, echoing loudly throughout the dance hall. Both Kou and Sou played at a much higher level than they had during our practice sessions. Undaunted, I honed my hearing and concentrated on the piano keys. Kou's violin was bewitching; Sou's cello rang out with deep reverberation. They felt closer to me than ever before. Through the piano, I was one with them.

Natsu

They say that as a Polish man, Chopin was fiercely patriotic and proud of his homeland, which had been continually on the receiving end of oppression and hardship. His style of music drew a line between court music, which had emphasized formal beauty and other passionate and experimental musical styles, giving those who performed his songs several variations of interpretation.

Do you play Chopin the Polish way? Go for an elaborate and precise Chopin? Or do you prefer the passionate, overwhelmingly emotional Chopin?

I didn't know which was correct. However, I wanted to perform in a way that would have a lasting effect on all who listened to my performance.

Play the treble like it's twinkling; hammer the bass as if driving a wedge in. The sound of our three instruments rose, heading for the climax, undulating in rounds. I rang out the final two chords and removed my fingers from the keyboard. Loud applause followed.

Everyone stood as they applauded. But despite getting through the song without missing any notes, there were many parts I failed to properly express. Nevertheless, I was genuinely delighted by the audience's raving applause. Even Miss Ayumi applauded without holding back, a pleased smile on her lips.

"Thank you, Kon." I looked up at her as I thanked her for being my page-turner.

"No need to thank me. You were amazing. It was completely different from when you were practicing. You're the type who blossoms in proportion to the number of people listening." She smiled weakly and reiterated, "You were really amazing." Negative emotions, contrary to her words, darkened her eyes.

Why do you look so sad...?

She quickly averted her glance when she saw I was about to say something. I faltered. How could I say anything when she was openly dodging me?

My playing well makes Kon sad?

Crushed under the weight of my doubts and confusion, I had no choice but to pretend I didn't notice.

♪♪♪

KON took a seat before the piano, timing it to match my return to the audience. She chose to play Listz's "Etudes D'execution Transcendante No.4 Mazeppa". As soon as her pure, clear sound rang out, I was overwhelmed by her outstanding technique. Kon used the full force of her arms to violently beat out the opening notes. Yet, contrary to what we witnessed, her sound wasn't wild at all. If anything, the rich sound resonated, expanding.

What skill.

Her range and connection of delicate sounds was enchanting.

Just when I registered that she'd played the romantic theme appearing midway through as a gentle whisper, she raced up the crescendo once again before dizzyingly dashing down it. I got goose bumps from her chords; they were like chiming bells.

How is she at this level when she's still in elementary school? Kon is sprinting full speed down a road I've barely even started on. This performance says it all.

I clapped until my hands hurt and stood from my seat about to go to her, when a sweet, low voice stopped me.

"Mashiro. Your performance was remarkable."

Prince Tobi.

"Thank you very much."

I think this is the first time he's spoken to me directly. Internally shocked, I turned to face him. His pristine blue eyes were wrapped in a warm glimmer as they locked onto me.

"Do you have any intention of attending a music school? I heard from Ayumi that you attend a normal public school."

"Ah, yes, I do. But my family isn't wealthy enough to afford one," I answered honestly.

His eyes rounded for but an instant before he furrowed his brow in disappointment. "What a shame. If you are serious about pursuing music, then—"

"Mashiro!" Kon ran over and leapt on my back, wrapping her arms around me. Forcing her way into someone else's conversation wasn't like her.

"Hi there, Kon. Your performance was elegant once again," Tobi greeted.

"Thank you." She stood between us, as if to protect me from Prince Tobi. She had a smile on her face, but the muscles in her dainty back were flexed with tension against her dress. "Mashiro, Sou and Kou said they wish to speak to you."

"They did? Th-Thanks. Um, please excuse me then." I bowed my head to Prince Tobi and left them.

Kon's intentions were as clear as day: *Don't get involved with Prince Tobi. It's Kon we're talking about. She must've had good reason to pry me from him. I sure hope she'll tell me why someday.* Praying that she would, I made haste to where the boys awaited.

Original Heroine's Results
Target Character: Tobi Yamabuki
Event: I'll Play for You
CLEAR ERROR

Target Character: ???
New Event: ???
CLEAR
◇◇◇

♪♪♪

THE party was over, so I departed with Sou. We weren't exchanging gifts this year.

"It's not a fair exchange because certain people buy expensive presents no matter the rules," I had protested.

Sou and Kon were disappointed.

Yes, I'm talking about you two.

The clock had only struck six, but the sun set early in midwinter—the sky outside had turned pitch-black aside from the Christmas illuminations.

"Can you pass by the hill on the way to Mashiro's house?" Sou requested of the chauffeur.

Oh yeah, he did say he wanted to take a detour on the way home.

Compared to how much he usually chattered to me about various topics, he was being awfully quiet today. Drained from our performance, I limply sank back into the seat. The silence between us was mysteriously peaceful. There was something comforting about not having to force a conversation.

Giving in to the car's vibrations, I absently stared out the window. The streamlined shapes drawn by the city lights continued downward at a slant. We were ascending the hill. I sighed in awe at how the lights of many houses in the distance looked like a swarm of fireflies.

"You can stop here," Sou said to the chauffeur.

"Yes, sir."

The car quietly stopped on the side of the road.

"It's a little cold out, but would you mind joining me outside?"

"Why?"

"Please?"

Sou got out of the car first and extended his hand to me. Taking his hand as if I were a princess, I braved the bitter winter air. Sou silently buttoned my coat up to the top button. Then he wrapped his scarf around my neck, took my hand, and began climbing the hill road. Walking some distance brought us to a wide-open clearing.

"This is the place. Isn't it pretty?"

"It is!"

Sou led me to the best spot to get an open view of the beautiful city lights.

"Mashiro, look at the sky too."

I lifted my gaze to the heavens, marveling at the abundant stars twinkling in the jet-black sky, as though they had been dabbed in with a brush. The suspended moon shone with a magical bluish-white glow.

"Wow…"

This is amazing. I can almost forget I'm standing on the side of an open road.

Sou watched me, wholeheartedly content, as I was enamored by the stunning scenery before us.

"…Hey, can I talk about the past…for a bit?"

"Sure." I returned my attention to him.

He smiled and slowly began, "Mom left us just around this time of year. It was snowing. I remember chasing after her, dashing outside barefoot. I was still five at the time, so I struggled to get my shoes on right. I was frantic, thinking Mom would be gone if I took too long. I ran and ran after her, even when she got into the taxi she had waiting outside and drove away. I thought she would stop the car if she realized

I was following… But it was no use. I lost sight of the taxi in no time."

His tone was matter-of-fact. The scene vividly painted itself for me. A young Sou, crying as he chased after his mother, probably after noticing the large bags she had waiting at the door. He must've cried out for her through his tears, enough to make his voice go hoarse.

"Less than a year later, Dad remarried the woman who's my current mom. Seems like they were already acquainted with each other, and her family's affluence was apparently a huge plus for the Shiroyama Group. Not long after getting remarried, Dad left for Germany the next year and hasn't been back to Japan since… They say that the woman who abandoned us is in Germany. What's Dad trying to do? I wonder why Reimi doesn't complain either. I don't understand how grownups think."

"Sou…"

I feared he might fade away at any moment. I squeezed his hand. He looked at me with a bitter smile.

"Even if I go to Germany, that woman never tries to see me. Maybe it's because she still resents me. Or maybe it's because she couldn't care less about me. Do you know why, Mashiro?"

"I don't know," I answered honestly.

How could I know? I didn't even want to understand how Risa was feeling as she abandoned a barefoot, five-year-old Sou on the snowy road. She must've been so anguished, to the point of wanting to die, after she lost her ability to play the piano; I could understand that much. But I couldn't believe she was capable of traumatizing the sole child she'd given birth to with the man she had loved.

"I see… If it's something even you don't know, it's obvious I wouldn't either."

"You want to see her," I accidentally said aloud when I saw his sad eyes.

He considered it for a moment before responding, "I'm not sure." He looked back at the sky. "You know, Dad told me about this spot right before he remarried. He said it was that woman's favorite place. One of her favorite things to say here was, 'Whether we have a boy or girl, let's have them play an instrument.'"

"I see," is all I managed to say.

My chest felt heavy, like it was being weighed down by a large boulder. His dad was probably trying to assure him that he was a child they wanted to have.

But then why isn't he with him now? Why, when Sou is this lonely?

Honestly? I wanted to hug Sou right there and then. But, feeling like it was wrong to hug him out of sympathy when I was unable return the kind of love he wanted from me, I couldn't take a step forward.

"...Sorry for telling you this stuff. I'm always relying on you."

"That's not true. I haven't been able to do anything for you." The second I somehow got my lips to curve into a mangled smile, hot tears rolled down my cheeks.

What good comes of me crying here?!

I bit the inside of my cheek, trying to stifle the tears, but once they were let loose there was no stopping them. Sou removed his gloves and wiped the corner of my eyes with his freezing fingertips.

"...I know you only view me as a friend, Mashiro. Even so, please let me say it." He took my cheeks in both hands, caressing them. My tears blurred his far too earnestly sincere gaze.

Don't say it. Don't make me waver any more than this.

"I love you. You are everything to me, Mashiro. Because I have you, I'm no longer lonely. Because you cry in my stead like this, I can forgive myself for still thinking about that person."

"I-I like you too. But—"

"Yeah. It's okay. I know." He removed his hands from my cheeks, turning away as if to stop me from saying the rest. "If we don't head back soon, your parents will worry. Let's go."

My heart knotted painfully in my chest as I watched his departing back.

It hurts. I'm in unbearable pain from not being able to return his one-sided feelings.

I still love you though, Sou. I've come to love you like family. I didn't fall in love with Hear My Heart's Sou Shiroyama, but with the lonely boy I found on the footbridge.

♪♪♪

AFTER that bittersweet Christmas, life returned to its normal hectic rush, and time mercilessly passed by. At the end of the year, Dad suggested going to the hot springs for the first time in a while, so we went for a one-day, two-night trip to a local spring.

Afraid to let my fingers grow sluggish, I brought the paper keyboard I made with all eighty-eight keys on it with me, pressing my fingers noisily across it inside the inn, which reduced Dad to tears from guilt for suggesting the trip.

"Let her be. Mashiro is seriously aiming to become a professional pianist," Mom forgave me with a smile.

Hanaka must've been lonely because she stuck by my side the whole time while I banged away on the paper keyboard.

♪♪♪

FOR Valentine's Day, I handed out chocolates to my usual group of friends. I tried my hand at making cocoa snowball cookies, and they turned out to be a hit. Hanaka resolved not to be fixated on making chocolate by hand, instead hitting up several stores until she found an acceptable chocolate. Shinji's first impression on me had been horrible, but I couldn't complain as long as he made my sister happy.

The girls all decided to give chocolates to Kinose and Hirata, leaving me no choice but to do the same.

Hirata jumped with joy, cheering, "I'm popular! I'm popular!"

I felt relieved every time I saw Hirata, a genuine elementary school boy.

"I'm giving you some because you've helped me out, are my friend, and finally, out of obligation," I deliberately reminded Kinose when I gave him his share.

"Do you have to point it out?" he grumbled, depressed.

Good, good! Continue to be disappointed in me!

I didn't give any to Sou or Kou. Simply because we were unable to meet up on Valentine's Day, but they still bothered to give me expensive cookies for White Day. I was perplexed when they showed up at my front door.

"What is this?"

Kou and Sou deeply sighed in unison.

"It's my way of ironically getting back at you for heartlessly forgetting Valentine's Day?" Kou offered.

"I planned to give you a present whether I received one or not," Sou stated.

They both had something different to say, but a similar dark aura rose behind them simultaneously. They taught me a good lesson: you need to fulfill your social obligations.

"I'm really sorry. I planned to give you some if we met up, but..." I apologized, whisper-soft.

"Huh? You're saying we had to come get it from you yourselves?" Kou demanded.

"That's not what I meant..." I fumbled over my excuses, making Kou sigh again.

"Fine. I'll come to get my share next year. I'll forgive you if you didn't give it to any other guys this year."

Half of what he said was so arrogant, I almost accidentally confessed that I had indeed given chocolate to other guys. I glanced beside him— Sou was holding his breath in anticipation of my answer.

I held my ground, responding, "I haven't! I don't have anyone to give chocolate to!"

What do I do if my choice just now flags Sou's Bad End? My heart thudded in my ears. Seemingly satisfied with my answer, they flashed me the most gorgeous smiles. *Ah, thank goodness. I don't sense the weird aura around them anymore.*

"What about you guys?" I wanted to ask, but I realized it'd only make things worse, so I grinned and tried to make it through the moment.

♪♪♪

APRIL rolled around once again. Finally, I became a sixth grader. I now stood at five feet tall, wore a bra, and had experienced my first period.

Yup, this is it. This is what it was like. I grimaced from the dull ache in my abdomen for the first time in February. In the past, I couldn't wait to catch up to my prior age, but a lot of annoying stuff accompanied growing up.

Mom shook her head emotionally when she saw that I had reached my older sister's height. "They grow so fast. You were such a tiny girl too. I hate how fast kids become adults."

"They really do. We're going to be empty nesters in no time."

Hanaka merrily laughed off our parents' sentimentality. "You're the reason why we've made it to this age in perfect health! You should celebrate that more!"

"But, Hanaka, what will you do? On her current path, Mashiro is going to get even better at the piano and eventually leave to study and play overseas!"

Instantly, Hanaka's expression dipped, her lips turning down at the sides. "HUH?! Don't even say that! I'm totally against it! Mashiro, reconsider living overseas this instant!" She clung to me on the verge of tears.

I quietly murmured, "I think Hanaka is going to get married and leave home sooner than I will."

Dad's eyebrows arched in alarm. "It's too soon for that talk!" He crumpled the newspaper in his hand.

I thought he'd say that.

Hanaka and I looked at each other before bursting into laughter over the poor newspaper.

♪♪♪

"I heard they're going to put close friends in the same class this year because we've got that big school field trip as sixth graders," Eri informed me on the way to school.

Would a school actually do that? What'll happen to the kids without close friends?

Not feeling it, I responded back halfheartedly. Eri and the girls were looking forward to the school trip—I saw it as nothing more than ruining my life.

I can't bear being away from the piano for three whole days. Maybe I'll fake being sick and skip it, had been my plan, but I couldn't go through with it when I knew it'd waste the deposit my parents paid. I was stuck with no way out.

Today was the opening ceremony for the new school year. I learned just how correct Eri had been when I checked out the class division announcements.

"Yay! We're all together again!"

"Isn't it great? We can form the school trip group with just us!"

Before setting foot inside the classroom of Class 6-3, I could already see everyone celebrating. Eri, Mako, Sawa, and Tomo, as well as Hirata and Kinose, had all been assigned to the same class. Last year I ended up in a different class, so I often did things on my own. I thought I was okay with being alone too, but there really is a joy in being with a group of friends you feel comfortable around.

Mr. Kumaja was my homeroom teacher once again, after a year apart. As I was about to go home, he called me back, "Shimao!"

What's he want? I thought, turning around.

With a serious face, he grabbed my shoulders and insisted, "Feel free to talk to me about anything! Don't worry too much about life!"

Whoa, scary. Please don't worry yourself too much either, Mr. Kumaja.

A lot of the kids in my school year kept a distance from me because I didn't assertively try to make friends or even interact with the ones I have. Maybe he was worried that I had ended up alone in my class last year because of that—yeah, he was definitely bothered by it.

"Okay. Let me start by asking you to let me practice the piano during our school trip's free time."

"That's a hard request to fulfill."

An immediate no?!

"I have nothing I want to talk to you about aside from that. Thank you for your concern." I bowed deeply and turned on my heel.

"Shimao! The piano is a fine hobby, but you're only a sixth grader once," he shouted at my back.

This is my second time being a sixth grader, I thought, a faraway-look in my eyes.

As for the piano, my bigger hands helped me advance through practice in less time. What used to take about an hour to master, I now did in thirty minutes. The solfège had paid off—it was easier for me to sight-read music.

At the moment, I was learning Beethoven's "Sonata", Chopin's "Etude", and Bach's "The Well-Tempered Clavier". According to Miss Ayumi, I had reached the level of a high school music student. But there are a ton of songs out there you can't clear just by playing them as they're written. Interpreting what the composer meant by their directions is necessary.

Miss Ayumi had instructed, "Learn about the country the composer was born in, the environment they were raised in, and what musicians and composers they have been influenced by."

"I really want you to start attending Seio for middle school, but… Why don't I discuss it with your parents?" she offered on countless occasions.

Our household didn't have the financial leeway to pay for Seio on top of the drain of Hanaka's tuition fees. Things were bad enough that Dad gave up going out drinking with his friends.

"No, thank you. I don't want to burden my parents more than I already have, so I will attend public school. But I haven't changed my mind about attending Seio for high school."

Miss Ayumi promised to support me as much as she could, even though she was disappointed.

♪♪♪

NOTHING else changed by becoming a sixth grader. My routine was practically the same as before. Go to school, home, Miss Ayumi's, and the Genda estate. Time zoomed by as I commuted between those four places.

Kon steadily grew more beautiful. I wondered how gorgeous she'd become as an adult. Just imagining it brought a silly grin to my face.

Apparently, Kou had grown taller than 5'4". Though smaller compared to Kou, Sou was growing into a fine physique as well. Imagining them attending a public elementary school sent me into a fit of giggles. I couldn't picture kids who didn't suit elementary school backpacks more than them.

Once May came, Sou requested that I gaze into his eyes and say his name for his birthday present. He did so much for me on a daily basis, how could I let something as simple as that be his only present? He'd given me an incredibly adorable keychain for my birthday last year. It had a golden bear attached to the chain. I'm only saying this here, but he looked like Becchin's brother to me.

I attached my house key to it so I could use it every day. I felt soothed by the cute bear each time I opened the front door.

"Hmm. You okay with just that?" I asked reluctantly.

"I'm okay with just that. Are you not?" He cocked his head, pressing his hands together.

I regret to say my heart throbbed. Not just throbbed, but thudded against my chest as if it were trying to make a run for it. And here I thought I'd been getting used to his unintentional killer lines and gestures that minded neither place nor time. Considering his attractive looks, he'd seriously make one frightening boy if these were actually calculated moves!

I accepted my fate as he sat on the living room sofa, looking at me with hopeful eyes.

"Okay, I'll do it. Here I go. You ready for it?"

"Yup, go ahead."

I leaned forward, gazing into his beautiful big eyes, inhaled, and opened my mouth like my life depended on it, "Sou."

"…Say it again."

"Sou."

"…Crap. I'm happier than I thought I'd be," he said bashfully, "I can't stop grinning, so don't look at me right now." His cuteness should be saved as a national treasure.

He's the one who asked me to do it! Why does he get to turn bright-red when I'm the one who did it? Now I'm going to catch his blush!

"GAH! I CAN'T DO THIS!" Distraught by his bashful face, I punched my fists into the cushion. He quit blushing and gave me a funny look.

Sorry, I couldn't withstand the sugary-sweet mood.

♪♪♪

SUMMER break came once again. I thought it'd be the start of another lonely piano boot camp until Kon invited me out.

"We don't get many long breaks. Want to go out together at least once?"

"I'll go! I really want to go!" I shouted immediately.

Kon happily smiled at my instantaneous answer. "Hehe, glad to hear it."

Knowing you have a reward waiting at the end of your hard work encourages you to work all the harder for it. At her suggestion, we decided to play at the seaside cottage the Genda family owned. I solemnly accomplished my self-assigned studying and piano quota with the circled day on the calendar as my motivation.

Just like that, our set date arrived. Overly excited, I awoke early, restlessly checking to make sure I had everything.

Bathing suit. Check. Hat. Check. Towel and beach ball. Check and check. Aaah, I'm looking forward to this too much! The time isn't coming soon enough!

"Mashiro! It looks like Kon is here to pick you up!" Mom called from the first-floor. I raced downstairs. She was five minutes early.

"I'm leaving now!" I exclaimed and dashed outside. Waiting in front of the house wasn't Kon's car, but that oh-so-familiar Rolls-Royce.

"Mashiro!"

"Long time no see, Mashiro."

The car window rolled down, revealing two people who shouldn't have been there.

Why are Kou and Sou here? Are you guys a set bonus whenever I spend time with Kon? I don't want this three for one deal anymore. And I'd planned on letting loose with Kon today during our private beach time too!

"How'd we get stuck with them again?" I climbed into the car beside Kon, pointing at the boys relaxing against the back seat as if it were only obvious for them to be here. Kou bent back my finger, nearly snapping it.

"I'm sorry. I was acting too suspicious with how excited I was yesterday; Kou saw right through me."

Kon was that excited to hang out?! My momentary joy was promptly replaced by resentment for Kou's perceptive senses.

"You know…you stalk Kon too much, Kou. With how much you follow her around wherever she goes…have you been diagnosed with a serious case of sister complex? To be honest, it's creepy."

"Shut. Up. Let me throw the question back at you. Why do you hate it so much? Do you have some sorta secret, guilty reason for not wanting us to tagalong?"

"I don't! I just hate that I can't relax with you around!"

Kon sighed heavily as our usual heated argument kicked up. Sou was staring at me like my clothes had caught his interest.

Disconcerted, I asked, "What? Are my clothes weird today?" I scrutinized my outfit. I was wearing a casual black, knee-length camisole dress with lace-up sandals. Nothing out of the ordinary.

"Nah. Was just thinking that you look good even in simple outfits. I don't want anyone else to see you."

As you'd expect, Kou was grossed out by how Sou delivered those honeyed lines with a straight face.

Kon pressed her hand against her head, muttering, "Maybe I should move to the front seat."

"Add that to the list of things you're not allowed to say!" I shouted at Sou.

"Haha. Your ears are red, Mashiro," Sou chuckled.

Damn him and his perfect composure!

♪♪♪

THE cottage was located an hour and a half by car from my house. The chic building standing beside a tiny inlet fascinated me. Above us was the bright-blue sky, and below it, the clear blue sea spanned farther than the eye could see. They were even more stunning up close than at a distance.

"What a gorgeous spot! Thanks for inviting me, Kon! Thank you for driving us here as well, Mr. Mizusawa," I thanked Kon, who was grinning, and our chauffeur, Mr. Mizusawa.

"You're welcome."

"You needn't thank me for such an easy task."

Mr. Mizusawa, Kou, and Sou carried our bags for us. I offered to help, but Kou stubbornly refused.

"There's nothing for you to help with. We've got it, so hurry up and change with Kon."

"Let's go, Mashiro!" Kon pulled me away by the hand, whispering in my ear, "Let Kou show you his good side sometimes."

He was trying to show off to me just now?! I thought he meant it as, "I could never entrust our stuff to the likes of you!" He's as indecipherable as ever.

We changed into our bathing suits in a room on the cottage's second-story. Kon put on a cute frilly-layered bikini. Even in a bikini, she looked neat and elegant with her porcelain skin and slender frame. I changed into a simple black tankini with white polka dots.

"Oh? Mashiro, isn't your chest pretty big now?! Not fair! We're still elementary school students!"

"H-Huuuh?! Not big enough for you to bring them up!" I reflexively

Natsu

covered up my chest.

"Wow, my heart just skipped a beat… I wonder if Kou will survive it," Kon muttered cryptically.

I hadn't paid it any mind until Kon had to go and mention it. Thanks to her, I felt hopelessly embarrassed. We went outside after I had tossed a parka over my bathing suit.

Mr. Mizusawa stayed on the beach as our lifeguard in case we ran into any trouble. He was wearing shorts and a white T-shirt so that his clothes wouldn't hinder him if he needed to dive into the water to save us.

Now that's a new look! I've only ever seen him wear suits, but he looks cool in casual attire as well!

"Thank you for looking out for us," I said, bowing my head to him.

"Please refrain from swimming too far out into the open sea," he answered, smiling kindly.

Kou and Sou had packed on more muscle in the last year. Their lean arms were well-defined. They were too blinding to look directly at.

Where am I supposed to look?!

"Mashiro! Over here! Let's swim together!" Sou exclaimed, unusually excited.

Kou was already in the water. Pushing his wet hair back was outrageously sexy. A diamond in a dunghill is still a diamond. Even if he's an elementary schooler, he's still a romanceable otome game character. My heart raced without consent.

This is why I didn't want them to come with us, I grumbled internally and steeled myself for what was to come.

"Let's go, Kon!" I pulled off the parka, tossing it under the beach parasol. I grabbed Kon's hand this time, and we ran to the water's edge. Naturally, we'd taken care of our warm-up exercises inside the cottage. "Here we go!" I announced, "One! Two! Three!"

We dived into the lapping waves at the same time, splashing white sea spray all over our heads. Amused with such a small thing, we looked at each other and laughed.

Sou and Kou were whispering to each other.

"…I'm glad I came."

"You couldn't be more right. I'm sure you know this, but don't go checking Kon out."

"I won't. You can't look at Mashiro either, Kou."

"What are you guys talking about?" I shouted from afar, instantly sealing their lips. Seeing the guilty look on their faces, I could easily gather they hadn't been talking about anything good. I hit the beach ball I had been carrying underarm at them. "Catch this!"

"…Whoa. Nice pass!" Sou easily caught my spike with a wide grin, setting off a game that the four of us played for a while.

Kou spiked the ball at me, but lightly tossed it to Kon. Ticked off beyond measure, I attacked him with the ball, smacking it with all my strength.

"Can you quit hitting the ball differently to me and Sou?"

"That's my line!"

The game ended up as a one-on-one match between me and Kou. Kon and Sou laughed the entire time from the sidelines as they watched us take the game too seriously.

The boys continued playing on body boards while Kon and I went back to relax on the beach. I feasted my eyes on them as they shone as dazzling as the sparkling sea.

They really are handsome, cool, and the best…when I get to watch them from afar.

♪♪♪

THE week after I'd played with Kon and the boys at the private beach, I went with Eri and friends to the community pool. Kinose and Hirata joined in for a fun time, rounding out our usual group of seven.

"Let's come again," Kinose invited at the end of the day. But playing in the water under the blazing sun drains a ton of energy! I always found myself dozing off when I tried to study in the evenings after hanging out.

So I politely refused, "Sorry, I have a lot of stuff to do."

Eri and the others were used to me turning them down and were unsurprised. I loved that about them. Friends who respect friends' space and time are the best, and few and far between.

The bathing suit Hanaka bought for me with her part-time job wages only got used twice.

Around the end of summer break, Dad suggested, "Why don't we go to see the fireworks as a family?"

It had been a long time since we had gone out as a family. I instantly agreed, but Hanaka slapped her hands together, begging for forgiveness.

"Sorry! I kinda have plans that day..." She had made prior plans with Shinji.

"Heh. Hana is going to pick her boyfriend over us. I see how it is," Dad pouted, responding immaturely.

I smiled wryly. "Nothing much we can do when he beat us to her. Let's go with just the three of us this time."

"Don't you have plans with Kon, Mashiro?" Mom chimed in from where she was frying food in the kitchen.

"You do?" Dad's shoulders slumped.

I grinned at him. "I don't. Take me with you to see the fireworks, Daddy."

"Haha. How can I say no to you? Since you want to so badly, let's go without Hanaka!"

Mom giggled at Dad's sudden rebound. Nothing made me happier than seeing my parents smile. Warmth filled me; then, for some reason, the warmth was followed by sadness. A lump lodged in my throat. Emotions of longing and a sense of having lost someone who was no longer with me welled up.

I felt like I had once laughed this very way with someone whose name and face I could no longer remember.

♫♫♫

THE enjoyable, productive summer break ended, giving way to the second school quarter. Second quarter's main event was the fall school trip, and Kyoto was our destination. I had always wanted to visit Japan's former capital. I might've visited it in my past life, but I couldn't recall, so I was genuinely looking forward to the trip—if not for the piano. Wavering between resignation and anticipation, I awaited the trip's arrival.

During my lesson last week, Miss Ayumi had taken my report that I would be unable to practice the piano on my school trip with a kind expression.

"I agree it's hard not to play for three whole days. But Mashiro, it's very important to your music to see and experience many things while you are impressionable, so you can store away how you feel to look back on in the future."

I'd lashed out at Mr. Kumaja, but Miss Ayumi's words had reached me.

...*I'm sorry, Mr. Kumaja.*

Leaves were only beginning to change their color. An endless number of places were on my want-to-see list: Maruyama Park, Kiyomizudera, Kodaiji Temple, Nijo Castle, Shinsen Garden, Mibuji, Kinkakuji, Ginkakuji, Sagano, Arashiyama.

Class groups consisted of six people. Our group was made up of three girls: me, Mako, and Tomo, and three boys: Kinose, Takata, and Mizoguchi. Takata and Mizoguchi were in the same soccer club as Kinose.

"Let's have a blast together," they'd greeted with pomp, but whenever it came to deciding our plans as a group, they flopped over on their desks, declaring, "We have no idea how to read a map or figure out the timetable. You girls can decide for us."

According to them, their heads hurt when they used them.

If you do nothing to improve it, it'll only get worse for you, I internally warned them.

Yet, "Temples? Not interested," the two of them complained whenever we tried to involve them.

The other four of us ignored them, finalizing our group schedule for the first day. We were going to take the western Kyoto course, traveling from Kinkakuji to Ryoanji and stopping at Ninnaji Temple. The second day would be the eastern course, going around Ginkakuji to Tetsugaku-no-michi—Philosopher's Walk—and ending at Nanzenji. Then we were going to buy souvenirs when we visited Kiyomizudera and Koudaiji during the morning of our last day. If you can't tell, our sightseeing list was full of temples and shrines.

"Isn't this perfect?"

"Yup. We planned out our days well!"

The girls high-fived, sharing in our sense of accomplishment. Then we looked up all the entrance fees and got our hands on the bus schedules, jotting down all the transfer and connection times as well. Naturally, I memorized the maps too. Mr. Kumaja was astounded when he saw how polished our finished trip plan was.

♪♪♪

"OH yeah, what're you gonna do during our free time on the second day?" Kinose quietly asked the day before our trip, after the teachers had finished checking our bags in the gymnasium.

"I plan to take a walk around Kyoto with the girls. They said they wanted to explore either Kyoto Station or Shijō Kawaramachi. What about you, Kinose?"

"Cool… Hey, can I take up some of your time after school today?"

"Okay."

Kinose's abrupt change in topic unsettled me; I had a hard time calming my restlessness before school ended. A lot of kids confess their feelings to the person they like just before the school trip. Eri was fired up, planning on taking her chances to confess to her crush Majima. Kinose had been trying to appeal to me since we were in the fourth grade. It wouldn't be strange for him to try to bring some sort of closure before we entered middle school.

He might want to talk about something completely different, I told myself off for overthinking things. *I'll be pretty embarrassed if I have the wrong idea.*

Unfortunately, my assumptions were right.

"I think you know already, but I like you, Mashiro," Kinose earnestly confessed to me in an empty classroom after school.

The setting sun dyed the space between us orange. He looked much like an adult when he was illuminated by the evening sunlight.

"I'm happy you like me. I mean it. But I've never seen you that way. I doubt I'll ever see you as anything other than a friend… I'm sorry."

His expression gradually withered before my eyes. My honest answer had hurt him. Even without romantic feelings, I still cared for him. He had especially looked out for me when I was alone last year. But I felt that I had to cleanly cut him down here and now if I was never planning on returning his feelings.

"…I know." He shoved up his bangs with a bitter smile. "I was fully aware you've never seen me as more than a friend. But I wanted to be free of these feelings… Now I have no regrets. Thanks, Mashiro."

You said those last words for me, didn't you? You're a good man, Kinose.

I changed my frown into an attempt at a smile. "Are you going to stop being my friend now? Am I asking too much by hoping you'll stay friends with me?"

"Nah. Not at all. Actually, I'd prefer it that way." He reached out and roughly ruffled my hair. "Don't make that face. And about our free time, Hirata and I will be joining you girls, so let's have fun as friends."

"…Okay. Thank you."

He walked half the way home with me.

"We're friends, so call me by my first name," he requested, so I called him by his first name, Rin, for the first time.

Eri and the others had started using his first name ages ago, but I could never bring myself to say it. Now we started calling each other by name, laughing as we bumped shoulders to keep the unpleasant awkwardness from lingering after the confession.

Like that, the day ended and the first day of our school trip began. I slipped on a long-sleeve tunic and skinny jeans, snatching a pair of comfortable sneakers as I slid into a cardigan. My outfit might prove hot for the midday temperatures, but it'd be just right for the evening.

"Mashiron! Morning!" Eri was waiting for me with a huge smile when I left the house with my heavy bag over my shoulder.

"Morning. Someone's in a good mood… Oh, let me guess—"

"Ehehe. I confessed my feelings yesterday, and…"

"And?"

"…He said he'll date me!"

"You did it!" We held hands, jumping up and down with joy.

Eri was so thrilled that it rubbed off on me.

If you make this cute and honest girl cry, I'll beat you to a pulp, Majima, I swore to myself.

"You did well!" I beamed at Eri and patted her head.

As soon as we arrived at the meeting place, I told my group of friends about what had gone down with Kinose yesterday. I requested that they look the other way and not poke fun at it.

"I thought you and Rin made a cute couple though." Sawa was disappointed, but the group agreed to heed my request after hearing the details.

We boarded the minibus after we'd finished our secret girl talk.

"Mashiro, over here!" Kinose waved from where he'd boarded first. We were supposed to sit with our group, so he was probably gesturing for me to sit next to him.

Sitting next to Kinose means Mako and Tomo, and Takata and Mizoguchi, will get to sit with each other, after all.

"You're early. Did you sleep well?"

"Like a log! What's wrong? You look sleepy, Mashiro."

As a matter of fact, I had played the piano the entire evening inside the Genda annex. I practiced nonstop for five hours until Dad had been worried enough to come get me. I think the leftover exhaustion still had its grip on me. Kinose was astonished when I relayed that to him.

"You practiced until ten?! No duh you're sleepy. Go ahead and sleep."

"Hm. But I crashed on your shoulder last time too. I'll try my best to stay awake this time."

"You worry about the small things too much, Mashiro. I'd be upfront with you if I didn't want you to do it."

Accepting his kind offer, I slept almost the entire way on the bus. Seeing me sound asleep on his shoulder got the girls whispering behind us.

"...How are they not dating?"

"Right?"

CG 19: School Trip (Kou & Sou)

"I am SO SORRY!" I did a ninety-degree angle bow as soon as I exited the bus.

Kinose laughed. "Where'd that come from?"

"I was trying to sleep without using your shoulder. I really was!"

When I'd come to, the bus had already arrived in Kyoto. And when I really came to my senses, I realized I had zonked out with my head on his shoulder. I must have some nerves of steel to use the boy I rejected just yesterday as a pillow.

"Okay, I'll give you the honor of buying me a soda at the hotel to make up for it," he joked, trying to ease my guilt.

He's such a good guy. I wonder why I didn't fall for him.

Our group members shot me a pitying look.

"I thought Shimao was more of the stuck-up prissy type."

"Me too."

Even Takata and Mizoguchi had commented on my behavior.

Hang on. Who's a stuck-up priss? It'd be horrible for someone to act high-handed and domineering despite being raised as a middle-class kid. Is that how I come off?

We dropped our bags off in our hotel rooms, attended orientation, and split into our groups. The evening hours drew closer, forcing us to hurry. We ran to the nearest bus stop. A number of buses were parked there, so we didn't have to wait long. After ooh-ing and aah-ing at Kinkakuji, which looked as if it were pulled straight from our textbooks, we solemnly took in the pristine grace of Ryoanji's traditional dry landscape gardens.

"How on Earth do they keep the place swept this clean?" Tomo marveled as she sat on the veranda.

The cool breeze felt nice. These places were probably packed full of people on public holidays and weekends, but we could comfortably explore because it was a weekday. People who were riding the same bus kindly chatted with us:

"Are you on a school trip?"

"Lucky! Have fun, kids!"

We thanked them with a smile.

The scenery was pretty, the buildings were stately and serene, and best of all, we got to revel in the accomplishment of fulfilling our sightseeing plans.

I'm so glad I came. Feeling like I was walking on air, I enjoyed my time visiting temples and shrines with my group.

All while forgetting a critical factor—this was *Hear My Heart's* world.

♪♪♪

GROUPS ate dinner together at the hotel restaurant. After dinner, we were supposed to return to our rooms to shower and had free time until 9:30 p.m. They forbade us from going to the other hotel floors but let us gather in each other's rooms to hang out. We were assigned to rooms in threes; girls were on the fifteenth floor while the boys had the sixteenth.

After we left the restaurant, our group leader, Kinose, offered to hand our reports in to Mr. Kumaja.

"I'll come too," I volunteered, receiving a puzzled look from him in return.

"Why? I can do it on my own."

"I'm sure you can, but I need to buy you that soda."

I had a feeling I'd seen a vending machine near the lobby.

He narrowed his eyes and muttered, "You're a stickler for keeping promises."

"Go on ahead without me, girls. You can lock the door. I'll knock." I told my roommates, Tomo and Mako, that I'd come back to the room after taking a detour.

From there, I accompanied Kinose to the lounge, where Mr. Kumaja was waiting. Kinose stood in line, swiftly reported our progress, and returned to me.

"Sorry for the wait. What should I have you buy me?"

"You haven't decided? How about cola? Don't you like carbonated drinks?"

"I do. But I'm full from dinner. Maybe I'll go with tea so I can drink it before bed."

"Good idea."

Mr. Kumaja called out to us as we were walking to the vending machine, discussing what to get. "Shimao! Do you have a moment?"

"Ah, yes." I turned around and ran back to him alone.

Beaming triumphantly, he put his hand on his hip and declared, "Did you see the huge piano in the lounge? I got you permission from the hotel manager to play on that piano for an hour starting at eight. But, because there are guests present, you're required to play an actual song, not practice pieces... What do you want to do?"

My mouth fell open.

I can play on the grand piano? At a hotel?

Part of me jumped for joy, while another part of me remained grounded, worrying whether it was truly okay.

"Mr. Kumaja... But is it all right for me to do that?" I asked timidly. He smacked me twice on the shoulder.

"I could tell how serious you are about the piano back during the summer camp. I really wanted to give in to your request back then. But I couldn't do much about it with only a day's notice. That's why I made the necessary arrangements long in advance this time! Surprised, weren't'cha? Bwahahaha!" he heartily laughed.

I sniffled. *He'll never understand how important the piano is to me!* I'd thought. I felt ashamed for arrogantly assuming he wouldn't understand. He most likely ran around asking the principal, other teachers, and the hotel staff on my behalf.

"Th-Thank you very much! I'm thrilled!"

Mr. Kumaja scratched his chin, bashful because he didn't think I'd be this moved by what he had done for me.

He's a great teacher in all regards! I almost cried.

"Sorry, can we push off your drink until tomorrow?" I apologized to Kinose, who had come over to see what was up.

"Of course. I'd rather hear you play the piano anyway!" he agreed easily.

I had Kinose wait in the lounge while Mr. Kumaja and I went to the front desk. The dandy, fifty-something male manager smiled upon seeing me.

"Miss Shimao, right? As a matter of fact, I have heard you play the piano once before."

I hadn't expected him to say that!

He has?! Where? When? How?!

My thoughts must've been written on my face because both Mr. Kumaja and the manager laughed. Of all things, he had been dragged by his wife—a huge fan of Miss Ayumi—to listen to our recital last year. He professed that he had been deeply moved and impressed by how Kon and I had performed.

"I have no doubt you've improved even more since then. I look forward to hearing you tonight."

"Thank you very much. I'll try to meet your expectations."

I followed him to where the grand piano was set up.

Wow! It's a Shiroyama SX Alpha!

The SX Alpha was the sister piano to the one I had performed on during the four-handed performance with Kon at the recital. It was a midsize concert piano, and I'd heard its key features were the pure pitch quality and vibrant sound. This would be my first time using one.

"Can I get right to it?" I asked the manager, after playing the C note to confirm the sound quality and level of tuning.

"You can start anytime you're ready," he generously agreed.

Lured by the sound of the piano, the hotel guests who were scattered about the lobby turned my way. Kinose settled into one of the lounge sofas and watched with anticipation.

I can do this! I pumped myself up and took in one big breath. *I'll warm up with a song by Brahms.*

Brahms – Intermezzo Op.118-2

I played the gentle predominant melody as though it were slowly riding the rhythm. Careful not to play with too much passion, I stroked the keyboard, imagining that I was sending my song as a letter to a faraway lover. High-notes resounded elegantly with my right hand's touch, as my left hand delicately instilled warmth into the keys. I took care to add ample vibration to the development section at the halfway mark. Following that, I loudly made the piano sing the theme, which returned at the end of the song.

"Marvelous!" The manager applauded me.

This is practice, not a concert, so I don't need applause. But it still feels good to be applauded. A smile escaped onto my lips.

Kinose and Mr. Kumaja were staring at me in mute amazement.

Wh-Why that look? Do they dislike Brahms? Maybe they'd be happier if I went with a familiar Chopin piece.

Chopin – Étude Op. 10 No. 4 C-Sharp Minor

My hands raced from one end of the keyboard to the other, my arms dancing above. To draw out a dynamic sound, I played each grace note like a ripple, making them overlap in a layered accentuation. I tore out the deep notes of the fortissimo part by playing with my whole body, and for the last part, I played as powerfully as possible. Finishing the song off with rich bipartite chords, I was astounded to find a crowd of people applauding loudly for me when I stopped.

"She's skilled."

"I wonder where she's from."

"Is she a famous child pianist?"

I was taken aback by the whispers I heard.

Um…have I drawn too much attention to myself? Is it okay for me to keep playing?

I looked imploringly up at the flushed manager, who gestured wildly with his hands, insisting I play more.

He's telling me to just keep playing I guess. If the manager is fine with it, I'll play more. This will help me hone my concentration more than normal practice does. My mind was as hushed as a calm ocean; my ears were filled with nothing other than the beat of the song I was about to play.

Beethoven – Piano Sonata No. 17 In D Minor, Op.31, No.2, "The Tempest"

They say that when Beethoven composed this song, he had

been contemplating suicide out of despair because his hearing was deteriorating.

The title, "The Tempest", is a reference based on hearsay; when an associate of Beethoven's asked how he should interpret the sonata, Beethoven responded by saying that he should read Shakespeare's *Tempest*.

Since I had the chance to play it, I decided to perform from the first movement through the third movement. The melody alternates brief moments of peace with extensive passages of turmoil. The occasional gentle, slower phrases are like the light of hope, seen through whirling despair. Contrary to the intense, surging waves of the first movement, the second movement is more relaxed and dignified. Firmly tethered to established sonata styles, the second movement softly develops into an almost lullaby-like melody from its slow, idyllic introduction.

People who had been listening where they stood started to take up seats around me. Some were even crossing their legs, relaxing as they listened.

I'd say most people think of the third movement when it comes to "The Tempest". Consecutive sixteenth notes fashion a heartrending melody; the staccato rings out with certain sharpness, and the bass is played with solemnity. The theme is presented numerous times by changing keys from G minor to A minor, D minor, C minor, B-flat minor, A-flat major, and then back to B-flat minor. I danced my hands across the keyboard, inducing despair amid its beautiful melody, yet also the burning desire of not wanting to give up on music. I removed my fingers at the end of the song, which had flown by surprisingly fast for a twenty-five-minute sonata.

"A great performance, just as I'd expect from you, Mashiro. You've gotten even better!"

"Yeah. It was a Tempest worth hearing."

Amid the wave of applause, I heard two voices I shouldn't have been hearing. I leapt from my bench.

"Huh?! Wh-Why are you guys h-here?" I fumbled my words, flustered.

No matter how I looked at the two boys, giving me an amused look as they gracefully approached me, they couldn't be anyone but Kou and Sou.

"Calm down. You sound like a twitterpated bird."

Kou's remark ticked me off as usual. On the flip side, it helped me collect my thoughts.

Anyway, they sure do show up anywhere and everywhere. Is it a game mechanic for them to appear whenever I play the piano? Hear My Heart's full title was Let Me Hear Your Sound ~Melody to My Heart~ after all.

"Shimao, are they your friends?" Mr. Kumaja inquired.

I quickly retreated to where he stood. "Umm…I guess you could say that."

"You guess?" Kou's attractive eyebrow shot up.

Watching me attempt to hide in Mr. Kumaja's shadow, Kinose quietly asked, "What's wrong? You okay?"

Aaah. Commonsense kindness is where it's at.

"Yes, they are my friends. Friends I'm super close to," I hurried to correct, but Kou's frigid gaze didn't change.

He abruptly stepped forward, grabbed my arm, and pulled me back to him, before I could even think to complain. Sou supported me, as I'd almost toppled over from Kou's forceful tug. But even he was giving Kinose an aggressive look.

My stomach! My stomach hurts, Mr. Kumaja!

"We are students from Seio Academy. We were invited to an opening performance at a newly built concert hall in the area, and we were surprised to find a friend of ours at this hotel." Kou masterfully masked his chilling gaze, using an honor student's tone to greet Mr. Kumaja.

Yuck. I've got goose bumps.

Mr. Kumaja's wariness dropped when he recognized Seio Academy's name and uniform. He grinned widely. "I see! I see! You're something else for having friends at Seio too, Shimao! I was stunned by your skill on the piano just now. You've done nothing but surprise me today!"

"What? But you look scared, Mashiro," Kinose said, confused.

"He uses your first name, huh?" Kou's ghost of a whisper reached my ears.

A black aura erupted from behind Sou as well, curling around him.

Please forgive me. Pardon me from any Bad Ends at least.

"I-I'm not scared. Just surprised because I didn't think we'd run into each other here. Umm, I'll go back to my room after speaking with them."

"If you say so. Okay, see you tomorrow," Kinose replied, still perplexed.

"Good night, Rin."

I accidentally blurted out his first name when he simply took me at my word, giving away our intimacy.

"Rin, huh?" Sou repeated this time.

Ah, checkmate. I just killed myself. I blankly gazed off into the distance.

Kou put his hand on my back and lightly pushed me forward. "Mashiro, let's have a nice long chat over there."

"Let's."

What charming smiles they were showing me.

Heroine's Results
Target Character: Sou Shiroyama & Kou Narita
Event: Invited by your Sound
CLEAR
◇◇◇

My two jailers kept watch over me as I thanked the manager. Believe it or not, he requested I play in the lounge again tomorrow. I immediately agreed to do it, then was escorted off to the booth seats deep within the lounge by Sou and Kou flanking both sides of me.

"...Are you dating that guy?" Sou questioned outright, in the booth seat across the tiny table from where I'd been made to sit. To make matters worse, Kou sat completely silent next to Sou with his long legs crossed. Tremendously terrifying, that boy.

Stuck in a stressful interrogation, I vehemently shook my head. "No way! He's a good friend of mine. Besides, isn't it a bit too soon to be talking about dating when we're in elementary school? I think it's too early for this stuff. Ahahaha," I laughed nervously.

They didn't even crack a smile. The heavy air between us seemed to suck all the oxygen out of the room.

"I see. I wonder how many *'good friends'* you have. Is it fun going around raising a guy's hopes before crushing them?" Kou remarked, in the imitation of a kind voice.

STAB!

The clash of his intense cynicism and tone nearly knocked me out. NEARLY. But I caught my footing.

Hang on. I can understand why Sou would get jealous and doubt my relationship with Kinose, since he's confessed his feelings to me before. But what's it matter to Kou? Plus, a line like, 'Is it fun going around raising a guy's hopes and crushing them?' is a horrible boomerang back at himself.

My thoughts must've been written on my face again because Kou glowered spitefully at me.

Ah, I guess it does matter to him. He's frustrated because he's the type who enjoys crushing normal people for getting too cocky. But I'll stand up for myself at least.

"I didn't get his hopes up. He confessed and I turned him down. I'm living only for the piano after all!" I flat-out declared. That should've left them with nothing else to say now.

But opposite to my expectations, Sou's shoulders drooped and his face filled with sadness, complicating the situation.

"Forever just the piano? You'll never need anything or anyone other than the piano?"

Ugh. I accidentally triggered Sou's past trauma. I can't say yes to that.

"No…um, at least until high school it is."

I mean, I'm not a robot. I want to fall in love too! With a decent, normal person matching my financial history, and who fits my actual age when I reach it again!

"Until high school, huh? An awfully realistic preference you've got there. Well, that plays in your favor though, doesn't it, Sou?" Kou turned a meaningful gaze on Sou.

Why would waiting until high school be better for Sou?

Sou wordlessly shook his head, glowering at Kou to shut up.

"…You haven't told her yet?" Kou muttered, sighed, then faced me again. "At any rate, you're on the dimwitted side when it comes to anything other than the piano—you need to be more cautious of what's going on around you. Don't get swept up by a stranger's flattery and empty promises."

I managed to pry myself free after getting an earful from Kou and returned to my room.

You tell me to be cautious, but you're the number one person I need to be the most cautious of in the entire world!

♪♪♪

AFTER that event, I kept an eye on the surroundings while continuing with our travel plans on the second and third day of the trip.

Who knows where they were going to pop up from next! I should've asked them how long they were planning on being in Kyoto for!

"Is a hit man after you?" Takata wound up asking me.

Kinose acted like nothing had happened.

He's such a good guy!

Mako and Tomo only laughed at my wildly suspicious activity.

"Shimao's one strange girl," Mizuguchi observed.

"Only just noticed?" the girls responded in unison.

Yup…thanks for your understanding.

Utter relief swept over me as I boarded the bus for home.

I sat down next to Kinose again and announced, "I won't fall asleep this time."

"You're seriously talented with the piano," he praised me in a whisper on the ride back.

Not everyone was aware I had played the hotel piano that night, or so he bashfully claimed as his reason for waiting until now to compliment me.

"I knew you played the piano, but I hadn't imagined you were that good… You're serious. I'm kinda ashamed of myself now."

"Thank you, but you praise me too much."

"No, I'm not. Those guys play some sorta instrument too, I bet. They said they attend Seio after all."

He was referring to Kou and Sou. I nodded. The corners of his lips softened into a smile.

"I'm glad you flat-out rejected me beforehand. Contending for you against those guys would've been impossible."

Unsure of how to respond, I didn't. I knew what he was trying to say. He likely felt distance between us when he saw how music connected me to Kou and Sou, regardless of our bickering.

"I'm sorry, Rin."

"I told you I don't need an apology. Help me out if I get a crush in middle school. We'll be even then," he jested.

Relieved, I smiled and replied, "Leave it to me!"

♪♪♪

EVERYONE seemed spent as the biggest school event in sixth grade came to a close. In a blink of an eye, as if someone had pressed the fast-forward button on life, second quarter reached its end.

I turned down the Narita Christmas party this year. Hanaka was bringing her boyfriend home after their date, so we were going to show him the Shimao family's hospitality.

I baked a three-tier cake with Mom in the morning, decorating it with fresh, stiffly beaten cream and lavishly topped it with the strawberries we'd splurged on. Next, we prepared the chicken and coleslaw salad, followed by several varieties of pasta and meatloaf. We snacked in the name of taste testing, which took care of lunch.

The doorbell rang just around five in the evening. Dad quickly snatched up a newspaper and plopped down on the couch. He began paging through it with feigned indifference.

What's his problem? He was just helping me set the table too.

Mom's shoulders trembled with stifled giggles at her husband's behavior.

"Good evening. Thank you for having me over tonight," Shinji greeted. "That looks like quite the feast! I brought this thinking you might like it, but do you drink?" He held up two six-packs of real beer.

Today he wore a white shirt and black straight pants with a casual jacket. Aiming to please our parents, he'd left out the gel and neatly combed out his hair. Hanaka was relieved to notice Dad's eyes obviously sparkling as soon as he caught sight of the six-packs. Her unusually stiff expression slipped away.

"Good for you, Dad."

"H-Hmph. Well, I can't turn down a guest's gift."

We raised our glasses in a toast around Dad, who'd apparently shifted into a tsundere character. Naturally, Hanaka and I were drinking soda instead.

"It's been a year since you got a job, right, Shinji?" I asked, trying to start a conversation.

He grinned at me. "Yup. Their training period is freakishly long, and I wasn't assigned a full-time position until this fall."

Our parents were relieved to hear the name of the company he was employed at. He was assigned to the sales department of a fairly well-known beverage maker.

"Seems like the perfect job for someone as friendly as you, Shinji," I commented honestly. Happiness softened his facial features into an expression that seemed truly comfortable.

"I sure hope so. I can't quit halfway and disappoint my parents who've raised me until now, so I'll work hard."

"You're a straightforward kid; that's rare to find these days," Mom remarked, impressed. Dad had a look of approval too.

That's Hanaka for you. She did have an eye for the right guy after all.

"Oh yeah, have you seen Tomoi lately?" Hanaka asked, as if she just remembered him.

"Nah. We haven't hung out much since graduation. He seems busy too." Shinji smiled wryly.

"Oh yeah," Hanaka blurted loudly. "Tomoi's a teacher. I heard he got hired at the middle school you'll be attending, Mashiro."

My eyes rounded. "He'll be a teacher at Tada Middle School?"

"Yup. I'm pretty sure that's what he said. You'll be Tomo's student next year, huh? Time sure passes fast," Shinji noted, making everyone laugh because it was a nostalgic comment that didn't suit his modern handsome guy appearance.

"Shin, you sound like an old man!" Hanaka giddily teased.

We enjoyed a peaceful and heartwarming Christmas evening together. After Shinji went home, our slightly tipsy dad stretched out on the couch muttering, "He's a good guy. Damn it."

♪♪♪

AROUND New Years, I was beginning to think that the third quarter would end uneventfully with me becoming a middle school student. One day after school, while I was under that misconception, I came across Sou for the first time in a while.

He was leaning against the railing on our special footbridge with the same tormented expression as the day we had met. The only difference was how much lower the railing stood next to him. Taller and more mature, Sou also didn't cry anymore.

An unsettling premonition came over me. There were dark shadows looming on his profile. He had an unnerving expression like someone who had been beaten violently.

Natsu

What happened?

The hammering sound of my heart echoed in my ears. Noticing me, Sou looked up, his eyes wavering with unshed tears. His lips soundlessly formed my name.

"...It's been a while. When did you get back from Germany?" I schooled my expression as I stood beside him. I last saw him before winter break began, when he'd told me he was going to Germany again.

"I got back yesterday."

"I see. So I guess you had an opening ceremony for the new quarter today."

"Yeah," he murmured, his lips stark white from the cold.

School ends before noon on opening ceremony days. It was now four o'clock.

"...Have you been waiting here since then?" I ventured, after debating whether I should.

I can't leave him be. Even if my feelings are just the result of some maternal instinct to protect him, the four years I've spent with Sou are very special. We've laughed together, cried together, and made music together.

Countless times I had told myself to push him away, but I couldn't do it. He mattered to me. I didn't have to love him romantically to care about him.

"Mashiro... Mashiro...Mashiro, I don't want to leave you!" Sou threw his arms open, capturing me and my backpack in a tight hug.

Hey, when did you grow into such a thick and toned body?

My cheek hurt where it hit his chest.

"You're frozen to the bone because you've stuck around in the cold. Come over my place so we can talk more comfortably, okay?"

"Outside is better. I don't know what I'll do if we end up alone together," he spat out painfully.

I led him back to a park near school as a compromise. Sunny weather had gloriously marked the morning, but it was replaced by the heavy clouds that had blown in. Specks too small and shapeless to call snow began to descend upon us.

CG 20: Farewell (Sou)

ALTHOUGH the park usually came alive with children passing through on their way home from school, poor weather kept most away today. We went under a small gazebo, good enough to protect us from the falling snow, and sat next to each other on an old bench. Poor carvings of kids in groups sharing an umbrella were etched into the round wooden table, most likely the work of elementary schoolers.

"What happened in Germany?" I boldly asked, resuming the conversation. We'd sat in silence for a long while, but that wasn't an answer to the problem.

Sou clenched his hands on top of his lap. "…They've decided to move me to Germany in April. I've been telling them how much I don't want to go since they first brought it up, but they told me to suck it up because I have no choice in adult decisions… Why? Why are they always so self-serving and selfish?!" he shouted bitterly, then turned to me. "I knew whatever I said to Dad and Mom was futile, so I've been thinking all this time about what I have to do to stay in Japan."

I was pulled in by the frenzied look in his eyes; I buckled down to firmly return his gaze. Whatever I had to do, I wanted to bring him back from the edge.

"I'm sure there's a good reason for it. Your dad's not the type to force you to do something you hate without a reason, right? What did he say?"

"Their reasons don't matter to me."

"Sou!"

I shook his arm, trying to get him to drop his obstinacy. He jumped, shuddering as if I'd struck him with a hot iron.

"…I'm thinking of asking my grandfather on the Morikawa side to intervene. I've never met him before, but he might help me out."

"What are you talking about?"

Morikawa was Risa's—the mother who gave birth to him—maiden name. This was the first time I'd heard of him having a grandfather on her side, but I was more surprised by what he said next.

"I'll give up being a member of the Shiroyama family. I don't need that family if it means I can no longer be with you, Mashiro."

His hasty conclusion drained the blood from my face. I wholly doubted that a grandfather, who decided he didn't need to meet his own grandson, would happily take Sou in. I was terrified of what could push him to make such a grave decision so readily. He was going to throw away his family.

Is it me? Am I why Sou has gone mad?

"Hold your horses. Let's think this through calmly. You can't do—"

"I can do it! It'll be harder for me to silently watch from a distance, enviously, as you grow up and become more and more detached from me!"

I gasped at the wave of Sou's violent emotions. But most of all, I felt sheer regret; I had pushed him to this terrifying breaking point. I should've let go of him sooner.

How can I stop him from acting so rashly because of his emotions? What can I do?

Well-attuned to my hesitation and fear, Sou grabbed my hands, holding onto them tightly. With urgency in his eyes, he peered at my face.

"Are you okay with this, Mashiro? Will you be fine with me leaving Japan? If I never come back again?"

"…That's not the problem here."

"Mashiro."

"How I feel is not the issue at hand, now is it?! Think more seriously about yourself! Talk after you've thought about the consequences it'll have in the future, not just the present! What'll you do when you go to the Morikawa's? What about the cello?"

"If I have to give up the cello to be with you, I'll do it."

It's undeniable that Sou loves the cello. Did he believe he could fool me when I'd heard the beauty of his music countless of times? Fool me after we played together?

"Something's wrong with you... You've lost it!"

A child's attachment is what's controlling him right now. "I don't ever want to be abandoned again." With that thought consuming him, he's clinging to me. I'm Risa's replacement. But he'd definitely deny it. He'd never admit that this wound, gouged deep enough to numb him, is what compels him to go this far.

Filled by an impulse to comfort him, I tightly hugged him back. An unbearable urge to reassure him that I'd always be with him fought for supremacy within me. But there's no way a mere elementary school girl such as myself could say those weighted words. Comforting him with the words he wanted to hear out of empty sympathy would only betray him in the end.

I don't know what I'll say if I keep feeling his warmth like this.

I tried to withdraw my hands to put distance between us. The usual Sou would've apologized and let me go. He didn't this time. Instead, he strengthened his embrace before I could resist.

A gentle, sweet aroma wafted from his silky hair. Squeezing my eyes shut so hard that it hurt, I placed my hands on his chest.

I have to say something horribly cruel to him now. I'm positive he'll come to despise me. Whether he detests me to the point of never wanting to see my face again, or he comes to begrudge the memories we made together—I must. I don't want to close off his future based on momentary feelings.

"...I hate you."

"What?"

"I hate your guts, Shiroyama."

"...You're...lying." Sou's arms limply fell from me. I felt like yelling in frustration; his brokenhearted expression screamed that he didn't believe me.

I've always only ever wanted to see him smile. Every moment, I wished for him to continue smiling happily forever. Yet I'd gone and stabbed a sharp dagger into his soft heart, then twisted the blade.

I mustered every fiber of my being to craft a stony expression.

Don't cry. He'll catch on if you cry now.

Gritting my teeth, I shoved myself off the bench.

"Do as your parents say and go to Germany. Grow up," I hurled dryly at him as he sat there dumbfounded.

"Ma...shiro."

"Don't come near me. I can't waste my time looking after you anymore. Don't place the burden of the responsibility for your future on me."

"You're...lying... You're lying, aren't you, Mashiro?!"

Large teardrops poured from his jet-black eyes. He wheezed painfully through the sobs, reaching out for my hand like his life depended on capturing it. I stepped back to escape his touch.

"I'll never forget you...Shiroyama. Thank you for falling in love with me. Please continue straight down your own path in life. Stay well even in Germany."

"Agh... I don't want to hear that... Please stop...Mashiro!"

Sou was beautiful even with a face marred with tears. He was the greatest boy in the world, possessing both talent and charm.

I'm sorry for hurting you. I'm so, so, so sorry.

I dealt the final blow. "Farewell."

The monotonous tone in my voice had no longer sounded like it belonged to me.

Seeing the warm light die in his eyes, I turned around. Frantically enduring the desire to run away, I walked slowly out of the park. I didn't run until I'd walked some distance away.

A lump caught in my throat while snowdrops hit my cheeks painfully.

This is nothing. My pain is nothing compared to Sou's.

I finally arrived in front of my house and fished around my pockets for my keys. An icy key hung from the golden bear I'd received from Sou.

"...Nngh. Aah. Aaaaah."

Swallowing back the sobs welling up in succession, I shoved the key into the keyhole with shaking hands. The key struggled, missing the hole again and again, swaying the bear each time.

At last inside the entryway, I was engulfed by the still space of the empty house. Guest slippers had been left on the floor, as if to mock me. I couldn't stop thinking of the first time Sou had come over. After that first day, he'd always shove his feet in those slippers before making his way down the hallway.

The first time he had come over was Valentine's Day. Sou waited for me in such light clothing, it'd chilled me just to look at him.

"If we're friends, will you be with me forever, Mashiro?"

His younger voice rang in my mind's ear.

"Sou...Sou!" I collapsed on the floor and wept, screaming out the name of my irreplaceable friend.

I wanted to be with you forever. Even I wanted to be together forever.

How long had I sobbed for? I stumbled to my feet and dragged myself to the living room to make a single phone call.

"Hello? ...Hello?"

The lump caught in my throat again upon hearing Kon's voice.

"K...on? It's...Mashiro."

"...What happened?" I heard a small gasp through the receiver.

Roughly scrubbing away my tears with my sleeve, I asked Kon for a single favor.

Heroine's Results

Target Character: Sou Shiroyama

Event: A "Farewell" for Your Sake

CLEAR

◇◇◇

Epilogue (Kon)

RIGHT after Mashiro called me, I found Sou's house number through Kou. An elderly maid answered the phone.

"Master Sou hasn't returned home yet," she said dolefully.

"He hasn't? All right. I will call again later then," I cheerfully responded.

I called Nonaga on the internal house line as soon as I hung up. "I want you to bring the car around. Yes, right now."

Mashiro's fears were on the money it seems. Please don't move now.

I dashed out of my room.

♪♪♪

ONLY one park was built close to Tada Elementary School. I had Nonaga drop me off nearby and told him, "I'll be back soon."

Opening my flowery umbrella to block the snow, I headed straight for the gazebo. Amid the growing darkness, streetlights dimly illuminated the area. Sou was exactly where Mashiro said he'd be. He stared at the palm of his hand, unmoving, like a statue.

"Shiroyama."

His head jerked up and he spun toward me. I wasn't who he was waiting for. I quietly sighed at his obvious disappointment.

"If you're waiting for Mashiro, she won't be coming. I'll take you home by car. Let's go."

"...Did Kou ask you to do this?" His lips curled in a self-derisive smile. "Mashiro relied on Kou for this? …Asked him to look after poor little Sou? What a piece of work we are."

Mocking Mashiro on top of himself—I snapped. "Cool it. Do you honestly believe Mashiro would do something like that?" I shook my head and stared at him. "That girl told me she'll never see my brother again. She directly asked me to do this as a favor. She wanted me to make sure you got home safely."

"…Huh?" Sou's eyes widened, betraying his confusion.

"If you seriously believe Mashiro relied on my brother for this, never go near her again."

"Wha—"

"You don't deserve Mashiro if you honestly believe she can thrust away someone dear to her and hurt them without suffering herself," I declared bluntly, without pausing. I hurried him since he remained unmoving with bewilderment plastered on his face. "Come on, it's cold. Hurry into the car. You're welcome to wallow in despair, but can you save it for home?"

"Haha…you're harsh."

"I wouldn't be in a place like this if she hadn't asked me to. Hurry up." I kicked Sou's sneaker with the tip of my boot.

"You're pretty violent, aren't you? Weren't you Kou's esteemed princess?"

"I'm not some exaggerated fairy-tale princess." I looked up at the sky to show my exasperation with him.

He smiled wryly and finally got to his feet. I pushed him into the heated car and instructed Nonaga where to go. Sou acted docile, as if he were but an empty shell of himself.

"…Mashiro cried."

"What?"

"She was crying, telling me how she relentlessly hurt you with the words she never wanted you to hear. That she had no other choice but to do it."

"……"

"I just told you what I promised I never would, so keep it between us."

"Okay… Sorry."

"I don't want your apology."

I shrugged as his eyes returned to life. Sou gnawed his lower lip hard as he glared at the sky for a period of time. Then he let out a long sigh and blinked back his tears.

"What have I done? …I was always thinking that I never wanted to be the one to make her cry. But I was so focused and bothered by my own feelings that I ignored hers. I forced her to say those things, when she's been nothing but kind to me."

"Yeah."

"…I'm going to Germany. Will you tell her sorry for me?"

"Nope."

"Huh?" Shock flickered across his face.

I gave him a smile. "You should write her a letter or something. You can even call her. You'll be an adult someday. It's not like it's set in stone that you'll never see her again."

Sou gaped at me for a long moment before his shoulders shook with laughter. "Your thought process is just like Mashiro's."

"…You get zero points if that's meant as a pick-up line."

"Huh? How could it be?"

I turned away from Sou's repulsed face. The words he'd said without much thought had shaken me up more than they should have.

Did it show on my face?

I slowly ran my fingers over the face reflected in the car window—my face, which didn't bear the slightest resemblance to Mashiro.

♩♩♩

WE let Sou off in front of the Shiroyama estate, and I sank back into the seat.

"Can you take the long way home?"

"Yes, my lady," Nonaga replied, then asked, "Shall I put some music on?"

"Yes, let me see—"

As I was about to ask for a song—

"I want to hear that one."

That man sits down right next to me. A perfect dent forms on the seat under him.

"Tchaikovsky's 'Pathétique'. Isn't it the perfect song

for today?" The man merrily folds his arms in front of his chest, his golden hair swaying.

"Put on Tchaikovsky's 'Pathétique'. We should have the Berlin Philharmonic's rendition on CD."

"Yes, my lady."

Happy? I raise an eyebrow. The man's lips curl into a satisfied smile. He begins to swing his index finger around to the music like a conductor's baton.

"Aah, what marvelous bliss... Mashiro's grief was indeed a sweet, sweet delicacy, Kon. Pure sorrow and regret flavored it most splendidly."

I silently stare at the snowflakes hitting the window. Dazzling white that slices through the darkness to pelt us.

"You fulfilled your role properly this time too. I'm very pleased with you. The story would be ruined if one of the princes left the stage. Now the game can continue." He narrows his eyes like a cat.

Sharply glaring at him, I soundlessly move my lips, "I will win...in the end."

"That's how it's gotta be! The stronger the light of hope, the deeper and more complex the taste of despair becomes." He smirks and swirls his finger. The next second, the space beside me is empty.

"Lady Kon? Did you say something?"

"No. I've had enough. Stop the song."

"Yes, ma'am."

♪♪♪

I have four years left until the promised time limit. Tobi Yamabuki gets his hands on the original game heroine when she wins the Seio Music Competition and manipulates her. Bearing the title of the sole heir to the Genda Group, he whispers sweet nothings in her ear, downright lies to ensnare the naïve girl he wants to market and profit off of as an up-and-coming female pianist.

The hidden route ends by hinting Tobi, who has never opened his heart up to anyone, might actually become serious about her. There's a single fork that leads to a Bad End: Failing the music competition.

If the original heroine doesn't win first place, Tobi cruelly tosses her aside after making her serious about him.

"I'm sure he will return for me," she assures herself.

Players were outraged by the CG of Kon waiting on the beach every day for his boat to return from England. "This is horrible even for a Bad End," they wrote furiously online.

If I find myself on that bad ending, I'll never be able to bring her back to me again. That's the one thing I must avoid at all costs. No matter the means I must use, I must win.

Clearing the game's Tobi Route is the one condition I've been given.

Aaah, Rika. I want to see you. Smile again for me, say my name—not that person's.

*I'll do anything—**anything**—to make that happen.*

Afterword

HELLO, I'm the author Natsu. Thank you very much for reading this book. I'm really happy to be able to deliver the English translation of this story, which I had published on a web novel site in Japanese, to you like this.

What made you want to read this story? Was it because you like otome games? Light novels? Or were you after the classical music elements? I believe everyone has different reasons for reading a story, but it is my greatest hope that you were entertained until the end.

As for the heroine, Mashiro, you can say her good traits are that she's earnest and puts all she has into whatever she does; her bad traits being that once she becomes obsessed with something, she's the type of girl who loses sight of everything else. Her first life ended at the age of eighteen. The first pieces of the story are put together in this "Elementary School Arc," where after she receives a second chance at life for some unknown reason, Mashiro fumbles her way forward in a world that is eerily similar to a game she knew very well.

This arc revolves around Mashiro's daily life and the piano, along with the two heroes who get involved with her and their constant bittersweet encounters. And then there's the friendship with Kon, the only other person who has been reincarnated into the game world, who holds all the secrets. I hope all the readers have enjoyed this story that has been packed with the various spices of life.

The last part of the "Elementary School Arc" might have been shocking to fans of Sou, but this is a vital step in forming the groundwork

Natsu

for "Sou's Arc." Please read their stories through until the end.

The illustrations, which added further color and appeal to the story, were taken on by the artist Shoyu. From the cover to the character page, along with all the insert images, every illustration perfectly fits the vision I had. The main characters appear at the beginning of the story as children and gradually grow up to become more mature-looking, so I hope you are satisfied by the wonderful illustrations that vividly show these diffcrences.

I'm also deeply grateful to everyone involved in the publication of this novel. And most of all, I'm grateful to readers who have honored me by going as far as to read this afterword too. Thank you very much!

I hope we meet again in the next volume, which covers the "Middle School Arc."

Natsu

LITTLE PRINCESS IN FAIRY FOREST
STORY BY: TSUBAKI TOKINO
ILLUSTRATION BY: TAKASHI KONNO
STANDALONE | OUT NOW

Join Princess Lala and Sir Gideon as they flee for their lives from the traitor who killed the royal family and wants to wed Lala! Gideon is willing to do anything to protect his princess, even if it means engaging the mighty dragons in combat! Tsubaki Tokino's fairy tale inspired Little Princess in Fairy Forest!

BEAST † BLOOD
STORY BY: SATO FUMINO
ILLUSTRATION BY: AKIRA EGAWA
VOL. 1 OUT NOW

Biotech Scientist Euphemia's world suddenly gets flipped upside down when her sister hires a sexy alien mercenary to be her bodyguard!

THE ECCENTRIC MASTER AND THE FAKE LOVER!
STORY BY: ROKA SAYUKI
ILLUSTRATION BY: ITARU
VOL. 1 OUT NOW

Yanked into another world full of dangerous magic and parasitic plants, Nichika does the one thing she can to survive: become the apprentice to an eccentric witch!

THE CHAMPIONS OF JUSTICE AND THE SUPREME RULER OF EVIL
STORY BY: KAEDE KIKYOU
ILLUSTRATION BY: TOBARI
STANDALONE | OUT NOW

Mia's a supervillain bent on world domination who lacks tact in enacting her evil schemes! Will the lazy superheroes be able to stop her?

THE WEREWOLF COUNT AND THE TRICKSTER TAILOR
STORY BY: YURUKA MORISAKI
ILLUSTRATION BY: TSUKITO
VOL. 1 | OUT NOW

"I don't care if you are a man, let me court you."
Rock's whole life is shaken when a werewolf shows up at her shop in the middle of the night...asking for more than just clothes!

OF DRAGONS AND FAE: IS A FAIRY TALE ENDING POSSIBLE FOR THE PRINCESS'S HAIRSTYLIST?
STORY BY: TSUKASA MIKUNI
ILLUSTRATION BY: YUKIKANA
STANDALONE | OUT NOW

After being dumped by a dragon knight, Mayna sets out to prove that fairytale endings aren't only for princesses! See how this royal hairstylist wins over the dragon kingdom one head of hair at a time!